C000096086

Black Looks

by

John Money

A Black Looks Novel

Text copyright © 2000, 2019 John Money
All Rights Reserved

Published by Regency Rainbow Publishing
Cover by Maria Spada Design at www.mariaspada.com

Preface

The very first draft of Bill and Franklin's somewhat adventurous meeting, still called Black Looks even back then, was quite literally penned – two biros and a whole heap of notebooks – back in 1994.

It was undoubtedly a first draft and not even close to being fit for publication, but far more importantly for me it was the first full-length book that I had written and completed, and it also brought life to two characters in particular. The middle-aged waster with the sharp but whisky-sodden mind, William Wilberforce Taylor, and the ever-unlucky teenager with mental talents hidden even to himself, Franklin Richardson, became somehow real to me.

They went on to feature in short story scraps and then a second novel which has now been published in a much-updated format – The Dark Side – and also in many mental discussions and debates in my own mind. Real or what?

It all started with Black Looks, though, and now I have revisited that ancient project and – hopefully brought the story of ten fretful days in the lives of the unlikely pair to new life. It's the story of how they met and how they discover that they complement each other – not that they ever publicly compliment their other halves. And it's now a story that contains the kernels of how their lives will grow.

Some of the characters in here will reappear in later works, some are here just for this one ride. All of them, though, are real to me, and (hopefully for you) they all play their parts in the journey that this story relates.

The third, all new, novel in what is now the 'Black Looks Series' is well under way, and who knows? Perhaps there'll be the occasional short story on the shelves one day, based on those idle scraps that I have penned – or more likely, typed – over the years?

Acknowledgements

The original 'first novel' was made possible by a campsite on the edge of the town of Oban in Scotland where time passed very, very slowly. I was encouraged by my then girlfriend Pamela M (you know who you are) and by the then manager of the Columba Hotel there. But...

My most sincere and full thanks and gratitude must go to the person I have found who surpasses all others, and who cares for me as we share our love.

Sara Avila has changed my life for the better in every way – despite MS affecting us both – and it is thanks to her that I felt the desire and need to resurrect this ancient story and breathe new life into it. Dear readers, turn your backs now if excess emotion disturbs you – because I just need to say to Sara, I love you and always will.

Inspirations and history aside, I must also thank everyone who has provided me with lovely feedback over the years, and I have to acknowledge your collective part in this story. Bill and Franklin salute you.

Regency Rainbow's agreement to publish the prequal to The Dark Side has been a great incentive to me, and their collaboration with cover designer Maria Spada has helped so much in the creation of this book.

Website addresses are listed at the end of this book.

Chapter 1

Bill Taylor had decided that enough was enough. Finally, irrevocably, conclusively and irrefutably. But not just yet.

He turned back to the bar and hailed a passing bartender. "Excuse me kind lady, I have a picture of the Queen who looks most displeased to be in the company of such a miserable reprobate. Perhaps you could separate us in return for a large measure of something warming?"

"Bill, you're drunk again." Mandy, the said passing bartender, smiled and took the crumpled twenty-pound note from Bill's outstretched hand. "What's your excuse today?" she asked over her shoulder as she reached for the whisky optic.

"Since when does a gentleman need an excuse to spend a couple of hours in pleasant surroundings, doing the things he is most good at?" Bill retorted amiably.

"You mean getting drunk, falling over and charming poor defenceless barmaids, I take it?" replied Mandy, returning with Bill's drink and change.

"Cruel, madam, very cruel," he said, smiling drunkenly, "Also rather accurate, I fear."

Mandy's attention was taken by a plea for service further down the bar. "Back in a minute, Bill," she said and wandered down to the youth, evidently suffering from dehydration, whose calls had become rather desperate.

"There but for the cruelty of the devil go I," Bill muttered to no-one in particular. He took a long swallow and shuddered slightly at the bitter, familiar taste.

At forty-nine, Bill Taylor had a great future behind him. Everyone said so. He was undoubtedly intelligent; despite the ravages of alcohol he still retained a certain handsomeness that seemed to be defying time, and he was a natural charmer. Without a doubt (anyone in his local public house would tell you the same) he was one of the most liked people in the neighbourhood; always willing to lend a hand (when sober enough to do so), always there with a kind word when it was most needed, and, although no-one knew where it came from – he didn't seem to work, after all – he was always most generous in matters financial.

The only thing about William Wilberforce Taylor that annoyed people (his sister to the point of apoplexy) was that he refused to take life seriously. "He could have been something!" was her normal plaintive cry, as if he were not something already. "He just wouldn't take things seriously at school. He could have had a great future. He just won't listen."

Mary's visits had become a form of living hell for Bill, but he endured them with good humour and a slight (make that large) increase in his daily whisky consumption. This particular week was one of those times. Mary had arrived, unannounced, and most unwelcomely Thursday evening, immediately launching into a tirade against alcohol (Bill thought that he had been relatively sober when she had arrived), slovenliness (Bill had accumulated the best part of three weeks' dirty laundry in his bedroom), and hygiene (she swore that something inside moved when she opened the fridge door). Her mood worsened appreciably when Bill suggested that maybe the bacon was grazing on the lettuce.

Having endured the haranguing for the better part of an entire hour, he excused himself and dragged himself into the sanctuary of his bed. This morning he had woken early, a mental safety device provoking this unusual experience, and had taken himself off to a local coffee shop via the newsagent before his sister was able to take up the diatribe once more.

When the Mucky Duck (how Bill loathed the modern trend in pub names) had opened he had been their first customer. Ten hours later the establishment was filling up once more, this time with the evening trade, and Bill had yet to persuade himself that he could face his sister.

Normally Bill would have been in the company of other members of the 'Losers Club', a small band of regulars who took their drinking as seriously as anything else in their lives. Tonight, they were away at a beer tasting do together with the landlord and head barman while Bill, not a beer-drinker, had declined their repeated attempts to cajole him into following suit. As the clock reached nine-thirty it became clear to Bill's fuddled brain that the club were going to be making a night of it and, without the company that usually stimulated him, he began to think about making a move for home. Outside, unforecasted thunder boomed loudly, and the rain began to patter even harder against the pub's large windows.

"Perfect," Bill muttered and reached for his overcoat.

* * * * *

Franklin Richardson, seventeen, was hurrying home. He was also wet-through, late and – in all probability – in deep trouble.

This was nothing new to Franklin. He was *always* in trouble. It followed him around with the same efficiency as his shadow. It was not that he *deliberately* set out to cause it, just that trouble seemed to find him – wherever he was, whatever he was doing.

Two weeks previously he had taken his foster parents' prized Dobermann for a walk. The normally placid and extremely well-behaved dog had slipped its lead and savaged a neighbour's equally prized miniature poodle. Despite the fact that Franklin had risked life and limb separating the dogs, he had been blamed.

Just last week he had decided to try to get back into his foster parents' good books by doing the washing in their absence. Everything had been going well until the second load. The catches on the ancient machine's door had chosen that moment to succumb to the pressures of age. The resultant flood had soaked every downstairs carpet, shorted the electric cooker and came perilously close to drowning their evil-tempered cat.

Of course, it was Franklin and not planned obsolescence that was to blame.

And now it was Friday night. The first time he had been allowed out since the great flood, and he was late home. If only his watch hadn't picked tonight to stop, unnoticed. And if only he hadn't won three replays on the Addams family pinball machine in the arcade.

"Oh well," he sighed to himself, quickening his pace and pulling his collar tight around his neck as the unexpected storm also gathered pace, perhaps this will be the last straw. *Perhaps*, and here he crossed his fingers, *perhaps the Harts would finally decide they couldn't foster him any longer*. Anyway, he'd be eighteen and officially free from care in six months or so. He'd make it... surely?

The Harts were the latest in a long line of foster parents stretching back to his earliest childhood memories. If they weren't the worst foster parents he had been 'cared for' by, they were certainly in the all-time top three.

Of his earliest years he knew nothing other than what he had been told by a succession of social workers. Apparently, he had been found as a baby outside a police station in Leyton, in London's East End. He was a well-cared for, healthy six-month old. A cursory note, presumably written by his real mother, simply stated that his name was Franklin and that he was to receive the 'best possible care'. Nothing else; no excuses, no clues as to her identity.

He was found there by a young constable returning from her night shift. Of course, he had no recollection of her, but carried her surname to this day. From the police station he was taken to a local hospital and from there to an orphanage. There he stayed until he was first fostered.

They were a young West Indian couple and Franklin being, to use his own words, as black as the ace of spades, had appeared an ideal choice. They were childless, and he was a godsend to them. Of his vague memories of them it was their generosity that he remembered most clearly. He was showered with kindness, consideration, love and any toy he wanted. For his fifth birthday (an assumed December date) he was presented with a vast Scalextric track which had been laid out in his already overcrowded playroom. A dozen or so friends had been invited from his school, and he still recalled the day as one of the happiest of his life.

It was less than a month after the party that his now constant companion, trouble, struck. In a hurry to get dressed for school (he had been playing with the Scalextric track since 5.30 in the morning), he had dropped one of the cars on the stairs. Sometime during the morning, Mrs Jackson, his foster mother, had begun carefully and slowly descending the stairs with an armful of washing.

The remainder of the descent had been far more rapid and resulted in Mrs Jackson breaking an arm, a hip and losing three teeth. When Franklin had arrived home from school, he found Mr Jackson in the front room along with Miss Blake from the Social Services department. He vividly remembered crying, sobbing that he was sorry, when he learned what had happened. Nobody blamed him, least of all Mrs Jackson when he visited her in hospital that evening.

It was probably this last fact that caused such a great shock when, two days later, he found himself back at the orphanage. Everyone there assured him that it was nothing to do with the Jacksons no longer wanting him – simply that Mrs Jackson was in no condition to cope with him. He didn't believe them at the time and even now wasn't sure.

He still recalled the Jacksons; even at five years old he was aware of the term 'adoption', and for some time he held out hope that when Mrs Jackson recovered then he would be returned to them, and that they would adopt him. It had never happened.

Franklin spent another year at the orphanage before a second set of parents, the Duvals, were found for him. He recalled his time with this pair far more vividly. Former flower-power teenagers, they had finally succumbed to the institution of marriage but still held on to many of their hippie ideals. They were white and had apparently had a hard fight to be selected as foster parents to a six-year old black boy.

Unfortunately (for Franklin) they wanted to care for him less as a pseudo-son than as a symbol of their open, non-racist, non-sexist, non-ageist ideals. He remembered being presented to a never-ending succession of their friends, colleagues and family with phrases like 'We don't even notice he's non-white now.'

Even at six he was aware of racism, and this inverted form troubled him deeply – although he was unaware of the complex reasons behind it at that time. He quickly tired of being their status symbol and was equally fed up with eating lentils and bamboo shoots. After six months he decided that enough was enough. This time he engineered the trouble.

Whenever he was wheeled out at parties he would misbehave abominably; when they began their 'We don't even notice' speech he would complain loudly that they called him a 'little nigger boy' when people weren't around; he broke crockery when 'helping' with the drying up; he was, quite simply, as obnoxious as his six-year-old mind could conjure.

In less than a month the Duvals had lost as many friends as they had plates and Franklin was summarily returned to a somewhat disappointed Miss Blake.

Thereafter he underwent the often less than tender administrations of a dozen other couples. The care he received ranged from token acceptance, through total disinterest, to occasional abuse. The latter, thankfully, had never escalated to sexual abuse, but he had got used to being treated, at times, as an unpaid servant – and even as a handy target when tempers flared.

Trouble followed him like a faithful but unwanted dog. He had mortified a pleasant enough, law-abiding, couple by accidentally wandering out of a shop with them, carrying a two-pound bar of Cadbury's Dairy Milk – and been arrested by the store detective.

He had run over, on his mountain bike, the prized pet rabbit owned by the daughter of another, normally mild-mannered, couple.

At the placement before his current situation he had nearly burned their house to the ground making toast.

His latest social worker, Ms. Thomsett (call me Jenny), decided that the toaster incident was the last straw. Forgetting for a moment her liberal, 'never-smack-them' attitude, she decided that he should be placed with a couple who were 'specialists' in handling problem children. Despite Franklin's protestations – both of his innocence and age – he had arrived three weeks ago at the Harts.

Mrs Hart was a shrewish woman who looked fifty but was probably in her late thirties. She cowered when Mr Hart was around but took her craven revenge out on Franklin when he wasn't.

They had an obnoxious, overweight daughter, Rose, who Franklin alienated on their first encounter when he suggested that she must be 'the original big Hart'.

Their other progeny was Raymond ('don't you dare call him Ray'), who was twelve but with a mental age far lower than his physical years.

And then there was Mr Hart. He was a large man, a shade under six feet tall, and a good deal over twenty stones in weight. He was also the most evil-tempered, violent and racist man that Franklin had ever met.

Franklin, himself, was also tall – a shade under six foot himself (although to him that was 180 centimetres) – but the sheer physical bulk of Hart was intimidating. The incidents with their Dobermann and washing machine brought out in Hart the meanest of mean streaks that Franklin had ever experienced. Had he not been so agile, he was sure that Hart would have hospitalised him.

Hart was also a heavy drinker and had extremely regular habits in that direction. It was for this particular reason that Franklin knew he was once more in trouble this Friday. Mrs Hart worked all Friday evening in the local Tesco, re-stocking the shelves ready for the Saturday rush. Mr Hart, on the other hand, spent all Friday evening at the local working men's' club (Franklin had never had enough nerve to point out the paradox in this – Hart never worked). Hart wouldn't leave the house for his evening's drinking unless the Hart children had someone to look after them. In between foster children the Harts hired the services of a sitter, but when they were 'caring' it was the duty of the 'caree' to sit the obnoxious brats.

Hart always left at eight o'clock sharp. It was now turned half past nine, and their sitter, Franklin, was still half a mile from the house. Franklin hadn't even called to say he'd be late, his phone lacking credits and his brain lacking willingness in any case. He was in *deep* trouble. He broke into a half-hearted trot – he wasn't sure he even *wanted* to reach the Hart residence.

As he passed the Mucky Duck pub he briefly noticed an older man stumbling through the door, pulling his overcoat tight around his neck. '*I bet he isn't scared just because he's on his way home,*' he thought.

Noticing the black youth trotting past, Bill Taylor thought exactly the same thing.

Turning into Earls Avenue, Franklin could see the front door of the Hart household, a place he could never call home. It was partially open despite the storm. He slowed to a walk, breathing deeply and bracing himself for the worse storm – the one still to come.

He was fumbling with the catch on the gate when Hart's voice ripped through the storm.

"You!"

Franklin started, this guy was in one *mean* mood.

"You little black *bastard*!" The booming voice reached a terrifying peak. "Get your black arse in here *now*!"

Franklin froze. His eyes rose to meet Hart's bulk, nearly blocking the now wide-open doorway. He had heard of the flee-or-fight reaction in a recent biology lesson. Now he *knew* what it meant. Freeing the catch, he pushed open the gate, its neglected hinges squealing in protest over the noise of the lashing rain.

"I said..." Hart began once more.

Franklin stared back at him, not moving, rain running off his nose, his chin, his hands. "Don't call me that," he said quietly.

Hart hadn't heard him over the noise of the rain. "*What* did you say, boy?"

Louder, Franklin repeated his words. "Don't call me that."

Something in Hart snapped – Franklin could almost hear it. "You little black *fucker*!" Hart screamed at him. "I'll call you what I fucking like, you little black whore's son." He began to step forward, his right hand clutching a long leather belt, the buckle shining in the light of a sodium lamp a few metres down the street.

Franklin watched him approach. His pulse was racing, the adrenaline pumping. He knew, really *knew*, that this was it. Hart, fat as he appeared, had the strength of the proverbial ox. He had also passed beyond mere meanness to outright fury.

As Hart reached a point just out of arms reach and drew back the belt, Franklin finally made up his mind. '*Fight be buggered*,' he thought. Spinning on his heels he raced away up the street.

Behind him he could hear Hart's astonished roar. "Get back here, you black bastard!"

'*He said it again*,' thought Franklin. He paused, slowing his pace and peered behind him. He was amazed to see Hart breaking into a rolling trot. The image of a hippo in full stride crossed Franklin's mind before he realised that Hart had achieved a fair pace and was closing in on him fast.

"Oh, shit!" he yelled, pumping his legs into a sprinter's pace. He raced back the way he had just a few minutes earlier trotted home, passing the Mucky Duck at a pace that Usain Bolt in his heyday would have been hard pressed to attain.

Whirring up Dukes Road he almost collided with a weaving figure he recognised as the drunk who had stumbled out of the pub earlier. Swerving past him he yelled back "Sorry mister!"

Bill Taylor focused bleary eyes on the rapidly retreating figure. "Looks like the Devil's on your tail, young fellow," he said aloud. Then to himself, "Lucky you, lad, I've still to face mine."

Five minutes and three long streets later, Franklin slowed to a walk and then stopped, gasping for breath, beside an articulated lorry. He doubted whether Hart could even walk this far, much less run it, but spent the next minute in the relative darkness beside the lorry, scanning the street behind him. Eventually he decided that Hart had given up the chase.

What now? he wondered. He was drenched, obviously homeless, rapidly becoming cold (despite his exertions), and, most importantly, totally confused.

He considered calling Ms. Thomsett and explaining the situation but could easily imagine her turning up and dragging him back to the Harts. He dismissed that idea immediately. It was then that he noticed a new feeling – nascent as yet – growing within him. He was free. Cold, wet, homeless maybe – but free.

He also realised that he was tired. Days of caring for the Hart brats, endless errands, a post-adrenaline downer, and the mad dash to escape had taken their toll. He had decided that he would call one of his friends, ask if he could crash for the night, when he noticed the rear doors of the lorry's trailer.

The catch was closed but there was no lock. It must obviously be empty. Scanning the street for prying eyes, he cautiously tried the handle. It opened noiselessly, and he peered into the gloomy interior.

A nearby street lamp showed him that the trailer was, indeed, empty, with the exception of a few dust sheets.

Looking around once more, he vaulted into the back of the trailer and pulled the door closed behind him. At the back of his mind he could imagine waking to the roar of the diesel as it carried an unnoticed cargo, himself, to destinations unknown. The idea appealed to him. After all, compared to returning to the Hart household, a trip to Hell would appeal.

Stripping off his saturated jacket but leaving his equally damp trainers on in case he needed to get out quickly, Franklin laid down among the sheets and closed his eyes. In five-minutes he was asleep.

*****

Saturday 7th June 2014

When Bill Taylor awoke Saturday morning he was not unduly surprised to find himself curled up under his bathroom sink, wrapped somewhat less than warmly in a slightly damp bath towel. He was still fully dressed, with the exception of his overcoat, the sleeve of which he could see in the doorway out of the corner of his eye.

Gingerly uncurling his six-foot frame into a sitting position that did not involve his head coming into contact with the sink, he leaned back against the bathtub. He yawned, stretched and groaned as several vertebrae and a knee groaned in sympathy at the sudden movement.

He braced both hands beside him on the tiled floor and winced as a sharp stabbing pain coursed through his right hand and along the arm to his elbow. He raised the hand in front of his face and attempted to focus his blurred eyes on the offending appendage.

Once again, he was not unduly surprised to find three slivers of glass imbedded firmly in his palm. His daily lifestyle often found him waking with various, often glass-inflicted, wounds.

Leaning forward slightly, he brought his left hand up and began to pluck at the shards. Both hands were shaking slightly and as he fumbled, cursing, in an attempt to extricate the glass, he tried to focus his mind back to the previous evening.

Blank spots in his normally retentive memory were rare even considering his high intake of alcohol but he was not overly concerned. From what he could recall so far it would appear that the injury had occurred after he arrived home. At least that meant that he wouldn't be required to make copious apologies in the Mucky Duck when he returned later, and nor would he be paying for breakages that he had caused there.

However, it did mean that the breakage had occurred here, at home, and he fervently prayed that it was after Mary had left. His drunken behaviour and his besotted reputation locally both drove his sister to distraction, but if he damaged anything in what had been their family home, her frustration and pique made the former Tory dragon, Margaret Thatcher at her most virulent, seem like a pussycat. Or maybe 'blue tit' would be more appropriate.

The shakes had temporarily made the extraction of the glass impossible. He studied the wounded right hand once more. The shards appeared to be thick and very slightly concave; they were each about an inch or so long and had entered his palm close together, just above the fleshy part where the thumb is joined. There were parallel scratches across the face of the palm ending at the points of entry which, together with the glass, formed a surreal (but near perfect) chevron of sergeants' stripes.

He gave up in his attempts to extricate the invasive silicon and decided instead to investigate the circumstances of its appearance in his flesh. He shuffled sideways onto his knees and winced once more as pain registered in his head and spine. He wondered whether he had, possibly, fallen and bruised his back – and whether it might be connected to the hand injury.

Deciding that, as yet, he couldn't trust himself to stand erect without falling into either the bath or toilet bowl, he crawled on his good (albeit shaky) left hand and knees to the doorway where his overcoat has spent an equally uncomfortable night.

The journey that far was so painful that Bill began to wonder whether someone with a particularly cruel sense of humour had knotted his spine during the night, or, more likely, whether it was broken. Were it not for the feeling in his legs, and, as he was increasingly aware, pain in his shoulder muscles, the latter was seeming more than possible.

On reaching the doorway he used his good left hand to pull himself up until he could sit back on his feet. Cradling the damaged right hand in his lap, he pulled the overcoat fully into the doorway.

Bright (in his befuddled, hungover state; too bright) sunlight filtered across the threshold from a window at the top of the stairs. It immediately illuminated dark stains on the front of the overcoat. The right sleeve was solidly stained from cuff to elbow and there were more splashes across the front of the garment.

The overcoat was an expensive, light-brown mohair; a present from Mary the previous Christmas. Despite the contrasting dark brown colour of the stains, Bill immediately had no doubt as to what they were – blood. He dropped the coat hurriedly; drunk or sober he couldn't tolerate its metallic smell or taste when splattered across cloth or clothing.

He looked back down at his right hand, resting in his lap. The scratches along the palm were shallow; they had barely broken the skin. Despite the depth of the punctures the shards of glass were clean where they protruded from the flesh. There was no way that the injury to his hand could have produced the extent of staining visible on his discarded overcoat.

Ignoring the blinding flashes of pain in his head and back, he quickly scanned the rest of his body for sign of damage. Only when he reached his face did he find any further indication of his vital fluids having escaped their normal corporeal seclusion.

As he wiped his hand across his face, fierce pain leapt from the bridge of his nose – directly into the most sensitive pain receptors in his brain. For a moment he thought that he had used his glass encrusted right hand for the task and had subsequently amputated his proboscis. Only when he looked at the left hand that had *actually* caused the reaction did he realise that he must have a badly damaged nose.

It might not explain the presence of glass in one hand, but it could well explain the presence of so much blood on his coat. He had broken his nose after falling off a bar stool three years previously, and the subsequent blood flow had ruined a perfectly good pair of suit trousers.

He gingerly probed his nose with the undamaged left hand and, despite the pain it caused, heaved a sigh of relief when he felt bone and gristle shift under his fingers. Without doubt he had broken the thing again.

He sat back on his heels for a full minute, waiting for the pain to subside, then hauled himself to his feet with considerable assistance from the doorframe. Upright, he swayed back and forth for a few seconds until he felt his sense of balance return, and then shuffled his feet across towards the bathroom mirror.

He peered at his bleary-eyed reflection. The nose was, indeed, very puffy and there were two dark circles appearing around his already dark eyes. There was a little blood dried and matted into his neatly clipped moustache, and he assumed he had used his overcoat to mop the rest from his visage.

He crossed to the sink and ran cold water onto a washcloth with which he tenderly removed the remaining blood from his face. When the task was finished, and he was leaning against the wall urinating noisily into the toilet basin, he realised that he would have to get the coat cleaned.

It had cost Mary over five hundred pounds and he could imagine her reaction if he were to leave it where she could find it in this state. He realised that it was Saturday and that the local dry cleaners would be closed. Rather than drag his hungover and battered body into the town centre, two miles away, he resolved to have it cleaned first thing Monday. Mary, especially after their row the previous day, wouldn't return until the following Thursday. There was no rush.

He flushed the toilet, wincing as the glass in his hand brushed against the handle. He would go downstairs and find some whisky to steady the hands and then locate some tweezers with which to remove the offending shards.

Still swaying slightly, he stepped from the bathroom, pausing only to gingerly stoop and pick up the blood-stained garment in the doorway. He crossed the landing to his bedroom and ambled inside to find, on his bed, a stack of neatly ironed shirts. He couldn't remember the last time he'd seen his iron let alone use it, and, correctly, assumed that Mary had gone through his laundry while he had been out the previous day.

Sitting heavily on the end of the bed he awkwardly undid the buttons of his shirt. He removed it and examined it for further blood stains. Other than a small splash on the right cuff it was spotless. He was mildly surprised but then recalled the foul weather of the previous evening. If the accident had happened just after he had reached home, his overcoat would have been buttoned to the collar and protected the rest of his clothes.

However, that also indicated that he had not had a chance to remove the coat before the accident, and that, surely, meant that Mary would still have been present when it happened.

He cursed mildly as he pulled on a clean shirt. If that were the case, Mary would no doubt give him Hell when they next spoke. There was probably one of her acerbic notes already waiting for him in the living room.

He fumbled for some minutes, attempting to button the shirt with an unfamiliar left hand – and one that was shaking, at that. After scanning his crumpled trousers for more blood stains and finding a welcome dearth, he decided that they would service him for another day and left the bedroom to begin his search for a large nerve tonic.

He paused at the head of the stairs to steady himself before the descent. Mary had once expressed astonishment that he hadn't fallen down them when he was 'inebriated' and he hadn't, at the time, the nerve to tell her that he had far closer calls with such an accident when he woke the day after being 'inebriated' and relatively sober.

The landing was bathed in a murky sunlight which contrasted starkly with the gloom of the hallway at the foot of the stairs. In some of Bill's more self-deprecating moods he likened his morning descent from near sobriety at the top of the brightly lit flight to near certain inebriation after reaching its gloomy foot, as his personal trip from Heaven to Hell. Although sometimes it seemed like the journey was from Hell to Heaven.

He thought of the analogy again this day as he cautiously descended the thirteen steps. He idly wondered why thirteen steps were so common in a flight of stairs in modern houses but then realised that he wasn't superstitious and never would be. Reaching out, he touched the wood of the stair rail to make sure and then grinned wryly to himself.

At the foot of the gloomy flight he stepped from the last stair expecting his foot to meet the thick pile of the hallway carpet. Instead, it struck an unseen object some three inches above the carpet's surface and he stumbled wildly forward. His already precarious balance in complete disarray, Bill clutched at the tall dresser to his right, unwittingly bringing his damaged hand into contact with its hard and unyielding surface.

Yelping loudly as two of the three razor sharp shards slid easily and deeper into his hand, Bill then fell heavily onto his backside, yelping again as pain coruscated along his already bruised spine.

14

He sat stock-still for a full minute, eyes closed tightly, while the various pains subsided. When he dared open the lids again, he realised that he (or, come to that, Mary) had left the living room light on all night. The doorway was parallel to the foot of the stairs, directly opposite his current position, and in the thin shaft of light that was cast from underneath the closed living room door he could see the object that had caused his latest accident.

It was a shoe. Black, low-heeled and obviously a woman's. *Mary's?* he wondered, leaning forward to pick it up.

He never paid much attention to the way women dressed unless, of course, they were alone, working or drinking in a bar – and found his company tolerable. Mary, he imagined, was always alone, but failed miserably with the last two criteria.

His hand touched the back of the shoe and he recoiled. It was sticky to the touch, and in the dim light he could see that his thumb and index finger were now coated in a dark substance.

Forgetting for a moment his aches and pains, he scrambled to his feet and groped blindly for the hallway light switch somewhere on the wall behind him. Successful, finally, the sudden harsh glare momentarily blinded his still-sensitive eyes. When they had adjusted, he stared downwards; first at the offending shoe and then at the stains on his left hand.

Both were covered in a sticky red substance. The dark curtain that blanketed his memory of the previous night after his return from the pub lifted momentarily and he could suddenly recall Mary's face. Her eyes were wide, bulging, and although the sudden memory was soundless, she was shouting, screaming at him, her face contorted in rage.

The flashback ended as suddenly as it had begun, and he leaned against the nearest wall, gasping for breath.

'So that was it,' he thought, *'I obviously fell over or whatever when I came in; Mary flipped and landed me one with her shoe.'*

Quite why she left the offending (and offensive) weapon behind her when she departed, Bill couldn't imagine. Reaching down once more, he gingerly picked up the discarded and bloody shoe. Carrying it between the already blood-stained finger and thumb of his left hand, he awkwardly turned the handle of the living room door, cursing all the while his own stupidity, and mentally berating Mary for her unusual and out-of-character flash of violence.

The door swung open, neglected hinges squealing softly. The lighting in the living room was subdued – Bill had found that after falling asleep, drunk, on the sofa from time to time, waking to 100-watt bulbs became painful.

Nevertheless, the gentle light was more than sufficiently capable of revealing the nightmare that was now his living room. As his eyes unwillingly registered the carnage before him, Bill was dimly aware of thinking, *Not a living room – an abattoir.*

His sister's body was sitting against the far wall. She was drenched in blood, her prim white blouse, now ripped, covered to the waist in a sickly red mess. One sightless eye stared directly at Bill as he stood, open-mouthed, in the doorway.

Mary, like her brother now, was open-mouthed. She, though, had little choice. The jagged end of the neck of a whisky bottle protruded from between her teeth. The remainder of the bottle had disintegrated around her neck, wicked shards puncturing both cheeks, her left eye. A particularly large splinter had severed her jugular, although Bill immediately doubted whether she could have survived even with the vein intact.

He looked down at his hand, his head reeling, stomach churning. "Oh, dear lord," he murmured aloud. He began to shake his head. "I couldn't have," he exclaimed louder. He was dimly aware of noticing the bottle's now ragged label; Teachers. "I don't even drink that brand."

He focused again on Mary's ruined face, the blood thickly coated over her chin, neck and blouse. Without realising that it was about to happen, he vomited, violently; a thick liquid stream which splattered across the carpet and over his dead sister's outstretched legs. Dull, multicoloured spots swam across his vision as his stomach contracted, and the remains of its contents spewed forth.

Panting heavily as the convulsions passed, he shook his head once more, trying to regain his senses.

Another flashback sparked across his mind. Last night. The front door opening as he fumbled with his key. Mary. And a man. He couldn't focus clearly. A man dressed in black. Except for a, what? White shirt? Under a black jumper? Possibly. Mary, saying over and over, "I told you he'd be here!"

It winked out of his mind as quickly as the first had and once again he was left gasping.

What the hell had happened? Had he really attacked her? If so, what of the man? If he, Bill, had really killed his sister, where *was* the man?

Bill clutched at a suddenly appearing straw. He had been drunk – obviously blind drunk. Had the man attacked him, broken his nose, and then killed Mary? Is that why no police had been called?

But no, he was an intelligent man and the truth, or at least the only plausible explanation, was far simpler. Mary had been disgusted with him when he had arrived home after she had arranged (?) for someone to visit. The man had left. They had rowed (he remembered her screaming, rage-contorted face from the first flashback). His nose had been broken by Mary – either as she flew at him or as she tried to defend herself. He had found a bottle – Teachers somehow, even though he never drank the brand – and he'd attacked her.

The brand of the whisky immediately nagged at him. He was positive that he never drunk it – sure that he wouldn't have bought it. Mary wouldn't have presented him with anything more alcoholic than a wine gum. So, had the man brought it with him? If the man was a friend of Mary's, Bill doubted it.

The reality of the situation returned to Bill with a jolt and he turned, staggering out of the room, desperate suddenly not to focus on his sibling's ravaged features. In the hallway he slumped onto the stairs oblivious to the pains in his head, hand and back. Had he *really* killed his sister? Should he call the police and give himself up?

Images of him locked away (*Away from drink*! his subconscious screamed), newspapers, courts, *cell bars*, swam before him. He tried to consider his options.

Call the police? Tell the truth? Run – and keep running? An alibi? But the mysterious stranger would be bound to spoil that. Along with half of the regulars at the local.

The only thing that he could possibly decide for certain was that he wouldn't – couldn't – end up behind bars. It was not as if she hadn't, at least in some ways, deserved it. Could he plead justifiable homicide? Or was that only in America? He certainly hadn't been in full control of his senses – but would that carry any weight?

He tried to calm his fevered mind, briefly wondering at the lack of grief that he felt for Mary. His thoughts kept returning to the dark-suited, white-shirted man. He was one of three things: the killer, the witness or the alibi breaker.

Whichever he was, if Bill called the police or gave himself up, the man was a major problem. Bill, finally, reluctantly, reached a decision. Mary lived (had lived, he corrected himself) alone; she wouldn't be missed for some days. In addition, Bill needed time – time to think, maybe time to investigate the stranger, probably just time to make himself scarce.

He knew for certain that he wasn't capable of clear thought yet. A drink would help. Unfortunately, his current store of malt whisky – and one bottle of blended – was sharing a room with his sister's corpse and he *definitely* wasn't going back in there.

Getting up gingerly, he limped painfully through to the kitchen. Looking about at the cupboards, distractedly, he remembered the store of beer cans that he maintained for his occasional visitors. He crossed to the far wall and pulled open the cupboard next to the seldom-used oven. Half a dozen cans of Budweiser stared back at him. He plucked one from the shelf and fumbled, hands still shaking, with the ring pull. Succeeding at last, he raised the can to his lips and drained half of it in one pull.

Normally he wouldn't have been seen dead drinking straight from a can (a man has to set at least some standards), '*But,*' he thought, '*needs must.*' The lager was warm but as he didn't really taste it anyway it didn't bother him. He finished the can and immediately opened another.

After draining the second and third cans he paused and held his hands in front of him. The violent shakes had lessened to minor tremors. He was breathing heavily after swallowing the beer so fast, but that was ok – he was, more or less, back in control. He turned his attention to his wounded hand and gently removed two of the glass fragments. The third proved more difficult. As he tugged gently at its sharp, exposed tip the shard broke, leaving a sizeable chunk beneath the flesh.

He winced but guessed that it would have to do for now. He grabbed a fourth can and sipped at the beer as he crossed to the sink. He ran the water cold and plunged his right hand under the icy stream, gasping at the stinging sensation.

He left it there for a full five minutes, the stinging pain subsiding as his hand rapidly lost its heat. Satisfied that it was as clean as could be expected under the circumstances, he drained the beer and then dabbed the hand dry with a towel.

The hand throbbed dully, a counterpoint to his aching back, as he considered his first moves. This was complicated by the repeated flashes of his sister's dead face which insisted on crossing his mind as he stood in the bright kitchen.

Eventually, he reached a decision. He would go away for a while. Where? Bill couldn't decide that yet. He would pack a bag and wander out as if nothing was amiss. Make a point of being seen – it would be less suspicious.

Grateful for a plan of sorts he left the kitchen and climbed the stairs to his bedroom. The first thing that he saw was the blood-stained mohair coat, crumpled in a heap at the end of his bed. His first thought was to destroy this damning piece of evidence, but his mind recalled a far more damning piece of evidence sitting in his living room. He bundled the coat under the bed, more to remove it from his sight than to hide it, and then repeated the exercise with his discarded shirt.

He found a holdall in his wardrobe and filled it absent-mindedly with enough clean clothes for a week. He made one trip to the bathroom, returning with a washing kit of sorts and bundled this into a side pocket in the bag.

Checking the back pocket of his trousers he examined his wallet. It contained two credit cards, an ATM card (could he remember the PIN?), and eighty pounds in assorted notes. He would withdraw more cash on his journey. In his dressing table he located his seldom used mobile phone and put it together with his wallet, into a jacket pocket. He slipped the jacket on and stood wondering whether there was anything else he wanted.

It occurred to him that his passport might be useful, but he couldn't for the life of him remember where he'd put it. He hadn't used it since the UK had followed the sensible example of other European countries in terms of pub licensing hours and let pubs stay open all day.

He decided to forget it. He wanted to get out of the house fast – and besides, the passport was likely to be in his writing desk. The desk was in the living room. Living room? The room's name was no less inappropriate yet.

He picked up the holdall and carefully descended the stairs once more. He stopped before he reached the open door to the living room, setting down the bag at the foot of the stairs.

Closing his eyes, he reached around the door-frame and turned off the light. The curtains would have to remain drawn – he wasn't going in *there* again. It probably wouldn't draw any attention – in some of his more drunken days they remained shut for days on end. Besides, it was common practice when someone went away for a few days – even though it was a clear signal to neighbourhood burglars.

Closing the door, he almost chuckled as he imagined a burglar breaking in and finding a most horrible deterrent – Mary would have been formidable alive, dead she would scare any self-respecting burglar to death. He could almost imagine the body count growing daily.

As he stood outside the doorway, trying to work out whether there was anything else he needed to do, a third flashback hit him with all the force of the other two.

Mary, still screaming with rage. She was nearly incoherent, but one phrase hit him with tremendous force. 'If it's the last thing I do, William, I'll make you pay for wasting your life, *our inheritance*. If it's the very last *thing*!'

As her voice reached its crescendo the image vanished. Bill found himself back in the darkened hallway, arms crossed in front of his face as if warding off an attack.

Unlike the first two, the latest flashback had taken less toll on his body. His pulse rate was slightly up, but he was breathing normally. "*Enough!*" he whispered aloud. Grabbing the holdall, he opened the front door. Despite the fact that his damaged nose was incapable of smelling anything the fresh June air tasted good after the cloying atmosphere inside his house. He breathed deeply through his mouth as he locked the front door, calming his ragged nerves for the hours ahead.

20

"Bill!" The voice jolted him, and he nearly dropped the keys as he was returning them to his pocket. Looking around quickly, he saw Mrs. Jenkins, his next-door neighbour, peering over the hedge between their properties.

"Sorry, did I startle you?" she enquired, smiling inanely at him.

"Er, yes... no..." he stammered in reply, taking a deep breath to steady himself. "I was in a different world." '*Although not as different as Mary*,' he thought.

"Going away?" Mrs Jenkins asked, nodding at the holdall.

'*Doesn't miss a thing*,' he thought. "Er, yes, just a few days," he paused, "to the south coast" he added, an alibi, of sorts beginning to form.

"Oh, that's nice" his neighbour replied. "Time you had a break. Need me to water the plants?"

"No!" he exclaimed, rather more sharply than he intended. Controlling his voice, he added "Mary will be keeping an eye on them." He almost giggled when he realised just how true his comment was. '*Must be cracking up*,' he thought to himself.

"Oh, good," Mrs Jenkins said. She caught sight of Bill's swollen, discoloured proboscis. "What on earth have you been doing to your nose, Bill? Not another bar stool?"

He almost panicked but then regained enough composure to agree with her. "Er, yes, that's it. Same old story." He uttered a short, humourless laugh and glanced at his watch, anxious to be on his way, "Sorry Mrs. J., but I really must dash – train to catch."

"Oh, of course, Bill. Sorry to keep you – you know how I go on so. Well, have a nice time, be sure to send me a postcard." Her voice trailed off into the distance as Bill scampered through the gate, and with a cursory wave, hurriedly made his way along the street.

Without realising where he was headed, he found himself outside the Swan, (never would it be the 'Mucky Duck' to a halfway-sober Bill), a few minutes later.

Chapter 2

Saturday 7th June 2014

William Wilberforce Taylor, forty-nine, professional drunk, and possibly even murderer, decided that a large drink (or several) would be a good idea; a good start.

He shouldered open the door of the pub and stepped inside. The familiarity of the pre-noon Saturday lunchtime scene was immediately comforting. The nightmare quality from his waking moments to the present took on a new, surreal, quality. For the first time since he awakened Bill felt that he was finally in the real world. He also recognised that it was time for some serious thinking. First, though, a drink.

Transferring the holdall from his shoulder to his uninjured left hand, he wandered over to the bar where three of the most regular of regulars were sympathising, noisily, with a fourth.

It transpired that the fourth regular, Davie Kent, had received news which transformed his normal hangdog expression into an even more depressed and depressing sight. Eeyore on downers.

"I can't believe she's actually coming back," he moaned as Bill swung the holdall to the ground. Bill immediately, and correctly, assumed that Joan Kent, Davie's Amazonian wife, was returning to the domestic fold.

The three others were offering solace, richly spiced with amusement. Davie and Joan's domestic quarrels were a source of never-ending delight and they had been eager witnesses to a dozen or more incidents in the past eighteen months.

Amidst the choruses of 'shames', 'pities', and general words of sympathy, Bill's presence at the bar went unnoticed for a moment. He took the opportunity to gaze along the counter, wondering if any of these friends and acquaintances might provide some assistance in his plight. Collectively the group were known as the Losers' Club. With the exception of the never-married Bill and the occasionally married Davie, all were divorced.

At the furthest end of the group was Gerry Cooper. At fifty-four he was semi-retired but owned a tractor unit and undertook occasional work as a lorry driver. He was the undoubted Good Samaritan of the group, more-so even than Bill, and always willing to lend a hand to anyone in need. Bill mentally pencilled in his name as someone that might provide valuable assistance.

Next to him, Richard Bates was propping up the bar – or rather, was being propped up by it. Of the Losers' Club, he was the only one who drank more, and more consistently, than Bill. None of them could remember the last time they had seen Rich sober, but at the same time, he was far and away the most incisive and intelligent of the five – even drunk.

Davie, still bemoaning his ill-fortune, stood between Rich and Ewan. Although born in Spain, of Spanish parents and with an unmistakable Iberian complexion, Ewan considered himself Welsh. He had been named after his paternal grandfather who had hailed from the Rhondda, and after moving to London as a teenager, he had been desperately seeking to recapture his 'heritage'. Twenty years later he would still greet people with phrases such as 'Hey, how are you amigo, look you?', and in the same twenty years he had married, and divorced, four women, blaming his ever-roving, womanising nature on his Spanish blood.

He was the first to notice Bill's presence and, happy to divert his attention from the ever-more maudlin Davie, welcomed Bill with a warm hug.

"How are you doing, Billy boy?" he exclaimed.

Bill winced, both from the sudden crushing of an already bruised spine and from the hated epithet. Extricating himself from the would-be Welshman's bear-like grip, he eased himself onto a bar stool and removed his wallet from his jacket.

"Fine, Taff," he replied, "Good morning, losers one and all."

With the exception of Davie, who was still muttering into his beer, Bill's greeting was returned with the normal array of crude retorts. Somewhat drunkenly, Rich noticed Bill's damaged visage.

"William," he slurred, his right index finger pointing vaguely in Bill's direction, "You appear to be suffering from the Pinocchio syndrome. Your nose has grown."

"Very astute, that man," Bill replied, the excuse ready, "Apparently I must have drunk something, during yesterday's brief visit to these hallowed premises, which upset my system."

Before he could finish his florid and potentially accurate account a youthful voice piped up, "Yes, probably the fourteenth large whisky. Fell over again?"

Mandy, the young, intelligent and highly attractive barmaid (who doubled as a lead in each of the Losers' more lurid fantasies) had joined the group, sensibly keeping the bar counter between them.

"Very perspicacious, beautiful one," Bill acceded, "Now if you are quite finished denigrating my unblemished, if bruised, character, would you be so kind as to provide my compatriots with some alcohol?"

"Mine's a pint," said Rich immediately, never a slouch when a drink was on offer.

"Certainly, Sir," replied Mandy, extracting a personalised pint glass from the Losers' personal shelf. Rich had half a dozen of his own glasses behind the bar.

Returning to Bill's battered nose, Gerry had forsaken his bar stool and was peering myopically at it over glasses that spent most of their time hanging precariously onto the end of his own nose. "Looks broken," he declared at last, "Need a trip to the hospital?"

"Very kind, but a definite 'No' – thank you anyway, Gerald," Bill replied, already prepared for the offer. "It's really not as bad as it may seem."

Drinks had appeared before each of the group with the exception of Davie who had declined on the grounds that he should return home before Joan arrived to 'tidy up a bit'.

The other four had exchanged knowing glances. In Joan's absence, Davie was far from being the perfect housekeeper. Even if she were not returning until the *following* Saturday, Bill doubted that Davie would be able to get the house into a presentable state.

Although the company and camaraderie of his friends was more than welcome after the horrors of the morning, Bill knew that he had to think things through. Collecting his change from the bar counter, he stood with his drink. "Gentlemen, please would you excuse me for a few minutes. I need to meditate alone for a while."

Amidst a spattering of comments concerning the seriousness of Bill's hangover, and clutching a newspaper he had borrowed from Rich, he instructed the others to keep an eye on his holdall and retreated to a bench seat in the corner of the capacious bar. Settling himself painfully into the under-stuffed seat he spread the newspaper open before him and cradled the drink in his lap. He stared down at it before taking a sip. "Fine friend you are," he muttered before setting the glass down on the table.

Together with the whisky, the infusion of the normal, mundane Saturday scene after the horrors of his earlier, waking, hours, settled his mind. He began to consider the facts; desperate for some idea of what he was to do.

His first concern was Mary. Despite the evidence, despite the flashbacks – even despite his continued dread of his bullying sister – he couldn't come to believe that he had taken her life.

But if – and he was beginning to suspect that it was a very big if – he hadn't done the foul deed, then who had? There were only two suspects: himself and the mystery man. The only thing he could rule out was suicide!

He sensed intuitively that the mystery man might hold the key. From the second flashback he recalled clearly Mary saying over and over, "I told you he'd be here!". Despite the occasional blank spots in his memory brought about by a surfeit of alcohol, his recall was normally far above average. He couldn't recall a single time over the last week or so when Mary had mentioned inviting a stranger to his house. Come to that, Mary hadn't even mentioned that *she* would be arriving.

And if Mary had invited him, surely it would be someone that she knew well and trusted. He tried once more to recall the stranger's features, but except for the black clothing and what was, probably, a white shirt, the memory wouldn't surface. It was as mysterious and unfathomable as the man's presence.

This line of reasoning, he realised, was taking him nowhere. Despite the deep-down, heartfelt conviction that he couldn't have perpetrated such an act of violence, he could still not see another explanation. The only thing that was becoming clear was that if he were to be able to piece together the puzzle, he would need to find out more about the stranger – something that, in all likelihood, would be impossible were he to go to the police.

With that in mind he began to consider the next steps he should take. It might well be a matter of days before Mary, or her absence elsewhere, was discovered. But there was no way that he would enter the house again. He could, of course, find a way to dispose of the body, but he suspected that he couldn't do it alone, and was *sure* that he didn't have the capacity to deal with his sister in such a way.

His confused reaction this morning had been to run, and he began to believe that this had been the intuitively correct decision. He desperately needed time, both to get his own mind back in order – perhaps memory would return gradually – and also to consider the stranger and his part in this grisly affair.

He also realised that an alibi was out of the question. Even if the stranger proved to be no witness, he had still been present the previous evening, and the damaged state of Bill's body had been witnessed by too many people. In addition, he had already told his neighbour that he was leaving for a few days' break and he had been seen with the holdall.

He glanced in the direction of the bar and saw Gerry and Ewan pointing at the bag and obviously discussing its purpose.

Mentally shrugging in acceptance of his next course of action, he tried to work out were to go. In order to stay liberated in case Mary's remains were discovered quickly he would have to lay some sort of false trail. Were she discovered, there would be no doubt in the minds of the police that he was the culprit.

First, though, he needed to see if there was any information that he could gather in connection with the mystery man. Taking these two facts into consideration he reached the first positive, and fully conscious, decision that he had made since discovering his living room's hideous occupant.

He hated involving anyone else in his plan but couldn't see an acceptable alternative. He glanced, again, at the bar where Gerry and Ewan were still talking animatedly. Draining the last of his whisky, he folded the unread newspaper and, wincing at the effort, stood.

On his return to the bar the Losers, their number now depleted by one due to the return home of the ever-more morose Davie, had turned their attentions away from the likely cause of Bill's distended proboscis to the holdall.

"Deserting us, boyo?" Ewan asked in his inimitable Mediterranean/Welsh accent.

"Just for a few days," Bill replied, placing the newspaper back into Rich's overcoat pocket. "Mary's idea I'm afraid. She thought a few days in Brighton under her care would be of benefit to my smog-smothered constitution."

"Battered you into agreement, did she?" asked Gerry, pointing at Bill's damaged snout.

Bill didn't like this turn in the discussion and mumbled a non-committal reply before offering to refresh everyone's glasses as a diversion.

Before the discussion could be resumed, Rich provided a welcome distraction. "'S not your round, Bill," he said, swaying away from the bar. In an effort to extract a twenty-pound note from his back pocket, under the voluminous overcoat he always wore, gravity claimed his wavering form.

Amidst much hilarity, he was helped to his feet by Gerry and Ewan. While Rich regained both his composure and his balance, Ewan returned to the forthcoming absence of Bill.

"Brighton, is it?" he asked. He continued without waiting for a reply, "I've got a girlfriend down there. Beautiful, she is."

Leaving Ewan to reminisce, Gerry asked Bill a question he was delighted to hear. "Do you and Mary need a lift?"

Bill had wondered how he would request the favour from Gerry and mentally thanked the lord that his friend's good nature had saved him the effort.

"Gerry!" he replied, feigning surprise to cover his relief, "That is a most magnanimous gesture. I will gladly accept your services, for an appropriate fee, of course," he waved away Gerry's protestations and went on, "Mary has already departed, but she called before she left saying that I was to collect something from her house and to meet her at the station in Brighton. I would be most grateful for your assistance, kind sir."

"No problem," said Gerry, "And no fee either. What are friends for?"

Bill felt a small pang of guilt before he went on, "Her place is in Redhill," he said, "Perhaps if you could give me a lift there, I'll then make my own way to the station – I have a ticket."

"Fine, fine," replied Gerry, dismissively, "You want to leave now?"

Courtesy of Rich, a fresh whisky had been placed in front of Bill. "Most certainly not," he replied, warming to his part, "If I've got to spend an entire week in the company of my dear sibling, I should, at least, enjoy a last, pleasant drink in the company of friends." Feeling as if he had finally taken a step in the right direction, Bill raised his glass and toasted the Losers. "Good health, gentlemen. Remember me when I've gone."

Amidst a small chorus of "Good Luck" and "Cheers", Bill drained his glass and extracted another note from his wallet.

* * * * *

Franklin awoke with a start from a nightmare that he could all too vividly recall. In it, he was running through storm drenched streets, zigzagging through alleyways and darting across vacant car parks. Behind him as he ran, he could hear the thunderous footfalls of Hart, keeping pace and distance behind him.

In the dream he had begun to look over his shoulder every so often, expecting to see Hart dropping back. Hart didn't, and every glance that Franklin gave behind him brought the monstrous figure another few centimetres closer. Franklin looked from the evil, leering face to the weapon at Hart's side. Despite the storm clouds, a bright moon reflected incongruously off the ornate buckle of a thick leather belt. In the surreal light it appeared to drip blood and Franklin was becoming certain that it would soon be joined by his own.

The nightmare Hart kept repeating the same guttural threat over and over again: "Come back here, you black bastard. I've got to teach you a little discipline."

Despite his relative youth and fitness, the constant glances over his shoulder were drawing Franklin within reach of the lumbering beast behind him. His legs were beginning to tire and he started to feel the first waves of cramp in his thighs as lactic acid flooded his muscles.

He sprinted around a corner, barely beyond reach of Hart's belt and its blood-soaked buckle. It was a dead end. An alleyway blanked off by a sheer brick wall. Panicking, Franklin surveyed the walls on either side, his breath coming in ragged gasps. The walls were featureless; he was trapped. He was going to die at the hands of his evil foster father. In just six months he would have been freed from the 'care' system but now that liberation was about to be taken from him...

Behind him Hart began to swing the belt back and forth, the blood red buckle crashing into waste skips either side of the alleyway's entrance; the noise deafening in the confines of the trap.

Franklin waited for the first blow.

He had jerked awake as his conscious mind overruled the subconscious nightmare generator. The crashing booming sounds were real.

At first Franklin was completely disorientated. A thin, dim light spilled over him, courtesy of a small rectangular plastic window in the roof of the trailer. The loud booming noise was deafening in the confines of the enclosed metal room, and he came close to panic, scrabbling to his knees and clutching at his still-wet jacket, before memory came flooding back.

Hart. The flight. The lorry.

The booming, clanging noise stopped abruptly. Franklin became aware that he had been holding his breath and exhaled slowly, looking around him. He wondered, briefly, whether it really was Hart outside, seeking for a way in to him, but the angle of the sun indicated that it was near midday. He looked at his phone's clock app, but it was dark and dead, and he remembered its treacherous part in the previous night's ugly scene.

From outside he heard a final metallic thump and a man's voice.

"No, it won't come. The bloody trailer hook-up is stuck fast."

Another voice, also male, said something but Franklin couldn't make it out. The first voice returned.

"No, it's alright Bill. We'll just have to take the damn trailer with us."

Two doors slammed and after a short pause, a diesel engine roared into life, its echoes reverberating around the trailer, empty of all but a bewildered

Franklin. Dimly he was aware of wondering, last night, whether he would wake up on the road to a destination unknown. As the lorry lurched forward, and despite the near-deafening roar, Franklin smiled.

Any romantic notions Franklin may have harboured about his journey into the unknown were, however, soon dispelled. The lorry lurched violently at every junction and the steady drone of the diesel, combined with a constant vibration, were threatening to induce a migraine.

During a particularly long stop – at a junction, he assumed – Franklin wound a pocket-watch he always carried, a souvenir of a previous life. It wasn't because he was suddenly aware of the time, but to give him an indication as to how long the journey was taking, and ten minutes later when he checked, Franklin wished that he left the watch alone – he had been sure that an hour had passed.

Resigned to his plight and at the same time cautiously hopeful, Franklin passed his time by counting his belongings. He had the grand total of sixteen pounds and twenty-two pence in coins of various type, a replacement battery for his phone with as much charge as the one currently in the Samsung, a Swiss army knife with two broken blades, and his ancient diary-come-address book. It wasn't a princely haul, but he guessed it would be enough for a night in a youth hostel or YMCA, until he could work out some kind of plan.

He wedged himself into a corner of the trailer and waited.

* * * * *

In the cab, Gerry was trying to ward off Bill's over enthusiastic gratefulness.

"Bill, honestly. Not another word. It's no trouble at all."

"So you keep saying," Bill replied, doggedly, "But when you discovered that the trailer-hitch, or whatever the technical term is, wouldn't allow you to detach the rear half, surely it would have been easier to let me get a cab?"

Gerry sighed and glanced across at his passenger. In truth, driving with the empty trailer *was* a pain, but at the same time, the sheer pleasure of doing a friend a favour far outweighed the drawback. And especially as the friend was Bill.

Despite Gerry's well-known acts of kindness – all the assistance he had given others – he couldn't remember a single time when Bill had accepted help in any fashion. This was definitely an exceptional pleasure.

"Bill," he said, patiently, "Please. Not another word on the matter – and that's final! This is a pleasure."

"Oh, very well, Gerald," Bill replied, sighing, "But it really is most generous of you."

"Enough!" exclaimed Gerry, laughing.

"Sorry, sorry. By the way, how much do I owe you for your time?"

Gerry groaned. "Bill, for the last time, this is a pleasure, a favour; merely carrying it out is reward enough. Now, if you want to repay me at all, grab the Sat-Nav and see if you can find an easy route through South London."

Gerry was very well aware of all routes through South London – easy and otherwise – but he figured that it might keep Bill quiet for a while. Twenty minutes later he had decided that, maybe, it hadn't been such a good idea, as he gingerly reversed the articulated lorry out of a one-way street. For the next ten minutes he was forced to listen to Bill's stream of abject apologies.

They arrived at the outskirts of Redhill an hour later, Bill's Sat-Navigation notwithstanding. Gerry heaved yet another sigh of relief when Bill pointed to a small road on their left.

"That's the one," Bill said.

Gerry eased the lorry to the side of the main street they were currently travelling along. "Okay, Bill," he said, killing the engine, "I'll never get this rig up that street, so I'll wait here for you."

"Fine, Gerald, fine," Bill replied, searching his pockets for his keys. Eventually locating them, he clambered awkwardly from the cab and made off in the direction of his dead sister's house, leaving Gerry to keep a watchful eye on his mirrors in case a traffic warden came along.

It had been nearly two years since Bill had last visited his sister's home and he only recognised the house by the large 'Jesus Saves' poster in a ground floor window. Mary had been very keen on the church.

He let himself into the house and wandered through the downstairs rooms searching for a likely place in which Mary might possibly have kept an address book. After opening the twentieth drawer in his search, Bill began to think that Mary might carry her address book with her – in which case it was currently sharing his living room with her. And there was no way he was returning *there* to look for it.

On the point of giving up, he returned to the front door and cast his eyes around the hallway. They lighted upon Mary's house telephone – just as old-fashioned as his sister. It was sitting on a small shelf behind the front door, and, more importantly, on a small book.

In his haste to retrieve the book he dropped the telephone, the handset snapping neatly in two on the tiled floor. He realised that anyone now attempting to telephone her would find her telephone apparently busy and drop straight to the answerphone. Ideal.

He quickly scanned the address book, and with some surprise discovered that almost every page was filled with names and numbers, and that rather than following the normal alphabetical order, the names appeared to be grouped into categories. he realised that he knew very little of his sister's private life and was surprisingly dismayed by the sheer volume of names in the book.

He was standing in the hallway, still riffling through the pages when inspiration struck. At some point during his earlier search he had chanced upon a small, well-ordered file containing Mary's domestic bills. He hurried back into the front room and started the process of opening and closing drawers once more.

At the fifth attempt he located the file and flipped it open at the section headed 'telephone'. Mary had filed everything religiously (pun intended) and the most recent two bills were at the front of the section. Behind each of the bills were print-outs containing itemised lists of all calls made by Mary. Bill figured that the telephone number of the mysterious stranger must have been contacted by Mary recently, possibly even often, and comparison of the itemised numbers with those listed in her address book represented the best possible chance of him discovering the man's identity. For once he was glad that his sister had been even more anti-technology than he was himself.

He hastily, and unceremoniously, tore the print-outs from the file and stuffed them, together with the address book, into his jacket pocket.

Returning everything else to order, he glanced about once more, idly thinking that Mary would miss the place. Shrugging off the weird thought, he made his way out of the house studiously locking it behind him.

The sky was once more clouding over and another June shower began to spatter against his jacket as he hurried back to Gerry.

*****

In the back of the lorry Franklin had come awake as the engine died. He listened intently and heard a single door open and close. Aware that two men had entered the cab earlier, he waited. He glanced at his inaccurate watch and fifteen minutes later had decided that the two men must have slipped out of the same door of the cab. He was making his way cautiously to the trailer's rear doors when he heard the cab door opening once more.

He scrambled back to the corner as the diesel roared into life again.

*****

"Got what you wanted?" Gerry asked as Bill clambered into the cab beside him.

"Certainly, Gerald," Bill replied, panting slightly from the exertion of climbing the steep cab steps.

"Great. Where to now?"

"This really is most awfully kind of you..." Bill began.

"Oh, no," interrupted Gerry, "Not that again."

Bill chuckled, "Message understood. Ok, then. As a final favour, could you drop me at the British Rail station?"

"I thought you were off to Brighton?"

"No!" Bill exclaimed, more sharply than he had intended. "Or rather, yes. But by train; Mary's already bought my ticket, remember? Er... Shame to waste it."

"Nonsense," replied Gerry, "It's a nice run down to the coast," he was about to go on, but an increasingly agitated Bill interrupted him.

"Really Gerald, I couldn't impose on you any further," he said, waving away Gerry's protestations. "Besides, it's years since I travelled on a train." In desperation he added, "And were you to insist, then I would have to make my gratitude extremely obvious."

Gerry considered an hour and a half of Bill's non-stop gratitude and shuddered. "Well alright then," he relented, "The station it is – if you're absolutely sure?"

"I am," Bill replied, relieved. "Indubitably."

They arrived at Redhill station fifteen minutes later and Gerry pulled the lorry into a parking bay in the station car park, shutting the engine off as he did so. Bill was once more alarmed.

"Er, thanks, Gerald, but there's no need to wait with me."

"I know," Gerry grinned, amused that Bill didn't want to be seen off by him, "But you forget – I had a morning-after pint before we left; I'm busting." He gestured towards the public lavatories, situated just behind his selected parking space.

"Oh, thank goodness for that," Bill sighed, and then to cover his overt relief, "I mean, very convenient conveniences are they not?"

Gerry grinned, "A hedge would have done, but under the circumstances, yes." He extracted the keys from the ignition and the two men clambered out, Bill dropping his holdall in the process.

* * * * *

In the back, Franklin heard the doors open and, eventually, close. He scampered quietly to the back of the trailer and in the dim light scanned the doors for a handle. There didn't appear to be one.

He could vaguely remember pulling the heavy door closed behind him the previous night, using a rope attached to the top of the door. The rope was still present, and he tugged on it in the forlorn hope that it was somehow connected to a release mechanism of some type. The door rattled but didn't budge. He tugged harder with the same result. He was wondering whether to start banging on the door in the hope of attracting attention when the decision was made for him.

34

The door's handle rattled and suddenly there was watery sunlight spilling into the trailer. Blinking at the sudden brightness, Franklin heard a cultured, middle-aged voice.

"Well, well, Gerald. It looks as if you've acquired a stowaway."

* * * * *

Gerry and Bill had just reached the back of the trailer when they heard the first rattle of the trailer doors. They paused, Bill raising an enquiring eyebrow towards Gerry, who shrugged.

When the rattling recommenced, Gerry reached forward and flipped the unlocked door handle upwards. Gravity took over and the door slowly swung open to reveal a young, dark-skinned man, blinking violently.

At Bill's comment, Franklin began to stammer his excuses. "Sorry, man, I mean, mister... er, sir. I sort of climbed in last night..." he trailed off as Gerry waved him into silence.

Gerry looked at the slightly frantic black youth for a moment then gestured him out, offering his hand in the process. "I think an explanation is called for," he suggested. "Feel like a coffee?" His invitation also took in Bill who was standing beside him and clearly grateful for the diversion.

Franklin realised that he was gasping for a drink and, given the circumstances, he had little choice but to accept the offer. Taking the proffered hand, he vaulted athletically from the trailer. He could immediately see that both men appeared to be friendly and hung on fervently to the hope that if he told them of Hart, they might not take him straight to the nearest police station. 'And besides,' he thought, 'neither of the men looked as if they would be able to catch him if he made a run for it.'

"Sure," he replied in answer to the offered refreshments. Looking about him, he added, "By the way, man, where are we?"

"The beautiful Surrey town of Redhill, young man," Bill replied. "I'm Bill and this is Gerald."

"Gerry," said Gerry.

"And who might you be?" Bill continued, unperturbed.

Franklin wondered whether he should reveal his name but decided it wouldn't matter much either way if he was going to tell them his tale of woe.

"Franklin," he replied, "Franklin Richardson. By the way," he added, "I'm black." It was a comment he used when he was nervous in the company of strangers and accompanied by his beaming grin, it normally relaxed all concerned. He was delighted to see that it had worked in the current situation.

"Well, master Richardson," Bill said, grinning, "Let us see if we can find liquid refreshment courtesy of our National train network."

Gerry closed the door of the trailer and the trio wandered into the station.

Glancing along the platform, Bill observed, "That is either a place to purchase tickets or exactly what we are looking for." He pointed to a sign reading 'Traveller's Feast'.

Gerry ordered a large coffee for himself, a large coke for Franklin and a large whisky (somewhat predictably) for Bill. Following Franklin's hungry gaze, he added a cheese and bacon burger to the order, paid, and excused himself, departing in search of the toilet facilities.

Bill and Franklin carried the refreshments across to a vacant table in the furthest corner of the room and pulled up an assortment of chairs.

"Do you mind, Bill?" Franklin asked, nodding towards the steaming burger.

"Not at all, dear boy," Bill replied, "Sustenance before the explanations, and all that." He drained his whisky and returned to the bar for another while Franklin wolfed the snack.

He had just returned to the table with a large whisky in each hand ('a balanced diet', he remarked), when Gerry returned.

"Well then, Franklin," he began, perching precariously on a stool, "How did you come to get a free ride to Redhill?"

Franklin gulped down the last of the burger and regarded the inquisitive faces before him. They looked kindly enough. He wondered whether he should spin a tale of misery and suffering; play on their sympathy. It suddenly dawned on him that, at least of late, no exaggeration would be required.

He sipped at his coke and then began. "I suppose it started seventeen years ago." He looked up to see if either Gerry or Bill were about to protest at this potentially preposterous opening line, but they simply waited patiently for him to continue.

"You see, I'm an orphan, and in the care – huh – of the social services until my next birthday…"

He hadn't intended to, but somehow his entire life story spilled out of him, an occasional question from either Bill or Gerry, and a short break for refreshments, the only things to interrupt his flow. He vaguely realised that he had never told anyone this much about himself and now here he was spilling it out to two complete strangers.

He finished his tale by relating the events of the previous evening, concluding with his last waking thought, that he might find himself waking in the trailer on the way to an exotic destination, unknown.

"I don't know if Redhill qualifies as exotic," Bill remarked into the silence when Franklin finished speaking, "But I get the distinct feeling that it is an admirable beginning." He recognised a similarity between himself and Franklin but wasn't able to fathom what on Earth it might be.

"Is all this true?" Gerry asked, eventually.

"Sure, man. No shit…. I mean, that's right." Franklin replied.

"A pretty pickle, as they say," said Bill thoughtfully. "And what, young sir, do you propose to do now?"

Franklin looked at the two thoughtful faces. "Any ideas guys?" he asked, plaintively.

"Well," Gerry began, "Obviously we should first of all contact the social services…."

Franklin looked aghast, "No way, man! They'd just send me back to the Harts."

"Surely not if we explain?" Gerry countered.

"Won't do no good," Franklin shook his head emphatically, "They never believe me – never have. I'm just a troublemaker in their books. Ms. Thomsett is just about the worst social worker I've ever had." He looked beseechingly from Gerry to Bill.

"Even so," Gerry said, "You're still more-or-less a minor…"

"A moment please, Gerry," Bill interrupted. "I have a strong inclination to believe young Franklin. And even if only half of his latest troubles are true, I feel that some time should be set aside to work out the options."

Franklin nodded eagerly.

"Bill," Gerry said in his best schoolmasterly voice, "There isn't time. Franklin's already been missing for one night and, besides, you're off to visit Mary and Brighton; you should have left an hour ago at least, she'll be worried."

"No, she won't," Bill replied, positively, shuddering at the thought of her waiting for him. "And besides, I'm loathe to endanger the young man without at least considering his alternatives." He eyed the watchful Franklin and finally reached a decision. "Ever visited Brighton?" he asked. Franklin would be an even better diversion than Gerry had been so far in his escape.

Franklin's eyes widened in surprise and hope, but before he could reply, Gerry cut in.

"Bill!" he exclaimed, exasperated. "You can't be serious. I mean," he spluttered, "If nothing else, think how it would look if you were found in the company of some runaway on the South Coast. I shudder to think. Front page of the newspapers, police, reporters – it'd kill Mary."

"Nonsense," Bill replied calmly and once again positively. "The lad deserves a fair break. Besides, he's seventeen, coming up for eighteen – isn't that right, Franklin?"

Franklin was about to mention that his birthday was six months away when he noticed the look in Bill's eyes. "Yeah, that's right, man." he replied, a little uncertain.

Gerry's continued exasperation meant that he missed the surreptitious eye contact. "Bill, you're crazy!" he said, at a loss for anything else to say.

"Far from it," Bill replied, still calm, "I am merely a humanitarian, and if you really want to help an old friend," he went on, playing his trump card somewhat guiltily, "you will return to Walthamstow and forget you ever set eyes on young Franklin here."

Gerry was speechless and close to apoplexy, but Bill had caught him in a particularly soft spot. If Bill wanted help, and Bill *really* thought that he could, in turn, help Franklin, then *surely* he should go along with the idea?

"Oh, Bill," he sighed, knowing already that he would go along with his friend's daft scheme. "Just make sure that you don't end up in trouble yourself."

Franklin had watched the exchange fascinated. He wondered whether Bill might not be some kind of gay paedophile but dismissed the thought. Even if he was, and Gerry's reactions seemed to indicate the contrary, he would be no match for Franklin. He spoke up.

"Yeah, Gerry," he said, "All I need is some time to sort things out, and if I'm in Brighton no-one will come looking for me for a while." He glanced at Bill for support which was quickly forthcoming.

"You see, Gerry, Franklin merely needs a little time and space to sort out a particularly knotty problem."

"I still think you're crazy – both of you." Gerry replied. It was a token protest and he was well aware of the fact.

"That's settled then," Bill said in a business-like way. He offered his hand for Gerry to shake. "I know you are a man of your word, Gerald – a gentleman of honour."

Gerry groaned inwardly, any thoughts of reporting Franklin's last known whereabouts (without mentioning Bill, of course) drained from him. "Oh well, if you really think that it's for the best..." he said, shaking the proffered hand.

Bill winced as Gerry's lorry driver grip clamped down over the remaining shard of glass. Gerry didn't notice, too preoccupied with rolling his eyes heavenward and shaking his head sorrowfully.

"Well," Bill said after reclaiming his damaged mitt, "You had better be on your way, Gerald." He was anxious that Gerry didn't find out that he had no intention of departing for Brighton.

Gerry looked at his watch. Four thirty; he could be back at the Mucky Duck inside two hours. Perhaps a few pints would help him forget his friend's foolishness. "Ok," he agreed, "Just be *careful* – both of you." He rose and fished his keys out of his pocket. "Bill," he added, "Don't forget to send us a postcard."

Bill got to his feet as well and patted him companionably on the shoulder. "Of course not," he said, gently guiding Gerry towards the door, "I'll see you very soon." He wondered, though, whether he would ever see him again.

Gerry took a couple of steps and then turned back to face the still seated Franklin. "Good luck, son," he said to him, "And if you do get stuck with Bill for a couple of days, make sure he doesn't get *too* drunk."

"Thanks, man," Franklin replied, genuinely grateful and still a little surprised at Bill's hold over his friend.

Gerry waved and wandered out onto the platform. Halfway back to his lorry he stopped and laughed aloud. He could just picture Mary's face when Bill turned up with a six-foot tall black youth in tow. Still chuckling to himself he climbed into his lorry and began the tortuous journey back through the London streets.

Inside the bar Bill ordered himself another large whisky and a coke for Franklin. Setting the drinks on the table, he sat and stared thoughtfully at the boy for a full minute.

Franklin, accustomed to such close scrutiny, tried his best to ignore him. *'The guy seemed ok,'* he thought, and although he had planned to bug out just as soon as he could he now decided that maybe, just maybe, he might hang around for a day or two. The guy was, after all, smart and compassionate. Maybe he really could be of assistance.

Eventually Bill broke the silence. "Franklin," he said. The boy looked up. "I have read in some of the more reputable newspapers that in order to have a youth or child trust you, you must first show them complete trust yourself. Would you agree with that?"

"Lost me there somewhere, man," Franklin replied, confused with this new and sudden shift in the conversation.

Bill tried a different tack. "Ok," he said, "Let's start by me saying that I really think that I might be of some assistance to you." Franklin shrugged noncommittally. "In turn," Bill went on," I think that you might likewise be of some assistance to my good self."

Franklin raised an eyebrow, a little suspicious and a little surprised, but remained silent.

"In order for us to be of such mutual assistance, I believe that we should trust one another."

"That ain't easy, man," Franklin commented with feeling.

"No, I can imagine," Bill continued, patiently. He decided that he should risk a small disclosure to test the water. "I'm not, in actual fact, heading for Brighton."

Once more Franklin registered slight surprise but said nothing.

"In fact," Bill plunged on a little desperately, "Like yourself, I need to... shall we say, *disappear* for a few days; time to think and all that."

"No shit, man?" Franklin was genuinely surprised. "What's going down?"

Momentarily baffled by the phraseology, Bill frowned and finally translated the question. "Oh, I see. Well, I can't really go into too many details," he explained, mentally cringing after his earlier comments about mutual trust, "But let's say that I may have a spot of bother – serious bother – and that it could well come to pass that the constabulary will be enquiring as to my whereabouts."

Franklin was equally confused by Bill's mode of speech, but eventually got the drift. "You reckon the filth will be after your ass soon, right?" he asked, now thoroughly interested.

"Yes, that is, in less colourful terms, most certainly what I'm trying to say. For that reason, I've led everyone to believe that I'm departing for a few days in Brighton. In actuality I'm thinking of heading North."

"Wow!" Franklin was enthralled. "That's really wicked; just like in the films. You're on the run and trying to cover your tracks." His voice rose in excitement.

Bill looked around, alarmed. "Shh!"

Franklin simmered down a little, "Sorry, man," he whispered at near full volume. A sudden thought struck him. "But why do you want to help me out if you're on the run and already in trouble yourself?" he asked, rising slightly from his seat.

Frantically signalling for Franklin to quieten his voice, Bill replied, "I'm beginning to wonder."

"Sorry, man," Franklin replied, sotto-voce.

"Well, I look at it this way," Bill continued when Franklin was settled back in his seat, "We both appear to be in the same proverbial boat. Providence seems to have brought us together and I really believe that we may be of use to each other in the short term."

Suspicion flared in Franklin's mind. "Hey, man, you're not gay or anything, are you?" his voice carried an implied threat.

"What!" Bill exclaimed, nonplussed. "Oh *that*. No, definitely not. I meant useful in more, er, practical terms."

"Such as?" Franklin asked, not thoroughly placated.

"Well," replied Bill, a little unsure himself, "Let's say that I'm not exactly worldly-wise – streetwise, I believe the term is these days. You appear to have that quality."

"Ok," said Franklin, accepting the reply at face value, "And what do I get out of this?"

Bill was still unsure of his own motives. "Well, to be frank, er, Franklin, I could simply just telephone the police..." he regretted the remark as soon as it had left his lips.

Franklin's eyes blazed. "Oh, right. Yeah. I get it, man – you're just like all the rest." he grabbed his jacket and began to rise.

"No, look, sorry." Bill pleaded in a forced whisper. He glanced around; no-one appeared to have taken any notice of them. "Sorry," he repeated, beseechingly.

Franklin paused, one arm through his jacket sleeve. "Go on," he said darkly. Normally he would have simply got up and left, but there was something about this man that fascinated him – especially the admission about being 'on the run'.

Bill groped for words. "I'm sorry about that," he said eventually, "I wouldn't do that – call the police – I promise. Please, this is very difficult; stay a while and listen." For some reason, totally inexplicable as it was, he felt that he needed someone like Franklin around. His logical, rational mind screamed that it was foolhardy; completely senseless and a potential great danger to his freedom. But a deeper, primal intuition overrode the pleas.

"I'll explain," he began, "But not here, it's too public." He drained his whisky and stood, motioning towards the door as he did so. "Let's take a walk."

Franklin weighed up the options. He could run, he could simply stay where he was and trust that Bill wouldn't phone the police. In the end curiosity, and a nagging magnetism towards the man, won through. *'Curiosity,'* he thought, 'killed the cat, – but what the hell, they had nine lives, didn't they?' He slipped his other arm into the jacket. "This I've gotta hear," he said.

Chapter 3

When they left the station, the older man pausing to check that Gerry's lorry had, indeed, departed, Bill had no idea what he was going to tell the young man. He said nothing until they had found a bank and had withdrawn three hundred pounds from the ATM, the pair walking a little apart in an uneasy silence.

"This is all part of the misdirection," Bill commented, replacing his wallet. "I want people to believe I travelled south."

Franklin had been content to wait for Bill's explanations, but this seemed nothing new. "So, what's happening?" he asked impatiently.

Bill motioned towards a side street and Franklin followed, a little reluctantly. At the end of the street a small cemetery, neglected and overgrown with weeds, loomed on their right. Bill climbed through the broken railings and, checking that they would be alone, perched himself on a rickety wooden bench that was still slightly damp from the earlier shower. He shrugged the holdall from his shoulder and gestured to Franklin that he should also sit.

"What the hell," muttered Franklin, seating himself at the opposite end of the bench.

Bill sat in silence for a while, staring at the ground immediately in front of him. Franklin was about to give up and leave the man to his mysteries when Bill began to speak.

Up until the time the words began to spill from his mouth Bill still wasn't aware of what he was going to say. He was troubled by his apparent need of Franklin's company and it was only when he suggested to himself that perhaps this was going to be some kind of quasi-religious confession, that the words began to flow.

"I think," he began, pausing to find the right words, and failing, "That you may be in the company of a murderer."

He looked up to see what reaction his admission had brought from the youth. Franklin looked back at him expressionlessly. "Go on," he said.

Bill returned his gaze to the ground at his feet and, as objectively as he could, described what he remembered of the previous day and all that had happened since he had woken in his bathroom that morning. When he had finished, he sat in silence his gaze still directed ground-wards, wondering why on Earth he had told this virtual stranger his dark secret, and, equally, wondering what Franklin's reaction would be.

Franklin, too, sat in silence for a while. He had been trying to second guess Bill's story before the man had started to speak. He had never imagined that it could have been so serious. Nevertheless, an irrational part of his mind not only believed Bill's story, but also believed Bill innocent of the crime.

"Shit, man," he said eventually; quietly, "I guess you *do* have a good reason to get away for a while." Bill didn't react. Franklin's mind whirled. Then a prior comment Bill had made jumped into his mind. "That's what you meant by all that stuff about trust, wasn't it?" he asked.

"Remarkably perspicacious." Bill finally looked up at Franklin. Seeing his blank look, he explained, "By which I mean, 'quite correct'. Now that I've told you, should you decide to follow on, you'll know that I won't do anything to jeopardise your situation." He paused before going on. "For some unknown, and highly illogical, reason, I have just told you that I have possibly murdered my own sister. I've told you this because, equally illogically given that I don't know you from Adam, I somehow trust you. Should you decide to 'turn me in' or whatever the modern parlance would have it, that is your choice. I wouldn't blame you. Equally, should you decide to shun my offer of assistance under the circumstances, I wouldn't blame you for that either. But rest assured that my intentions, as is said in other circumstances, are entirely honest and honourable."

Both parties sat for a while, staring at one another; two minds reeling with their respective thoughts and emotions.

Eventually Franklin laughed. "Hey man, you're really straight, ain't you?"

Bill, without knowing why, smiled and nodded in response.

"Don't know why, man," Franklin went on, shaking his head as if not believing his own mind, "But I really don't think you did it." Bill looked a little surprised. "Shit, it looks like we're both due a little break."

Franklin's laughter subsided, and the two men regarded each another once more. "So, what's your plan, Bill?"

Bill wondered at Franklin's ability to absorb his story so readily before he replied to the boy's question. '*In for a penny*,' he thought. "Well, I've acquired Mary's address book and telephone bills," he explained, "I had considered taking a couple of days going through them to see if I could identify the stranger. I was going to simply take a train heading northwards and see where I arrived."

Franklin nodded. "Sounds a great start, man," he agreed, "But where do I fit in?"

It was Bill's turn to grin. "I hadn't actually planned on *anyone* else fitting in," he replied, "But I just have the feeling that our mutual difficulties may well be solved should we stick together."

Franklin thought for a moment before replying. "I suppose I've got nothing to lose," he said. "Hey, man, it might even be fun – on the run with a wanted man!"

"Hmm," Bill said. "Just one thing. Could you drop that awful American accent?"

"That's a deal," Franklin replied, "As long as you keep your words down to a *maximum* of four syllables."

Bill laughed. A weight was slowly lifting. '*God knows when*,' he thought, '*But I actually think that things might work themselves out*.' He stood up quickly, once more the business-like Bill. "Well, time waits for no man. Let us depart." He offered his hand to Franklin.

Franklin took it and grasped it tightly. Bill winced once more. As Franklin hurriedly let go, Bill tucked the damaged hand under his left armpit, still grimacing.

"What's wrong?"

Gingerly, Bill held out his hand for Franklin's inspection. The boy examined it before reaching into his pocket. As he withdrew his Swiss Army knife Bill tried to draw away. Franklin, however, had anticipated the move, and clung tightly to Bill's fingers.

"This won't hurt a bit, man," he said, extracting a blade awkwardly with his free hand.

Bill closed his eyes, trying to avoid thoughts of tetanus or worse. A moment later he felt a pinprick in the palm of his hand, followed by gentle pressure. His hand was released.

"Nothing to it," Franklin said.

Bill opened his eyes and stared at his palm. The glass was gone, a small, neat, cut in its place. "Thank you," he said, "But, please, next time, warn me – I can't stand the sight of blood."

Franklin refolded the blade and tossed aside the sliver of glass. "Definitely not the killer type, are you Bill?"

"No," Bill replied, both ruefully and truthfully.

"By the way, Bill," Franklin said, "I'm real short on cash...."

Bill waved his words away. "That, Franklin, is no problem."' He reached into his wallet and extracted two twenty-pound notes. "Call it surgeon's fees," he said, handing them to a protesting Franklin. "I reckon you'll pass for eighteen-plus," he added, "Before we depart, I think I'd better have a post-operative drink. You're buying."

Franklin shrugged, grinned, and accepted the notes. "We'd better make us some plans while we're at it," he suggested.

"True," agreed Bill, "And also, we'd better buy you some clothes and things if we're going to be away for a day or three."

"Need any more surgical work?"

* * * * *

Wandering back in the general direction of the station, Bill and Franklin first stopped in a chain store dealing exclusively in the latest 'street' fashions. Despite Franklin's continued protestations, Bill insisted on him buying sufficient clothes to last a week.

"He's just arrived from Romania," he told a bemused shop assistant.

"Oh," she replied, "He speaks very good English."

47

Bill and Franklin retreated to the High Street, both giggling. "Man, you're a bust," Franklin commented.

"Oh, dear Lord, pray for the English language," Bill moaned, raising his eyes heavenwards.

"Sorry, man... er, Bill."

They spent a further half an hour purchasing toiletries, and a small amount of 'medicinal supplies' which amounted to two litres of Scotland's finest. At six o'clock, the High Street shops now closing, they strolled into a pub close by the railway station. The unlikely pair had each fallen into a companionable frame of mind, comfortable with each other's presence, but both still unsure of themselves. Although it went unsaid, both felt as if they had known each other far longer than the single afternoon they had been together. Under their extreme circumstances, it worried neither of them one iota.

At the bar Bill ordered a large whisky and an orange juice for Franklin. Franklin, not averse to the occasional lager, began to protest, but Bill had launched into another improbable spiel.

"Yes," he was explaining to an attentive barman, "The lad's still in training, but I reckon he'll be the new Usain Bolt. Marvellous times he's been clocking. Of course, I used to be a miler myself; maybe you've heard of me...."

Franklin groaned, collected the orange juice and retreated to a pinball table in the furthest corner of the bar. A few minutes later he became aware of Bill's presence.

"Quite finished with your athletic memoirs?" he enquired, glancing at Bill.

"Absolutely. Impressive, was I not?"

"Incredible, more like," Franklin replied, grinning, "You should write stories."

The game finished, and Franklin followed Bill to a table near the door where they had left their bags. "By the way," he asked, "What *do* you do?"

Bill cradled his drink between his hands for a moment. Franklin noticed that he had added another measure or two to the glass. Answering Franklin's question, Bill said:

"To tell the truth, very little. The inheritance I spoke of, has successfully enabled me to avoid the drudgery of the nine-to-five routine. In fact," he added, "It's enabled me to avoid work altogether."

Franklin looked impressed.

"Don't get me wrong," Bill continued, "I have occasionally exerted the odd grey cell. The odd short story here and there; compiling the odd crossword – that sort of thing."

"Easy money, eh?" Franklin commented.

Bill thought for a moment. "Too easy, sometimes." he replied. "What do you do?"

"I'm seventeen, Bill," Franklin whispered in reply, "You know, school age?"

"Oh, of course," Bill said, "You look so much older. Will anyone miss you there?"

Franklin shrugged. "Not for a week or two, anyway," he said, "I'm not exactly regular there."

Bill grinned at Franklin's show of embarrassment "That's rather useful," he said.

"Anyway, Bill, what are we going to do now?" Franklin asked, rapidly changing the subject.

"First," replied Bill, "Another drink." He rose from the seat.

"Er, haven't you had enough yet?" Franklin asked, recalling Gerry's parting comment.

Bill smiled. "Franklin. Have you heard the term 'practising alcoholic'?" Franklin nodded. "Well, I don't need to practice anymore. You'll soon learn that," he added, patting Franklin on the head and walking to the bar.

Franklin smiled at his retreating form. '*I must be mad,*' he thought, '*Homeless, a runaway, and now teamed up with an ageing, alcoholic, maybe-murderer.*' He shrugged. "What the hell," he said, aloud.

Bill returned with a very large whisky and a half pint of lager for Franklin.

"I told him it was a celebratory drink after you'd broken the national junior record this afternoon," he explained. Franklin groaned but gulped the lager gratefully.

"I vote," Bill went on, "That we take the next train into town then take a taxi or something to Kings Cross or Liverpool Street, and see what takes our fancy. How does that sound?"

Franklin shrugged. "Sounds fine," he replied.

* * * * *

They finished their drinks and, despite Bill's protestations that 'one for the road, or rather, tracks, wouldn't hurt' made their way immediately to the station. At the ticket counter, Bill spent some minutes trying to fathom out why a 'Cheapday Supa-Sava Return' was actually cheaper than a one-way single ticket.

"But madam," he explained to an exasperated employee, "I don't want to return here."

Franklin, highly amused by the exchange, unlike three potential travellers queuing behind Bill, eventually ended the dispute by buying two tickets from the automatic ticket vending machine close by the station's entrance.

He led the still protesting Bill onto the northbound platform. "We really shouldn't be drawing too much attention to ourselves," he pointed out.

Quietening down slowly, Bill contemplated this for a moment. "Yes," he agreed eventually, "You are quite right, young Franklin. And perhaps we would do best to consider that point on our journey."

They waited in silence for the City bound train, each contemplating their forthcoming journey and the implications of their particular, unexplained sudden departures.

The train arrived, miraculously on time in Franklin's opinion, just as the heavens opened once more. Slightly bedraggled, the pair wandered through two carriages as the train left the station, searching in vain for empty seats. Before entering a third carriage, Bill passed Franklin his holdall.

"Would you mind carrying this for me?" he asked.

Franklin took the bag on the grounds that he had little choice. He clumsily followed Bill through the door into the next carriage and paused to rearrange his load. When he looked up he groaned aloud and closed his eyes. Bill was hobbling up the central aisle, clutching his left thigh as if supporting an artificial leg. He hurried after him to see what the old fool was up to this time.

Bill had reached a seat halfway along the crowded carriage and had launched into another of his ludicrous stories.

"Yes, lost it in Iraq; 1997 it was. I was with the Special Forces. Of course, the Yanks needed the expertise of the British; couldn't hack it on their own, you know?"

Franklin watched in disbelief as an elderly man, obviously an ex-serviceman, struggled to his feet and guided Bill into the vacated seat.

Deciding that he wouldn't be able to keep a straight face, Franklin squeezed past the elderly gent and piled the luggage into an alcove by the door. As the train rattled and swayed towards the heart of the capital, he tried desperately not to listen to Bill and the retired army officer swapping campaign stories. He imagined that somewhat less than half the tales were true – even the genuine army man seemed prone to sprinkle bullshit liberally into his reminiscences.

At Victoria Station, Franklin was forced to wait on the platform for a full fifteen minutes while Bill and the elderly gent exchanged addresses and a few final anecdotes.

"Bill, you are crazy!" he exclaimed after the grinning, and still limping, Bill had re-joined him.

"Nonsense," said Bill, his expression radiating smugness, "It's merely a little diversion to help pass the time. And anyway, it's not Bill, it's Major Harold Egerton."

"You are..." Franklin spluttered.

"The word you are looking for, I believe, is talented. If not that, then incorrigible."

"Sounds right," muttered Franklin, handing Bill his holdall, "Does the Major think he can manage his own bag?" he enquired.

"I know it's difficult given your racial origins, Franklin," Bill replied, smiling and taking the bag, "But do you think you could stop giving me those black looks?" With that he turned smartly on his heel and strode off for a dozen paces before remembering that he had been seriously injured nearly two decades before. He limped the rest of the way to the ticket barrier.

51

Franklin followed – what choice did he have? – shaking his head but grinning broadly. Being on the run with Bill promised to be fun.

Outside the station Bill lurched through another performance, a small wave of totally misplaced sympathy taking him to the front of the queue for taxis.

As Franklin followed Bill into the taxi, a large and obviously obstreperous lady asked him whether he was 'really in the Major's company'.

"Certainly, madam," Franklin replied, "In fact, I'm his batman."

Bill chuckled as Franklin closed the door behind him. "You are learning fast, young Franklin."

It took a couple of minutes discussion, the driver muttering and grumbling all the while, before the pair decided to head for Liverpool Street station. The deciding factor being Bill's recollection of a 'decidedly charming little ale house, just around the corner'.

The Saturday evening traffic, coupled with road closures in the City following yet more bomb atrocities, made the journey a slow, tortuous affair. Bill and Franklin passed the time trying to decide on an initial destination. It took some time before either realised that they didn't have the foggiest notion of the potential destinations that were *even* available from the station.

They arrived there a little after eight o'clock, Bill placating the still-grumbling driver with a large tip.

"I say we retire for a small drink and then locate a suitable train," Bill suggested.

"And I say we should find out where we're going first," Franklin countered. "At this rate, we'll end up spending the night on the platform."

"Oh, very well," Bill conceded reluctantly.

They entered the station and peered up at the vast array of indicator boards in the middle of the station's concourse. They dismissed Chingford as being too close, Cheshunt on the grounds that they didn't know where it was, the Hook of Holland since neither had a passport, and finally settled on Cambridge.

"The air of *academe* should certainly assist us in our planning," Bill reasoned.

Bill left Franklin with the baggage and went in search of two tickets. When he had failed to return from the ticket office after ten minutes, Franklin gathered up the bags and went in search of him.

He found Bill embroiled in another altercation with a hapless member of the railway's staff.

"But, young sir, I am *positive* that you'll find a 'Cheapday Supa-Saver Return' much cheaper than a single," he was saying.

"Oh, no," said Franklin, "Not again."

"Sir," the young man behind the counter said in tones of forced patience, "I can assure you that this is not the case. On the other hand," he went on, "If you happen to have your Senior Citizen's Railcard with you–"

"What!" Bill exclaimed, "I'll have you know, impudent youth, that I'm–"

"Excuse me," Franklin interrupted, desperately, "Remember, no scenes," he whispered urgently in Bill's ear. To the exasperated man behind the counter he said quickly, "Just two singles to Cambridge, please."

Muttering under his breath, the man pressed a couple of buttons, two tickets dropping onto the counter. "That will be twenty pounds eighty pence," he said, coolly, "Please."

Keeping the irked Bill at arms' length, Franklin paid for the tickets and pocketed the change. "Now," he said, taking the still protesting Bill by the arm and leading him out of the ticket office, "How about we spend the half hour wait having a drink?"

This succeeded in quieting Bill, who agreed with the minimum of further fuss. '*I really am learning*,' thought Franklin.

When they were seated in the station bar Franklin turned his attention to the night ahead. "Where are we going to stay?" he asked.

"What time will we arrive?" Bill countered.

"If it's on time, a little after ten o'clock," Franklin replied, peering at the indicator boards outside the window.

"In that case," Bill decided, "We'll stay at any hotel with a bar. We'll still have time for a couple when we get there."

Franklin shook his head and grinned. "What was that word you used to describe yourself?"

"Talented?"

"No. The other one."

"Ah," Bill said, "Incorrigible."

"That's the one."

Bill laughed and sauntered to the bar for another whisky. '*I really could get to like that boy,*' he thought.

* * * * *

They boarded the train without Bill further upsetting the railway staff and found a carriage to themselves. When the train lurched into motion Franklin turned his attention to their disappearance. "We've got to make sure that we don't leave a trail," he said.

"True," Bill replied, considering the implications, "Although we're not exactly an inconspicuous pair of travellers, are we?"

"That shouldn't be a problem," Franklin countered, "After all, with the exception of your friend, no-one knows we're travelling together. To everyone else, we've disappeared totally separately."

"And Gerald is totally trustworthy," Bill added before Franklin could ask the question. "Anyway, streetwise young man, what else should we be wary of doing that might lead an inquisitive nose in our direction?"

Franklin considered this for a while before replying. He was not nearly as 'streetwise' as Bill imagined when faced with covering a trail, but there were some obvious things that sprang to mind.

"Firstly," he said, "And most obviously, we can't use our real names if we check in anywhere."

Bill listened in silence. He was somewhat chagrined – the thought hadn't occurred to him.

"And of course, you won't be able to use any credit cards or even our mobiles. Cash is the only option," Franklin went on.

"Well both our phones are dead anyway, but what about ATMs – bank cash cards?" Bill asked, worried.

"Those too," Franklin said, warming to his role.

Bill was immediately even more worried. "That might cause a problem or two," he said, "This," he added, extracting the card from his wallet, "is our only source of the folding stuff."

"Ok," Franklin replied, "Let me think for a minute." He sat back, lapsing into silence. This was definitely out of his range of experience, but he couldn't help thinking that he owed Bill some return for his trust and generosity. He turned his mind to the quandary while Bill fiddled nervously with the problematic plastic.

"Well," he said, eventually, "I think we've got two courses of action open to us." He paused, both for effect and to get his words into order. "Firstly, no-one's going to be looking for either of us for a while; especially you. If you take as much as you can from the bank tonight, we'll be long gone before anyone bothers checking up." He sat back looking pleased with himself.

Bill shook his head. "There's a daily limit on the amount I can withdraw," he explained, "I've already used up today's allowance."

"Ok," Franklin said, expecting something of the sort, "You can do it first thing tomorrow. By the way," he added, "How much is the limit?"

"Three hundred a day is what my dull bank allows me," Bill replied, "It won't keep us going for long if it's the last time we can use the card."

"Fair enough," Franklin said, thoughtfully, "Ok, how about we make it look as though we're heading west for a few days, making withdrawals as we go?"

Bill considered this. "It'll work for a few days," he conceded, "But who knows how long it will be before Mary is discovered? She could even be front page news tomorrow." He was even more worried than before. "Any other ideas?"

"Yeah," replied Franklin, still thoughtful, "Alright then, first we check the papers tomorrow. If there's no news, we'll risk one withdrawal in Cambridge."

Bill shrugged, then nodded.

Franklin chose his next words very carefully. "Can you really, I mean, deep-down, *really* trust your friend Gerry?"

Bill agreed immediately that he could. "But why?" he asked.

Franklin explained. "In that case, you could mail him the card. He's a lorry driver; he travels all over. He could make withdrawals on his trips and mail the cash on to you at pre-arranged pick-up points." Franklin sat back, pleased with himself and more than a little surprised.

Bill, too, was surprised. It was an extremely clever idea. However, he was reluctant. He'd already dragged Gerry further into his plans than he felt comfortable in doing. It wasn't that he had any doubts about placing trust in his friend – he simply didn't want to involve him in an affair that could potentially cause a great deal of trouble for all concerned.

"Your plan, young sir, is extraordinarily clever. I'm without doubt, tremendously impressed," he began, "But I'm loathe to involve the man in question." He went on to explain his feelings.

Franklin, at first revelling in Bill's praise, felt his spirits drop. "Do we really have a choice?" he asked when Bill had finished.

Bill studied his young, earnest face. 'Do we?' he asked himself.

"Bill?"

I fear that you are right," he replied eventually. "As I've said, I'm rather loathe to involve Gerald any further, but we will most certainly require money – especially if we are to conduct an investigation into the mystery man's identity." Resigning himself in the face of an otherwise impossible situation, he added, "I'll telephone him first thing tomorrow – from a landline close to where we withdraw the readies."

Franklin sighed with relief and settled himself back into the seat. It occurred to him that sometime during the afternoon and evening both he and Bill had begun to talk as if they would be 'on the run' together for some time – not the day or two that had been mentioned during their first meeting at Redhill. He was surprised to find that this pleased him no end.

Bill's thoughts were following the same train, and he had begun to realise that, however intelligent he supposedly was, Franklin's fast and practical mind would be an absolute requirement were they to succeed in eluding discovery – or worse, capture and arrest.

Their private reveries were disturbed by the carriage door sliding back. "Drinks, light snacks, refreshments," a voice boomed loudly and somewhat unnecessarily in the near empty carriage.

"A splendid idea," Bill said, his face brightening as his eyes took in the approaching buffet trolley.

The steward set the brake when he reached the two men. "Good evening, gentlemen. Can I tempt you with something?"

Franklin was about to request a sandwich or two, when Bill spoke.

"Just a glass, please," he asked pleasantly.

"Pardon?" the steward said, puzzled.

Bill fished around in the holdall at his feet, eventually extracting one of the bottles of whisky he had purchased earlier. He held it up. "Yes, just a glass. They may be plastic, but beggars can't be choosers, and it's so unseemly drinking from the bottle, don't you think?"

"Er, sorry, sir," the steward replied, "It's not company policy to give away eating and drinking utensils for people providing their own refreshment."

"Ah," Bill nodded sagely, "The old 'company policy' bit. Be that as it may, young man, the gentleman announcing the departures at Liverpool Street referred to me as a customer rather than a passenger. Therefore, I must assume that I have purchased at least a small part of the national railway network. That being the case, I feel that a single glass, albeit plastic, would undoubtedly represent a fair value for my purchase."

The steward looked at him dumfounded. "Er..." he began.

Bill rose and extracted a plastic beaker from the stack atop the trolley. "Thank you, young man."

The steward, still gazing open-mouthed, looked across at Franklin in search of some sense. Franklin merely smiled back at him and repeated Bill's thanks.

"Oh, well," the steward mumbled, regaining a little of his composure, "If that's all, I'll just be, er, on my way." He unlocked the brake and wandered off, still shaking his head.

"I know," said Bill when the steward had left the carriage, "Incorrigible." He poured a large measure into the beaker and sat back contentedly.

Franklin smiled at him, shook his head, and followed in the direction of the departing trolley, returning a few minutes later with three rounds of sandwiches. He offered Bill the choice and he selected one commenting that he 'hadn't eaten all day'.

Franklin wasn't surprised. It would be hard to squeeze food past the constant string of glasses Bill always seemed to have at his lips.

They spent the rest of the journey in a companionable silence, punctuated only by the occasional sound of whisky gurgling into a plastic beaker.

They arrived in Cambridge at twenty past ten, some fifteen minutes late. Franklin was pleased – it re-affirmed his faith in British railway travel's inefficiency.

* * * * *

Back in Bill's house, Mary's single, sightless eye appeared to be focussed on his ornate wall-clock. Had anyone been present to witness it, they would have sworn that a grin spread over her ravaged features.

* * * * *

Bill led the way through a number of small Victorian streets, Franklin hurrying to keep up. "It's just along here," Bill explained.

They arrived outside a small bar. "You know this place?" Franklin asked, surprised.

"Oh, of course," Bill replied.

"I just got the impression that you didn't travel much," Franklin commented.

"No, I don't," Bill agreed, "But I did spend four years here at the university," he explained. "I wonder if dear Mrs. Somerville still owns the establishment." He pushed open the door and went inside.

Franklin, fascinated by the revelation that Bill had spent a number of years at the university, hurried after him as best he could under the burden of bags. "What did you get a degree in?"

Bill paused in the narrow hallway that led from the front door to the bar. "Oh, I didn't actually get the degree," he replied, "Sent down, and all that; Mary was not impressed to say the least. But to more-or-less answer your question, I studied computer science." he continued on his way.

"So you know all about computers?"

"Well, a little, and that was twenty-odd years ago. To be quite frank. I learned more about Turing than the blessed machines themselves."

Franklin was a tad disappointed; for a moment he had a vision of Bill hacking into computers all over the country, setting up false identities, transferring cash into covert accounts... For such a brief vision, the possibilities had seemed endless. "Oh, well," he sighed.

Bill had pushed open another door ahead of them. A deep, powerful and ('*probably,*' Franklin thought) female voice filled the corridor.

"Why, I don't believe it. It is, isn't it?" Not waiting for an answer, the disembodied voice continued. "William Taylor. Why it must be ten years. You haven't changed a bit. William, my boy, come in, come in. What happened to your nose? Get William a large whisky, Tony. Let me take your bag."

Franklin peered over the stationary Bill's shoulder. Moving towards them in a wave of rolling flesh was one of the biggest women that Franklin had ever seen. "Mrs. Somerville?" he whispered.

"Quite so, dear boy," Bill dropped his holdall and spread his arms wide as Mrs Somerville reached him.

'*If he means to hug her,*' Franklin thought, '*he'll need to stretch his arms another foot or three.*'

Bill and Mrs. Somerville embraced clumsily, the large lady fussing over him all the while. Eventually, satisfied that it really was the William Taylor that she had known all told for some thirty years, she stepped back.

"That reminds me," she said, "I still haven't got the stains out of our spare room carpet from the last time you were here." Her face wasn't designed for frowning and the mock sternness in her voice carried no reproach whatsoever.

"Oh, yes," Bill replied, grinning from ear to ear, "A reunion party, was it not?"

"I'm truly surprised you can remember, William. But never mind, come in and tell me all that you've been up to." She finally noticed Franklin as Bill reclaimed his bag and stepped into the surprisingly spacious bar. "And who's your young friend?"

"This, Mrs. Somerville, is Fran... Frederick." he explained. "He's a foreign exchange student from darkest – excuse the pun – Africa. I'm showing him around."

Franklin, now Frederick, groaned inwardly. He could barely remember where Africa was on a map.

"Well, come in, come in," the lady enthused, "Any friend of William is a friend of mine."

Franklin stepped over the threshold and discarded his bags. "Very pleased to meet you, Mrs. Somerville."

"Oh, doesn't he speak lovely English," she cooed.

"Bill, William that is, taught me everything he knows," Franklin replied, casting the jovial Bill a very dark look.

"Isn't that nice. Now, you must come and sit down and tell me all about what the pair of you are doing here." With that she turned and waddled in a surprisingly nimble way back to the bar. "Tony, have you poured William's drink yet?" She located the whisky and handed it to Bill as he joined her. "And what would young Frederick like?"

Franklin asked for, and quickly received, a foaming pint of lager. He sat on a stool, sipping the cool liquid as Bill and Mrs. Somerville exchanged ten years' worth of news. '*So much for travelling incognito,*' he thought.

During the half hour that followed, Franklin discovered quite a lot about himself. He had arrived in England a little under a year ago, he was eighteen, the son of a tribal chief in Kenya, and was studying the English language in order that he would be able to return home to educate his fellow tribe's people. He just hoped that he would be able to remember it all were the need to arise.

Eventually the conversation turned to their immediate plans. Bill turned his charm up to full volume.

"Well, Mrs. S., we were going to stay with a former colleague for the coming night," Bill explained, "but I'm afraid he is rather unwell." He made a great show of looking at his watch. "And now the time is getting late, we really must depart and find alternative accommodation." He finished his drink in a decisive gulp and made to rise from his stool.

"Nonsense!" Mrs. Somerville exclaimed, "Oh, William! You should know by now that my bed is always available for you."

"Mrs. S., what are you saying?" Bill replied, grinning.

She blushed deeply as she realised what she had inadvertently said. "Oh, William. You are..."

"Incorrigible?" Franklin suggested.

"Quite right, Frederick," agreed the still blushing lady. "Now, I've only got one spare room, but there'll be ample room for you both. I insist that you stay here tonight. Besides, William, there's still so much for us to catch up on. Agreed?"

"You are most generous, Mrs. S.," Bill replied, "If you are quite sure...?"

"It's agreed then."

Franklin yawned. The hectic day had caught up with him.

"Oh, the poor lad's tired," Mrs. Somerville tutted, sympathetically, "Tony, show him up to the spare room."

"Yes," agreed Bill, "Go and get some sleep Frederick, we shall have a busy day tomorrow."

Franklin nodded wearily and retrieved their bags. "Thank you for your generosity, Mrs. Somerville," he said as he followed Tony out of the room.

As he mounted the stairs behind the barman, he could hear the landlady's delighted squeal. "Oh, isn't he polite," she was saying, "So much like you, William."

Franklin shuddered at the thought and trudged wearily onwards.

"Your'n friend's a real character, ain't he?" Tony commented as he showed Franklin into the spare room.

"Yeah man, you can say *that* again!" Franklin agreed.

"I ain't seen the old girl that 'appy in years," Tony added.

Franklin smiled. "Bill has that effect on people."

Tony showed Franklin the route to the bathroom and bade him goodnight. Back in the spare room Franklin chose the twin bed furthest from the door, undressed and climbed under the duvet. He hadn't realised how tired he was and in seconds he was sleeping. He woke briefly, the bedside digital alarm clock displaying 3:30 when Bill staggered into the room and collapsed onto the other bed.

"Night, Bill," he muttered sleepily.

"Night, Frederick."

Franklin drifted back to sleep to the gentle snoring of his roommate.

Chapter 4

Sunday 8th June 2014

Bright sunlight was streaming through the window when Bill shook Franklin gently awake the next morning.

"Good morning, Franklin."

"Frederick," Franklin muttered. He yawned. "Wha's the time?"

"Eight o'clock, and breakfast will be waiting I warrant," Bill replied cheerfully.

Franklin opened bleary eyes and was surprised to see Bill washed, changed and wide awake. "How on Earth do you manage it?" he asked.

"Years of practice, dear lad. Now, up and at 'em. We do, indeed, have a busy day before us."

With a little coaxing, Franklin found himself in the bathroom. Still yawning, he climbed under a steaming shower and luxuriated in the warmth. Twenty minutes later, refreshed if not fully awake, he returned to the bedroom to find Bill poring through a stack of Sunday newspapers. The floor was littered with the colour supplements and a plethora of junk advertisements.

"Awake now?" Bill asked.

"More or less," he replied. "Anything in there?"

"Not a word as far as I can see. We'll risk the one cash withdrawal here in Cambridge if we can find a laptop with a news channel that still agrees with the newspapers."

"Okay," Franklin nodded, "Besides, it's not as if we're here incognito, is it?"

Bill looked a little shame-faced. "No... I shall have to be a little more circumspect in future. Anyway, what is done, is done. Let's breakfast."

With that they made their way downstairs and Franklin followed Bill through to a kitchen from which emanated the distinctive and mouth-watering smells of a fried breakfast being prepared.

"Good morning, Mrs. S.," Bill greeted the landlady.

"And a good morning to you, William and Frederick," she replied from the vast cooker at which she was preparing their meal. "Sit yourselves down, it'll be ready in a jiffy."

Bill and Franklin sat at a long kitchen table and were treated to the biggest breakfast that Franklin had ever seen before. Bill, between mouthfuls of bacon, sausages, eggs, mushrooms, tomatoes and toast, kept up a steady chatter, regaling Mrs. Somerville with tales from the past. The lady, despite her vast bulk (or maybe because of it) nibbled at a couple of slices of dry toast and responded with oohs and aahs.

When they had finished eating, Bill excused himself for 'a small errand in the town', and Franklin sat back, belly bulging, sipping a third mug of strong black coffee.

"And how do you like England?" he was asked when Bill had left.

"Er, fine," he said, uncertainly, before remembering his role.

Ten minutes later Bill returned to find Mrs. Somerville listening with rapt attention as Franklin described the methods his tribe employed to capture tigers. Mrs. Somerville looked up as he entered the kitchen. "Frederick has been telling me such wonderful tales of his life at home," she remarked.

"I bet he has," replied Bill, making a mental note to inform Franklin that tigers were never *found* in Africa, let alone trapped. "However, we must, I'm afraid, be on our way; so much to do and all that."

"Oh, of course," Mrs. Somerville replied, "Your meeting with the Chancellor, wasn't it? And on a Sunday too!"

"Quite so," Bill agreed, Franklin nodding in automatic agreement, without for a second understanding anything. "How much do we owe you for our accommodation and the most splendid breakfast?"

"Why William, don't be silly," the landlady replied, aghast.

At the end of a five-minute debate a compromise of sorts was reached, Bill stuffing a twenty-pound note into a charity box on the bar.

Franklin collected their bags and joined Bill at the front door of the pub. "Of course I promise to write, Mrs. S.," he was saying. "And I definitely won't leave it so long before my next visit."

Franklin eased past them as they shared a mismatched embrace, and stood, blinking, in the June sunlight.

"Oh, I nearly forgot," Mrs. Somerville said, disentangling herself from a wheezing Bill. She hurried off to the kitchen and returned a moment later with a bulging carrier bag which she handed to Bill. "It's just a snack or two to keep you going," she explained, "And just you mind you look after young Frederick." She stepped out into the street and embraced the highly embarrassed young man, unable to defend himself with his arms full of their luggage.

Ten minutes, a dozen assorted promises and two hugs later, the door closed – and Bill and Franklin stood alone in the street.

"They broke the mould when they made her," Bill remarked.

"You sure she didn't just sit on it?" Franklin replied, wondering whether she hadn't cracked some of his ribs.

Bill laughed. "Tigers, indeed."

They set off in the general direction of the railway station, Franklin attempting to work out what Bill meant by his last remark.

On route they discussed the relative merits of a variety of possible destinations before deciding on Norwich or its environs, on the dubious merit of having been very close to the place where Bill, thirty-one years previously, had lost his virginity to the daughter of a – what else? – publican.

In an effort to forestall further hostilities between Bill and British Rail, Franklin insisted on buying their tickets while Bill waited outside the station's ticket office. He didn't have the heart to tell Bill on his return that he had been persuaded to purchase two Cheapday Supa-Sava Returns on the basis that they were cheaper than the two singles that he had asked for.

Once comfortably seated on the train, Bill turned his attention to his dead sister's address book and the telephone bills he had removed from her house back in Redhill. The print-outs detailing calls made during the six-month period listed over two hundred calls lasting longer than three minutes and he set Franklin the task of listing the most popular ones – those made most often – in order. He began to browse through the oddly-ordered address book.

Half an hour into the journey Franklin paused in his somewhat frantic scribbling. "There seems to be three numbers called far more often than the rest," he informed Bill, handing him a scrap of paper on which he had listed them.

Bill looked at them for a moment, having not a little difficulty in deciphering Franklin's untidy script. "Hmm, well you can discount the third one," he said, slowly, "Because it's mine. But that does come as a surprise." he added.

"Why's that?"

"Well, for the life of me," Bill explained, "I can't recall taking more than a dozen calls from Mary in the last two years, let alone two quarters. How many are listed?"

Franklin checked through his calculations. "At least thirty," he replied.

"Curiouser and curiouser," Bill said before showing Franklin his own notes. "You'll see that she organised the book according to categories," he explained, "Some of them are obvious – family, suppliers, services and so forth – but there are a couple of very odd entries." He pointed to two words circled on the page.

"B. church and W. church," Franklin read aloud, "Was she particularly religious?"

"To be honest," Bill replied, "I'm not really sure. She certainly used to attend a church, but she hadn't mentioned anything about it for some time."

"Do you remember what it was called?" Franklin asked, "It may explain the 'B' and the 'W'"

Bill tried to recollect the name of the church. "You may be right," he said eventually, "If my memory serves me correctly, she used to attend St. Wilhelmina's or some such. That might well explain the 'W'. However," he went on, "I can't recall any mention of her changing her affiliations."

"Can you find the two most often called numbers in the book?" Franklin asked.

Bill nodded and thumbed through the dog-eared address book, glancing back and forth between it and the two scribbled numbers. "I think we can rule out family, services and so forth... Ah, here's one. It's under W. church – a single name, Phillip. Means nothing to me." He resumed his search.

"I wouldn't mind betting that the other number is in the B. church section," Franklin remarked.

Bill flicked forward through the book to the relevant page. "Very perspicacious," he nodded, the number being first in a list of twelve or so. "Or very lucky. It's here alright, next to another single name – Jonathon." He showed the page to Franklin.

Franklin studied it. "All single names," he said thoughtfully. "Any of them mean anything?"

Bill scanned the list. "Not a one."

"There is one thing," Franklin said, slowly, "It's the last section in the book, probably the most recent. Did she join anything recently?"

Bill shook his head, "Not that I know of," he replied, once more a little surprised that Franklin had spotted something that he, himself, should have noticed. "And I definitely can't recall her mentioning a new church."

Franklin had turned back to the printouts. "Read out a couple of the numbers on that page," he suggested. Bill did so.

After a pause Franklin, his voice excited, said, "They're here – all fairly recent calls too. Read out some more."

Five minutes later they sat back and looked thoughtfully at one another. All fourteen numbers appeared on the printed lists and the most recently recorded calls were made up almost exclusively of the same fourteen.

"Seems my sister had a new interest," Bill observed, "And with only one exception all of the numbers are 0207 – which, before you were born, indicated central London, and the City at that. There's no guarantee these days, but a lot of the older numbers still follow that 0207 versus 0208 trend."

"So where does that leave us?" Franklin asked.

"To be perfectly honest, dear boy, I'm not at all sure. But I think that we should make a casual call or two – at least we might be able to ascertain the name or location of the church for what it might be worth."

"Looks like we've got quite a lot of calls to make," Franklin observed. "Don't forget Gerry and the cash withdrawals."

Bill winced slightly at the thought of further embroiling his friend. "True," he replied, "We shall make it our first priority. At the earliest opportunity I shall find a landline telephone. We'll share the load."

Franklin, revelling in his role of detective, grinned and settled back in his seat. "This should be fun."

Bill, apparently alone in being aware of his immediate problems, replied wryly, "Quite." He too sat back. Half an hour later they arrived at Norwich station. It was midday.

*****

In Walthamstow, Jenny Thomsett replaced the telephone receiver and heaved a huge sigh. She stood for a minute, eyes closed, counting slowly backwards from one hundred.

"Trouble?" her flatmate and lover, Susan, asked eventually.

Coming out of her enforced reverie, Jenny shuddered. "You could say that," she replied. "It's Franklin Richardson again. Apparently, he's run away."

Susan, also a social worker, knew all about the exploits of the troublesome Franklin. "Doesn't surprise me."

Jenny knew what was coming. They had argued long and hard over his placement with the Harts; Susan had been dead-set against it.

"He's just too much of a bully," Susan went on, "And whatever you say, Franklin's a nice lad. Smart, independent; he's not the sort to tolerate a big oaf like Hart for long."

"Alright, alright," Jenny snapped, aware that she had made a mistake. "I'd better get on to the police."

"When did he disappear?" Susan asked.

"Well," Jenny began, "Hart says he didn't turn up last night, but I get the impression he wasn't being entirely honest. For all I know he could have run off last week."

"Don't blame the poor lad," Susan said, a little too smugly for Jenny's taste.

She ignored the comment and lifted the receiver. "Perhaps I should try one or two of his friends from the arcade before I call in the police," she mused, turning the handset over and over.

"Oh, let them do it," Susan replied, referring to the local constabulary, "It *is* Sunday remember."

Jenny pondered the idea for a moment. She and Susan had planned to spend an idle lunchtime in their local. She had spoken to one of the regulars during the week and he had promised to loan her a couple of books on her latest pet subject, computer theory. Finally, she decided on a compromise.

"We'll take a look in the arcade on the way to the pub. If no-one knows anything, I'll call the police from the arcade, okay? I hope Bill Taylor has remembered those books," she added.

Susan wandered up behind her. "Typical Libran," she said, smiling and kissing the back of Jenny's neck.

* * * * *

Bill and Franklin emerged, blinking, from the railway station, and Bill's eyes darted eagerly from side to side.

"Don't tell me," said Franklin, "We'll just find a quiet little pub and have a quick drink before we start?"

"I've said it before, young lad, and I'll say it again," Bill replied, "Very perspicacious." Spotting a likely watering hole further down the street, Bill began to march purposefully towards it.

"Incorrigible." Franklin said to no-one in particular and, smiling, followed him.

"We might as well settle here for a while," Bill reasoned when they were sitting in a cosy corner of the pub, drinks before them. "Gerry is bound to be at the Mucky Duck now, and if these people in the address book are all church-goers, they will still be at their morning worship."

Franklin couldn't quite work out how Bill always seemed to find an excuse for avoiding the task at hand whilst still being able to find one for settling down in a pub somewhere. He said so.

"Oh, it's really quite simple," Bill explained, "When one has spent as much of one's life in the surrounds of countless hostelries as I have, the rest of life seems to fit around their licensing hours and environs."

"I'm beginning to wonder if that isn't true," Franklin admitted. "But aren't you worried about leading this poor little orphan astray?"

Bill returned his grin. "My dear Franklin, you already show a very old head on your broad, youthful shoulders. I'm beginning to get the distinct impression that it is you that is leading this poor wretch astray."

"Bill," Franklin replied, sipping his lager, "I very much doubt if that's possible."

For the next two hours they cross-questioned each other about their previous experiences, Bill doing most of the talking and the vast majority of the drinking. When the publican called out that the afternoon cleaning was going to begin in a few minutes, they gathered up their belongings and wandered back out into the June sunshine.

"I think," Bill mused, "That if we are to hole-up here for a few days, since you say using our phones is out of the question, we should procure a map of the region and select a nice, quiet place to lay our heads."

Franklin, used by now to Bill's hidden meanings, said, "Okay, I get it. Franklin should now go and locate a newsagent and buy a local map, right?"

"What a good idea," Bill replied, smiling from ear to ear. "Absolutely splendid. In the meantime, I shall locate a suitable telephone and begin our nefarious investigations."

"Gerry first." Franklin stated, aware that Bill was still reluctant.

"Oh, of course," Bill replied, thinking not for the first time, that Franklin was far more intelligent than most people, Franklin included, would credit.

They located a suitable telephone together in a supermarket, and Franklin left Bill with the luggage while he went to hunt down a local map. Bill spent a full five minutes wrestling with his conscience before finally dialling his friend's number. Any hopes of a reprieve, albeit temporary, were dashed when the telephone was answered on the third ring. *Bloody mobiles*, Bill sighed.

"Good afternoon. Who calls?" came the familiar reply.

"Gerald, It's Bill."

"Bill! How the devil are you?" Gerry asked.

"Fine, fine. How's everyone there?"

"Missing your repartee, of course," Gerry replied, "And that young social worker was in here with her girlfriend – apparently you had promised to loan her a book or something."

"Slipped my mind," Bill said, a little impatient to begin the delicate discussion.

"Never mind," Gerry went on, barely pausing for breath, "I said you'd be in next Sunday. Anyway, how's Brighton? And how did Mary like the young lad? Is he still in tow?"

"Gerry!" Bill interjected before the list of questions could grow to enormous proportions.

"Sorry, Bill. What's up?" Gerry asked, immediately sensing Bill's discomfort.

"To answer your questions, Gerald," Bill replied, stalling for time, "No I won't, I've no idea, she hasn't met him, and, yes."

It took a while for Gerry to assimilate this information. Finally, the penny dropped. "You're not in Brighton?"

"Correct. But don't let anyone there overhear you."

"Don't worry, I've stepped outside. The lad didn't mug you or anything?"

"No, of course not," Bill snapped. This was proving harder than he imagined.

"What's up, Bill?" Gerry asked, his voice becoming serious.

Bill sighed. "Gerald, I have a problem," he began. "I think I need your assistance, as much as I don't want to."

"No problem."

"At least let me explain, Gerald. This is hard enough as it is."

"Sorry, Bill. Go on."

"Gerald," he began, "I don't want you to become involved, but I fear that I have little choice. I need to use the services of someone that I can trust. You fit the bill better than anyone, and if anything goes wrong then I'm truly, truly sorry," he paused. "Gerald my friend, for reasons I will not go into, I'm, shall we say, 'laying low'."

To his credit Gerry didn't ask a single question while Bill outlined his requirements in terms of cash supply. When Bill had finished, he waited for a barrage of questions. They didn't materialise.

"Okay, Bill," Gerry said after a short pause, "Seems you're in trouble of some sort. Of *course* I'll do what I can." Bill winced. "Send me the card and the number; give me a call in a day or two with a mailing address and I'll get the cash to you." He paused again. "Bill," he asked eventually, "how bad is it?"

For a moment Bill nearly told him everything. Instead he replied, "It's bad enough, Gerald. But Franklin is also, as you know, in a little trouble of his own. Between us I think we'll be ok. He's very sharp and I think we've also discovered something already that might help to cure the problem."

"Okay," Gerry replied. Bill could imagine him standing outside the Mucky Duck nodding pensively, "But Bill?"

"Yes?"

"Stay safe and keep in touch. You've got a lot of friends here. Whatever the problem is, I'm sure we can all help."

He was going to deny it but instead, merely said, "Thank you, Gerald. I appreciate that, and I'll be sure to be careful. Thank you once again."

"Don't forget to call," Gerry finished.

"I won't, friend, I won't," Bill replied. They hung up.

He was still staring at the telephone when Franklin walked up. Together they stepped outside.

"I found a map," Franklin said, brandishing an ordnance survey glossy in front of Bill's bruised nose. "How did it go?"

"As much as I don't like it, I'm pleased to say that he'll help us. *And* he didn't ask any questions."

"A real friend," Franklin remarked.

"Quite so," Bill replied, sighing. "Now, to business." He handed Franklin a list of the fourteen 'B. church' telephone numbers and two phone cards. "Start dialling."

They each called seven of the numbers with the same result. Not a single reply.

"That's odd," Franklin said as they stood once more in the sunlight outside the supermarket

"Maybe not," Bill mused. "Apart from one number, they are all 0207, so probably City of London numbers. It could be that they are work phones."

"True," Franklin agreed, "In which case we'd better try again tomorrow." He paused, "Or Tuesday – tomorrow's a Bank Holiday."

Postponing further investigations, they retired to a nearby park, settling themselves on a shaded bench and pored over the ordnance survey map while sharing some of Mrs. Somerville's generous rations. After some deliberation, Bill turned to Franklin. "How about Wroxham?"

"I thought Wroxham was in Wales," Franklin answered.

"No, that's Wrexham," Bill explained, "Wroxham is just a small village over here." He pointed to its location on the map. "Don't you take geography at school these days?"

Franklin looked a little sheepish. "Well I should have," he explained, "But I don't seem to be able to settle to it. After all, it's the fourth school I've had in two years."

"What!" Bill exclaimed, genuinely surprised. "Don't they keep you at the same school? I mean, I know that you, er, change parents from time to time, but education and all that; it's important."

Franklin, embarrassed, shrugged. "It's no big deal. I've gotten used to it."

"It's reprehensible, is what it is," Bill went on, disbelievingly, "You're a smart, intelligent young man. You certainly deserve a decent education. Were we not in our present predicament, I would most certainly contact your whatever she's called, and complain most vehemently."

"It's not just her," Franklin explained sheepishly, "I've had problems in school..." he trailed off.

"Such as?" Bill enquired.

"Well, there was the fire...."

"Oh, I see. Your, what is it? 'Troubles'?"

"Something like that," Franklin replied, sullenly.

Bill was momentarily surprised. It was the first time Franklin had shown the least of negative emotions about his chequered past. For the first time since he had met the youth, he realised that Franklin was little more than a boy. A wave of something somewhere between pity and sympathy struck him, shocking in its intensity.

"Oh, Franklin," he said, trying not to sound the way he felt, "It's time you had a decent tutor."

"Oh yeah?" Franklin said, still sullen.

"Why, yes," Bill replied, positively, "I've embroiled you in my troubles and it appears that we are, to use the vernacular, 'lumbered' with one another. We can profitably use our spare time extending your knowledge."

72

Franklin was a little nonplussed. "How do you mean?"

"Despite appearance," Bill explained, "I have a modicum of knowledge in a wide variety of areas. If I'm to continue to be in your company, involving you in my problems, the least I can do is impart some of it in your direction."

"A sort of glorified field-trip?" Franklin asked, surprised at Bill's offer for reasons he could not yet fathom.

"Look upon it as an ongoing, private tutorial."

It was a side of Bill that Franklin had not seen and would not have believed existed. He was only too well-aware of his own lack of formal education and he had surprised himself with the ideas he had come up with during their day or so together. Bill's offer would, under other circumstances, have been met with derision, but he was beginning to realise that there was more to the man than met the eye. "I think you're a bit late for that," he said eventually.

"Nonsense," Bill replied. For some reason, he felt elated. He had found a way in which he could return the favours that Franklin was heaping upon him merely by his presence. He shrugged the alien thought aside. "We shall start tomorrow once we are settled into some lodgings in Wroxham. If nothing else, it will help to pass the time."

Franklin shrugged, thought for a moment or two, then grinned at Bill's earnest face. "Okay, man, consider me your charity."

Bill smiled back in delight. "Now, young man, let us away into the wilds of Norfolk."

An hour later the pair were standing at the end of Wroxham's main street, a taxi and its driver disappearing in the general direction of Norwich, the latter happy in the knowledge that he had just received a ten-pound tip for the journey.

"You tip too much," Franklin reprimanded Bill.

Bill was counting the notes left in his wallet. "At that you may have a point," he replied, "I can see that we may well find it necessary to conserve funds until Gerald pulls through."

Franklin was beginning to feel guilty – he had almost no money left of his own. "And you're supporting me," he said.

Bill looked shocked. "Nonsense!" he replied. "Your bright ideas are worth far more than any patronage I could offer. Don't ever let me hear you say that again!"

Franklin shrugged. He was out of his depth. "Whatever you say, man."

"Tell you what," Bill suggested, "On the grounds that I am well aware of my gender, how about you repaying me by dropping the 'man'. That will be reward enough."

Franklin laughed aloud. "You got it."

Bill shuddered. '*Trying to teach this boy English,*' he mused, '*is going to be much harder than I thought.*' Sighing and shaking his head in mock despair he suggested that they find an inn for the night.

Making their way down the main street Franklin commented, "Roy must be a popular dude."

Bill looked around. Over half of the shops bore the name 'Roy's'. "Not *a* Roy," he explained, "It's a family name, they used to own half the village, and maybe still do for all I know."

"You know Wroxham, too?"

"A little," Bill conceded, "I used to spend weekends here."

"Oh, the publican's daughter," Franklin surmised.

To his credit, Bill blushed a little, "Something along those lines," he admitted.

"We're not going to end up staying with another of your long-lost friends, are we?" Franklin asked, worried.

"No! Of course not," Bill replied. He decided not to mention that the family of the ex-girlfriend had departed some years before. He was already feeling regret that he couldn't see them – or at least, her – again. "We'll just take the first couple of rooms that we can find."

Franklin considered their plight for a moment before remarking, "Should we really be seen here together?"

The question caught Bill by surprise. He suddenly realised that Franklin's presence was a little more precious than he had imagined.

"No," he replied thoughtfully, "No-one will be looking for us as a pair." The answer was out of his mouth long before he realised that it was also true.

Franklin thought about this for a moment. "Sounds right," he agreed.

They walked on in personal, perplexed and thoughtful silences for another ten minutes before arriving at a small guest house. A short gravel drive led up to the front door where a sign proclaimed that there were both 'vacancies' and a 'traditional Norfolk welcome'.

"Looks ideal!" Bill said.

It took Franklin a further ten seconds before he saw another, smaller sign. 'Licensed Bar'. "I thought you might say that," he said, grinning.

Bill led the way into the house, leaving Franklin to follow with the luggage. He found Bill inside talking animatedly with a mature, blonde, country type who's spectacles incongruously matched her fine hair.

"Of course," Bill was saying, "Young musicians these days, especially ones with the precocious talent of young Frederick, need to get away from the pressures of performing in front of thousands of screaming fans every night."

The middle-aged blonde, Maisie as they were to learn, simpered alarmingly as Franklin entered. "Quite," she agreed, "It must be a terrible pressure for the poor lad."

As she hurried around, forcibly extracting Franklin from the luggage and beginning to haul it up a steep staircase, Bill turned and gave Franklin his most earnest, toothpaste commercial, grin.

"Oh, no, Bill," Franklin groaned. "Okay, what instrument? What do I play?"

"Why, young Frederick, you are a rock star! No instrument other than your wonderful voice."

"Bill!" Franklin exclaimed in a loud stage whisper, "You were only in here for a minute before I arrived! Besides which, I'm tone deaf."

"Doesn't matter, doesn't matter," Bill said soothingly, still grinning like a cat that got the creamery, "And besides, I've told the dear lady that we're here incognito. All part of the cover. What do you think?"

"What do I think!" Franklin tailed off, "You're... you're..."

"Incorrigible?"

"I was thinking more of a pillock!"

"You must remember to save your voice," Bill admonished as their new landlady returned, slightly red-faced from her exertions.

"Your rooms are this way," she wheezed, gesturing towards the stairs.

"Why, madam, you are so kind," Bill said graciously, following her directions. "By the way, what time do you open your quaint little bar?"

Franklin groaned inwardly. He followed Bill up the stairs, pausing only to smile magnanimously to the still simpering Maisie. After all, he didn't want her to think that rock stars were all self-centred, stage-struck ruffians, did he?

* * * * *

Jenny Thomsett glared at her flatmate. Susan gave her an 'I told you so' look and returned her gaze to the latest issue of Cosmo on her Kindle

"As I said, miss, did you think that Mr Hart was being entirely honest when he spoke to you?"

She glared at the young policeman once more. She was beginning to feel as if she were being accused of some hideous crime. "I don't know!" she snapped. The day, the *Sunday*, her one day of rest, was disintegrating around her ears.

The call from Hart had got her out of bed an hour earlier than she would have liked; her investigations at the arcade had drawn not only a blank, but some highly insulting personal comments; the old drunk, Bill had apparently swanned off to Brighton completely forgetting about the books; the police had *finally* dispatched some spotty PC who had taken two hours to reach the flat; and on top of it all, Susan had descended into one of her obnoxiously smug and condescending moods. '*Hart be buggered*,' she thought, '*When I get hold of young master Richardson, he'll wish he'd never been born.*'

"But would you say that Hart's word is trustworthy?" the ardent PC Blake continued.

Jenny shuddered, striving gamely to restrict her answer to phrases that included no Anglo-Saxon epithets, "No, I bloody well wouldn't. He's a bastard," she replied, failing miserably in her efforts.

"In that case, miss, may I..." the young policeman droned on unperturbed.

Jenny shuddered once more and, ignoring both the constable's drone and Susan's barely concealed smirk, wished every possible bad luck on the errant Franklin.

"So," Franklin asked, "How do you propose we spend our time?"

They were sitting on the bed in Bill's bedroom and Franklin was feeling the first stirrings of boredom.

"An idle mind does, of course, need exercise," Bill replied, "But I feel that the remainder of the Sabbath should be spent in more Bacchanalian pleasures."

Franklin looked blank.

"By which," Bill explained, "I propose to retire to the bar and engage the fair Maisie in conversation. Why don't you have a wander around the village?"

"Trying to get rid of me so that you can have your evil ways?"

"No such thing, dear boy!" exclaimed Bill in mock horror, "I merely imagined that you would like a break from my eloquent conversation and sparkling wit."

"Shining wit, more like it," Franklin replied, grinning.

"What? Oh yes, crude spoonerisms," Bill said reproachfully. "Definitely time for a break." He handed Franklin a twenty-pound note. "You never know, you might find a pinball table or some such."

Franklin accepted the note reluctantly and grabbed his jacket. "Er, what time do you want me back?"

"How do you mean?" Bill asked, nonplussed.

"Well... When should I come back?"

"Dear boy, you are most certainly old enough, if not ugly enough, to use your own judgement. As much as it might benefit you, I am neither your guardian or your father. Do as you see fit – but if you do return with an attractive young lady on your arm, do remember to ask if she has a friend who is attracted by the older man."

Franklin laughed. "Thanks, man... *Bill*," he said, genuinely. "I'll see you later."

Bill watched the young man go and was struck by how assured he seemed. In just a day or so Franklin had become part of his life. His departure brought home the realism of his own situation and he was surprised at how, in the lad's presence, the depth of his problem seemed to become somehow surreal.

It was threatening now to overwhelm him, though, and he hurriedly rose, straightened his tie, and made for the bar. '*The whisky would help,*' he thought.

Chapter 5

Franklin stepped out into the early evening sunlight. A cool June breeze was sweeping across the flat, open landscape, and he hurriedly buttoned his denim jacket to the collar.

As far as he could recall there were a number of pubs along the main road through the village, and another couple near the boating centre where the taxi driver had dropped them. He walked to the end of the drive and took a couple of steps in the direction of the village before he stopped. He looked around him, taking in the lush soon-to-be-summer greenery; the small quaint cottages, a bicycle left casually by a garden gate, unchained.

He finally realised what had made him stop and look around. It wasn't the picture postcard prettiness of the village, nor was it the spectacular sunset, blazing red and gold under wisps of fluffy shower clouds. It was simply noise – or rather, its absence.

Franklin was a city boy through and through. He'd visited the 'countryside' countless times over the years, and yet he couldn't ever remember a quieter time. And for the past day or so he'd been in the company of one of the world's greatest talkers. Even when they had been sitting in a companionable silence, it had been accompanied by the sounds of a train on its tracks or the hum of a car engine.

He drew in a deep breath, soaking up the subtle smells and tastes of the country air. Combined with the near silence and fiery setting sun, it contrived to drain all the tension from his young body. He shuddered slightly, pleasurably.

The draining of the stress and the tension from his body left him a little light-headed, the same tingly sort of feeling he normally only experienced after three pints of lager. He was also a little surprised. He hadn't even realised he'd *been* that tense.

Instead of continuing into the village, he about-faced and began to wander aimlessly along the lane and soon came to a stile. It provided access to a footpath that ran alongside a field on the right and a small wood on the left. He leaped easily over the stile, the sudden relaxation lending a greater spring to his normal athletic form.

Halfway along the path he found a fallen log. Without anything in mind, he sat down and faced the still setting sun. In the shade of the woods the breeze couldn't reach him, and the last rays of the sun were warm on his face.

Unbuttoning his jacket, he fumbled in the many inside pockets before finding a battered cigarette packet. He seldom smoked, deploring the habit on one hand, but enjoying an occasional cigarette whenever he felt at peace, which was seldom. The packet had been soaked, dried, crumpled, and was generally the worse for wear. Inside, however, one of the cigarettes was, with a little straightening, halfway smokable. He perched it in the corner of his mouth and searched through his pockets once more, eventually locating an equally crumpled box of matches. These, too, had been soaked during his walk home and subsequent flight Friday night, and it was only after eight attempts that he finally managed to draw a reluctant flame from one of the matches. He raised it to the cigarette and drew deeply, coughing lightly as he usually did.

Resting his forearms on his knees, the cigarette dangling lightly from his left hand, he closed his eyes, the process of relaxation reaching near perfection. He let his mind wander idly, concentrating on no particular topic of thought, revelling in the quietude of the moment.

He couldn't remember being so much at ease for a long, long time. Certainly not since he had been introduced to the Harts – maybe never. Taking a final, long drag from the battered Marlboro, he ground it out beneath his foot and carefully covered the butt with earth; someone, sometime (he couldn't remember who) had taken pains to instil the virtues of the 'Country Code' in him.

The quietness, coupled with the reverie, had brought about a subtle change in his thought processes. As his mind came, reluctantly, back to the present, he suddenly began to see his situation more clearly, more realistically.

It almost came as a complete surprise to him when he realised that, here he was, a seventeen-year old runaway in the company of a man who was almost a complete stranger, and possibly even a murderer. Up until now, he realised, it had really been little more than a game to him; at the most extreme, merely a way of avoiding the bullying Hart, a way of taking a break from the all-too-harsh realities of his ordinary day-to-day situation.

But now, as his mind finally began to focus clearly on the realities of the situation, he began to see it for what it was.

Sure, he could end his involvement now. Ok, he'd be in trouble, but he doubted in all honesty that he'd be sent back to the Harts. It would only take a phone call to the lugubrious Ms. Thomsett and he could be back in London before midnight.

But what then? And what of Bill?

It also came as a shock as he suddenly realised just how much he liked the man – more than liked, really, *respected*. When was the last time he had felt like that about anyone? He didn't know. And was this guy really a murderer? Franklin couldn't reconcile that with what he knew of him. So, ok, he'd only known him for thirty-six hours, but in all that time and under, what was becoming clear, fairly desperate circumstances, he had seen nothing to indicate that Bill could even be aggressive. Exasperated, maybe, and Franklin smiled as he recalled Bill's frustrated conversation with a railway ticket clerk. No, he just couldn't see Bill as another Crippen or Christie. And there was something more, as well. A gut feeling, intuition, whatever. Something inside him was telling him – screaming at him – that Bill was innocent. Or at least, innocent of murder.

So, should he go back? Or should he stay with Bill for a while – wherever that might lead them? Life was becoming full of surprises. It was with yet another burst of surprise that he realised that the choice was that simple. If he went back it would be to some minor trouble, to some all too normal uncertainly about his future, and to the normal daily grind. If he stayed with Bill for a while (and it only *need* be for a while – until he decided otherwise) then could there *really* be any more trouble? Was there *any* more uncertainty? There certainly wouldn't even be a passing resemblance to his normal daily life.

He became aware of his decision without consciously making it. Besides, he genuinely liked the man. He just couldn't believe that Bill was guilty of any crime other than excessive bullshit – and he never even used that to hurt anyone. Bill needed the help, and for the first time that he could remember, it was him, Franklin, that was providing useful thoughts and ideas for someone. He really could help Bill; really wanted to.

Despite the seriousness of the situation, as he'd thought before, this *could* be fun. He also thought that maybe, just maybe, he could learn something from the man – something or some things that would be far more useful than all his school lessons put together. Besides, Bill had shown him trust – and trust in a depth and purity that he'd never witnessed before.

'*I don't exactly owe him,*' he thought, '*but he does deserve my help.*' A final surprise surfaced in his adolescent mind. '*Somebody needs me.*'

He shook his head suddenly, as much in shock as to clear it. "Bill," he said aloud, "Whether you like it or not, you're stuck with me. At least for now," he added.

Feeling more in control, more his own man, than he had ever felt before, he rose, stretched his long limbs and, whistling tunelessly, sauntered back the way he had come.

The sun had finally disappeared beneath the flat, stark horizon and the cool breeze reached into his clothing as he leaped over the stile and back into the lane. He paused for a moment and re-buttoned his jacket. As he was about to step off the verge a car, headlights blazing, screeched around the corner behind him. He leapt back as it roared past, throwing dust and roadside grit up against his legs. As the car disappeared around the next bend, he could just make out a couple of words, loosed by the driver through his open window. "Black bastard."

Franklin sighed, images of the enraged Hart dancing across his mind. "Some things never change." He gave a half smile and stepped back into the road, this time listening intently for the sound of an approaching engine. He walked slowly, easily, into the village.

* * * * *

Wandering down the main street in Wroxham, he passed by two pubs after checking to see if either had pinball tables. At the third, craning his neck

82

to look over the frosted glass in the lower half of the window, he spotted the familiar shape of a table, and wandered inside.

There were half a dozen men seated at the bar chatting quietly amongst themselves, occasionally passing a comment to the bewhiskered barman. They all looked up as Franklin entered.

"Evening, gents," he said amiably, crossing to the bar.

There were one or two grunts and a genuine 'hello' as he passed the seated customers, their eyes to a man, following his progress. When he reached the broad and ancient bar the barman eyed him carefully.

"Evening, young sir," the man said, his accent broader than any Franklin had yet heard since his arrival in the area.

"May I have a pint of lager?" he enquired, politely, trying to ignore the eyes boring into his neck.

"Sure you be old enough?"

"What?" Franklin feigned surprise then smiled as if used to such 'mistakes'. "Oh, yeah. Of course. Twenty-two. I've got my ID card here somewhere if you need–" he added.

The barman shrugged, cutting him short and, collecting a pint jug from the bar, began to pour the drink.

"Don't get many of your type in here," a voice said by Franklin's ear.

"Londoners?" Franklin asked, guilelessly, turning to the overweight, middle-aged local sitting on the stool beside him.

The barman banged the foaming jug on the counter and turned a baleful eye on the man who had begun to answer Franklin. "That'll be enough, Jack!" he warned him.

"Well–" Jack began.

"Enough, I said!" the barman reiterated.

The local shrugged, deciding against further comment, and turned his attention back to the game of dominoes he had been playing against his neighbour.

The barman watched him carefully for a minute before turning his attention back to Franklin who was watching proceedings with a wry, resigned smile. "Two pounds fifty pence, please sir," he said.

Franklin handed him the twenty-pound note that Bill had given him earlier. "Sorry I've not got anything smaller," he said, "And thanks." He held the barman's gaze for a moment.

The barman nodded, and Franklin sipped his lager while his change was being counted out of the till, making a mental note that this would be his first and last pint in this establishment.

"On your own?" the barman enquired when he returned and counted the change into Franklin's outstretched hand.

"Er, no," Franklin replied, pausing in an effort to recall the latest piece of bullshit (or cover story) Bill had used. "With my manager. We're taking a break for a few days. Staying with Maisie along the road."

The barman nodded sagely. "Oh, manager, is it? We get a few like you up here."

Franklin was amused but suppressed a smile. Bill seemed to be able to create the perfect cover without trying.

"Now, you've definitely fallen on your feet at Maisie's," the barman went on, "Fine lady. Just you make sure you treat her right."

"No problems," Franklin replied, relaxing a little. '*In for a penny,*' he thought. He extended his hand. "The name's Frederick, by the way."

The barman paused a moment, seemingly surprised at the gesture. Eventually he took the proffered hand and shook it firmly. "And I be George," he replied, "And these here lads are Jack, Michael, Jack Junior, Peter, Frank and Simon."

For the most part, the locals relaxed perceptibly and there were a number of nods and 'hellos', only Franklin's immediate neighbour ignoring the introductions.

"Pleased to meet you," Franklin said, smiling at the seated men. "And now, if you'll excuse me, I'm addicted to these things." He pointed towards the pinball table.

George nodded. "See you in a while."

Franklin wandered over to the table, setting his glass on a nearby window ledge. With the exception of Jack everyone seemed friendly enough and he was revising his opinion of the place. After checking through the rules of the unfamiliar game, he inserted a pound coin and begun to play.

84

Half an hour later he was still playing. Two of the younger locals, attracted by the sharp bang emanating from the machine whenever a replay had been achieved, wandered over. Pausing for a gulp of lager between games, Franklin noticed their presence. "Hi," he said, "Jack Junior and Simon, right?"

Simon nodded. "Just Jack," Jack Junior replied, and, in a quieter voice, "I may be his son, but I'm not that keen for it to be public knowledge." He smiled ruefully.

Franklin nodded and grinned. "Yeah, I bet," he said.

The two lads were the youngest of the regulars, both in their early twenties Franklin guessed. They both wore a look of small-town boredom that Franklin, despite his city upbringing, had seen before. He was a little surprised when he felt a wave of sympathy for the pair – several years their junior, he had probably experienced more than the twosome combined. If only they knew what he was involved in now! To cover himself he said, "Fancy a game?"

"We're not in your league," Jack, nee Jack Junior, replied. "You must play a lot."

"Too much, sometimes," Franklin replied, ruefully and truthfully – a memory of Hart's enraged face coming back to him. "Anyway, it's real easy when you know how to get the jackpots," he went on, "I'll show you."

With the minimum of coaxing, the two locals joined in and an hour later they were still playing. To Franklin's gall and amazement, Simon, still untalkative, had just won two games in a row. "Not so hard, is it?" Franklin asked them.

Jack laughed. "Not at all. Thanks Freddy."

Franklin smiled to himself. Normally he didn't take kindly to his name being shortened to Frank, as some people insisted on doing, but somehow, he quite enjoyed his alias being familiarised in that way. "Anyone care for a drink?"

Jack shrugged and offered Franklin his empty glass. "Why not?" he replied, "The night's young."

"It's a nice offer, Freddy, but I'm a little bit short at the minute," Simon said, blushing slightly.

It was the longest speech he'd made in Franklin's presence and he was still surprised at how shy the lad was.

"No matter, man," he said, "My treat." For the first time he looked at Simon squarely. "Hey," he said, looking across at Jack and then back at Simon. "You two are brothers, right?"

Jack laughed again. "Half-brothers," he explained. His expression darkened as he half turned and nodded towards Jack Senior at the bar. "We have the genial Jack-the-jerk in common."

Franklin had already sensed Jack's ambivalence towards his father and smiled back at him. "Sorry, man," he said quietly.

Jack grinned again and proffered his glass. "Lager please, Freddy," he said, "I'll cover Simon," he added.

Eventually, amidst much haggling, Franklin managed to persuade the pair that it really was his treat. He returned to the bar clutching three empty pint mugs. "Three pints of lager please, George," he said when the barman strolled over to him.

"Certainly, Frederick," the barman replied, taking three fresh glasses from the shelf. "I see you're teaching the lads a thing or two," he added, nodding towards the pinball table.

"They learn fast," Franklin agreed. "Too fast!" His gentle laugh was interrupted by a slightly slurred voice at his side.

"They're all good at that sort of thing," Jack Senior interjected, "*Them* types."

"Enough of that, Jack!" George snapped, "I told you."

Jack's voice dropped to a mumble, but one that was calculated to be heard throughout the bar. "Prob'ly leading m'boys astray already."

"And you don't?" a cultured voice asked from along the bar.

Franklin looked at the speaker. It was either Frank or Peter, he couldn't remember which. The man had piercing blue eyes and was currently staring at the half-drunk bigot standing next to Franklin, with open contempt.

"Wha's that s'posed to mean?" Jack asked aggressively.

"You're pathetic," the man replied, levelly.

Franklin stepped back hastily as Jack slid unsteadily to his feet, his stool clattering to the floor in the process. "No-one calls me that!" he shouted along the counter.

A brawny arm shot across the bar, George gripping the drunk by the shoulder. "I warned you fair and square," he said, darkly. "Now, out."

Jack struggled for a moment before his addled brain realised that he didn't have an alternative. "Ok, ok," he said, swaying slightly despite the barman's grip. He turned enough to stare directly at Franklin. "I told'ya them blacks are nothing but trouble."

"Get out now!" George roared at him, pushing him towards the door despite the intervening bar surface.

Jack staggered, regained his balance and looked at the staring faces. As George moved to round the end of the bar, he choked off another comment and staggered through the pub's doors.

Franklin, his heart pounding, looked around at the remaining customers. Jack's former domino partner, Michael, started at the bar, Frank or Peter was shaking his head in disgust, Jack Junior was staring at his toes, his ears red, Simon looked angry, staring at the door his father had just reeled through.

"Sorry about that," It was George's voice, breaking through Franklin's shock. "He gets like that," George went on. "Now," he cast a glance along the bar, "Perhaps we can get back to some civilised behaviour."

Franklin noticed that George's gaze had settled on Michael, who was still staring at the bar.

"It's no problem," Franklin replied, sighing. "I get used to it." He detected a wry smile from Frank/Peter.

As George went back to the task of pouring their drinks, Simon touched Franklin lightly on the shoulder. "I'm truly sorry," he said.

Franklin tried to wave his apologies down, but the shy Simon continued. "He's a bigot and he's not the only one. There's a few here like that," The lad's eyes settled momentarily on Michael. "But we're not *all* like it," he added.

Franklin looked at Simon, noticing as he did so Jack Junior behind his shoulder. The look of shame that emanated from the pair jolted him. '*And I think I've got problems with* no *father*,' he thought. Instead of iterating that concept he smiled, slowly, ruefully, but with a genuine warmth. "No problem," he said quietly.

He turned back to the bar shrugging off the disturbed and disturbing emotion within him. "Well," he said, brightly, "Would anyone else care to take a drink from a poor nigger boy?"

There was a moment's shocked pause before Frank/Peter laughed, loudly. "Why not," he replied, his eyes sparkling with a dark humour, "I'm not proud."

The comment, full of irony and self-deprecation, broke the gathering layer of ice as effectively as any ice-axe. With the exception of the still taciturn Michael, everyone in the bar accepted a drink.

Franklin returned to the pinball table another twenty pounds lighter, but considerably happier. He was just grateful that he'd kept the change from the last set of rail tickets he'd bought.

At eleven o'clock, George's powerful voice suggested that they all drink up and by midnight Franklin, still with Simon and Jack in tow, finally found himself on the street. Not used to more than two or three pints, the five he had inside him created a pleasant, gentle buzz, and the mood of quietude and calm from earlier had returned. He was young, free and happy.

"That was fun," he suggested.

Jack agreed. "Almost all the way." He was more than a little drunk but far more agreeable for it than his father was, even sober.

Simon, despite half a dozen beers, still remained shy. "I enjoyed it," he said, "Hope you're around for a while."

Franklin nodded, realising that he meant it when he said, quietly, "Yeah, me too," despite all that had gone on that evening.

They said their goodnights, promising to meet up the following evening, and went their separate ways.

* * * * *

When Franklin let himself into the guesthouse, he was not unduly surprised to find Bill seated comfortably at the bar, deep in conversation with the still simpering Maisie. As he strolled, a little unsteadily, into the cosy room, the equally cosy pair looked up.

"Why, it's Frederick," Maisie positively squealed, "Come in and sit with us a while. Tom, here, has been telling me all about you."

'Tom?' thought Franklin, before realising that Bill had at least shown a little sense by adopting an alias. As he took a seat at the small bar, he wondered just what Bill had been telling the lady.

"Well, Frederick, have you been relaxing? I hope no-one recognised you." Bill said, amiably.

"Yes and no, er, Tom," he replied, "Other than one idiot, I've had a very pleasant evening."

"Idiot?" Maisie enquired, worriedly.

Franklin nodded. "Just some overweight local with an underweight mind. Jack, his name was."

Maisie nodded knowingly. "That'll be Jack Parsons," she sighed, "the man's an oaf. He's already seen off two wives and he's *always* in trouble. I don't know how his sons put up with him." She took her glasses off and polished the already immaculate lenses on the front of her blouse.

"Simon and Jack. I've met them. Nice lads."

"Oh yes," Maisie agreed. "They didn't recognise you?"

"No," Franklin replied, honestly, "And I didn't let on."

"That's a boy," Bill interjected, grinning at his young friend. "Just what the doctor ordered. Fancy a night-cap?"

"If it's all the same, I'd better turn in," Franklin replied, trying but failing to give Bill a black look, "I have to watch the throat and all that."

After a prolonged round of 'goodnights' he left Bill and Maisie to their tête-à-tête and went up to his room. The lager conspired with the day's exploits and he was asleep as soon as his head touched the pillow.

* * * * *

Monday 9th June 2014

The following morning he woke, ravenous, and showered quickly before wandering downstairs in search of breakfast. It was a little before nine o'clock and he was surprised to find Bill wide awake, bright eyed, and tucking in to another vast breakfast.

"Good morning, Frederick," he said between mouthfuls, "How are you this fine day?"

"Great," he replied, although in all honesty, his head was aching, dully. He didn't know how Bill managed it.

They ate in a companionable silence punctuated only by Maisie's anxious, and totally unnecessary, enquiries as to the quality and quantity of their meals, and once when a plate was evidently dropped or knocked off a worktop in the kitchen – followed, of course, by Maisie's abject apologies for startling them and her *very* quiet self-recriminations. At ten o'clock they left the guest house and strolled into the village. They discovered that it was a Bank Holiday when they tried to go into the Post Office – something that neither of them had realised but a local newsagent was open and Bill was able to purchase some envelopes and postage stamps, and mailed the cash card to Gerry, along with a note of Maisie's guest house which he had apparently okayed with the lady as a convenient mailing address.

With that task completed, they wandered through the village until Franklin spotted a pair of old-fashioned telephone kiosks and they then repeated the previous day's exercise with the telephone numbers. When they met up again ten minutes later, only Bill had made any contact.

"The third name on the list," he said, "Paul, whoever that might be."

"Did you speak to him?" Franklin enquired eagerly.

"Hardly," Bill explained. "It's the number of one of the larger merchant banks. I know the place – there must be a dozen or more Paul's working there so a forename is not sufficient for our purposes. Besides, as it's apparently a Bank Holiday virtually no one is actually at work anyway. No wonder we have had the very minimum of contact success."

Franklin nodded in agreement. "I can't see any link between a bank and a church anyway."

"You *do* have a lot to learn," Bill replied, wryly, "But for the purposes of our exercise, I quite agree. This Paul is obviously connected to the church somehow, but I'm sure that his working at a bank has no particular significance. I'll cross him off the list."

They decided to try the remaining thirteen numbers later in the day on the very unlikely off-chance that someone might be working Bank Holiday overtime, or that one or two of the numbers might prove to be residential..

"What we need now," Bill said, "Is a decent bookshop."

90

"Oh?"

"Yesterday, dear lad," Bill explained, "I made you a promise."

Franklin still looked blank.

"Today," Bill went on, "we start your proper education." If he had expected a protest, he was surprised.

Franklin simply nodded and said "Okay."

"Oh, well, what subjects should we start with? How's your grasp of your mother tongue?"

"I'm fair at English," Franklin replied, "And maths for that matter. It's pretty much everything else."

"Doesn't narrow it down too much, does it?" Bill thought for a moment. Eventually he shrugged. "Oh well, let's see if any book-selling shop is open despite the holiday and see what takes our fancy."

They spent the next hour finding a suitable shop – mercifully open – and subsequently, suitable books.

"Fits in quite well, doesn't it?" Bill asked Franklin as they emerged from the shop with three bags full of text books.

"I suppose so," Franklin replied, darkly. Bill had spent ten minutes explaining to the shop owner how Franklin's career kept him away from school, and how he, Bill, was both the lad's manager and private tutor. "I'm supposed to be twenty years old!"

"I did say it was 'further' education."

"I don't think 'French for beginners' is exactly degree course material."

"Have you never heard of joint degrees?" Bill asked amiably.

They arrived at the guesthouse and set up 'school' in Franklin's room. The afternoon was spent with Franklin deeply engrossed in French, Geography and History, Bill disappearing occasionally 'for sustenance' and returning in a whisky-hued haze.

Franklin was pleasantly surprised when Bill tapped him on the top of his head with a pencil and pointed at his watch. "Six o'clock, young scholar, and school's out."

He had found Bill to be an ideal tutor, explaining a number of tricky points in a concise, easy to understand way, never talking down to him. He was also amazed at the breadth of Bill's knowledge.

Bill, himself, was also surprised. Franklin had not only buckled down, but when he asked Bill a question the answer was quickly assimilated. He had surmised that the lad was intelligent, but he had no idea that he was as smart as he was proving to be. He wondered how it was possible for him to have reached seventeen with such a lack of general knowledge. '*If only...*' he had thought once or twice during the afternoon. He had also smiled ruefully to himself once or twice. It was the closest he had ever come to feeling the least bit paternal.

They wandered downstairs in search of something to eat, Bill explaining to Franklin the meaning of demography, and arrived in the lounge to find Maisie laying two places at a table by the window.

"Good evening, boys," she trilled as they entered the room.

Franklin cringed slightly but Bill switched up a gear and crossed quickly to the beaming lady.

"And a very good evening to yourself, dear lady." Bill kissed the back of Maisie's hand.

'*Oh, really!*' Franklin thought, smiling at his friend.

Maisie simpered alarmingly and shooed the pair of them to the table, supplying menus as she went. They ordered and chatted quietly through a thoroughly pleasant meal.

"I get the distinct impression," Franklin commented at one point, "that the portions are in direct proportion to the amount of bullshit you spin."

"You mean 'charm', Frederick," Bill replied, peering over the top of a mound of butter-soaked new potatoes, "But I believe that you may well be right."

When Maisie brought them a pot of steaming coffee at the end of the meal, Bill invited her to sit with them. The squeals of delight and the general fluttering that resulted from the offer made Franklin wonder just how the lady would react if she were ever invited to Buckingham Palace.

The conversation turned to 'Tom's' exploits in the music business and Franklin excused himself after his first cup of coffee. '*Either that, or burst into fits of giggles myself,*' he thought.

"I said I'd meet up with Simon and Jack," he explained, instead.

"Oh, of course!" Maisie exclaimed. "It must be so nice to meet up with ordinary people."

"Yes," Franklin replied, eyeing Bill, "It does make a pleasant change."

"Don't you worry about us," Bill replied, cheerfully avoiding Franklin's gaze, "Maisie and I will be fine, won't we dear?"

Maisie giggled girlishly, and Franklin beat a hasty retreat before his own laughter surfaced.

When he entered the pub, he found Simon alone at the bar. He looked up when Franklin came in.

"Hi, Freddy,"

"Hello, my man," Franklin replied, and to George who had just emerged from a back room, "A pint please, George, and one for Simon."

"Evening, young sir," George replied cheerfully, reaching for two recently washed pint glasses, "And change for the pinball machine, would it be?"

Franklin laughed, "Yes please George, I've got to remind Simon here, who's the best."

"Where's Jack?" he asked Simon when their beers had arrived.

Simon's smile disappeared, and a haunted look replaced it. "Our dad's got him cleaning off a boat. Seems he's not too keen on us getting to know 'your type'. Jack'll be along presently."

"Sorry about that, man. If it's any easier, I'll leave you to it."

"No way!" Simon almost shouted back, then, moderating his voice as George looked up sharply, "I mean, no; it's his problem, not yours."

"Okay, man, no sweat. Let's have a game. At least that's one bastard," he pointed at the pinball table, "that I can get the better of."

Simon smiled once more, "We'll see," he replied and followed Franklin to the machine.

Jack Junior came in an hour later and wandered over to the pinball players. "Evening, Freddy, Simon," he greeted them, "Sorry I'm late."

"Hi, Jack," Franklin replied, "No problem. Sorry about the bother with your old man."

Jack, unlike Simon, didn't seem to harbour any bitterness. He shrugged off Franklin's comment. "No worries."

Leaving the pinball machine to cool down they took a table near the door and swapped their life stories, Franklin, a little guilty, spinning them a yarn about his fictional music career, and he was grateful when he told them that he didn't want to talk much about it and found that the brothers didn't press him.

For their part Jack did most of the talking, Simon occasionally interjecting with a barbed comment about their father. Jack Senior, it transpired, ran a less than successful boat hire business – Parson's Pleasure Cruises – and his general air of bigotry and antagonism did little to endear him to potential clients and most of the locals alike.

"If they say they're friends of our father," Simon said at one point, "then they're not worth knowing."

Jack it transpired, was the elder of the two and was being 'groomed' to take over the business when their father either retired or 'more hopefully', as Simon put it, died.

"The way I figure it," Jack explained, "the way he talks to people, it's going to be sooner rather than later."

Their life stories complete, they replenished their drinks and returned to the pinball table where they spent the rest of the evening. Neither Jack Senior or his sometime friend Michael made an appearance, although Peter/Frank wandered in shortly before closing time and bought the three lads a drink.

Once again, they agreed to meet the following evening and Franklin strolled back to the guesthouse relaxed and in high spirits. He remembered as he let himself in the front door, that he and Bill had forgotten to call the remaining thirteen telephone numbers. He would remind him.

He found Bill sitting alone at the bar and nursing an empty glass.

"Now there's an unusual sight."

"Why, hello Frederick," Bill said, looking up, "And less of the cheek, please, my youthful scholar."

Franklin laughed, "Where's the adorable Maisie?"

"The lady that you so accurately describe as adorable has just popped along the road to borrow something," Bill replied, a little evasively.

Franklin looked once more at Bill's empty glass and from there to a small optic rail behind the bar. The whisky bottle was empty. "Oh, you didn't?"

"You will make a fine detective, young man," Bill replied, "But no, I didn't. Maisie insisted. She was feeling most guilty when she realised that she had run out."

"Okay," said Franklin, "I believe you. And talking of detective work, we forgot the other telephone calls."

"Not entirely," Bill replied, smiling, "There's a note on your pillow to remind you."

"Hmm," Franklin remarked, pointedly, "I don't suppose while you were upstairs you thought of loaning Maisie your remaining store of liquid luggage, did you?"

"Oh, I wouldn't dream of it," Bill replied guilelessly, "It would break the dear lady's heart if she thought she wasn't needed."

Franklin raised his eyes heavenwards.

"And before you say it," Bill continued, "Yes, I know – I'm incorrigible."

Franklin laughed. "Ain't that the truth."

"I think, perhaps, that tomorrow's lessons should include a little English grammar," Bill remarked.

Maisie returned while the pair were still laughing and beamed at the scene before her. "It's so nice to see old friends enjoying each other's company."

Chapter 6

Tuesday 10th June 2014

The following morning dawned damply, and Bill and Franklin deferred their planned stroll into the village, filling their morning with more tuition. At four o'clock that afternoon the rain was still falling steadily.

"Only in Britain could there be such a thing as torrential drizzle," Bill remarked gloomily.

Franklin grunted in agreement, yawned and stretched. "I'm exhausted. This learning business is hard work."

"But rewarding nonetheless, I trust?"

"Yeah. And kinda fun."

"Well," Bill went on, "I think you've done enough for today. Rain or not, we'd better sally forth and recommence our investigations."

"Good idea," Franklin agreed. After several hours in his room, even a damp walk would seem refreshing.

They scurried through the downpour to the telephone booths and repeated the previous morning's exercise. The results were depressingly similar despite it being a normal working day. This time it was Franklin that made one contact.

"They're a large firm of stockbrokers," Bill explained when Franklin told him the name of the company he had contacted. "Other than their involvement in the financial services field, I see no real link between them and the prior number – and it certainly doesn't help our investigation any."

"Perhaps we should try the rest during the evening?" Franklin suggested.

"Why not?" Bill consented gloomily. He hadn't realised just how much he was pinning his hopes on the telephone numbers.

They returned to the guesthouse for dinner, Maisie fussing around them when they reappeared, bedraggled, before her. As they ate another enormous meal their moods lightened a little and when they set off once more into the village, Bill was back to his usual ebullient self.

"It could of course be that, with the exception of one or two numbers on the list, the persons concerned travel a lot, or that the numbers are only useful at particular, maybe even pre-arranged, times."

Franklin shrugged. "If that's the case then we simply keep trying. Different times, different days."

"Agreed."

That evening the exercise bore no fruit. Bill returned to the guesthouse and the eager Maisie, and Franklin made his way to the pub in search of Simon and Jack, both enjoying quiet restful evenings.

* * * * *

Wednesday 11th June 2014

Wednesday also dawned wetly and they spent it as they had the Tuesday, eating, learning or teaching, telephoning and drinking. Franklin, for his part, was quite content with the pattern developing but he noticed that Bill was becoming a little restless. When he returned from the pub that evening, he broached the subject while Maisie was busy in her kitchen.

"Why so edgy?"

Bill thought for a moment before replying. "We're not getting anywhere with our investigations for one thing, and for another, it can only be a matter of time before my dear, departed sister is discovered. I've no idea what the consequences of that might be."

Franklin blinked in surprise. He'd completely forgotten about Mary.

* * * * *

"He can't have just disappeared into thin air!" Jenny was becoming more exasperated by the day and PC Blake's latest report wasn't improving her temper any.

"No-one anywhere has seen him, miss," the policeman went on.

"Officer," Jenny said patiently, "It's Wednesday evening, Franklin has been missing at least five days – *someone* must have seen him."

"Not according to all of our investigations."

"And just how much 'investigation' has been done?" Jenny demanded.

"Well, as you're well aware, we're very undermanned," PC Blake went on sheepishly, "But I've managed to spend at least an hour a day on it."

"An hour a day! You're dealing with a seventeen-year old runaway for Christ's sake. For all we know, that animal Hart could have killed him and hidden the body somewhere."

"Now that really would be corrective punishment," Susan interjected lightly.

If looks could kill, Jenny would have been arrested on the spot. "Not funny, Suze!"

"Quite so, miss," the policeman agreed, secretly grateful for Susan's intervention. "But I'm fairly sure that Hart hasn't done anything. Our only witness, the neighbour, saw Franklin sprinting away and Hart just isn't capable of running, let alone sprinting." he tried to sound reassuring.

Jenny sighed, her anger leeching away. "It's just not *like* Franklin. He might appear to be forever getting into trouble but he's normally very responsible."

"Personally," Susan said, "I think that running away from Hart *is* being responsible. How many different stories has he told you, officer?"

Blake grunted. "Four at the last count. I think he was trying to cover for not reporting Franklin missing on the Friday night."

"Well he's certainly being taken off our list," Jenny commented.

"At least something good has come out of it," Susan remarked; and before Jenny could reply, "Anyone care for a coffee?"

* * * * *

Thursday 12th June 2014

When Franklin appeared at breakfast on the Thursday morning, Bill was opening a letter.

"Gerry?" he enquired.

A stack of banknotes fell from the envelope. "Quite so," Bill replied, extracting a sheet of paper and unfolding it. Checking to see that Maisie was still busy in the kitchen, he read the letter aloud.

"'Dear Bill, you silly old...' I'll skip that bit, 'Here's the cash as arranged. Don't forget to tell me if you're moving on. I posted this in Coventry where I got the money from. Hope it's far enough away. Also, hope you know what you're doing. I doubt it, but I hope so anyway. Whatever else you do, take care. Your friend, and don't forget it, Gerry'."

"A friend indeed," Bill commented, folding the letter and putting it in his jacket pocket. He gathered up the banknotes and counted them. "More than I thought," he added, "There's five hundred here; he must have added a little of his own. Very kind, but a misplaced gesture. Remind me to phone him after breakfast."

"You're lucky," Franklin commented.

"Very. It's a useful lesson for you," Bill replied. "Value trust in others beyond all else." He held out five twenty-pound notes. "And talking of trust, take these."

Franklin began to protest but Bill waved him into silence. "Think of it what you will, but don't consider it to be charity."

Franklin shrugged and accepted the cash. "Thank you," he said, pointedly. He pocketed the money as Maisie entered with their breakfasts, her spectacles rather foggy with the steam rising from their plates.

When she had returned to the kitchen Franklin pointed at the plates. "Is it my imagination or are our portions getting bigger?"

"It does appear that way, doesn't it?" Bill replied.

"I'm beginning to wonder what you two get up to when I'm not around."

"A gentleman never tells," Bill replied, smiling around a fork-full of bacon.

When they were drinking their coffee, Franklin wondering whether he would ever be able to move again, Maisie brought Bill several newspapers.

"Sorry, Tom," she said, handing him the bundle, "I'm afraid they didn't have a copy of The Times."

"Not to worry, dear lady, it's a dreadfully boring journal anyway," Bill replied.

He spent the next twenty minutes scanning the pages for any indication that his sister's bloody remains had been discovered. "Not a thing," he reported eventually, "By the way, what day is the Walthamstow Guardian published?"

"Thursday, I think," Franklin replied. He thought for a moment. "Oh, I see. You're wondering if there'll be any news about me. Perhaps Maisie has a laptop I can check on?"

"Let's not leave any electronic traces, but you're quite right. Let's away to the telephones – I'll ask Gerald to send me a copy."

* * * * *

While Bill spoke to Gerry who was evidently having a day off work, Franklin tried the remaining telephone numbers on the 'B' church list – once again without response. When they had both finished, they decided to postpone the day's lessons and retreated to a small coffee shop.

"What did Gerry have to say?" Franklin enquired when they were both seated.

"Oh, the usual," Bill replied, "You know – be careful, are you sure you know what you're doing, that sort of thing. He also said that he has mailed some more cash, this time from Exeter. I think he's enjoying the intrigue, and he's certainly dying to know what we're up to."

"Did you remember to ask about the local paper?"

"Yes," Bill replied, "that's what took so long – he went through it while we were talking. I take it you don't mind me telling him a little more about your good self?"

"Of course not," Franklin replied, "Any friend of yours and all that."

"I also told him that we'd be here for another few days. Is that ok?"

The question surprised Franklin a little and he shrugged while he pondered its import. "Fine by me."

"When do you think that we ought to move on?" Bill continued.

It occurred once more to Franklin that Bill was holding a great deal of faith in his opinions. He thought carefully for a while, anxious in his own mind to give value for money as it were. "Well," he replied eventually, "I don't see any harm in staying for a few more days. Our story has been accepted easily enough. There is one factor though."

"Go on," Bill prompted when the lad paused again.

"Well, if either of our... *problems* make the newspapers, I don't think that we should move on immediately."

Bill pondered this for a minute. "Of course," he nodded at last, "Too suspicious!"

Franklin nodded. Given that they weren't known to be together, he couldn't really imagine that it would be a problem, but, there again, you couldn't be too careful. Besides, he was enjoying it here in Wroxham.

Bill was like-minded. Maisie provided most welcome home comforts and Franklin was noticeably becoming more relaxed and self-assured in their new surroundings. "That's settled then!" he agreed.

Deciding to further postpone the lessons until the next day, they spent the rest of the daylight hours wandering around the village and Franklin was surprised when Bill only insisted on visiting one pub.

Their first positive decision had the effect of further relaxing the pair and Bill, especially, was in high spirits during their evening meal back at the guesthouse. Franklin listened, enthralled, as Bill described his university years and his laughter, when Bill explained how he had been sent down after a drunken night's roistering, brought Maisie scampering from the kitchen at a run.

When they had finished their coffees, Bill's liberally laced with brandy, Franklin was a little reluctant to leave, but he (or at least, Freddy) had agreed to meet Simon and Jack.

"I've really enjoyed today," he informed Bill, seriously, as he put on his jacket.

Bill was thoughtful for a moment. "And I also, young man. Thank you."

Franklin left Bill in Maisie's capable, if a little smothering, hands and wandered out into the night.

When he reached the pub, his relaxed mood slipped a little when he spotted Michael, Jack Parson Senior's cohort, at the bar. Deciding to ignore his presence altogether, he ordered a pint from George and asked whether the landlord had seen either Simon or Jack.

"Aye, master Frederick," the landlord replied, "Simon was here a short while ago. He said to tell you that he'd be a little late. 'Bout nine o'clock, he reckoned."

Franklin thanked him, paid for his pint, and made for the pinball machine.

His relaxed mood seemed to assist his playing ability and he had just gained his fourth replay when Simon and Jack appeared. He was between games when they entered and looked up at the sound of the door opening. He was surprised to see them enter, arguing. When Jack spotted Franklin, he broke off from the heated discussion.

"Enough!" he said to Simon, and then: "Evening, Freddy. Fancy a pint?"

Simon was about to continue the debate, but seeing Franklin, he shrugged and lapsed into silence after a cursory wave in his direction.

"Evening Jack, Simon," Franklin replied, "I'd love one."

Simon wandered over to the pinball table while Jack purchased the lagers.

"Problems?" Franklin asked.

Simon looked up at him, his eyes blazing momentarily before he sighed deeply. "The usual," he replied.

"The old man?" Franklin prompted.

Simon nodded. "Yeah. He's been like a bear all week, but this afternoon..." He paused.

Franklin said nothing, waiting for the lad to go on.

Simon straightened his droop-shouldered stance and continued. "This afternoon he came back to the boatyard drunk. He's sleeping it off now. He was rambling on about nothing; not making any sense. All of a sudden he went for Jack with a club hammer."

"Jesus, man!"

"Good job the old bastard was drunk. Fell over his own feet before he got close enough to do any damage."

Jack returned with the drinks.

"Thanks," Franklin said, accepting one of the pints, "Just been hearing about your troubles."

Jack shrugged. "Something and nothing."

Simon began to protest but Jack, his voice calm, stopped him. "It's not Freddy's problem."

"Don't mind me," Franklin said, "Problems are problems."

"That's what we were arguing about," Simon explained sullenly, "I say we should just get out and leave the old shit to it."

Jack shook his head vehemently. "No way. I aim to have that yard someday. Someday soon, at that."

Simon began to argue once more, but Jack silenced him with a look. "Let's beat this black show off," he suggested.

The tension drained perceptibly from the air and Franklin laughed. "No chance, white trash." He pressed the credit button three times. "A pint says I'll outscore the pair of you combined."

Half an hour later Franklin was in credit by two pints.

"There's no Irish blood in your family?" Jack enquired, "Only you've got the luck of them."

"Luck be buggered," Franklin replied, laughing, "But I suppose it's the red hair that gives me away?"

They were still laughing when the pub doors clattered open.

Everyone in the pub fell silent and turned towards the doors as Jack Parsons Senior staggered through them.

"Oh, shit!" Simon groaned softly. He took a step towards his father before Jack Junior laid a hand on his shoulder, stopping him.

"Wait!" he whispered urgently.

Their father stood inside the doorway swaying from side to side and blearily scanned the pub and its occupants. Eventually his eyes settled unsteadily on his sons.

"There y'are, y'little bastards!"

George moved around the end of the bar watching the drunk all the while. Parsons was oblivious to his approach and after a moment of mental effort spoke up again.

"Come here you little shits!" he roared at the boys, "Y'were s'posed to cook m'dinner."

The mixture of anger and the pathetic whining quality of his voice combined to bring a sense of revulsion to Franklin's mind. "Pathetic!" he muttered quietly.

"Wha's that?" Parson's voice rose again. "Y'little black bastard! S'your fault they're not looking after their own father," he gestured vaguely with his arm. "All the same, your lot. Tole you before."

He staggered around a table, his right fist balled. "Teach'ya t'lead m'boys astray," he roared.

Franklin took a step backwards, quickly scanning the nearest tables for a weapon. He needn't have bothered. Before Parsons could close the gap between them, he was simultaneously grabbed by George and Peter/Frank who had appeared from nowhere.

"Oh no you don't, Jack," George said as Parsons struggled to free himself. Peter/Frank whispered something into Parson's ear that Franklin couldn't make out. The struggles ceased.

Jack Junior had positioned himself in front of Franklin and seeing that his father was now comfortably restrained he stepped forward to him.

"You are a pathetic, drunken, slob!" he spat at his father. "I won't bother asking you to apologise; and I certainly won't apologise for you."

Parsons went to make a reply, but a twist of his arm from George silenced him.

Jack stared at his father for a moment, shook his head in undisguised loathing, and turned away. It was clear to Franklin that Parsons was too far gone in drink to really understand what was going on but his own loathing of boors and bigots like Parsons was strong and well defined.

"You're shit, man," he said darkly. "Nothing!" He, too, turned away.

Deciding that enough was enough, George spun the now silent man around and pushed him forcefully towards the doors. When Parsons staggered, falling to one knee in the process, the landlord dragged him upright by his collar. At the door, without bothering to turn Parsons to face him, he said, clearly and slowly:

"Jack Parsons you are a disgrace. A disgrace to your sons, our village, this pub. And mostly to yourself. Now, get out and stay out. You needn't be coming back."

Michael, Parsons' erstwhile friend, made to protest but George, one hand still on Parsons collar, glanced over at him. "And that will go for you too, Michael, if you don't decide to quieten down." The man fell silent.

As the landlord opened a door with his free hand in preparation of throwing the drunk into the street, Simon stepped up behind them.

"Father," he said quietly.

As Parsons turned at the sound of his younger son's voice Simon brought his arm back and delivered a roundhouse punch that connected squarely with Parsons' jaw.

The drunk flew backwards into the street and Franklin swore afterwards that he'd seen Parsons' feet lift off the floor.

In the sudden, shocked, silence that followed, the sound of Simon's fist connecting with his father's jaw seemed to reverberate around the bar.

Every eye had turned towards Simon and he suddenly looked around, seemingly as surprised at his own actions as everyone else. He looked down at his right hand and, even from ten feet away, Franklin could see that it was already discolouring and swelling.

George snapped out of his own shocked silence as Peter/Frank quietly clapped Simon's efforts.

"Now, young Simon," he said to the lad, a glance at Peter/Frank curtailing the applause, "I won't condone what you've just done, and if you do anything like that again in here, you'll be barred just the same as your father. But this time, and under the circumstances, I'll let it go."

Simon, still seemingly a little stunned, simply nodded.

Jack and Franklin walked over to him. "You're for it now," his brother told him.

"He won't even remember," Simon replied, shrugging as if he didn't care either way. "He had it coming."

"Don't bet on it, brother," Jack went on, "But I'll keep an eye on him."

George had walked over to the bar and now came back carrying a tea towel in which he'd wrapped most of his supply of ice cubes. "Let's have a look at that hand," he said to Simon.

Peter/Frank had gone to the door and now closed it. "He's staggered off," he reported in his normal cultured tones. "Well done, Simon."

The boy glanced over and acknowledged the comment with a shrug. He winced as George examined his hand.

"Nothing broken, I'm thinking," the landlord reported eventually, wrapping the injured hand in the ice-cold cloth. "And now, can we all please settle down and enjoy the rest of the evening?"

Jack nodded, and the three lads walked over to the bar. Peter/Frank joined them.

"Anyone care for a beverage?" he enquired.

Jack and Simon both nodded. "Thanks," Franklin replied.

George poured the drinks. "That'll be twelve pounds exactly please, Peter."

'Thank god for that,' thought Franklin, mentally assigning the name to the face. When he accepted his own pint his hand shook slightly, slopping the foaming beer over his feet. Jack, too, took his beer unsteadily. Only Simon seemed unaffected.

"Bad business," Franklin muttered, "Sorry to have caused you that sort of hassle."

Simon looked up at him, surprised, "You caused it?"

"Well–" Franklin begun but Jack interrupted him.

"Don't think it for a minute. He's always like that."

Peter nodded in agreement. "A thoroughly reprehensible character."

Franklin went to apologise once more but he suddenly realised that it was probably true. The man really was a boor. He hadn't realised just how bad home life must be for his two new friends. "Sorry, anyway," he said, glancing from one half-brother to the other.

Jack nodded, seeing the apology for what it was. "As I've said," he replied, "the old bastard won't last much longer. If he can turn Simon here to violence, sooner or later he'll do it to someone that won't be as gentle."

Simon looked at his brother who was grinning ruefully. He laughed and raised his injured hand. "Didn't feel that gentle."

"Didn't sound that gentle, either," Franklin added, smiling himself for the first time since Parsons' appearance.

"Personally," said Jack, "I think it was just an excuse for getting out of losing at pinball."

"I can still beat you both one-handed," Simon replied. "Come on, let's find out." He unwrapped his hand and walked over to the machine.

Franklin and Jack picked up their beers. "Join us?" Franklin asked Peter. "Why not?" he replied.

By the end of the evening, Franklin was once more in a relaxed mood. Parsons was trouble, obviously, but he was Simon and Jack's trouble. When they parted outside the pub, both he and Peter offered to accompany them back to the boatyard in case there was any further trouble.

Franklin didn't know about Peter's feelings on the subject, but he was certainly relieved when the offers were declined.

* * * * *

Friday 13th June 2014

The hallway clock was chiming-in Friday when Franklin let himself into the guesthouse. Maisie's laughter trilled in the bar, and Franklin smiled to himself. Deciding against the early night that he had planned, he walked through and joined Maisie and Bill.

"Ah, the very man," Bill said, as Franklin sat down.

"Oh?"

"Thomas, here," Maisie explained, "has made me a very kind offer, but he'll need your co-operation."

Fleeting thoughts of Bill proposing to Maisie, with him as best man at the wedding, flashed through Franklin's mind before Bill took up the narrative.

"Maisie's sister runs a guesthouse in Great Yarmouth," he explained, "and with both ladies running such businesses they seldom get time to see each other. I suggested to Maisie that she visit Mabel tomorrow while we look after the shop. Our poor landlady is in any case having one of her – how did you say it, Maisie, my dear? Oh, yes, one of her 'tired days'." Beside Bill, Maisie was nodding. "You don't mind, do you?"

"Oh, Tom," Maisie admonished him, "Let Frederick answer for himself."

Franklin shrugged, smiling. "Why not?" he replied, "It should be fun."

"Oh, that's lovely," Maisie beamed, "I'll just pop through the back and telephone her. She'll still be up."

"You don't really mind, do you?" Bill enquired while Maisie made the call to her sister.

Franklin shook his head. "Of course not. Given that we're the only guests, it shouldn't be too difficult."

"Ah," Bill replied, "There is just the matter of the half a dozen that arrived this evening."

Franklin suddenly remembered four large cars parked just beyond the house. "Half a dozen?"

"Ten to be precise. Can you cook?"

Franklin groaned with good humour, "You are a... a...."

Bill never learned what he was thanks to Maisie's timely return.

* * * * *

Six hours later, Franklin stood bleary-eyed in the kitchen while Maisie fussed around showing Bill where everything was.

"Are you sure you don't mind?" she enquired for what, to Franklin, seemed like the twentieth time in as many minutes.

"Dear, dear lady," Bill replied reassuringly, "It is the least we can do to repay your overt kindness."

Privately, Franklin thought that the least they could do was to remain in bed. Shortly afterwards a car horn tooted outside and Maisie, her gratitude profuse, was hustled out of the front door by Bill.

"Methinks the lady doth protest too much," he said, returning to the kitchen.

"And methinks," Franklin said, yawning loudly, "That some silly old sod doth make too many daft promises to innocent landladies."

"Do I detect an ounce or two of complaint?"

"Make it a ton or two and you'll be getting closer."

* * * * *

The first couple appeared for their breakfasts a little after seven o'clock and Franklin gradually woke up as he struggled with frying pans, saucepans full of scrambled (and occasionally incendiary) eggs, and coffee pots. Bill waited at the tables, playing *mine host*, with a gusto that surprised Franklin.

At ten o'clock when the last guest had wandered back to his room, Bill returned to the kitchen with half a dozen dirty plates and two coffee mugs.

"That was easy enough, wasn't it?" he enquired.

Franklin gave him a baleful look. "For who?"

"For whom, dear boy," Bill replied, cheerily. "Any chance of a bacon sandwich? Oh, perhaps not," he finished when Franklin gave him an even darker look. "Shall I wash up?"

Half an hour later, with the exception of two blackened saucepans, the kitchen was once again as spotless as it had been when Maisie had departed. Bill collected the mail and newspapers, Franklin setting himself on a stool with a steaming mug of coffee.

"Gerry's letter there?" Franklin enquired.

Bill nodded, opening the letter simply addressed to 'Tom'. He counted the notes into his pocket, balling the envelope, and turned his attention to the newspapers.

Franklin picked up copies of the Daily Mail and Daily Express and joined Bill in scanning the day's output for news of Mary's murder. They then checked Mary's laptop for online news, but half an hour later they were happy that no such discovery had yet been made.

In lieu of schooling, on the grounds that they were, after all, working, Bill spent the next couple of hours trying to teach Franklin the intricacies of cryptic crosswords with indifferent success. After that, the rather superstitious date took centre stage.

"Isn't it tricksy-something?" Franklin responded when Bill asked him whether he knew the correct   name of the phobia.

"You're thinking of triskaidekaphobia," Bill smiled, "But that is actually just a fear of the number thirteen. Well done for at least remembering that it was tricksy!"

Franklin shrugged, "I didn't remember it properly, though. Anyway what is the Friday the thirteenth one? Maybe I'll remember that instead."

Bill laughed, "Given that it's paraskevidekatriaphobia, maybe not. Although the alternative might be more memorable for a callow youth such as yourself. That's friggatiskaidekaphobia."

Franklin gawped, "Frigga... thing... as in f–"

"As in Friday, in truth," Bill interrupted, "Although to be fair to you, the frigg part is certainly derives in that way, and is undoubtedly just what you were thinking."

"Okay, okay," Franklin grinned, "Maybe I'll give it a miss for now anyway, but man! Just how the f... how the *hell* do you know all these monster words"

Bill's grin widened, "That, dear boy, is because I do *not* suffer from hippopotomonstrosesquippedaliophobia." He roared a laugh as Franklin's jaw almost bounced off the table-top, "And before you ask, yes it is a real word, and it means an irrational fear of long words. Rather appropriate, don't you think – hippopotomonstrosesquippedaliophobia?"

The young man eventually found his voice, "There's nothing irrational about that fear! Isn't it time you went and had a rest? I know my ears need one!"

At two o'clock Bill retreated to the bar and settled down with a copy of the Daily Telegraph and a large whisky. On the grounds that one of them should be on the premises at all times, Franklin was volunteered to venture forth and make the daily round of telephone calls.

He returned, his mission unsuccessful, to find Bill on the telephone himself.

"Of course, dear Maisie," he was saying, "We didn't expect you back earlier than eight o'clock anyway."

Franklin groaned as images of burnt steaks and cremated chicken crossed his mind.

"Bill," Franklin said, desperately, when the phone call was over, "I really don't think I'm good enough to cook evening meals."

"It's no matter, young Franklin," Bill replied cheerfully, "I'll handle that. Believe it or not I'm quite a dab hand with a steak."

"And you made me cook a dozen breakfasts?"

"Didn't I mention my culinary prowess earlier?" Bill replied guilelessly, "I thought you *wanted* to cook the breakfasts..."

"I…" Franklin began.

"Have a drink, dear boy," Bill interrupted, "You've earned it."

When Bill had eventually managed to pacify Franklin, the pair spent the remainder of the afternoon in amiable conversation. Franklin spoke of his likes and dislikes, hobbies, sports and music. Bill, as ever the main contributor in a two-person conversation, created vivid and, to Franklin, hilarious word portraits of his friends and acquaintances. Throughout the afternoon Bill drank steadily, Franklin becoming ever more amazed at his capacity. Shortly before the first guests reappeared in search of their dinners, Franklin interrupted one of Bill's anecdotes.

"Why do you drink so much?"

Bill looked nonplussed for a moment, his gaze moving backwards and forwards from Franklin to his glass. "Well," he began thoughtfully, "I could be trite and simply say 'because I can', but your question deserves a little more effort." He paused again before continuing. "If truth be told, I'm extraordinarily shy." He looked up to see if Franklin was about to protest. Franklin merely raised an eyebrow. "The whisky, (literally 'water of life', or 'uisge-beatha' in Scottish Gaelic did you know?), helps. Or at least, that's how it started when I was in my teens. I suppose, now, that I'm too afraid of returning to my former shy, introverted state should I stop drinking."

Bill had surprised himself by his admission; something that he had studiously ignored for many years – especially around his sister. He was more surprised by Franklin's reaction.

"Okay, that makes sense," the young man replied, "But why don't you try quitting for a while? You know, just to find out?"

Bill smiled back ruefully. "Good question," he replied, "but I feel that maybe, despite all my fears of timidity, it might run a little deeper."

"By which you mean you can't. Give it up, I mean?"

"Perspicacious as ever," Bill agreed. 'Why,' he thought to himself, 'can a young, inexperienced, culturally different person like Franklin induce more self-shame in two sentences than Mary in twenty-some years could ever create?' Shelving his thought, he added aloud, "And do you disapprove?"

Franklin, to Bill's further surprise, laughed. "Hell, no. It's a free country, and as they say, it's 'because you can'. You're about as harmless as they come. Now, if you were like Hart after a beer or two..."

"Perish the thought," Bill replied, shuddering, "Violence has never been in my nature." He paused for a moment before adding quietly, "That's why I really can't believe that I did for my sister."

Franklin's smile disappeared. "Yeah," his own voice quietening, "That's why I can't believe it either."

The next couple of minutes were spent in quiet contemplation before Bill slapped his hands together loudly. "Enough morbidity, and enough dissemination of my reprehensible habits. Let us begin the preparations for the culinary delights that will await our guests!"

*****

For three hours, Franklin waited tables, prepared vegetables and generally made himself helpful while Bill dashed around the kitchen, displaying remarkable aplomb. They were sitting in the kitchen, idly picking at a plate of surplus vegetables, the last guests sipping their coffees, when Maisie walked in. Franklin had, earlier in the day, predicted her first words.

"That's a beer you owe me," he said to Bill when the lady trilled, "Oh, thank you both so much!"

Bill laughed and greeted their landlady. "Welcome home, Maisie my dear. Your establishment is, as you can see, still in one piece and it has been a most entertaining diversion for us."

Maisie simpered around the pair, gratitude pouring from every pore while Bill related their days' activities. When Franklin returned with the last diners' coffee cups, Maisie was arguing quietly with Bill.

"I insist," she said decisively, "You've done more than enough already."

Franklin could briefly imagine Bill having offered to look after the guest house for another week, before his fears were dispelled when the man spoke up.

"But, Maisie, I'm not even sure that I want to go out for the evening."

"Nonsense," the lady replied, "You haven't been out a single evening since you arrived here, and you've said more than once that you'd like to have a quiet drink with Frederick."

"He has?" Franklin enquired, grinning as Bill blushed a little, flustered.

"Most definitely," Maisie replied, looking from Bill to Franklin, "And you've most certainly earned a reward for your kindness today. I promise you my... tired spell has passed." To emphasise her point, she took her glasses off and pointed at the front door somewhat myopically.

Bill made a couple more protests, studiously ignoring Franklin's grin, but eventually had to relent. "Ok," he said, raising his hands in mock surrender, "Besides, I appear to *owe* the young lad a drink in any case."

They were almost forcibly prised through the door by the still-profuse Maisie and found themselves in the darkened street beyond.

Franklin heaved a huge sigh. "Thank god for that," he said, "I think Maisie's gratitude is harder to take than skivvying in the kitchen."

Bill laughed. "I don't think you're too far wide of the mark," he replied, "Now, where's this wonderful public house you have taken to frequenting?"

"Normally wonderful," Franklin replied. As he led Bill into the village, he related the Parsons incident from the previous evening.

"A real charmer," Bill commented when Franklin had finished.

"Not so unusual," Franklin replied, "Sometimes I get to wondering just what makes someone such a bigot – colour, creed, that sort of thing. Drink, maybe, a bad parent, no parents. But all in all, I think that maybe all of those things or some of those things or none of them are to blame – that some people are just like that. It's there from the start – maybe even in all of us."

They had reached the pub door and as Franklin reached for the handle the sound of the gunshot cracked into the night and the glass panel of the door disintegrated into a deadly shower. Franklin pitched backwards, his scream choked off almost as soon as it began.

Chapter 7

Friday 13th June 2014

In the Mucky Duck Gerry was desperately trying to turn the conversation away from runaway teenagers, without success.

Jenny Thomsett had arrived a little after eight o'clock with Susan in tow and had immediately launched into a bitter tirade concerning the irresponsibility of teenagers, the ineptitude of the police, and the lack of respect for over-worked social workers. When the name Franklin had appeared briefly in the monologue, Gerry had immediately become interested. His usual defence against the young social worker's tirades was to depart in the direction of a fruit machine (any of them would do), but now, she had his full attention.

When he enquired, during a brief lull in Jenny's ranting, as to the nature of the incident she was referring to, the pieces quickly clicked into place.

Franklin Richardson, she explained, forever a trouble maker, had disappeared a week ago on the grounds, apparently, that he was terrified of receiving a beating from his foster father of the moment, one Mr Hart. She went on to describe PC Blake in, what to Gerry, were surprisingly colourful terms, and ended by bemoaning the problems the 'little sod' was causing her at work.

Gerry wasn't sure whether the term 'little sod' referred to Franklin or the policeman but decided it didn't matter. He was relieved to hear that the enquiries into Franklin's whereabouts were cursory to say the least and made a mental note to inform Bill when they next spoke. However, a comment from Susan alarmed him greatly.

"Since when do you take an interest in us poor social workers, Gerry?" she asked him.

While Gerry was floundering for a suitably innocent reply Richie, drunk as ever, alarmed him even more.

"Yes, good point that, Susan," he said, "Given Gerry's normal description of social workers."

"Thank you, Richard," Gerry replied darkly. To Susan he said, "It was just that I recall seeing a young black lad hitching on the M3 the other day."

Jenny was immediately interested, and Gerry cursed his own lack of imagination. Why hadn't he simply said that he'd enquired because he was bored or something?

"When was that exactly?" Jenny asked him.

Gerry was wondering whether to try to confuse the issue and decided that, given his rather stupid comment already, it might be worthwhile. "Monday," he replied.

"What did the lad look like?" Jenny went on.

"Well, I only got a brief look," Gerry replied, carefully, "But he was quite tall, sort of athletic-looking."

"Could be," Jenny mused. "What was he wearing?"

'In for a penny,' Gerry thought before replying, "Denim jacket, jeans, trainers I think."

"Doesn't narrow it down much," Jenny replied, "But it must be worth a little investigative time. Suze, go phone Blake."

"Yes, ma'am," Susan replied, saluting her friend and smiling as Jenny continued her interrogation.

"Which way was he heading?"

"South."

"And where does that take him?"

"Well," Gerry replied slowly, "Southampton. But I really think it would be too much of a coincidence; there must be hundreds of runaways that could match his description."

"Yeah," Jenny replied, sighing, "In fact there are thousands."

Gerry, satisfied that, at worst, he was being merely misleading was warming to his task. "Does he know anyone down that way?"

"No..." Jenny began, then paused. "Hang on! I Think you've cracked it. I know it's a long shot and all that, but there **is** one person he knows down that area."

Susan returned from the telephone and informed them that PC Blake would stop by a little later. Jenny filled her in with Gerry's information.

"What's the name of the old girl that retried to Southampton?" she asked her friend.

"Miss Baker?" Susan suggested.

"Uh huh," Jenny shook her head and thought for a moment. "Blake! Miss Blake."

"Who's that?" Gerry asked.

"She was Franklin's social worker when he was young. She still keeps in touch with him – a miracle given the problems he's caused her, in my mind. She retired four years ago and moved down there a little later."

"Could be, I guess?" Gerry suggested, happy with the coincidence.

Jenny opened her battered briefcase and brought out an equally battered mobile phone. She studied a couple of pages for a minute before cursing. "Damn! The only number I've got for her is a London one. Who's in the office tonight, Suze?"

"Steffi," Susan replied, "Should I call her?"

Jenny nodded peremptorily, and Susan saluted again before pulling her much smarter phone from her pocket.

Jenny, now thoroughly absorbed by the possibilities that Gerry's revelations had induced, explained that the addresses of former 'carers' were held in the office. Steffi should be able to provide a telephone number.

"Why didn't anyone think of contacting Franklin's friends before?" Richie asked, ever contentious.

Jenny blushed slightly. "I did, sort of," she replied, "I contacted his school friends and the kids where he used to hang out, but I'd forgotten about Kathy Blake. It's got to be three years since Franklin last saw her, but now that you mention it, I'm pretty sure that they kept in touch."

Susan slipped her phone back in her pocket a moment later. "I've got the address," she reported, "but no telephone number."

Jenny nodded. "Directory enquiries?"

"Ex-directory."

"Thought so." It was not uncommon for former social workers to move away and guard their new-found privacy in this way. "Oh well," Jenny went on, "It looks as if we've got a day by the south coast tomorrow."

116

Susan groaned. "Why not leave it to the police?" she suggested. "I was planning on visiting my brother tomorrow."

Jenny shrugged. "As you like."

"Ok, ok," Susan knew the tone Jenny had used and quickly decided that she couldn't stand the reproaches that would follow for the next few days if she didn't go with Jenny. "I'll call him and tell him I'll make it next week." She pulled her phone back out.

"Of course," Jenny said sweetly, "And thank you."

"What's wrong with the police checking it out?" Gerry asked her when Susan made her way to the door in search of a better signal.

"After the way they've handled things up here," Jenny replied grimly, "I haven't got an ounce of confidence remaining. Besides, if Franklin doesn't want to be found, I can't see him admitting his presence if the police turned up at the door."

"But wouldn't this Miss Blake turn him in?"

"I doubt it," Jenny explained, "She left under rather a cloud. She began to question some of the placements we were making and was carrying out quite a lot of personal investigations into some of the foster families. When she recommended that a couple of children be removed from one particular couple, the police were involved, and it even made the national newspapers. Seems her information about the couple was wrong – there was a terrible fuss."

Given Franklin's description of the Harts, Gerry could easily have sympathised with Miss Blake's efforts. He decided that it would be unwise to mention it. "What should I tell the copper when he turns up?" he asked instead.

"Oh, I wouldn't want you to lie to them. Just tell them about noticing the boy, and what he looked like."

Gerry smiled to himself. 'No lies?' he thought. Despite being happy with the way his earlier slip had turned out, he was still glad when Davie and his re-united wife Joan entered the pub and joined them.

"Good evening, everyone," Joan boomed, several people nearby flinching noticeably. "David," she went on, "buy everybody a drink." Richie, wisely, stifled a laugh.

PC Blake arrived half an hour later and spent ten minutes taking a brief statement from Gerry while trying to avoid the smug looks and barbed comments emanating from Jenny Thomsett.

* * * * *

David Phillips, twenty-five and a part time freelance journalist, who secretly hoped to become a full-time novelist who would one day outsell JK Rowling – or at least, Stephen King, scribbled frantically in the notebook he always carried. Surely the story of a teenage runaway, spiced up with police bungling and self-styled investigative social workers would earn him a by-line in next week's local paper? He listened avidly as Gerry spoke to the young policeman and wondered whether he should follow the Woodward-Bernstein Watergate tactics and tail the two women to the south coast the next day.

It might not be the scoop of the century, but the combination of human interest, infighting amongst the social services and his planned covert investigations would surely warrant a front page sixty-eight-point headline?

When the policeman left, muttering under his breath, Phillips decided to order another drink and sidled closer to the group at the bar in the hope of gaining a few more snippets for his story.

Oblivious to the spy in their midst, Jenny continued berating the local constabulary.

* * * * *

Three hundred yards away, Mary's corpse rose to its feet.

The body was supported by a panting, and very nauseous, Paul Jarvis. "Are you sure we're doing the right thing?" he asked a tall, gangling man who was standing in the living room doorway.

"Brother Paul," the man replied in sepulchral tones, "Our sister, Mary, has made the ultimate sacrifice for our church. Her faith in death as well as in life should be sufficient answer for you, and, what is more, shames you."

"Ok, ok, but why couldn't we have at least brought a couple of the others? She's not exactly a lightweight."

118

"Trust and your faith will give you strength," the tall man replied levelly, "Now, place our sister on the blankets."

Jarvis grunted with the effort of moving his hideous burden and thought, not for the first time, that Jacob and the Brothers of the New Church were getting in over their heads. Fancy rites and rituals were one thing, but he was beginning to suspect that he was now an accessory to murder – whatever the ever-more-weird Jacob might say. Were it not for his dire financial situation and the crimes he'd already committed in an effort to hide the fact, he would have left the Brotherhood weeks ago. And, of course, there was Jacob to consider. The man seemed to know everything, and, when all was said and done, without his help he'd more than likely be behind bars right now.

Paul glanced up at Jacob standing there in the doorway like a figure from the gates of Hell. His eyes, as dark as his hair and his dress, had become unfocussed, and Paul found himself speculating on the thoughts going on in Jacob's unfathomable mind.

What was his purpose? The Brotherhood had been formed by Jacob and had recruited members who all shared one common bond. Crimes – undetected crimes. Paul had spoken to a number of the others and their stories were remarkably similar to his own – fraud, theft, even blackmail, all on a large scale, all to cover their individual failings and obsessions. Jacob promised absolution and new-found wealth through faith, and from time-to-time outsiders would appear – never part of the Brotherhood, staying in touch for a short time before disappearing once more. After they left, each member found themselves somehow richer, somehow closer to saving themselves.

Mary had been one such outsider, and Jacob had promised the Brotherhood riches enough to end their collective misery thanks to her involvement. Then, last weekend, Jacob had called Paul and told him that their normal Sunday meeting had been cancelled; Mary, he had explained, had been 'martyred' in their cause. He offered no further explanation.

Until that morning. Paul had been sitting at his desk in the City when his telephone rang. Jacob's voice had explained in crypt-like tones that he required Paul's assistance, that Mary's own 'assistance in their cause' had not been in vain and arranged to meet Paul at a tube station in the East End.

They had met, and Paul had been led to this house, Jacob explaining *en route* that the plans Mary and himself had so carefully laid had somehow not worked. Jarvis now wished that Jacob had been a little more forthcoming. When he'd entered the house and seen her grisly remains, he had nearly fainted, only Jacob's deep reassuring voice bringing him back from the edge of welcome oblivion.

Whether it was the shock of seeing this hellish corpse or not, he wasn't sure, but when Jacob had gone on to explain the circumstances surrounding Mary's death, he had seemed to say that Mary had committed suicide. Seeing her, Paul somehow found that hard to believe.

He let the corpse fall to the floor, onto the blankets that Jacob had laid out, shuddering when he heard the sound of breaking glass.

Jacob had also spoken of a brother, at first confusing Paul – one of the Brotherhood or Mary's brother? He guessed at the latter – settling on the guess because Jacob never allowed questions when in full flow. The brother had spoiled their plans by doing what was expected of him, Jacob had continued, confusing Paul still further. When Jacob had finished speaking, Paul had asked, what seemed to him, a perfectly obvious question.

"What are we doing here?"

Jacob had laughed, a sound that always made Paul shudder. "Why," he replied, his eyes sparkling with a dark humour, "we are merely going to take Mary to a safer place."

As he continued wrapping the body in the heavy blankets, Paul concentrated on not panicking. A thousand questions seemed to be hammering at his skull. *'Did Jacob murder Mary?'*, *'How many of the other outsiders met the same end?'*, *'Just what was Jacob doing?'*, but one question had a far louder voice. *'Just how much trouble am I in?'*

When Paul had finished wrapping the corpse, he tied the ends of the hideous package with lengths of string and knelt back on his heels recovering his breath. Jacob stepped into the room and, bending, laid his hands on the blanket.

"You have served us well, sister," he said, "And now your brother will play his unwitting part." He paused before adding, "When we find him."

Paul, although he had never met Mary's brother, immediately felt sorry for him. He still couldn't work out who had killed the woman, or why – it could even have *been* her brother himself – but the threat in Jacob's voice was so dark, so hellish, that he couldn't help but feel sorry for the man. Jacob *would* find him – Jacob *always* found what he was looking for.

"And now," Jacob said, rising to his feet, "Let us take her to the car."

"What car?" Paul asked, already guessing that the 'us' meant him.

"Mark awaits us outside," the man replied, softly.

"I didn't hear..." Paul began, but stopped short. Jacob wouldn't explain anyway, and he might as well save his breath. Grunting once more with the effort, he hauled his revolting burden upright.

Struggling outside he kept repeating to himself, over and over, '*I'm mad. Should go to the police. Can't go to the police. Be jailed for the frauds if not this. I'm mad...*'

Ten minutes later the house was once more locked and silent, and Paul was left alone at the end of the street as Jacob, Mark and their lifeless passenger sped away into the night. As the reality of what he had just done and witnessed made itself felt past the barrier of shock, he began to shake violently before vomiting into the gutter.

He was dimly aware of a passing voice, "Another drunk from that blasted pub!" Paul wished, desperately, that that was the case.

* * * * *

Mrs Jenkins closed the curtains. Bill had asked her to keep an eye on his house and she had been doing her neighbourly duty in his absence with a thoroughness far beyond the call.

Now she was close to panic. She had watched the two men enter the house, vaguely recognising the taller of the pair but unable to place him. Although she had listened intently at the adjoining wall, she had heard nothing save one loud thump. The men had left the house some minutes later, the shorter of the two carrying an extremely suspicious burden and muttering to himself constantly.

A car that had drawn up outside a couple of minutes earlier had been approached. The boot was opened, and the suspicious 'parcel' placed inside. It drew away taking the tall man with it, and the other stranger had walked up the street before stopping suddenly, doubling over, and vomiting into the road.

Mrs Jenkins had watched it all and now the car was gone, even the stranger who had been left there had walked away, and she still hadn't phoned the police. She *should* have phoned when they were still inside, or, if not then, when they had reappeared. Cursing herself for an ageing fool, she ran to the telephone she had left in her kitchen and, reading the number from the bulletin board, dialled the local police station.

*****

PC Blake had just left the Mucky Duck and was radioing in the possible sighting of the runaway, Franklin Richardson, on the M3, when he was interrupted by the dispatcher.

"Where exactly are you, 341?" she asked him, "Over."

"Bottom end of Princes Street, outside the Mucky Duck, over," he replied.

"Ok, proceed to number 47 Princes Street, 341, possible break in. Suspects have left scene. Car on its way but you'll be quicker. See a Mrs Jenkins at number 45, over."

"Got that, control, over," He replaced his radio and checked his watch. He only had forty minutes of his shift left. He hoped this wouldn't take long, he was planning to take his girlfriend to the new Indian restaurant later. Quickly explaining things to his beat partner who had been enjoying a swift pint inside the pub, they made their way down Princes Street at a brisk pace.

Mrs Jenkins was waiting for them at her front door. Spotting the two officers she ran down the path and began a garbled explanation of what she had seen before Blake was able to stop her.

"Ok," he said, soothingly, "Slowly, now, start again."

The frantic lady began her explanation again and with a little coaxing the police officers finally determined that the lady might well have witnessed a crime. Blake radioed in a message to that effect and enquired where the patrol car had got to.

"RTI en route," the dispatcher had replied. "Another car on its way, should be there in fifteen minutes, over."

Blake groaned after checking his watch again. Twenty-five minutes left. "Ok," he said to his partner, "Let's have a look." And to Mrs Jenkins, "Do you have a key?"

When the neighbour had located the item the two officers went into Bill Taylor's house. Ten minutes later, CID cars racing to the scene, Blake phoned his girlfriend from Mrs Jenkins' house and told her to forget about their planned meal. This could well be a long night.

"Bloody Friday the thirteenth!"

Chapter 8

Time seemed to slow down for Bill Taylor. He was just about to agree with Franklin's idea that inside all people there was an element of evil, when the shotgun blast had crashed into the night. As if in slow motion, he saw Franklin silhouetted against the bright light shining through the pub door's window, and watched the glass disintegrate, blowing outwards in a sparkling, deadly shower.

He saw Franklin pitch backwards, heard the beginnings of a scream, choked off, and watched Franklin's now limp body twist in the air before landing, face down, at his feet. Shards of glass pattered against his chest and arms, and he was dimly aware of another body hitting the ground at the foot of the wrecked door.

As the echoes of the blast reverberated into the night, as an enraged shout began inside the pub, time returned to its normal fleeting pattern. His shocked mind reeled, and his eyes lost their focus. He swayed forward.

A second, louder blast, another scream, brought Bill back from the brink of oblivion. He gasped, his heart thundering in his chest. He shook his head and his vision swam back into focus. He brought his gaze down to the ground immediately in front of him.

Franklin's form was stretched out face down on the pavement, his arms extended above his head as if frozen in a dive. He made no sound and, as Bill stared down, horror creeping into his shocked mind, he saw dark liquid begin to run freely over the flagstones under the boy's head.

An image flashed into his mind – Mary, her face punctured in a dozen or more places by wickedly sharp shards of glass, an eye spewing forth a colourless, jelly-like liquid around a razor-sharp glass fragment, blood pouring, spouting, from her throat, a hissing, mewling noise spilling from her mouth.

The flashback snapped out of existence and, uttering a strangled cry of horror, he dropped to his knees beside Franklin's stricken body. Oblivious now to the shouting and screaming from the pub, he reached out with a hand that shook alarmingly and grasped the boy's shoulder. Taking a shudderingly deep breath, he pulled hard and Franklin's limp form flipped over onto its back.

"Oh, dear God," Bill whispered into the night.

His vision blurred once more, the shouts and screams drifting away, and oblivion welcomed him. He pitched forward, unconscious, sprawling beside Franklin's blood-soaked body.

* * * * *

Bill awoke with a start, cold liquid splashing his face. "What…" he tried to jerk upright, but a wave of dizziness forced his head back to the pavement. His mind gradually came back into focus and he became aware of sights and sounds. Blue lights pulsing along the outside of the pub, someone nearby sobbing, voices, some raised in anger, and then, a quieter voice close by.

"It's okay, you just fainted," the voice said, soothingly.

He was lulled by the voice for a moment before his memory came flooding back. "Franklin!" he cried out, alarmed. He made to sit up, but hands held him gently where he lay.

"If you mean Freddy, Frederick, he's okay. Don't worry."

He tried to assimilate this information in the face of what he had seen. "He can't be…"

"Sure I am, you silly old sod," came Franklin's familiar tones.

The hands restraining Bill relaxed their grip and he sat up and looked around. The hands, he saw, belonged to a young man in uniform, a paramedic. Behind him, another uniformed man was holding bandages to Franklin's head. Franklin himself was sitting up, one hand nursing the opposite arm.

"Welcome back," he said to Bill, grinning wryly.

"What happened?" Bill asked, dimly aware that he thought that it was a question only used in books and films.

Happy that Bill was adequately recovered, the paramedic left him while Franklin explained as best he could.

"Seems Parsons finally cracked. Apparently, he came into the pub a few minutes before we arrived, he charged in yelling something about his sons then pulled out a twelve bore."

"But what about you?" Bill asked, still thoroughly confused.

"The first shot was aimed at Simon. He was running for the door and it caught him in the side; he crashed through the door as I was about to open it. It was the door that hit me."

Bill shook his head, relieved but still shocked. "How is your young friend?"

Franklin pointed to another figure, this one sitting against the pub wall. Simon was conscious but in obvious pain, his T-shirt shredded and blood-stained, another paramedic tending his wounds. Before Franklin could comment, a further uniformed figure emerged from the surrounding chaos and squatted down between himself and Bill.

"Good evening, gents," he greeted them in broad Norfolk tones, "I'm Sergeant Baxter. If you're up to it, I'd like to ask you a few questions about this sorry incident."

The sight of a policeman had already begun to induce feelings of panic in Bill and he noticed that Franklin, too, had become uneasy.

"Er, we really didn't see anything officer," he explained, hurriedly.

"So I've been told, sir," the officer replied, seemingly not noticing Bill's anxiety, "It's just that the lad here has apparently seen something of Parsons' violence before. I'm hoping he'll be able to throw a little more light on things."

Bill was about to protest but the paramedic tending Franklin's still bleeding head beat him to it.

"Sorry, sergeant," he interjected, "but the lad will need a couple of stitches in this first."

Baxter sighed in resignation. "Seems like all my witnesses are being carried off for someone's needlework practice. Ok then, gents, if you'll just let me have your names and addresses, I'll pop round tomorrow morning."

Relief flooded through Bill and he took a deep breath before replying, "We're staying with Maisie along the road there," he began, "I'm Tom and the dusky lad is Frederick. Do you need the exact address?"

"No, sir, indeed not," the policeman replied, smiling, "Maisie's my sister. I'll see you there tomorrow." With that he rose and, bidding them a somewhat inappropriate 'Good evening', left them.

Bill sighed deeply but refrained from commenting in the presence of the paramedic. For his part, the ambulance man applied a bandage around

Franklin's head and declared himself satisfied that the lad 'would live'. He left Franklin there with instructions that he was to sit quietly for a while and that he'd be back later to drive him to the local cottage hospital for a couple of stitches. He was also happy that there didn't appear to be any concussion.

Bill watched him leave and, when he was happy that he and Franklin were out of everyone's earshot, he turned to the lad. "That was a close call, young Franklin," he commented, "You had me worried there."

Franklin, the white bandage positively glowing against his dark skin, smiled back at Bill. "Had *you* worried?"

Bill moved across until he was sitting beside his young friend. "I think it is time we moved on," he said, sighing deeply.

Franklin looked back at him, surprised, "Why?"

"The police involvement. It worries me."

Franklin shook his head vehemently before wincing at a bolt of pain. "They won't be interested in us. That sergeant knew we weren't really involved. And, besides, it's only me that he wants to talk to."

"That is as maybe," Bill replied firmly, "but if they *should* make any further enquiries about either of us, they'll soon realise that something is seriously amiss. In addition, Mary will probably have been discovered by now; if they find out that either you or I are travelling incognito, with no clear aims in mind, I can quite believe that they will wish to investigate further."

Franklin nodded lightly. What Bill had just said made a great deal of sense. He smiled ruefully to himself as he realised that for the first time since they had taken off a week ago, Bill had recognised a danger quicker than he had. He was reluctant to leave Wroxham – he had begun to really enjoy their life there – but he had no intention of being taken back into care. And, besides, there was Bill to consider.

"Ok," he agreed eventually, "But I think it would look very suspicious if we left before seeing the sergeant in the morning. We should see him first then pack up and move out tomorrow afternoon."

Bill considered this for a moment before agreeing, albeit reluctantly.

"And we should leave a forwarding address with Maisie," Franklin added.

"What on earth–" Bill began.

"A false one," Franklin explained, hurriedly.

127

"Ah, quite so. Good thinking as ever, young man."

The paramedic returned while they were discussing possible destinations. "We're ready for your embroidery," he said, cheerfully, "How's your head feel?"

Franklin shrugged. "Feels fine. Just aching a bit."

Bill helped him to his feet and together they followed the uniformed figure through the crowd that had gathered at the scene.

"We didn't get this many people turn up at the village fete," the paramedic commented.

As they arrived at the ancient ambulance, a familiar voice rang out.

"Oh, my goodness! Thomas, Frederick, are you alright?"

"Hello, Maisie, my dear," Bill replied, "We are fine. Just a bump and a scratch."

The paramedic turned briefly, "A small abrasion on this one, but Thomas, was it? Well he seems fine other than some faint bruising around the eyes and that seems like an older injury anyway."

"It's nothing," Bill shrugged, "Just a bump I picked up a while ago."

Maisie fussed around the pair as Franklin joined Simon in the back of the ambulance. Bill eventually managed to persuade her to go home and wait for them there before joining the two boys in the back of the vehicle.

"She's not going to be a happy bunny when we tell her we're off," Franklin commented as their short journey began.

"You're going?" Simon asked.

"I'm afraid so, young man," Bill replied, "Work to do, and all that."

"Yeah, sorry man," Franklin added.

"Nothing to do with my idiot father then?" Simon went on.

Franklin shook his head and winced again, making a mental note to verbalise all of his replies for a day or two, "No. What will happen to him?"

"Baxter reckons he'll be charged with attempted murder," Simon explained, "As long as Jack and me agree to testify."

"Will you?" Franklin asked.

Simon laughed sourly and clutched his side. When the spasm of pain subsided, he looked Franklin directly in the eyes. "Try to stop me. Maybe Friday the thirteenth isn't so bad after all."

* * * * *

Saturday 14th June 2014

Franklin and Bill arrived home at one in the morning, Simon remaining in the cottage hospital where the pair had been entertained by a stream of surprisingly varied swear words emanating from Simon as each of the shotgun pellets were prised from his flesh.

Maisie was waiting for them, a large whisky already poured for Bill and an equally large Brandy 'for the shock' for Franklin. He took it reluctantly, wincing at the bitter taste as he swallowed it. Bill had no such reluctance and downed the whisky in one. Maisie, by now used to Bill's drinking habits, refilled his glass immediately.

"Thank you, my dear lady," Bill said, sipping at the second drink, "And not just for your kindness and concern tonight, but ever since we arrived, so fortuitously, on your doorstep."

Maisie, despite her natural tendency towards scatter-brained behaviour, was nevertheless very sharp and immediately detected a hidden message in Bill's comment. "That's very kind of you, Thomas," she replied slowly, "but is there something else?"

Bill paused before replying, seeking the correct words. "Very true," he replied, "I fear that Frederick and I will be moving on tomorrow. Work and all that," he added, reverting to the excuse he had used earlier with Simon.

"Oh dear," Maisie said, clearly upset at this development, her fingers pushing her fine hair back, "It's nothing to do with this Parsons business, is it?"

"A little," Bill conceded, deciding to use their cover as an additional excuse, "Frederick really doesn't need this sort of publicity, and I must look after his interests first and foremost."

Maisie sighed to cover her disappointment. "You're quite right, of course. But I'll miss you terribly."

"And we will miss you, dear lady," Bill replied, "But we'll be sure to stay in touch."

"Where will you be going?" Maisie asked.

"South," replied Franklin.

"West," Bill replied, simultaneously.

"South west," he corrected, "Torquay, to be precise." He and Franklin had already decided to make for York as their next stop, on the grounds that its historical influence would be conducive to Franklin's studies, and that it was on the main rail line to London should the need to travel back quickly arise.

Maisie sighed once more, accepting Bill's motives but surprised at the depth of disappointment she felt. "Oh, well," she said, rallying herself, "I'll pop out to the shops in the morning and prepare you something for your journey."

"As ever, madam," Bill replied, "you cater to our every need in ways that far exceed the expectations of the greatest of optimists."

Maisie giggled girlishly, delighted as ever at Bill's flattery. Blushing slightly, she at first dropped a glass before she refilled a fresh one for 'Thomas' once again.

Franklin, feeling a little gooseberry-like, and not a little tired by the events of the evening, decided to retire. He left the others chatting amiably and collapsed into bed without bothering to undress. He slept immediately.

* * * * *

In London, Saturday morning dawned bright and clear, although those adjectives could not be used to describe Jenny Thomsett. The previous night's drinking had got a little out of hand and as she woke, memory came flooding back. As well as the drinks they had already consumed during the early part of the evening, they had all hit the bottle hard after hearing that Bill Taylor was missing, presumed either dead or a murderer.

She knew him in passing and couldn't believe that he was capable of murder; a view shared by everyone in the pub. Only Gerry had seemed taciturn on the subject and all had ascribed this to shock. He was, after all, one of Bill's closest friends.

The drinking had escalated after that and the party had returned to Richie's flat after the pub closed where even more alcohol was consumed. Jenny recalled that Susan had more-or-less carried her home. She shuddered when she imagined what Susan would say to her when she awoke. She looked across at Susan's still somnolent form in the bed beside her and wondered, not for the first time, why Susan put up with her erratic and often irresponsible behaviour.

She decided to placate her in advance and rose as quietly as possible to make toast and coffee. When she returned with the breakfast on a tray, Susan was stretching luxuriantly under the covers.

"Good morning, piss-head," she said amiably when she noticed Jenny standing by the bed, "Oh, lovely. Breakfast in bed."

"I thought you deserved it," Jenny explained.

"Quite right too," Susan replied, smiling and accepting the tray. "Mind you, it was a bit of a shock hearing about old Bill."

"You don't think he's killed someone, do you? Someone said there was litres of blood splattered around his place. No body though."

"Who knows?" Susan shrugged, "But Bill's whereabouts, alive or dead, are not our problem. We've got a little black runaway to locate."

Jenny groaned, Franklin's disappearance having temporarily slipped out of her mind. "Oh God! I'd better phone the train station and find out the train times to Southampton."

"Good idea," Susan replied around a mouthful of toast. "And while you're at it, book us into a hotel for the night. I don't fancy travelling there and back in a day, and a dirty weekend on the coast might be fun."

"Yeah, why not?" Jenny replied, "And if we do find young Franklin, I'll get him to pay for it for all the trouble he's caused." She left Susan to her breakfast and began phoning round the hotels in Southampton.

* * * * *

Outside the flat David Phillips, erstwhile investigative journalist, was having third thoughts about his scoop, second thoughts having departed hours earlier.

He had followed the two young women when they had left the pub the previous night and had been dismayed when they were accompanied by a number of the other locals. His dismay was compounded when they all went in to a flat together, but he had, at least, heard that it wasn't their flat.

When they had emerged two hours later, Jenny obviously drunk, he had followed them here. Satisfied that they were staying for what remained of the night, he had returned to his own flat and picked up his car. He parked a little way down the street and sipped coffee from a thermos he had also collected when he had gone home.

Although the weather had cleared up, the nights were still cool at this time of year and Phillips had spent several uncomfortable hours alternately dozing and shivering. Sometimes simultaneously.

It was now 8.30 and he was beginning to attract attention from pedestrians. He wondered how long it would be before a policeman turned up asking awkward questions. He unscrewed the top of the long-empty thermos in the impractical hope that it had mysteriously refilled itself and quickly discarded it in favour of a cigarette. It was the last one in his packet and he lit it reluctantly with his Zippo. He had found the packet in the glove compartment, and the Marlboro, already rough to his tastes, was now stale. He coughed heartily and wondered whether he had enough time to pop along to a newsagent's and buy a fresh, and preferably low tar, packet.

He was still wrestling with the pros and cons of the problem ten minutes later, when the door to the block of flats opened and the two social workers emerged hand in hand. Galvanised into action, and once more optimistic about his chances of a big story, he reached for the ignition keys and turned them. The starter motor whirred in near silence and then stopped completely. Beginning to panic, he scanned the dashboard. One light glowed faintly alongside the battery light. Somehow he had spent most of the night sitting in the car without realising he had left the lights on.

He dived out of the vehicle and scanned the street just in time to see his quarry turn a corner a couple of hundred yards ahead of him. Cursing, he hurried after them.

* * * * *

132

In the nearby police station PC Blake was also cursing. He had been seconded to the CID investigation of the Bill Taylor case and had spent all night on the telephone trying to locate the man, or anyone that might know where he was.

The locals that had drunk with Taylor had informed Blake that he was holidaying in Brighton with his sister. One had even given Taylor a lift to Reigate station, but no-one knew where he had gone precisely, and he had discovered, to his horror, that there were more than three hundred hotels in the Brighton area – and those were just the ones listed in the online directories. Further digging had turned up CCTV footage from the Brighton station, though – around four hundred hours' worth.

He had started phoning the hotels first at seven am and in an hour and a half since then he had contacted only thirty, not even one tenth. And *those* calls were on top of another twenty he had made to hospitals both here and on the coast. He had now been on duty for over fourteen hours and had dreamed up at least three dozen grisly ways of murdering Home Secretaries who instigated cuts in police manning levels.

Checking his phone, he noticed that he still had half an hour before he would be relieved. Sighing and cursing alternately, he started tapping the phone once again, dialling yet another number.

* * * * *

Unaware of the now wheezing would-be journalist behind them, Jenny and Susan arrived at Walthamstow Central tube station in good spirits. The distractions of breakfast in bed and the prospect of a night's fun on the coast had succeeded in deflecting Susan's attention from Jenny's behaviour the previous night. Susan was now clearly looking forward to the trip and had spent the walk to the station planning their evening's entertainment.

Jenny, whose stomach was a little unsettled after the previous evening's drinking, was a trifle horrified at some of Susan's plans, but agreed to them with false enthusiasm, eager not to upset her partner.

"And tomorrow morning, we'll have breakfast sent up to our room – the works: bacon, sausages, eggs and all that – together with champagne and fresh orange juice. How's that sound, Jen?" Susan babbled on.

"Great. Really good," Jenny agreed hoping that Susan didn't notice the green tint to her face. "Anyway," she went on, anxious to change the subject, "We'd better get a move on. The train leaves Victoria at ten o'clock, we've only got an hour or so."

"Don't fuss," Susan replied amiably, pausing beside the newsagent's kiosk, and thumbing through magazines and newspapers, "We've got plenty of time."

Jenny waited impatiently while Susan bought enough reading material to last a week let alone a weekend, and when Susan eventually returned, having spent a minute stuffing the magazines into her overnight bag, Jenny hustled her down the elevator.

* * * * *

Behind them Phillips, who had been grateful for Susan's delaying tactics as a chance to regain his breath, followed them on to the waiting tube and sank gratefully into a seat. Knowing that the journey would take forty minutes or so, he wondered whether he should risk taking a short nap. He closed his eyes while weighing up the alternatives and was snoring quietly within a minute.

He woke with a start as the train pulled in to Warren Street station, his confused, sleep-addled brain convinced that this was Victoria. He dived out of his seat in panic and leapt through the doors onto the platform the second they opened. Looking frantically about for the girls, it took a few seconds before he realised his error.

He lunged desperately at the now closing doors as the train prepared to leave the station. He was partially successful – he managed to get one arm and a foot wedged between them.

The driver re-opened the doors and Phillips stumbled gratefully back into the carriage. He glanced at the girls who, he realised, were watching his performance with much amusement. He smiled back at them and returned to his seat, deciding that he would have to be extremely careful from now on if they weren't to realise that he was tailing them. He briefly wondered whether Woodward or Bernstein ever had this sort of problem.

When the train pulled in to Victoria station he rose hurriedly and ran up the stairs, determined to lose himself in the crowd on the mainline concourse. He already knew where they were headed for and the chances were that there would only be one obvious train that they would be catching. Scanning the indicator boards, he was pleased to see that he was correct and sighed with relief. There was still fifteen minutes before the ten o'clock to Southampton departed and he sauntered over to the ticket office, scanning the crowd for his young ladies.

Spotting them already standing in line at the nearest queue, he walked past them to the furthest and stood in line. It moved quickly, and he arrived at the window a couple of minutes later. Reaching in to his pocket he pulled out his wallet and was about to ask for his ticket when he realised to his horror, that the wallet was empty. Groaning and mumbling apologies, he moved away and scanned the station.

He didn't have a credit card to his name, the result of an unpaid student loan four years earlier but did have a bank cash card. All he needed now was a bank with an ATM. In desperation he asked a passing BR Transport policeman who directed him towards a bank 'just around the corner'.

It took him five minutes to locate the bank and he stood in line for a further couple of minutes behind other eager cash hunters. After mistyping his PIN, causing another bout of panic, he eventually, and very gratefully, gathered up the requested banknotes and sprinted back to the station. He glanced up at the station clock on his arrival and groaned aloud when he saw it registering 9:55.

Rejoining the queues at the ticket office he managed to persuade two people to let him jump forward and eventually, clutching tickets and change, dashed towards the distant platform. He arrived just as the guard was closing the barrier and hurtled past him, ignoring the half-hearted request to check his ticket.

The train was an ancient plain blue-and-off-white thing and he hurled himself on to it just as the doors began to close. He stood for a while, trying to regain his breath and praying that the two women were not in this particular carriage watching his repeat performance of the fiasco at Warren Street.

Scanning the rows of his fellow travellers, he was pleased not to notice his quarry. Later in the journey he determined to check on their location, but for the time being, he needed a rest. He crossed to the nearest available seat, slipped out of his jacket and slumped gratefully into the threadbare upholstery. As the train rolled gently out of the station he began to doze once more, his mind filled with dreams of the money and fame his headline story of the 'social services scandal' would bring him.

*****

At the same time some 100 miles further north, Franklin woke and immediately wished he hadn't. His head was pounding fit to bust and positively thundered as he carefully sat up in bed.

The nurse at the cottage hospital had warned him that this was likely and had supplied him with some strong pain killers – 'industrial strength' was the term she had used. Franklin checked the pockets of the shirt he was still wearing and located the plastic strip. He popped two of the tablets into his hand and dry-swallowed them, ignoring the bitter taste. He decided to lay down for a while until they took effect and was still dozing lightly when Bill quietly entered the room half an hour later.

"Good morning, young man," he said quietly when Franklin's eyelids fluttered carefully open. "How is the cranium?"

"If you mean my head," Franklin replied, yawning softly, "It still aches a bit, but, other than that, it's fine."

"Glad to hear it. Now, Sergeant Baxter is downstairs chatting to his sister and has requested your presence if you're up to it."

Franklin began to rise but Bill signalled for him to stay where he was. "He did say *if* you were up to it," he explained, "We could always say you're not and then depart before he returns later…"

Franklin decided not to shake his head vehemently, just in time. Instead he replied, "Uh huh, we agreed last night. It would only make us look more suspicious when we do go. Besides, I really don't know much about what went on last night, and I doubt if they'll bother to check up on us after we leave."

"Ok," Bill agreed, still obviously worried about the involvement with the police but resigned to the good sense in their earlier agreement to co-operate. "I'll go back down and tell him you'll join us shortly."

He left a little reluctantly and Franklin, as quickly as his head would allow, washed and changed before joining the trio downstairs.

* * * * *

PC Blake yawned hugely as he slammed the door to his locker and was happily grinding his knuckles into his eyes, daydreaming all the while of a long, long sleep when a voice startled him.

"Oh, there you are, Dave."

Blake turned to the figure in the doorway. "Please, not another list of hotels," he pleaded. The voice belonged to DS Craig, an often irascible but somehow likeable member of the CID squad stationed in the same building.

Craig grinned, "No, definitely not – and thanks for all your help. No, this is just a bit of news; thought you might be interested."

Dave Blake shrugged noncommittally. Right now the only news he wanted to hear was that his bed was ready.

"We've just got a report in from the City of London crew. They've found a body and it looks as though it's Mary Taylor. What with the clothes we found under Bill Taylor's bed and his sudden disappearance I think it's a safe bet to assume we are now looking for a murderer, not a missing piss-head."

Despite his bone-deep tiredness, Blake was suddenly much more wide-awake. "Are you sure?" he asked.

"As much as we can be at this time," Craig replied, shrugging slightly in a gesture that probably meant 'What else could it be?'. "And," he added, "the first reports back from the lab confirm that the blood on the overcoat, shoe and living room are from the same person. Once we get the results from the corpse we'll know for certain."

Blake shook his head thoughtfully.

"What's up, Dave?"

He looked up at Craig, the thoughtful look intensifying as he did so. "Well," he said slowly, "It's just that I met Taylor a few times and he really didn't seem like the type..."

Craig laughed. "That's what they said about Shipman, Christie and Crippen," he said, "And if you want to get your transfer to the CID confirmed, you'd better drop the personality assessments pronto." He had said this lightly, but Blake detected a very serious piece of advice being offered.

He nodded, "Thanks for the gen, sarge."

Craig smiled at him again. "Go get some sleep, son," he suggested, "I've had a word with Bill Baker and he's okayed it for you to help out a bit more on this one, so when you come in this evening, come straight up and see me or Joey Evans and we'll sort out where you can be of most assistance." With a cheerful wave he slipped back out into the corridor and left a suddenly much happier Blake to collect his coat.

*****

Franklin heard quiet laughter coming from Maisie's front room as he descended the stairs and paused a moment before entering, composing his features into what he fervently hoped would pass for nonchalance. As he walked into the room, he quickly scanned the assembled company and, to his relief, saw that everyone was wearing expressions of amusement as Maisie busily recounted stories of her and her brother's childhood pranks to Bill.

She was just finishing off a tale that apparently concerned a very long stick, a fishing net and an irate farmer's apples when her brother glanced up (somewhat embarrassed by the tale of lawlessness) and saw Franklin on the threshold.

"Good morning, young sir," he said cheerfully, "And how are you feeling this morning?"

As was usual for him in the presence of the constabulary, Franklin felt a moment of non-specific guilt (although in this case there was undoubtedly a very large element of *very* specific guilt) and he cleared his throat before replying in what he hoped was a cheerful way.

"Morning," he said. "A bit of a headache, thanks, but at least the bruises don't show." He flashed his broadest grin and was mightily relieved when the sergeant joined in with Bill's raucous laugh and Maisie's slightly nervous giggling.

"Come and sit down, my poor boy," she said when she had regained her composure, "I'll fetch you some coffee."

"Thanks, Maisie," he replied, easing himself down into a vacant armchair.

"Well," Sergeant Baxter began when Maisie had departed for the kitchen, "Tom, here, has told me who you are and why you're here, and I quite understand why you don't want any fuss and bother so I'll keep this brief."

Franklin glanced at the erstwhile Tom and saw a degree of tension in Bill's face that was a little unsettling. "Oh," he said, forcing another smile on the policeman.

"Simon and Jack Junior have told me all about the little rumpus in the pub last night," Baxter went on, "and it's clear you're not really involved. On top of that you obviously didn't see what actually went on in there – although I'm sure you felt it," he paused and chuckled to himself, pleased with his witticism, "so all I really need to know is whether you want to bring any charges against old man Parsons."

The question threw Franklin for a moment and he stared gormlessly at the policeman before he realised that, as long as he declined the offer, there wouldn't be any further involvement with the local bill. "Oh," he started before composing himself once more, "I mean no, definitely not. Er… thank you." He glanced across at Bill and wasn't unduly surprised at the barely concealed look of relief that registered on his friend's face.

Baxter had been holding a notebook open on his knee and after enquiring as to whether 'the young sir is really sure?', he replaced it in his uniform pocket.

At this point Maisie returned with a tray filled with steaming mugs of coffee, her spectacles foggy again in a way that was becoming charmingly familiar, "Oh, have you finished?" she asked her brother as he stood up.

"That's right, sis," he replied, "And since I've got at least a hundred forms to fill in thanks to old Parsons, I'd better be heading back to the station house."

139

"Oh well, that's nice," Maisie replied, setting down the tray, "I'll see you out then, George." She headed for the doorway.

"Well, I might have had another coffee if you'd insisted," her brother said a little disappointedly. He obviously wasn't looking forward to the chores ahead.

"Nonsense," the lady replied, "Father might have let you get away with a little scrumping, but he'd turn in his grave if he thought you weren't doing your duty." The last part of the sentence drifted back from the doorway through which Maisie had resolutely disappeared.

"The bum's rush, they call that, don't they?" Baxter asked Bill, who grinned and nodded in reply. "A right bully, that sister of mine. Still, nice meeting you both and I'll see you around soon," he added, trailing after his sister.

"Most certainly, sergeant," Bill replied cheerfully.

"Yeah," Franklin added, "And thanks."

Baxter's replies were cut short by Maisie. "Do come on, George. I've got to prepare Franklin's breakfast."

Franklin shot an alarmed look at Bill. "She called–" he began but Bill interrupted him with a frantic wave.

They waited in silence for nearly two minutes while Maisie and her brother said their goodbyes at the front door. When it closed Franklin surged to his feet, ignoring the pain in his head and crossed quickly to where Bill was sitting. "She called me Franklin, man," he whispered urgently.

"I know," Bill said softly, sighing, "I'll explain in a minute or two." He motioned towards the door where Maisie was at that moment re-entering the room.

Franklin gave him a long, quizzical stare before returning to his own armchair.

Maisie breezed into the room and handed Franklin one of the coffee mugs. "There you are," she said brightly, "Now, if you'll excuse me for a moment, I'll just get your breakfast under way."

"Er, thanks," Franklin replied.

She smiled sweetly at him and, taking one of the coffee mugs with her, departed once more for the kitchen.

The second he heard the first clattering from the stove Franklin put his coffee mug back on the side table and shot to his feet. "How does she know my name?" he began, somewhat frantically, "And what about yours? Does she know-"

Bill also rose to his feet and waved Franklin into silence. He paused for a moment, eyes closed, composing himself, and then sighed. When he re-opened them, he fixed Franklin with an open stare. "My young friend," he began, "It is altogether possible - I might say that it is even likely - that I can teach you a few basic facts concerning the nature of history, geography, maths and so forth. However, the most valuable lessons I could ever impart to you would be those concerning human nature and life in general."

"But-" Franklin began.

"Hear me out," Bill interrupted.

Franklin shrugged and lapsed back into a fraught silence.

"I've already tried to teach you something of the nature of trust," Bill continued, "And I think I've also learned a little from you on that score," he paused and smiled, "Another lesson I need to impart concerns truth and the difference between lies and what are colourfully and euphemistically called white lies."

"But-" Franklin tried again, unable to see exactly where Bill was leading but getting faint warning signals.

"Please?" Bill interrupted once more. When Franklin fell silent again, Bill went on, "There is also the question of judgement of others. Last night, after you had retired, I had a very long talk with our charming hostess and discovered that my judgement of her was both very accurate and also completely wrong."

At this Franklin looked very alarmed but Bill shook his head and smiled. "Don't look so worried, I meant that I had been wrong in the best of ways. It would appear that our Maisie is rather more... *shrewd* than either of us has given her credit for. She had, for example, quickly decided that our story of Tom the manager and Frederick the rock star was a complete fabrication."

"Then why didn't she let on?" Franklin asked, unable to contain himself any longer, "And why didn't she tell her brother? Or did she?" he added, more agitated by the second.

141

Bill laughed and then looked serious once more. "Do not fret, young man. To answer your questions in reverse order: No, she has not informed her brother – she didn't do that because of what I told her last night; and finally, because she felt that whatever the truth really was, it was a matter for us alone."

Franklin breathed a sigh of relief. "Ok," he said after a few seconds deliberations, "What did you tell her last night?"

"Well," Bill replied, "A couple of minutes ago I mentioned that there is a difference between lies and white lies. The story we had told her was of the latter category, I believe, but – and this is the lesson we had both better learn – when all is said and done, whether it had been a white lie or an outright lie, it is still a lie. I'm not trying to preach to you, but it remains a fact. Lies do not work and the longer we stay in any one place, whatever pretext we use will not hold water indefinitely. Especially when someone as shrewd as Maisie is the target for our pretensions."

"Ok, man," Franklin said, still not mollified, "I hear what you're saying, but all you've told me is *why* you told her that we were 'lying' to her; you ain't told me *what* you said to her."

"Remember that I also mentioned trust as a valuable lesson?" Bill asked a little tentatively.

"Yes..." Franklin replied slowly.

"Well, basically, given that it appears that we *can* trust Maisie..." Bill hesitated.

"Yes?"

"Everything." Bill shrugged.

"W... What?" Franklin stammered, "You mean that you told her..."

"Everything," Bill finished for him.

"But how do you know we can trust her, man?" Franklin asked desperately.

"That's trust for you. You can't know if someone is trustworthy. But the mere fact that she didn't let on to her brother must support my feelings."

Franklin's mind was in overdrive. "But are you sure that she's not on the make or something? You know, blackmail or whatever?"

Bill laughed. "Maisie?"

Franklin paused and then smiled too. He nodded. "Not Maisie," he agreed, "And I kind of guess that that's got nothing to do with whether she's shrewd or not, right?"

Bill smiled, relieved beyond measure that the young man had understood. "I've said this many times, young Franklin; you are very perspicacious – and a fast learner to boot."

Franklin was surprised to find that he really did understand what Bill had tried to explain. He could almost hear a mental 'click' as it snapped into place, and he wondered, not for the first time, what sort of change was going on inside him. There was, of course, an element of doubt attached to trust – as Bill said, you can never *know* – but he was surprised, now that it was done, that he felt an element of relief in Maisie knowing of their true stories. "Ok," he said eventually, "Where does that leave us now?"

"En route to the breakfast table," Maisie said brightly from the doorway, "You poor thing."

"You didn't exaggerate about my problems?" Franklin asked Bill as he followed Maisie towards the waiting meal.

"Did I need to?"

Franklin laughed, "I guess not."

A thought occurred to Franklin as he seated himself in front of a steaming pile of various fried foods. "Does all of this mean that we don't have to leave here?" he asked.

Bill and Maisie exchanged glances before the former replied. "Maisie seems to think that we might well be able to stay on here for a while and, I must admit, her arguments for that motion are undeniably persuasive – but even our most wise hostess has agreed that it would probably be unwise."

"At least in the long term," Maisie agreed.

"Nevertheless," Bill continued, "Another day or two here shouldn't hurt, and, besides, we must consider our plans in a little more detail before we select a course of action."

"And there's the telephone to consider," Maisie added.

Franklin raised a questioning eyebrow at Bill, his mouth, bulging with breakfast, being unable to form the question.

"Yes," Bill explained, "I have told Maisie about my late sister's telephone book and she has kindly offered us the use of her landline telephonic apparatus in order that we may continue our investigations."

"Not before time, too," Maisie admonished, "You have been very lazy following up a good lead like that book."

"Maisie is very fond of detective novels."

"I've always fancied myself as a bit of a Miss Marple," Maisie agreed.

"Although a much younger one," Bill added.

Maisie giggled happily, "Oh, Bill!"

Franklin chuckled around a half-eaten sausage and had to be firmly slapped on the back by Bill before he could regain his breath. When he could speak again, he asked, "So what do we do now?"

"As Maisie has so accurately observed, we are bound to be running short of time. So, when you have completed the demolition of that food mountain, we shall repair to the sitting room and consider our options together," Bill took in Maisie with a glance and Franklin began to wonder, not for the first time, just what Bill thought of the lady.

While Franklin finished his breakfast, Maisie busied herself in the kitchen – only one crash of dropped crockery and the mildest of curses interrupting the noises of busy-ness – and Bill wandered into the village in search of the Saturday newspapers. He returned laden with the journals and a small square box wrapped in decorative paper and bearing a small red ribbon tied into an ornate bow. Franklin met him in the sitting room where Bill was hastily concealing the package under the coffee table nearest to the fireplace.

"Bill," Franklin said softly, causing his friend to start and spin round in an effort to disguise his activities.

"Why, young Franklin. Did you, er, enjoy your repast?"

"What's in the box?" Franklin asked, grinning at Bill's embarrassment and totally ignoring his question.

"Box?" Bill asked, guilelessly.

Franklin nodded and pointed to the brightly coloured wrapping paper clearly visible behind Bill's right leg. "The *gift* box, just there."

"Er, nothing," Bill stammered, "Or rather a small token... Make that a small, er, demonstration of my gratitude to the fair Maisie."

"I'm definitely beginning to wonder about you two," Franklin beamed from ear to ear.

"How do you mean?" Bill asked, feigning ingenuousness.

"Well, all these late-night chats, revealing our true identities, and now we've decided to stay on a while..."

Bill sighed deeply and checked over Franklin's shoulder to make sure that Maisie was still in the kitchen before replying, "Well," he explained, blushing slightly, "I must admit that I have developed something of a soft spot for our gracious hostess..."

"And that's another thing," Franklin added, half-seriously, "When you woke me this morning you were talking as if we were still leaving today and yet you and Maisie seemed to have already decided that we weren't."

Bill looked genuinely surprised, "My dear boy," he exclaimed, "Nothing could be further from the truth. It was always to be as much your choice as ours – I mean mine – if you were adamant that we should depart hence I would not have hesitated for one iota. You do, after all, have just as much to lose as my poor unfortunate self if we were to be traced."

Franklin was surprised at Bill's thoroughly concerned reaction, "Whoa," he said in an effort to placate the man, "Just a joke – but thanks anyway."

Bill sighed with relief, "Sometimes I feel far too old to understand the youth of today."

"But not too old to... what's the word? Oh, yes – *court* the youth of yesterday?" Franklin teased.

"Franklin!" Bill exclaimed, but his protestations were cut short by the return of Maisie.

"Are you two squabbling again?" she asked cheerfully.

"No, not at all, dear lady," Bill replied, surreptitiously sliding the present underneath the coffee table with the heel of his right shoe.

"Good," Maisie replied in business-like tones, "Now, we really must try to sort out our plan of action. Have you been through today's papers yet? And surely you two could use my business computer to check things as well?"

Franklin felt an immediate sense of relief that someone was finally taking charge of their planning. He also felt a great deal of surprise that it was Maisie but *somehow* it seemed right. He shook his head in reply as Bill waffled through a half-hearted excuse as to why the task had yet to be properly started, let alone completed.

"Well then," Maisie said, interrupting Bill's flow, "that must be our first priority." She bent and collected the journals from the armchair where Bill had hastily deposited them, and then divided them into three piles. "We'll split the qualities between us, William, and Franklin can have the tabloids. Then I'll fetch my laptop."

Franklin was too amused to feel affronted and dumbly took the proffered pile from Maisie.

They sat in silence for twenty minutes, the only interruption coming when Maisie expressed concern that Franklin was spending 'a little too much time' combing the third page of one of his stack – hastily denied by Franklin.

When the last page had been dutifully scanned, and the laptop perused for twenty minutes, Maisie collected the newspapers and disappeared into the kitchen to brew fresh coffee 'to sustain them through the discussions'.

While she was busy Franklin decided that he should ask a question that had been playing on his mind for some time – one that had only been brought into focus by their more than usually studious examination of the national press. "They're bound to find her soon, aren't they?" he asked, quietly.

Bill, who had been gazing into the middle distance, barely registered the question before replying, "Quite so."

To Franklin it was obvious that his friend had been thinking of just the same thing. "What do you think will happen when they *do* find her?"

Bill recollected himself and turned an earnest, serious gaze on the lad, "I believe," he said slowly, "that it will undoubtedly make front page news. They'll issue a very poor photograph of my good self to the press and probably accompany it with a release that says that I am a dangerous, desperate criminal." He paused, "And that I am wanted in connection with one of the most brutal murders this century."

"You really didn't do it, did you?" Franklin asked quietly.

Bill smiled slightly, "As ever..." he said pausing for Franklin to complete the sentence.

"Perspicacious?" Franklin smiled quietly back at Bill.

146

"Quite so. No, to answer your question. Last night, after copious amounts of the water of life, I retired in a most pensive and thoughtful of moods – my disclosures to Maisie and her responses must have contributed – and lay awake for some time." He paused here in his explanation and changed tack for a moment, "Have I mentioned to you – I'm sure I must have – that I experienced a number of what are popularly known as 'flashbacks' before I left Walthamstow?"

Franklin nodded his reply, not wishing to interrupt the flow.

"Well," Bill continued, "Whilst laying there last night, a fourth came to me. It was as vivid as the others and what it showed me is as much responsible for my change of mind and attitude as anything Maisie has demonstrated." Bill paused again, searching for the right words to describe what he'd seen. "I *think* that it showed me something altogether quite extraordinary in one respect – which I'll explain further in a moment – but it also showed me that it *was* the stranger, this man in black, that dealt the fatal blow – and, in a way that, given what I was unfortunate enough to observe last Saturday morning, was totally unconnected to whisky bottles." Bill paused and glanced up at Franklin.

When he was sure that Franklin's reaction was as he expected, he continued, "Some of what I am about to impart must, of course, be speculation – it was, after all, just another flashback – and not a very long one at that. From what I recall, the whole thing was a 'set-up' of some sort – one that went wrong when I came home earlier than expected. Mary had guessed that I would, or saw me coming or something, and she was screaming at the stranger that she had 'told you he'd be here'. Somehow, I tried, drunkenly, to stop what was going on. However, the one thing that was as clear as the finest of Waterford crystals, was that the stranger – may his God curse him – stabbed Mary. He appeared to be aiming for her throat but in her rage and with me grappling with him, the intended target was missed. I remember, now, the knife entering her mouth. I don't know whether the bottle was an afterthought to mask the mistake or part of the original scheme to implicate me, but either way it will certainly achieve both of those ends."

Franklin, unable to contain himself, broke in, "All you have to do now is contact the police and tell them what happened – you'll be off the hook!"

Bill looked up at him again, his eyes sombre, "I'm aware that you might think that – I even contemplated it myself – but consider two things. Firstly, the bottle will most certainly have disguised the stab wound, but, far more importantly, there is still no *evidence* that I wasn't the only person there. Only two people, as far as I can recall, witnessed the event – or three if you include Mary – and it is me that would be the only person anyone would expect to be present. I can't see the stranger coming forward to admit his involvement, let alone his culpability, and, equally, I can't imagine anyone even believing that he was there." Bill paused once more and sighed deeply, "Just about the only thing I can say for the flashback is that it has convinced me of my innocence." He tailed off into a brooding silence.

"And in that," Franklin added, "Nothing new comes to light – I already knew you hadn't done it."

"And I also," Maisie added from the doorway.

Both Franklin and Bill looked across, surprised at her presence, and both grateful for her comment.

Bill suddenly re-gathered himself, cleared his throat and said brightly, if a little artificially, "Very well then, what next, my dear lady?"

* * * * *

For the next ten minutes Maisie fussed around the room in her unique style arranging coffee mugs, finding pads of notepaper, pens and a vast platter of biscuits, while Franklin excused himself and wandered upstairs to wash again and change.

Bill sat alone amongst the activity, on the surface scanning the Daily Telegraph crossword, but inwardly wrestling with his conscience. In truth (how the word echoed around his head guiltily) he had lain awake the previous night trying desperately to recall the events of seven days previously. He was convinced that he hadn't murdered his sister, but the risks that he was taking – involving not just Franklin and Gerry, but now Maisie – meant that he must find hard evidence that his belief was true. It hadn't happened. His mind refused to release the information that he knew was locked away somewhere. When he had begun to speak a few minutes earlier, that was precisely what he had intended to say but something – something dark within him – had taken over. For the first time since his early teens he had lied – not 'exaggerated the truth', not 'told a white lie', not 'bullshitted' as common parlance would have it – but lied. Lied with a capital 'L'.

Now he sat wondering about the compulsion that had come over him, and what it meant. Did it imply guilt? Was there a sub-conscious voice, unheard, screaming at him to admit that he had done it? But, there again (and this really was important), there actually had been a stranger present.

He brooded in silence, his mind swimming with thoughts and emotions ranging from a suspicion of guilt to a positive, inherent feeling of innocence, through to a desire for confession and a plaintive inner whine that demanded that his conscience be left alone.

When Franklin returned and settled himself into an armchair, and Maisie pronounced that the preparations were complete, he raised troubled eyes and a troubled mind to the room and persons around him, with a prayer – fervent and deep-rooted – that soon, very soon, he really would know for certain what had happened one week before.

* * * * *

Franklin, gingerly dabbing water across his very sore forehead, was feeling unsettled but he couldn't quite pinpoint where the feelings of unease emanated from. After all that had happened the previous weekend – his flight from Hart, the lorry ride, meeting Bill and their subsequent journey north – he had been surprised at the ease with which he had settled into his new routines and surroundings. Certainly, there had been no element of the current feeling of unease that he was experiencing.

Last night's shock had most definitely caused a degree of disorientation, and he and Bill's subsequent decision to move on had also contributed to a feeling of disappointment. It was this last fact that disturbed him now. If, as they had now decided, they weren't going to be moving on (for a while, at least), then *surely* he should be feeling relieved or elated or... something. What he was sure of was that he certainly shouldn't be feeling uneasy.

Maisie's somewhat surprising introduction into the equation might well contribute a little to the unease he was feeling – although retrospectively, he wasn't as surprised as he might have been.

Bill's flashback should also have brought a sense of relief – that Bill was now sure that he hadn't been responsible for the murder of Mary (although Franklin had never really had any doubts) should also have allowed him a little more freedom of thought – no suspicions, no doubts.

Franklin paused in the act of drying himself and stared thoughtfully at the towel. Bill had seemed to be unlike his usual self this morning. But why? Was it Maisie, finally taking control of their situation? Was it Bill's sudden lack of self-doubt? Was he, Franklin, jealous of the blossoming relationship between his new friend and the ever-friendly Maisie?

He shook his head gingerly. Whatever the reasons behind his unease, he was suddenly sure of one thing. All of this – the whole situation – was leaving him far out of his depth. He looked up at his reflection in the mirror above the wash-basin. "Oh well," he said to himself, mentally filing his doubts away for the time being, "No use worrying. Just go with the flow."

He dropped the towel, liberally spotted with flecks of dried blood, into the laundry basket, and pulled on a clean polo shirt, wincing slightly as yet another bruise made its presence felt. Composing his face into a relaxed state with not-inconsiderable assistance from the mirror, he unlocked the bathroom door and headed downstairs for the discussion that would be shaping his future – for a few days at least.

* * * * *

Maisie was now thoroughly enjoying herself. Bill's admissions to her the night before had not come as a complete surprise – she had never believed the man's cock-and-bull cover story – but she was a little shocked at the seriousness of Bill's situation. When he had finally gone to bed (not very long before dawn) she had stayed awake for another hour wondering what she might be getting herself into. In the end, her own brand of logic had prevailed. For the first time since her... *condition* had been diagnosed she was feeling both useful and capable. A few dropped mugs and plates were nothing compared to picking up her mental capabilities and helping her two guests, and most especially the ever-charming and really very likeable Bill.

She didn't believe that he had committed the crime – not because of its unlikelihood, nor his recollections this morning (she didn't for one minute believe *that* story at all) – but simply because he was Bill (or Tom). They had spent most nights during the previous week, sitting and talking into the early hours (and in Bill's case, drinking her whisky stock dry), and during those many, many hours, he had regaled her with stories, tales and his experiences. It had been as early as the second night when she had realised that here was a charming man – although she doubted 'man' was the description – 'little boy' might well be better.

When he explained, last night, that they would be moving on, she realised just how much she had been dreading the moment. She had decided, then and there, that when Franklin (poor lad) went to bed, she would make one final effort to get to the truth behind this unlikeliest of couples.

She felt a small pang of guilt about pressing Bill for that truth while he was still evidently shocked and upset by the events of the evening, but it was, after all, very important to her.

When he finally, reluctantly, confessed she had been delighted (at his trust), shocked (at the possibilities it raised) and – what was the last emotion? – somehow... *protective* all of a sudden. If only she could admit her own frailty to him... but perhaps one day she would have to, and was that really so awful to a man such as he?

Now, gathering notepads and pens from her little office, she smiled to herself. Bill Taylor had awakened long-forgotten feelings inside her. She would ensure that, whatever else happened, they would run their course. She giggled girlishly to herself as the word formed again in her mind. *'Love*?!'

* * * * *

The discussion (or 'campaign meeting' as Maisie termed it) began with a delay when Bill was sent to collect the telephone book and print-outs but progressed rapidly from there. For his part, Franklin who had little to say or do, simply sat quietly growing ever-more amazed at Maisie's quick grasp of their problems, and the ease with which she saw ways around them.

The grandmother clock in the hallway was halfway through its noon chimes when Maisie decided that they had achieved enough 'for now' and handed both Bill and Franklin hastily written 'scripts' for their first tasks.

The key to their problem, Maisie insisted, was to properly contact at least one member of the mysterious church organisation. The difficulties they had already experienced in attempting to do so were dismissed as a lack of real effort.

When Maisie had excused herself 'to powder her nose', half an hour earlier, Franklin had suggested that she bore a passing resemblance, in character but not looks, to the ancient politician, Margaret Thatcher. He nearly choked on his coffee when Bill wistfully replied, "Yes. She really is quite wonderful at times."

The script that Maisie had devised was really quite simple. Instead of merely asking to speak to the person by name, the men were to insist they speak to the person and also mention that it was 'vital information in connection with the church'. Together with their scripts, they were also handed a hastily constructed rota.

"Since the list of telephone numbers is the key to the whole business," Maisie explained, "It is vital that we solve this part of the mystery – to some degree at least – first."

"But my dear lady," Bill had protested, "The cost of the calls alone will be astronomical! And what if you have other guests?"

Maisie smiled warmly at him. "In the first instance, William," she replied, "I have all the money I am ever likely to need and a telephone plan that offers unlimited calls in any case, and in the second, I'm closing the guest house for a week – it's very quiet at this time of year just before the school holidays, anyway."

She waved away all of Bill's further protests and curtailed the argument by leading him to the telephone in her office to begin the first round of telephone calls.

She returned to Franklin who was busily trying to memorise his version of the telephone script.

152

"And now, poor lad, what of your problem?"

"Huh?"

"It's obvious that we must do something to assist you – throw them off any possible scent, that sort of thing. Any ideas?"

Franklin shrugged, "I don't think they'll really be that bothered."

"Not the point," Maisie stated firmly, pressing her glasses firmly up the bridge of her nose, "We must, of course, ensure that they don't link you with William. Without being rude you are, shall we say, a little dusky, and much younger than William to boot. If it were known that you were in his company, you would both be much easier to spot."

"True," Franklin agreed slowly, impressed despite himself, "What do you suggest?"

"Well," Maisie replied, "William has mentioned Gerald's assistance. Perhaps you could send him a postcard saying something like 'I'm ok.' and he could post it to the social services girlie from some remote part of the country."

Franklin laughed, "You are wicked!"

"I'm... Oh yes, street talk for clever, isn't it? Well, thank you, but no. Merely practical." Maisie replied happily.

"I don't suppose..." Franklin began.

"If I've got any postcards? Of course, I just happen to have one here." Maisie produced a picture postcard depicting rolling hills, suitably anonymous to have been photographed anywhere in the British Isles.

Franklin took the proffered card. "Thank you, Maisie," he said sincerely, "Glad to have you with us."

Maisie simpered, her fingers toying with her fine locks, "My pleasure," she replied, "Now I'll pop into the kitchen and prepare you both some lunch."

As she bustled out of the sitting room, Franklin watched her go and chuckled softly to himself. Somehow, either Maisie's involvement or the mere fact that they were finally applying themselves *properly* to their problems, was having a beneficial effect. For a while, at least, the unease he had been experiencing earlier dissipated and he sat back, happily concocting a message for Ms Jenny Thomsett.

Jenny was woken from a deep sleep by a persistent tickling sensation near her left eye. She paused a moment before letting daylight into her muzzy-brained head, and briefly took stock of her whereabouts. The vague underlying sensation of rapid motion was sufficient for her to remember that she and Susan were on a train, on the way to Southampton to undertake some business (or pleasure, if you took Susan's view).

She opened her eyes cautiously and was greeted by Susan's startling blues. "Wassup?" she mumbled to her girlfriend.

"Just an early alarm call. We'll be in Southampton in about twenty minutes," Susan replied, flicking her black hair (recently used to tickle Jenny awake) back into place. She made room for Jenny to struggle awake and upright.

Jenny stretched languorously in her seat, expecting cramped muscles and joints to complain, and pleasantly surprised when they didn't: she wasn't used to the relative comfort of the old Southern Trains express service after spending most of her time in London travelling on the cramped, dirty and seemingly ancient commuter stock.

"Still twenty minutes?" she asked.

Susan nodded vigorously, "Just enough time for you to help me finish this." She held up a magazine crossword up for inspection in front of Jenny's face.

"A crossword?" Jenny asked when she was finally able to bring her sleep-bleary eyes into focus.

"Beautiful, wonderful, sensitive human being," Susan nodded.

Jenny smiled in spite of herself, "Are you sure you couldn't have let me sleep on a while like him?" A less than gentle snore was emanating from somebody near the back of their carriage.

Susan, smiling, shook her head, "Uh-huh. And besides, I know how long it takes you to wake up. You'd only be grumpy when we arrived, and I don't want anything to spoil our dirty weekend."

"Romantic weekend," Jenny corrected her, "And don't forget that we're also here to find young master Richardson."

"Oh, that won't take long," Susan replied dismissively, "I'm really looking forward to seeing the hotel."

Jenny considered this for a moment and was surprised to find herself thinking more or less the same thing. She really *was* looking forward to their break, "Yeah," she said at last, "Me too, Suze."

Susan grinned happily, leaned forward, pecked Jenny on the nose lightly, and then thrust the magazine into her hands. "Fourteen across; five four and five – 'Battered girl found in the garden', any ideas?"

Jenny laughed as she looked down at the puzzle. "Oh yes," she replied, "It's really very appropriate."

"Well?"

"Black-Eyed Susan. Which is what you'll be if you wake me up too early tomorrow."

* * * * *

The train rolled smoothly into the station a reassuring ten minutes late and Susan, with the enthusiasm of a ten-year old kid on a picnic, was first off. Jenny, struggling with their holdall, followed.

Behind them, barely awake, Dave Phillips trudged after them, partially refreshed from his slumbers but in desperate need of a toilet. The previous night's coffee had taken its toll.

"Let's find the hotel!" Susan exclaimed as they passed a dozing ticket collector, momentarily waking him from his accustomed Saturday afternoon snooze.

"Fair enough," Jenny conceded, an unfamiliar sensation of excitement trying to make itself felt, "There's a taxi rank over there." She pointed towards a row of dilapidated cars all of which were busily destroying the ozone layer as exhaust fumes drifted lazily in the early afternoon sunlight.

Susan nodded and dashed across the station's forecourt towards the leading vehicle. Jenny had barely struggled through the doors of the station before Susan returned.

"Apparently it's only a couple of minutes' walk," she reported, pointing in the vague direction of a looming hill. Without waiting for a reply of any sort she began to make her way towards the station car park's exit.

"Ok, then," Jenny muttered, smiling despite herself, "We'll walk there."

Behind her Phillips sighed in relief. He had not considered what would happen should his quarry have taken a taxi when they alighted from the train. Trying to ignore the increasingly uncomfortable pressure on his bladder, and mentally praying that Susan's two minutes was not a figment of a disinterested taxi driver's imagination, he followed the women as casually as he could.

When, a mere five minutes later, Jenny and Susan arrived at the New Rotterdam Hotel, it would have been hard to distinguish whether Jenny or Phillips was the more relieved. The hill, running directly out of the town centre was steep and more than a little busy. The holdall, weighed down with Susan's reading matter, had cut quite deeply into Jenny's palms and made her wonder just why she'd even bothered buying her a Kindle the previous Christmas. Breathing deeply and more than a little aware of just how out of condition she was, Jenny dropped the offending bag on the gravel forecourt of the hotel and leaned against the gatepost. "I don't care whether this is the right place or not," she gasped, "We're staying here."

"Looks nice," Susan replied.

Jenny had to admit that it did. Despite its relative smallness compared to the other hotels in the street it was undoubtedly very smart. When she had recovered her breath, she stooped and picked up the holdall. "True," she said, "Let's dump this stuff and get our business finished with."

Susan preceded her into the hotel lobby and signed in while the landlady, a somehow fittingly small person, informed Jenny of the house rules – which basically amounted to 'don't smoke on the premises', 'come and go as you please' and 'if you want anything at all, just ask'. Within five minutes they were unpacking in a small room overlooking the hill.

At about the same time Phillips, squirming in discomfort, was being told that, unfortunately, the hotel was fully booked.

* * * * *

Gerry Cooper paused in front of the ATM and fished around in his pocket for the small, rectangular piece of plastic that was, as far as he knew, Bill Taylor's only access to cash. He was thoroughly delighted to be helping his old friend in his desperate need and in no way hesitant in believing Bill innocent of the crime the police were now openly accusing him of.

Earlier that Saturday morning a police officer had called at his flat and asked him a number of innocuous questions concerning Bill's disappearance and he had had no trouble in fending them off, his conscience content in the certain knowledge of Bill's lack of culpability. After the officer had departed in a resigned manner, he had washed and shaved, decided to forsake his normal trip to the Mucky Duck, and climbed into his cab.

During the previous week he had visited a number of different towns and cities throughout the country and had studiously extracted the cash Bill was obviously in desperate need of. Today he had simply travelled across London a few miles to perform the task – no discernible pattern would emerge from his withdrawal here in London, he reasoned.

Despite the clarity of his conscience, his fingers still trembled slightly as he fumbled the card into the slot in front of him, and his stomach reeled in perfect harmony with the two or three dozen butterflies that appeared to have taken up residence there.

Taking a deep breath to steady his twitching digits, he carefully punched the four numbers he had committed to memory and begun the transaction idly wondering why people insisted on calling the four-digit code a PIN number thereby making it 'a personal identification number number'.

The maximum amount he could extract from the machine was £300 in any day and, when requested by the impersonal display to do so, he keyed in that figure. He glanced around a little nervously as he waited for the machine to spew forth the cash and so didn't notice when an unfamiliar message appeared on the screen. When he judged that the machine had taken a little too long to complete the transaction, he brought his attention back to the display.

'Sorry, we are unable to complete your transaction. Please contact your branch.'

The message, glowing green in the hazy sunlight, momentarily took him aback. Bill had insisted that there was in excess of five thousand pounds in his current account, and that meant that he could withdraw the maximum amount every day for at least a fortnight. This was only the sixth time he had carried out the operation. Something was obviously wrong.

The truth dawned on him suddenly. The police had obviously instructed the bank to freeze Bill's account – to cut him off from his only source of cash.

The card had been returned and was poking out of the slot in the front of the machine. He reached out with a mental shrug '*I did what I could, Bill,*' and he was a little surprised to find himself slightly relieved that his own part in Bill's continuing disappearance was at an end.

He was fumbling the card back into his pocket, wondering whether to destroy it or perhaps mail it on to Bill, when the hand fell on his upper arm.

"Good Afternoon, Mr Cooper," a voice said quietly into his ear, "Would you be so good as to accompany me back to the station?"

"Oh, shit!"

"I take it that means yes?" the voice continued, unperturbed.

Gerry took a shudderingly deep breath and finally summoned up the courage to turn and view his captor. It was the same officer that had visited him that morning. "Sorry, Bill," he muttered to himself, and nodded to the officer.

"Good, lad," the policeman continued and pointed to a car parked a little way down the busy street, "Shall we go? This shouldn't take long."

Sighing once more, Gerry allowed the officer to lead him to the waiting vehicle.

* * * * *

Paul Jarvis stood nervously by his desk and stared down at the hand-written note laying untidily on his blotter. He stooped and picked it up, re-reading it for the fifth time since he had discovered it on his chair earlier that morning.

The somewhat antiquated style of the writing identified it immediately as being from Brother Jacob and though its contents were alarming enough in

158

their own right, the fact that it had been hand-delivered in a plain, unmarked envelope worried him far more. Just how much access did the strange man have? The office in which he was standing was accessible only via the main doors to the building and anyone wishing to visit this particular department would also have to know the six-digit entry code for the inner door. Somehow Brother Jacob or another of the fraternity had circumvented all of the security measures and left the missive for him to find when he entered the office.

Stranger still, even *he* hadn't known that he would be coming into work this Saturday morning until his restless nightmare-full sleep had finally been disturbed by an aggravatingly cheerful milkman.

He scanned the note for a sixth time. Only one phrase disturbed him greatly: 'Be prepared, my brother, for a visit from the constabulary; never let down your guard and remember the friendship of the church.'

In itself it seemed innocuous, but Jarvis could clearly see the hidden threat behind the words. He could already quite imagine a visit from the police – it had featured in several of his nightmares the previous night – and, yet again, he began to contemplate ways that he might extricate himself from the weird, dangerous church that he now appeared to be trapped within.

The intercom buzzer, strident in the near-silent office, nearly induced a heart attack. Panting and suddenly covered in sweat he dropped the note back on to his desk and reached out with a trembling hand to depress the 'respond' switch on the intercom.

"Yes...?" he croaked before clearing his throat and repeating the word.

"Mr Jarvis?" the downstairs receptionist's voice queried.

"Er... Yes."

"I have a gentleman on the telephone. I'm not sure if the call is for you, but he wants to speak to a Paul and said it was urgent business to do with the church. Since you're the only Paul in today, I thought I'd see if it was for you."

Jarvis took a deep shuddering breath. "Yes, thanks. It is. Please put it through, Stan."

His mind raced as he waited for the telephone on his desk to ring. '*Well*,' he thought, '*when Brother Jacob says something, he always seems to know in advance that something is going to happen.*'

159

The telephone rang, and he took another deep breath, hoping that his voice would appear steady and calm. He lifted the receiver and slowly brought it to his ear. "Yes, officer?" he said, "How can I be of help?"

"Officer?" a cultured voice questioned.

It took Jarvis a few seconds before he realised that the caller was in no way connected to the police.

"Hello?" the voice came again.

He tried desperately hard to place the voice but to no avail. He was aware that telephones often distorted voices, but he still felt fairly certain that the caller was not one of the brethren. Neither was it one of the clients – so why was someone calling in relation to the church?

"Yes?" he said, cautiously.

"Is that Paul?"

"Yes..."

"Good gracious!" the voice exclaimed before falling silent.

Jarvis was now thoroughly confused. "Who is this?" he asked.

"Er, one moment, please," the voice returned.

He heard the handset at the other end of the line being placed noisily onto a hard surface and then a muffled voice calling for someone else. His initial alarm began to fade behind the growing sense of curiosity. He waited a little less than patiently for the voice to return.

* * * * *

Bill couldn't believe his luck. When the evidently nervous young man at the other end of the line confirmed that he was, indeed, Paul, his mind went blank. The young man then asked him something, but Bill's mind was racing, and he merely asked the person to wait a moment. It had occurred to him that he didn't have the faintest idea what he should do or say next. Dropping the handset onto the tiny desk he stood up quickly and poked his head out of the door.

"Maisie! Franklin!"

He was somewhat amazed to find himself hopping from foot to foot while he waited for them to come to his call. Apparently, that sort of behaviour

160

didn't only happen to characters in books. Maisie appeared first, dish cloth in hand, closely followed by Franklin, incongruously holding a half-eaten sausage.

"What is it, William?" Maisie asked.

"I've found one of them!" Bill exclaimed in a loud stage whisper, "What do I say now?"

"Wow, man! That's great!" Franklin said around the other half of the sausage.

Maisie immediately took charge. "Let me deal with him," she said, "I've been thinking about what comes next."

Bill at once stepped aside and ushered an increasingly excited but very business-like Maisie into the room. He and Franklin crammed themselves into the doorway and waited impatiently for her to begin the next stage of their investigations.

Maisie, for her part, took a moment to compose herself and then delicately lifted the handset to her ear. "Sorry about the delay, sir," she began, "May I first confirm that you are a Mr. Paul Smith?"

Franklin and Bill exchanged puzzled glances while Maisie received her reply.

"Oh, of course, silly me!" she exclaimed after a few seconds, "That's right, it's Mr Jarvis, isn't it? I was looking at the wrong list." She paused again, and Franklin and Bill once again exchanged glances, both clearly impressed by Maisie's evidently successful ruse.

"Yes, Mr Jarvis. I will let you know what I'm calling about in just a second but, as you must appreciate with a matter so, shall we say, delicate as this, I must verify that I'm speaking to the correct person. Now, could you please let me have your full postal address."

Once again, she paused, this time with pen at the ready. After a couple of seconds, she started scribbling furiously on the reverse of Bill's telephone script which was still laying on the desk. Franklin muttered a joyous 'Yes!' from the doorway, while Bill, mouth agape, could only shake his head in amazed delight.

Maisie replaced the pen on the desk and then with a quick "Could you just hold on for another second?" covered the mouthpiece of the telephone with her free hand. "Anyone think of anything else we need to know?" she whispered to the two men.

Bill continued shaking his head, but Franklin immediately dropped into a thoughtful silence. After a moment he started talking rapidly and quietly, "How about we ask him to confirm his personal mobile number, and where he works – now that he knows someone is on to him, and if he thinks it's suspicious, he might avoid his home, or at least any strangers calling on him?"

"Excellent thinking!" Maisie trilled and returned the handset to her ear. She repeated Franklin's questions to Jarvis and once again began scribbling on the script as she received the reply. After a few seconds she simply dropped the receiver back into its cradle. "Well, I couldn't think of any way to allay his suspicions," she said by way of explanation, "And that seemed the simplest way to end our discussion." She beamed at the two overjoyed men.

Bill, freeing himself from his bemused silence rushed forward and dragged Maisie out of the chair. "That was marvellous, my wonderful lady!" he exclaimed, joyfully, and planted a less than delicate kiss on her suddenly highly surprised lips.

"Why, William!"

"Franklin! Would you fetch the little box from underneath the coffee table?" Bill asked the grinning youth, still clutching Maisie by the shoulders.

"Sure," Franklin replied, and he descended the stairs chuckling to himself.

While they waited for Franklin to return Bill talked excitedly with Maisie, alternating between the possibilities her discovery had brought about and lauding praise upon the lady's head.

"William!" Maisie finally protested, smiling at the amount of pleasure she saw in Bill's features – and from an inner warmth generated by the all-too quick kiss. "Let's wait until Franklin returns then find out what this 'little box' has to do with anything before we start to plan our next move. And, by the way, my shoulders are beginning to lose feeling."

Bill sighed in part contentment and part frustration before releasing his grip and agreeing, "Yes. As ever you are quite correct my dear, dear lady. It's just such good news; the first positive step–"

"William!"

Bill laughed as he realised that he had started prattling once again. "Sorry," he said and made a gesture indicating that his lips were now (or at least, for the time being), sealed.

Franklin returned to the sound of Maisie's delighted giggling, bearing the delicately wrapped gift box. He handed it to Bill and determined to stay in the room while Maisie opened it, fascinated by whatever it might contain. Bill looked at him for a second and realised immediately that nothing short of a small explosion or a large fork lift truck would remove the youth. He frowned at Franklin as a token protest to his presence then turned back to face Maisie. "My dear lady," he said to her, "This is just a very small token of my gratitude for your kindness. In view of the help you have given me this very day, it now seems somewhat inadequate, but I hope you like it."

"Oh, William," Maisie cooed, accepting the small package, "I know it's what everyone says, but you shouldn't have."

Carefully, Maisie tugged at the red ribbon and laid it aside. Then, with equally delicate movements, she gently eased the brightly coloured wrapping paper apart to reveal a plain, white cardboard box. The lid was taped securely shut and Maisie brought a pair of scissors into use to free the final bonds. She turned and laid the box on the desk top before carefully removing a large wad of soft tissue paper. Franklin, despite his height, had to stand on tip-toes to maintain a reasonable view.

Suddenly, Maisie's hand shot to her mouth. "Oh, William," she murmured tremulously, "It's beautiful!"

To both Bill and Franklin's surprise, she spun round and hugged Bill tightly. Franklin took the opportunity to peer into the open package. Nestled inside on a further wad of tissue paper was a small crystal horse, elegantly sculpted and gleaming in the early afternoon sun. He glanced across at Maisie's face, almost buried on Bill's broad shoulder and was not unduly surprised to see the gleam echoed on her face, where a couple of small tears streaked across her pink cheeks. Surprised at both Bill's evidently carefully chosen gift and Maisie's very emotional reaction, he retreated silently from the room and went back to the dining room.

Smiling quietly to himself, he made his way through to the kitchen and finished his coffee, before washing up his breakfast dishes. He was drying his hands when he heard footsteps in the hallway and he wandered into the sitting room. Maisie was once more her normal, composed self, although grinning from ear to ear in a confusing mixture of happiness and embarrassment. Bill, still holding Maisie's hand, was also smiling.

"Hello, young lovers," Franklin greeted them.

"Enough of that, dear lad," Bill replied, amiably.

"Quite so," Maisie agreed, "We should settle down now and discuss what we are to do about our discovery."

Franklin nodded, slightly embarrassed himself about what he had witnessed, and sauntered over to his favourite armchair. "Fire away?" he suggested, settling into the comfortable seat.

"Firstly, a short comfort break," Bill interposed, "I shall return shortly." He lifted Maisie's hand, kissed it in a gentlemanly fashion and, bowing courteously, sidled out of the room, leaving Maisie to giggle girlishly behind him.

"Oh really!" Franklin groaned.

"Don't take on so," she chided him, happily, "He's just being his normal charming self. And besides, his little gift was so thoughtful and kind."

"Yes," Franklin mused, "That's been puzzling me. Why a horse?"

"Ah," Maisie replied settling herself into an armchair, "That is all to do with something I told William about a couple of nights ago. Ever since I was a little girl – which doesn't seem as long ago today as it did yesterday, I might add – I've always wanted to own a horse of my own. Due to a very unfortunate string of accidents, bad luck and now... well, never mind that, I've never been blessed enough to actually have my dream come true. In his naturally gallant fashion, your friend told me that were it in his power he would make sure that I could have my horse," Maisie paused and sighed, "I think that's why the little gift, as he called it, so touched me." She smiled a contented Cheshire cat grin and settled back into the cushions.

"I see," Franklin commented, quietly, finding himself impressed but not astounded by Bill's thoughtfulness.

Bill entered the room quietly and, after patting Maisie on the shoulder in passing, took his place in the comfortable chair nearest the large fireplace.

When he was settled, he looked across at his companions. "Well, what next?" he asked simply.

"Yes," Franklin added, unconsciously passing the question directly to Maisie.

The lady paused for a moment before replying then began to talk. "Well firstly, our good fortune in contacting one of the church members must count as a most important breakthrough in our investigations, and for that we should take a little moment to celebrate. Franklin, would you be so good as to pass the whisky bottle and a glass to William and pour my good self a large schooner of sherry? And, of course, help yourself to whatever you wish – there's some lager cooling in the fridge," she added.

"No problem," Franklin replied, rising.

While he sorted out the drinks Maisie lapsed into a thoughtful silence, broken only when she muttered a thank you to Franklin as he passed her the sherry. When all three were once again settled (Franklin having been dispatched to fetch a glass for his lager by Bill's disapproving frown), Bill raised a generous glass of whisky in front of him. "A toast, then, to our first success. To Maisie, who with her sterling planning and detective work would have put even her heroine, Miss Marple, in the shade."

"Why, William, thank you," Maisie replied and raised her own glass.

Franklin followed suit, the first time he could ever recall joining in a toast, and added a brief "Well done, Maisie!".

They each took sips of their drinks (although in Bill's case, 'sip' would hardly have been an appropriate description) before Maisie once again took up the discussion. "I think we must confront this Jarvis fellow in person," she began, "This, of course, is not something that William would be able to do – he might, after all, be recognised in town, and if the police are looking for him, that would be disastrous. Despite my own fondness for the stories of Agatha Christie, I don't think that I know enough of London to be able to comfortably travel there and find this man – and besides, sometimes these things need a man's touch," she paused and looked at Franklin, proffering him a kindly smile, "Therefore," she continued, "I think that Franklin should travel to the City without delay and try to find Mr Jarvis. Does that sound sensible?"

Bill was about to offer a small protest but was interrupted by the lad. "Very good," he said, smiling and evident impressed by the logic – especially as it pretty much matched his own thinking, "When do you think I should go?"

Bill tried once more to offer the protest but was this time silenced by Maisie's reply, "Well, I don't think that there's much point in travelling down today – if, as I suspect, he doesn't want to be found under these circumstances, especially after that odd call, then your best chance will be where he works and that will no doubt be an office that doesn't open on a Sunday. I can't imagine him answering his mobile to an unknown number."

Bill gave up in the face of insurmountable odds and merely listened as Franklin and Maisie planned the trip. Franklin was to leave the following afternoon, arriving in London on the Sunday evening in time to locate a reasonable hotel, close by the address Jarvis had given for his office. On Monday morning, very early, Franklin would travel to the man's private address and try to locate him there before he left for work. Failing that, he would travel to the office and try to gain entry on a pretext of some sort – 'possibly as a messenger', Franklin had suggested. If that, too, failed, he would then travel back to the residential address in the evening and wait there in case Jarvis showed up. They both agreed that it might be necessary to repeat the exercise over a number of days, and that Maisie and Bill, meanwhile, would continue with the telephone calls in order to try to locate another of the church members. Were they successful, they would phone Franklin on a new 'burner' mobile, and he could immediately try to get access to the person or persons they had managed to contact.

After the initial planning, the two of them spent some time going over finer details, checking on train departure times, allocating funds for the venture and so forth. Bill sat back, cradling the whisky and amazed and enthralled by the conversation going on before him. *'Friends like this,'* he thought, *'must be very hard to find. Very hard indeed.'*

It was nearly four o'clock when they finally finished and sat back contentedly. "Well, that's that settled," Maisie sighed, "And now I think we've all earned some relaxation time. I'll pop into the kitchen and cook up a little snack."

Bill roused himself, "No, madam. If I am to be left to sit idly by in the face of so much planning and mental activity, the least I can do is provide the rewards in the form of a little sustenance. And before you say a single word, dear Maisie," he added, mock sternly, "There shall be no arguments in this matter. I will brook no dissent." With that he marched briskly, if a little unsteadily, into the kitchen.

"Masterful, isn't he?" Franklin commented.

"Oh, yes," Maisie sighed happily.

"Oh, dear," Franklin moaned softly, grinning.

* * * * *

Susan stood at the gate of the New Rotterdam Hotel, enjoying the spring sunlight while Jenny returned the key to the landlady. When Jenny joined her, she pointed out a figure standing on the opposite side of the street, ostensibly reading a newspaper, "If that's what seaside air does to you, I think I'm glad we live in London."

Jenny looked at the young man. He was sweating profusely and panting as if he'd been running a marathon – unlikely given the bulky overcoat that he wore. "Yes," she agreed, "Even I didn't find the hill that hard to climb, and I was only carrying a single holdall – albeit one containing half of a newsagent's stock."

Susan grinned at her. "The exercise will do you good. Now, let's go find our Miss Blake." She opened the gate and turned towards the town.

"Funny, though," Jenny commented thoughtfully, following Susan through the gate, "I'm sure I know that guy's face from somewhere."

Susan glanced back at the figure, now desperately trying to gather loose newspaper pages from the pavement where he had dropped them. She shrugged, "Yeah, he does look kind of familiar. Funny how that happens isn't it?"

The subject was quickly dropped and then forgotten as the pair made their way back to the railway station where, Jenny had decided, they would find a taxi to take them to Miss Blake's retirement bungalow. Seated in the rear of the ancient Ford Focus, Jenny soon lost all sense of direction as the driver negotiated Southampton's maze of a one-way system. Beside her, Susan hummed a currently popular tune and Jenny was surprised that the normally annoying melody seemed quite pleasant in their current surroundings. Before the mood was broken by Susan's sixth repetition of the air, Jenny commented, "I hope we find the little sod."

"Umm," Susan replied, "Well I guess at least you wouldn't be fretting about him all weekend."

"Oh, it's not that," Jenny said, dismissively, "I'm definitely going to enjoy our little break. And besides, I'm sure Franklin can look after himself wherever he is. It's just that I still feel a little guilty about the whole Hart thing."

Susan looked across at her in amazement. It was the first time Jenny had admitted her partial responsibility for Franklin's disappearance in any way shape or form. She suddenly felt a little guilty about the earlier goading of her friend. "Don't worry, Jen. You weren't to know how it would turn out – and Franklin really can be such a nuisance at times."

Jenny surprised her further. "It's not normally his fault. I guess he's just unlucky."

Susan laughed quietly. "This sea air is really doing you some good. I could get used to this new, mellow Jenny."

Jenny laughed, self-consciously. "Oh dear. This will never do."

The driver interrupted their laughter. "We're there, ladies. That'll be nine pounds. Cash or card?"

They climbed awkwardly out of the ancient taxi and paid the driver with a ten-pound note who thanked Jenny most profusely for the one-pound tip she gave him. "He'll never make it in London," she observed as he drove happily off in a cloud of acrid blue exhaust fumes, "Far too nice."

"So true – but here we are then," Susan said, pointing to the large bungalow before them, "Looks like she did alright on her pension."

The building was large by any normal standards for a bungalow and was set at the end of a long curving drive. On either side a luscious lawn, green and healthy at the tail end of Spring, was flawlessly trimmed, and was surrounded by equally immaculate flower beds with early Summer blooms waving gently in the soft breeze. In front of the rose-bedecked porch leading to the front door a current registration Toyota gleamed a brilliant dark blue.

"Very nice," Jenny agreed, "Although I think most of the money came from her parents. They were quite a well-to-do family, if I recall right, although I think there was some friction with their only daughter when she went into the 'working class' career."

"I can imagine," Susan commented, "Although, somehow, I've never quite got used to the idea of being in a working-class career – I prefer to think of it as one of the 'caring' professions." She smiled at Jenny to see if her friend recognised her own words when they were spoken back to her.

Jenny nodded and was about to agree, when she realised that Susan was pulling her leg. She punched her playfully, "Enough, Suze, before the decidedly less than mellow Jenny makes her reappearance. Come on, then. Let's get this over with." She opened the wrought iron gate and entered the driveway.

Susan followed, admiring the carefully nurtured garden, and secretly hoping that Franklin *would* be present. It would ensure that Jenny didn't spend any more time over the weekend fretting about her ward – whatever she might have said to the contrary.

The drive was far shorter than Jenny had imagined, a trick, probably deliberate, of the setting of the garden and the angle the driveway took. When she reached the front door under its rose burdened portico, she paused, making sure that Susan was still with her – the young woman, lovely as she was, had a tendency to wander away just when she was most needed – and, satisfied that she was not alone (and dreading meeting the woman who had so terrorised her when she first joined the service), she pressed the doorbell.

Deep inside the building she heard the elegant chimes respond to her finger and then footsteps approaching the front door along a corridor. The door opened, and a familiar face peered out.

"Hello, Miss Blake," Jenny said, feeling a similar sensation to the one that had always crept over her when she had been sent to see her headmistress at school.

"Why, if it isn't little Jenny Thomsett," the remarkably robust lady trilled in reply when she recognised her caller, "And the lovely, practical Susan Smith. Do come in ladies, it's lovely to see you."

'*Retirement,*' thought Jenny, unaware that she was echoing Susan's thoughts, '*has certainly mellowed this old battleaxe.*' She followed the slight figure into the recesses of the bungalow, trying desperately to squeeze an answer in between a barrage of questions that Miss Blake was firing at them both. They were shown into a palatial sitting room and, after their jackets had been almost forcibly removed, were instructed to sit and make themselves comfortable while Miss Blake made them some coffee.

Left to themselves for a couple of minutes, Jenny and Susan first stared at each other and then burst into fits of hushed giggles. "I can't believe it!" Jenny almost squealed.

"I know!" Susan snorted, "She's so, so..."

"Nice!" Jenny whispered, sending them into another fit of giggles.

They were still laughing when their hostess returned with a silver tray bearing three delicate coffee cups and saucers and an equally ornate coffee pot. She placed it on a mahogany table in front of the two young ladies and beamed happily at them. "Well, you two do look well. Still shacked up together?" she enquired, candidly.

Jenny blushed, as ever embarrassed in some circumstances by her and Susan's relationship. Susan had no such qualms. "Yes, thank you," she replied, "And just as happy."

"Oh, that is nice to hear, dears," Miss Blake went on, carefully pouring the steaming brew into the delicate china receptacles, "And now," she added, handing each of them a cup, "What brings you to visit an old duck like me?"

Despite the distinct tempering of her nature, she still evidently retained the sharp, to-the-point, style of questioning that had led to her being nicknamed Torquemada by some of her juniors.

"Well," Jenny began when Susan evidently wasn't going to reply, "It's about a mutual little friend of ours."

"By which you must mean one of the little sods that we had to look after?"

"Quite so," Jenny replied.

"Don't tell me," the old lady paused. She thought for a minute then, "Stephanie Draper?" she suggested.

Jenny shook her head.

"Oh, well then, it must be Franklin Richardson."

Jenny and Susan exchanged surprised and impressed glances. "Absolutely," Jenny replied, "But how on earth did you know?" She wondered if this were confirmation that Franklin had, indeed, either been in touch, visited recently, or was even *actually there now*.

Miss Blake smiled, knowingly. "If you recall, Jenny, we only worked on a few cases together – and the only time you ever referred to our wards as 'little friends' was when dealing with particularly troublesome ones. I was merely reciting the list of those that fell into the category of 'troublesome', starting with the most obvious ones."

Jenny was astounded by the old lady's memory. Retired she might be; in her dotage she most certainly wasn't. "That's really very well remembered," she congratulated Miss Blake.

"Well, I didn't think you'd travel all this way just to see an old colleague," the lady replied, enjoying the sudden look of embarrassment that came over Jenny Thomsett's face. In order not to make her house-guest too uncomfortable, she went on, "What exactly can I do to help you with young Franklin?"

Jenny, relieved to be back on firmer ground explained how he had run away after Hart had evidently been bullying the lad. "We were wondering if he'd been in touch with you recently?" she finished.

Miss Blake sighed and shook her head. "I always told you that we had some people on our list of 'carers' that had no right to be there," she chided Jenny, "And Hart is certainly one pig of a man that I remember. I know Franklin was always getting into little scrapes, but I really don't think *I* would have placed him there." Deciding that enough pontificating was enough, she softened her tone before continuing, "I can quite understand that you must have been frustrated with him, though. But to answer your question, I'm afraid I haven't heard from him since just after he moved in with the Hart's. He called me a couple of times – mainly to say some very uncomplimentary things about your good self, I might add – but then I've heard nothing from him for the last few weeks."

Jenny, her cheeks still flushed from the reprimands, tried to concentrate the conversation on Franklin's current plight. "You haven't any idea of where he might have headed off to, do you? Any friends or anything?"

171

Miss Blake smiled sorrowfully, "No, my dear, I'm afraid not. Franklin was always on the move and I doubt in all honesty if you could say that he had any *real* friends at all. But he's a bright lad, far brighter than many people give him credit for," she took Jenny in with a meaningful glance, "And I'm sure he'll come to no great harm. To be honest, he's probably better off on his own than with that farmyard of a family. Besides, he's got to be coming up for eighteen soon, anyway, hasn't he?"

"Not for another six months," Jenny replied, automatically. Despite the evident mental power that the old lady still possessed in abundance, she was fairly certain that Miss Blake wasn't lying to her or in any way covering for Franklin. In a strange way that she couldn't define, she was almost relieved.

"Well," Susan commented, breaking a stretching and increasingly uncomfortable silence, "It would appear that either Gerry was wrong, or our little runaway has yet to arrive." She went on to explain the lead that their friend, Gerry Cooper, had given them, but decided, wisely, not to mention that for her at least the trip was far more involved in pleasure than business.

Miss Blake was suitably impressed by the dedication shown by Jenny and Susan, and Jenny felt that she had regained a few brownie points in the old woman's eyes by the time they bade her farewell and left her waving to them as they descended the drive.

With a final wave, they rounded the gatepost and made their way along the quiet street towards the town centre. When she was sure they were well out of earshot, Jenny breathed a huge sigh of relief. "I really thought that she had mellowed!" she exclaimed.

Susan laughed. "We should have known better. She's just as hard as ever."

"Granite," Jenny agreed.

"Diamond?" Susan suggested.

"Rough diamond," Jenny corrected her.

"Well," Susan said, changing the subject, "No Franklin here, and the old girl said she'd leave a message on out phones or at the hotel if he contacted her this weekend, so, what now?"

"Food and booze"' Jenny replied firmly, "After that little interview I'm in desperate need of a little food and a little drink."

"Make that 'a lot of drink', and I'm with you all the way," Susan agreed.

172

* * * * *

Dave Phillips had almost reached the point where he would rather give up his nascent career in journalism than pursue his quarry any further. After discovering the hotel fully booked, and with his bladder fast approaching the point of no return, he had waddled as quickly as he could to a decidedly seedy looking establishment opposite the New Rotterdam, optimistically sign-posted as 'The Haven Hotel'.

A surly, unshaven man wearing a vest and dirty kitchen checks had demanded money from him in return for a battered key which would let him into 'our box room'. He had scuttled upstairs and found the over-sized wardrobe and then made a frantic search of the corridors for a bathroom. After initially mistaking a cleaning closet for the intended room and having to replace half a dozen assorted mops within its murky recesses, he moved on to the next door and finally located his target. The bathroom was filthy, and the door had no lock, but to Dave Phillips, it was a view of heaven. He urinated noisily, accompanying the din with a variety of satisfied sighs, for what seemed like ten minutes, and, finally relieved, he re-zipped his fly and wandered back to the room.

The bed was predictably lumpy, and the bed linen looked as if it had not seen the inside of a washing machine for many a very long week. He determined that he would have to sleep on top of the sheets that night, and since he was running short of cash funds, would have to make do with the grotty little place for the rest of the weekend. His next task was to find out what the two women were up to and he crossed to the window in the vain hope that it would afford a view of the New Rotterdam's entrance.

That, it did not. What it did offer was a less than picturesque view of a side yard littered with black plastic waste bags, most of which were split open and currently providing sustenance for a large variety of the local fauna. He felt sure that a particularly large looking rodent was a rat and decided immediately that, could he find the time, he would be dining out.

Sighing, he fumbled the room key into his coat pocket and tramped downstairs. Five minutes later, after a slight altercation with the unkempt landlord who wouldn't let him leave with the key, he was standing opposite the New Rotterdam with a newspaper open in front of him, panting breathlessly. He had first dashed down the hill to a newsagent's and, desperate not to miss the departure of his quarry had also dashed back up. He had prepared himself for yet another long wait and so, when the girls appeared across the street almost immediately, he took this as a sign that his luck was finally changing.

The dark-haired one, Susan, walked up to the gate and stared across at him. He wondered whether she would recognise him but decided it unlikely. Fighting to regain control of his ragged respiration, he stared down at the open newspaper. The other girl, Jenny, he noticed out of the corner of his eye, joined Susan at the gate and they exchanged a few words that he couldn't make out, although he was sure that it involved him. Feeling a rising panic, he went to turn the page and managed to drop half of the paper onto the pavement. Cursing, he bent and scooped up the pages before they could escape and gathered them into an untidy bundle. When he next looked up, he saw the girls retreating forms some fifty yards down the hill. He scuttled after them as nonchalantly as a scuttle would allow.

When they reached the foot of the hill, he was just a few yards behind them, still on the opposite side of the road. They were, he guessed, making for the train station and so he crossed the main road recklessly, and made the other side well in front of them. He then slowed his pace and, praying fervently that they were going to be taking a taxi ride, he approached the taxi rank and lingered behind a lorry parked close by.

When he saw them climb into a battered Ford, he mentally praised himself. 'Phillips, you are brilliant!' He then realised that he would now have to persuade another driver to follow them were he to keep up the chase. Groaning he crossed to the taxi rank. The ancient Focus had been gone nearly five minutes before he gave up.

He trudged dejectedly back to the Haven Hotel, his only hope being that if they located the runaway, they would still have to return to their own hotel for their belongings before returning to London. He would just have to stay on watch for them until they did.

Gerry Cooper was not a happy man. An aggravatingly cheerful detective sergeant, Craig, he believed the man's name was, had been popping in and out of the interview room he had being detained in for the previous two hours. Each time he asked him variations on the same two questions. Where is Bill Taylor? And, how have you been helping him?

Gerry's replies had been monotonous and, had he been aware, he would have been happy to know that each time DS Craig left the tiny room, he swore loudly and kicked the filing cabinet in the corridor. His replies were respectively, a fairly honest 'I really don't know' and a thoroughly dishonest 'I'm not'. The matter of the bank card he dismissed by saying that Bill Taylor had owed him money and had given him the card to use by way of repayment.

Gerry was aware that the story was weak in the extreme, but without Bill Taylor to gainsay the tale, there was little Craig could do to disprove it. Fortunately, Gerry kept a fair amount of cash in his bedroom at home, tucked beneath a floorboard, so, when Craig asked him what he had done with all the money he had withdrawn during the previous week, Gerry merely told him that he had stashed it in his home in preparation for a cash purchase he had been planning for the following week. Gerry was delighted with his own ingenuity – the antithesis of Craig's emotions. The latter's mood took a substantial turn for the worse when a DC, sent to check for the cash at Gerry's home, returned with a plastic bag full of twenty-pound notes and mouse droppings.

Craig decided to try another tack. Breathing deeply to compose himself, he quietly opened the interview room door. His prisoner was leaning back in his chair, feet on the tiny desk, and whistling quietly.

"Cigarette?" Craig asked his prisoner.

"How kind," Gerry replied, accepting the proffered Marlboro.

Craig lit the cigarette and one for himself before settling into the other chair. He stared at Gerry Cooper for a full minute, Gerry returning his gaze with a half-smile playing across his lips. Finally, Craig broke the silence. "Gerry," he began, "You don't mind if I call you Gerry, do you?"

Gerry responded with a shrug.

"Let me explain my thoughts on this matter before I ask you just one simple question," the officer continued, "I think it is ninety-five percent certain that Bill Taylor murdered his sister Mary. From the stories we have gathered so far, the only possible motive seems to be one of sheer anger and frustration at the woman. Therefore, I do not believe that the crime was premeditated. With Taylor on the run, and people evidently helping him avoid capture, whatever sentence he will finally receive will only be lengthened because of this behaviour. You're really doing him no favours by keeping us away from him. In addition, you yourself are also running the risk of being charged with aiding and abetting the crime or perverting the course of justice – and the penalties for such are quite extraordinarily severe." The detective paused to gauge Gerry's reaction to this threat. Cooper's face was a complete blank and Craig filed a mental note never to play poker with the man.

"When I mentioned that I was ninety-five percent certain that Taylor really did kill his sister, I should also have added that, despite your cock-and-bull story about the cash, I am one hundred percent certain that you've been helping him. And that you know where he is, or at the very least, where he's been. Even if we do catch him and he gets off the charge, I intend to make damn sure you get to suffer for this little charade. Do I make myself clear?"

Gerry replied calmly. "Perfectly clear. Was that your question?"

Craig closed his eyes and tried to control the mounting anger inside him. "No," he said slowly, with deliberate forced calmness, "My question is simply this: Do you believe that Bill Taylor did it?"

For the first time the blank and calm expression left Cooper's face. He smiled and shook his head before replying. "Sergeant," he began, "Not only do I *believe* Bill didn't do it, *I know it*."

It was not the first time that Craig had heard that opinion that day, and he was irritated that he seemed to be in a minority of one when it came to the question of Taylor's innocence or guilt. He was going to ask Cooper why he was so sure but decided it really didn't matter. What was clear was that Cooper wasn't going to divulge any useful information sitting in this interview room. Before he had returned for his final words with the man, Craig had arranged for him to be released and then observed. He figured that the best chance they had of Cooper leading them to Taylor was to let him loose and see if he made a similar mistake to the one he had made with the bank card. He glanced at his watch. Cooper's telephones – landline and mobile – would, by now, be tapped, and three plain clothes officers were ready to tail the man.

Craig feigned weariness and sat back in the uncomfortable chair. He ground out the remains of his Marlboro and sighed deeply. "Very well then Gerry," he said, "As it appears you are unwilling in any way to co-operate with us, I'm willing to let you leave. On condition, of course, that you don't wander off anywhere where we might not be able to find you in a hurry."

Gerry was evidently surprised. "You're not going to charge me with anything then?"

"Oh, no," Craig smiled evilly at him, "That comes later. And that is a promise."

With the final threat hanging in the air, he stood and went to the door. He opened it and called for the uniformed officer waiting outside. "Constable, would you escort Mr Cooper from the premises?" Without waiting for a reply, and without another word to his former prisoner, Craig stalked off down the corridor.

Gerry found himself outside the station five minutes later, blinking in the late afternoon sunlight. Relatively pleased with his performance in the station he decided that his first stop would be the Mucky Duck – a pint or eight would be just the thing to get the taste of the place out of his mouth. Unaware of his new-found retinue, he walked briskly towards the welcoming alcohol.

* * * * *

While Maisie sat and read her way through the day's newspapers and Bill prepared their dinner, Franklin busied himself with packing his clothes and other necessities for the following day's journey. As he sat on his bed folding shirts and packing them into the sports bag that Bill had bought him almost exactly a week before, he felt a sense of release coupled with a terrible sense of foreboding that seemed ill-placed and alien.

He was undoubtedly looking forward to the 'mission', as Maisie now termed it, but he was worried. He didn't, for a start, know if he was up to the task of confronting someone who might very well be an accessory to a murder. For god's sake, he was only seventeen! There was also a sense of personal worry. He was going to be travelling back to the place close to where he, himself, was almost certainly the subject of an investigation of some sort. Were he to be recognised, he could well find himself back in the arms of the social services at best – and at worst, back in the dubious care of the Hart's.

This latter point didn't worry him unduly. For a start, the area he was travelling to was unlikely to put him in any immediate danger, and, besides, he was fast on his feet and swift to recognise dangers should they arise. He was far more worried about leaving Bill, and the problems that he might cause his friend if this Jarvis bloke ran to the police when he approached him. He didn't doubt for a minute, that Maisie was capable of looking after Bill in his absence, but there was a nagging feeling at the back of his mind that he couldn't quite place. *Somehow, someway*, he felt that Bill was more likely to be in danger without himself to protect him. From what, he didn't know. Nevertheless, the sensation of imminent danger wouldn't go away.

Finally, the packing now finished, he decided that he was merely being over-protective. He also decided, for reasons that he couldn't even begin to comprehend, that he would try once more, that very night, to take Bill into the village and make sure that, if everything went wrong, he would at least have spent one last evening alone in Bill's company. Happy to have arrived at that conclusion at least, he closed the sports bag and sauntered downstairs towards the enticing smells of good food and a peaceful evening.

Chapter 9

Saturday 14th June 2014

Bill and Franklin walked into the village in high spirits. Bill had prepared a meal which Maisie had described as 'Divine, like manna from heaven or ambrosia from the Gods'. Franklin had described it a little more prosaically as 'Really good, man'. They had dozed into the evening, a comfortable sense of peace and relaxation refreshing all three of them. When Franklin had roused himself, he found his headache had completely disappeared and he suggested that all three wander into the village.

Maisie would have none of it. Her perceptive powers were quite incredible, Franklin had thought. She insisted that he and Bill make the trip alone and that they were to make absolutely sure that they enjoyed themselves in the process. To Franklin's surprise, Bill agreed readily to the suggestion and, sober once more, veritably ran upstairs to wash and change.

The evening was bright and surprisingly balmy for so early in the Summer and they walked in silence for a while, enjoying the fresh country air – something which Franklin was still acutely aware of after his upbringing in the polluted atmosphere of the capital. They paused at the tiny hump-backed bridge which led into the village and looked down into the river that ran idly below them.

"This is a really great place," Franklin commented.

"Yes," Bill agreed, slowly, "Despite everything, I really feel at home here. In fact," he added, "When all this is over, I really might consider moving out here." He paused a moment before adding, "Of course, that does rather assume that we can verify my innocence."

Their moods darkened a little at that thought and Franklin sought to reassure Bill that everything would be ok. "Don't worry, with super-sleuth Maisie and her faithful black sidekick to help, we'll sort it all out."

Bill laughed softly, the shadow lifting and Franklin was relieved. He fumbled in his pocket and brought out a fairly new packet of Marlboro. Bill watched him light the cigarette with a match which Franklin cast into the river and then commented, "I didn't know you smoked."

Franklin looked at him in surprise. "Well, I don't really; just occasionally. Like, when I feel really good, or really at peace, you know?"

Bill nodded vigorously. "Quite right," he agreed, "I do partake of the occasional cigar myself. Hang on a moment, the newsagent's is still open." He left Franklin standing by the bridge and crossed the square to one of the Roy's shops on its furthest side. He re-joined Franklin a couple of minutes later with a large cigar which he lit with one of Franklin's matches.

"While we're alone," he said, "A toast – albeit in nicotine – to good fortune and speedy and successful conclusions to both of our troubles." He took a long drag on the cigar and blew a perfect sequence of fragrant smoke circles into the night air.

"I'll, er, smoke to that," Franklin laughed and attempted to copy Bill's actions. The little cloud of rather more acrid fumes disappeared into the evening air with no discernible pattern.

They spent the next ten minutes with Bill teaching Franklin the art of blowing smoke circles, Franklin consuming two more Marlboro in the process. When Franklin finally achieved a perfect circle, Bill declared that it was 'yet another lesson successfully taught,' and they resumed their stroll into the village.

When they reached the pub, Franklin and Bill both shuddered. Although the pub was obviously open, the front doors were both boarded up and it brought back vivid memories of the previous evening. Bill smiled ruefully and said, "I think I'd better open the door."

As Bill approached the door sideways, James Bond style, Franklin couldn't help but laugh. Images of shotgun blasts, blood and darkness lifted from him and he joined Bill at the door with a broad grin on his face. "After you, I think," he suggested.

Bill laughed too and opened the door wide indicating that it should be Franklin entering first. Franklin froze and took a sudden step backwards. Bill jerked the door shut and quickly pulled Franklin to one side. "What's wrong?" he asked frantically.

Franklin paused a moment and then laughed raucously. "Nothing," he replied, "I just wanted to see your face."

Bill was at a loss for words, "You, you...."

"Yep, that's me," Franklin chuckled. He grabbed the door handle and pulled it wide, "Come on, my man," he said, "You look as if you're catching flies."

"Incorrigible," Bill finally found his voice.

"No," Franklin commented, "That's you." He led Bill in to the bar.

George was behind the counter as normal, but the bar itself looked anything but typical. The ceiling was a mess, the plaster pitted with holes and large chunks of the surface missing altogether. Behind the bar, the ornate mirrors were missing and the wall, exposed for what Franklin believed was the first time in fifty years, were also cratered in the same fashion as the ceiling. A large section of the bar had been cut away, presumably blasted by Parsons Senior the previous evening. Even George, himself, was showing signs of damage. His right arm was swathed in a bandage that ran from shoulder to wrist.

When the landlord, already alerted by the opening and shutting of the door previously, spotted Franklin in the doorway, he hustled around the bar to greet him. "Master Frederick," he boomed, "Please, please come in. I'm so sorry about last night's bother. I saw you outside – all that blood." He peered closely at Franklin's bruised and lacerated forehead, "Young Jack has been in today – apologising for his old man, if you believe – and told me you were alright. But I was worried, I can tell you–"

"Whoa," Franklin interrupted the big man, "Look! No need to apologise, this wasn't anything to do with you."

George paused and smiled at his customer, "That's as may be, young man, but I still feel responsible in some ways–"

"Enough!" Franklin insisted, "The only thing you should apologise for is taking so long to pour me a pint!"

George laughed, "Well," he said when the laughing fit had subsided, "It's fair enough to know you don't blame me, but we really were very worried for you."

Franklin smiled at him, uncomfortably aware of the genuine concern that had been shown, "Please," he said, "I'm really very grateful, but enough's enough."

George nodded. For the first time he looked at Franklin's companion. "And this must be your manager?" he asked.

Franklin took a second before he realised that it was only Maisie that now knew of the deception. He felt a strong pang of guilt after the evident concern that he couldn't also confide in George but shrugged it aside as a necessary part of their continuing safety. "That's right," he replied, "George, this is Tom. Tom, George."

Bill walked forward and offered his hand to the corpulent landlord. "I've heard a lot about your marvellous hospitality," he said, "And I couldn't wait another moment to meet you."

The cultured tones had a surprising effect on the normally dour man. He adopted a most surprisingly obsequious posture as if he'd just been introduced to, and accepted by, royalty. "It's my pleasure," he responded awkwardly, "And now, I'd better serve you gentlemen." He retreated to the bar and awaited their order like an eager puppy. Franklin had to struggle to suppress the urge to giggle at the sight, but Bill took it in his stride with only the slightest of grins hovering around his mouth.

"The usual for Fr... Frederick, and a large whisky, straight, for myself," he requested.

"Certainly, sirs," George replied and busied himself with the drinks.

The bar was nearly empty, an elderly couple the only other people present, and Bill and Franklin exchanged amused looks, Franklin still struggling to suppress a fit of the giggles. George returned to the bar with the lager and a tumbler three quarters full of golden liquid. "These are on the house," he told them with a little more of his normal authority.

No amount of pleading by Bill would change the man's mind and he eventually relented with profuse thanks which were accepted in much the same way as he imagined a knighthood would be received from the Queen. Sipping at the whisky, he pronounced it 'Superb!' and averted his eyes while the big man unconsciously mopped his brow in relief.

Franklin had yet to take a sip of his beer in case the threatened giggles sent it spraying around the room. He was mightily relieved when Bill suggested that 'Frederick show him how these infernal pinball machines work'. He extracted a pound coin from his pocket and led Bill over to the machine in the corner of the bar, a little guilty about being relieved that it hadn't suffered damage in the previous night's disturbance. He took a minute explaining the principles of the game and then inserted the coin in the slot.

The garish music and flashing lights made Bill wince, but he was determined to find out what fascinated his young friend about the contraption. He watched Franklin for a full two minutes as the lad frantically pressed flippers, pushed the machine around and cursed loudly at every given opportunity. Finally, Franklin, losing the ball, stepped back, sweating profusely and announced that it was Bill's turn. "That," he explained, "is a mega-score. Hope you were watching, man!"

Bill stepped forward and stood at the unfamiliar contraption. He fired the pinball around the table and deftly caught it with one of the flippers. "No, man," Franklin interposed, "You're supposed to fire it here," he pointed to one of the machine's ramps. Bill shrugged and continued. He flipped the ball towards a particularly bright target and was rewarded by a ringing bell, several clicks and thumps and the ball returned gently to the flipper where he trapped it again. Five minutes later the ball was once again rested gently on the upturned flipper and he was preparing to fire it at another glowing target. Franklin had interposed a number of times with advice and remonstrations when Bill was 'doing it all wrong' but had latterly fallen silent.

Firing it successfully at the target he smiled in satisfaction and then surprised himself by cursing loudly as he missed the ball altogether when it was fired back at him. It disappeared inside the machine and the display indicated that it was now 'Player 1's' turn'. "How did I do?" he enquired.

Franklin was staring balefully at him. "You've done this before."

"Not at all," Bill replied, "At least ways, not for many a year, and they are much more complicated than when I last played." Franklin continued with the baleful look, "And, please," he added, "I've told you before. Stop giving me those black looks."

Franklin roared laughter.

They continued playing for a further half hour, Bill showing a natural (and, to the addicted Franklin, aggravating) talent for the game, interrupted only by Bill's couple of trips to the bar for further whisky. After Bill had beaten him for the fourth successive time, Franklin, sweating surrendered. "Let's break for a while," he suggested.

Bill was happy to do so. He could quite easily see himself hooked on the game and he had to admit that it was far more tiring than any stationary game should be. "A fine idea," he replied and led the way thirstily to the bar.

Franklin collected the remnants of his pint and was following Bill to the bar when the door opened, and Jack Parsons Junior walked into the pub. "Jack!" he called happy to see his new-found friend.

Jack looked over in surprise and made straight for Franklin. "Before you say a word," Franklin said as Jack reached him and opened his mouth to speak, "Don't you dare apologise!"

Jack paused, the concerned look dropping from his face, and smiled broadly. "Thanks!" he replied, seriously.

"How's Simon?" Franklin continued.

Jack's smile slipped. "He's okay. Sore, but okay. He'll be along in a while."

A gentle nudge from Bill interrupted Franklin's flow of questions. "Oh, yeah, this is, er, Tom. My, er, manager. Tom, this is Jack."

"Charmed to meet you," Bill replied, "I hear that you are one of the young fellows that have been keeping Frederick company."

"Oh, er, yes, I mean, nice to meet you," Jack replied, nonplussed by Bill's formal but friendly words.

"I really must buy you a drink," Bill went on, "After all you've done me no end of favours by keeping Frederick from under my feet for a few hours."

Jack laughed, especially as Franklin objected volubly to Bill's comment. "Thanks, Tom. A pint of lager, please."

"My pleasure," Bill replied, "And I suppose you'll be requiring more of the same?" he asked the still slightly piqued Franklin.

"For that, definitely," the lad replied.

Bill bought the drinks and they retreated to the bar stools that were placed along the end of the bar. "I hear your father was responsible for last night's shenanigans," Bill said to Jack when they were seated, "I do hope he hasn't been such a burden for you for too long?"

Jack, who was clearly delighted by Bill's company took five minutes to explain first-hand the tale of woe that was he and Simon's upbringing.

"It's no small wonder that you and Frederick get along so well," Bill commented when the narrative ended with the background to the previous night's incident.

Jack looked quizzically at Franklin.

"Didn't think I'd bother you with my problems," Franklin said by way of explanation, "You've enough of your own."

Bill was impressed by Franklin's response. *'That boy is growing up fast,'* he thought. To save any further problems for Franklin he interposed. "My little protege had a number of nasty incidents during his earlier years. It is one of the reasons that he is so successful now, I believe."

The conversation gradually moved on to other matters including the planned visit by Franklin to London, "I'll be back by Tuesday at the latest," he assured Jack and Simon, who had joined them after half an hour.

Eleven o'clock arrived all too early for Franklin, and even Bill seemed a little disappointed when George called for their glasses at quarter to midnight. They joined Jack and Simon outside the pub after Bill had spent ten minutes thanking George for his hospitality. Summer had begun to assert itself in no mean (but very British) fashion, and a light drizzle accompanied by a cool breeze soon had the quartet shivering in the dark. Simon sneezed violently then winced as his multifarious wounds protested.

"I think, young fellows, that is a cue for us to wend our weary ways homewards," Bill suggested.

"He means, time to go home," Franklin explained, unnecessarily, and the foursome parted with promises to meet up when Franklin returned to Wroxham after his 'business trip' to London. Bill, slightly unsteady on his feet, and Franklin, not much better, meandered back through the village and out towards the guest house. They paused once more en route by the bridge and Franklin voiced a slight fear that had been nagging at him since the afternoon. "I really hope I don't let you down, man."

Bill smiled at him. "That, my dear boy, you will never do. However things go in London, it cannot make matters worse for me. The worst you could possibly do is fail to make it any better – and even then, I doubt whether you will meet with anything but success."

Franklin considered the words and drew some comfort from the seemingly evident truth behind them. "Yeah, man," he said finally, "I suppose you're right. Now, if I don't get you home soon, I'll have Maisie to contend with and she might look at me over the top of her specs – and that is a really frightening thought!"

Bill laughed comfortably. "At that you may be quite correct," he replied, "Let us hence to the comfort of a warm sitting room and a warming drink."

They restarted their journey and five minutes later, a comfortably silent journey behind them, they returned to the house for what Franklin fervently prayed would not be the last time.

* * * * *

The drizzle which soaked Franklin and Bill in their way home had started earlier in Southampton and had developed into a steady downpour by the time Jenny and Susan, giggling, left the Duke of Wellington pub in the city centre. They had found a marvellous Indian restaurant earlier in the evening and spent the best part of three hours filling their faces with a wide variety of highly spiced food and ice cool lager. On leaving the restaurant they decided to pop into the first pub they came to for a night-cap and, more importantly, to get out of the steady rain. They spent another couple of hours in there, sampling a variety of cocktails until they found one that would suffice as a night-cap.

It was now midnight and they were eager to get back to their cosy room at the New Rotterdam hotel. Swaying precariously, they ascended the hill and fumbled with the latch on the gate. As they finally swung it open, Jenny waved Susan into silence.

"You Suze, sneeze? Er, sneeze, Suze?" she asked before hiccupping decorously.

Susan thought carefully about it for a few seconds then shook her head vigorously, "No!" she trilled and, dizzied by the motion of her head, staggered into the hedge.

"Coulda sworn ya did," Jenny said emphatically. "Musta been me," she giggled again and offered her hand to Susan who was still struggling to free herself from the privet. Together they staggered into the hotel, retrieved their key and wobbled their way up to their room.

Outside the hotel, sheltering as much as possible from the torrential rain, along the side of the hotel Dave Phillips sneezed violently once again. He had fallen asleep some hours before and had only wakened when the sound of the girl's giggling as they fumbled with the gate permeated his unconscious brain. He now realised as he checked his watch that he could have spent that time in his own room – it was clear they weren't going to be returning to London that night – and now he was soaked through, had no fresh clothes with him, and, on top of all of that, he was coming down with a cold. Groaning and muttering to himself he crossed the road to The Haven and spent ten minutes trying to wake the landlord to get back in. He stripped off in his room, drying himself as best as possible with the ancient hand-towel that he had found in the bathroom; the sound of the landlord's imprecations still ringing in his ears.

Deciding that, whatever happened, he would be spending the next night in his own bed, he lay on the covers of the hotel cot and, alternately shivering and sneezing, tried to get some sleep.

* * * * *

Gerry Cooper was drunk. Not intoxicated, bombed, inebriated or even pissed. Just plain drunk. When Mandy called last orders, even Ewan decided that he was far more drunk than Richie and given that Richie was currently impersonating a pinball as he staggered back from the gents, that was saying something. Since he had entered the pub that evening, Gerry had been the centre of attention. As in small communities everywhere, news of his 'arrest' had preceded him, and when he walked into the bar he was inundated with questions from all corners.

His tale of wrongful arrest, created by his imagination on the walk from the police station, was at the ready and he repeated it (albeit in various versions) several times during the course of the evening. As with any brush with the constabulary, he was treated much like a road accident victim that had miraculously crawled from the burning wreckage. Drinks were poured liberally in his direction, and he was, as he put it, far too polite to refuse a kind gesture.

In the furthest corner of the bar, PC Dave Blake, now dressed in jeans and a sweatshirt sat glumly watching the bacchanalian activities at the counter. When he had arrived at the station that evening, he had reported to DS Craig as he had been instructed to do and was told to join three other officers in keeping an eye on Gerry Cooper. He tried to tell his superior that he was well known to the man, but Craig seemed to be in a vile temper and in no mood to listen to him. So, from eight o'clock that evening he had been sitting in the Mucky Duck sipping at pints that were served to him with barely concealed hostility. The entire atmosphere in the usually friendly establishment had been somewhat soured by Gerry Cooper's tale of police incompetence and harassment, and a palpable wave of the same overcame him whenever he approached the bar or visited the gents.

The atmosphere hadn't improved when, out of boredom and as a diversion, he put a pound into the fruit machine and immediately hit the jackpot. He was now drinking his fifth pint, and the pile of tokens was still too heavy for him to put in the pockets of his jeans.

When Mandy rang the ornate brass bell signalling time, he drained his pint and wandered into the damp night. Across the street in an all-night cafe, the other remaining observation officer was sipping coffee and reading his Kindle. When Blake rapped heavily on the window pane, he gained a little satisfaction as the CID junior splashed coffee into his own lap. Swearing softly, the DC, Tim Stevens joined Blake on the pavement.

"Thanks a bunch, Dave," he complained, "Any developments?"

"Not a thing," Blake replied, sourly, "He's as pissed as the proverbial newt and yet hasn't had to buy a drink all night. Just keeps rabbiting on about how the 'bastards' kept him locked up all day, and so on. Not a single word about Taylor."

"Oh, well," Stevens replied a little more cheerfully, "At least you got to have a drink on duty. Besides, if he's that pissed, he won't be up to anything tonight; we might as well sod off home."

Blake weighed up the constable's logic. He desperately wanted to get out of the uniform branch and didn't want to mess up this chance to show his worth to the CID. But, there again, Cooper was definitely wrecked. There was no way he would give them any clues now. The usual side effect of several pints of lager came into play. "Yeah," he replied, "Fancy a curry?"

Stevens, seventeen stones of compulsive eater needed no second asking. "Come on," he said, setting off towards the red sign glowing damply in the darkness.

Inside the pub, Gerry was trying to prise a late drink out of the reluctant Mandy. "It's what Bill would have wanted," he insisted, "Besides, I've done everything I can to keep him safe. If he were here, he'd insist on it."

Suddenly, Gerry was once more the centre of attention. In his drunken state it did not take long to extract the story from him.

Chapter 10

Sunday 15th June 2014

Sunday was a morning full of hangovers. It dawned damply, the previous night's rain reluctant to leave and grey clouds keeping it company over the entire country.

Bill awoke early from a dream-filled sleep, his head muzzy and with vague recollections of the last dream. In it he could see Mary standing in a doorway frantically signalling to him in the muted language of hand signals. Their father had been deaf, but he couldn't remember using the sign language since the old man's death more than ten years previously. The dream had a haunting quality which stayed with him when he rose and showered.

He went downstairs with the remnants of the dream dragging around his ankles like an ethereal mist. Maisie met him at the bottom of the stairs, alerted by his heavy, early morning tread. She was solemn and held one of the Sunday newspapers. The dream sloughed off him in an instant as he realised what Maisie's grave demeanour meant.

*****

Franklin woke to a gentle tapping on his door and he struggled awake, his head aching for the second day running, but today from a mild hangover. "Come in," he called softly.

Bill poked his head around the door. "Good morning, young Franklin," he greeted him, "We have some news. Do hurry down."

Before Franklin could get his thoughts together sufficiently to ask him any questions, Bill had closed the door and departed downstairs. Stretching luxuriously and wincing as the bruises reasserted their presence, he fumbled his way out of the bedclothes and dressed as quickly as his aches and pains would let him. He struggled along the corridor to the bathroom and washed briefly. When, ten minutes later, he made his appearance in the sitting room, he found Maisie and Bill poring over the Sunday newspapers. Glancing at the grandmother clock he realised that he had slept late – it was half past eleven. "Mornin' folks", he greeted them.

Bill and Maisie looked around, Maisie's face a mask of concern and Bill looking somewhat more sombre than usual. "Good morning, Franklin," Maisie greeted him, "Come and have a look at these."

He moved quickly over to the coffee table where the newspapers had been spread out. On the armchair next to it he could see the Sunday Telegraph opened and folded so that a small two column story was highlighted. The headline ran 'Police seek murder suspect'. "Oh-oh," Franklin said, "I suppose this is about you?"

Bill nodded, "Yes. Three of the qualities have run the story, but fortunately only one of the tabloids."

"And even more fortunately," Maisie added, "They have only a very old photograph of William. He's hardly recognisable."

Franklin picked up the Telegraph and scanned the story. It was a standard police bulletin that had been marginally re-worked by the newspaper staff. It amounted to nothing more than telling the reader that the police were seeking a middle-aged man in connection with a murder in the East end of London. In addition, it mentioned that the search was currently centred on the south coast resort of Brighton. The photograph was, indeed, old and blurred sufficiently to be totally lacking any resemblance to Bill. Bill handed him the other three reports and he read each of them. They followed exactly the same pattern as the first. "Well, that's not too bad, is it?"

Bill shrugged, "To be perfectly frank, er, Franklin, I have not the faintest idea. I don't know anything about police procedures in these matters. I am relieved that I've always been intensely camera shy though. I just hope they don't pester the regulars at the Mucky Duck. There are bound to be a few more recent snaps amongst that crowd. In a way," he continued, "I'm relieved that the story has finally come to light. I was beginning to think it was all some awful joke."

Maisie turned and stood beside Bill, a protective arm linked through his. "It's such a worry though. Still, there is one very good piece of information to come out of this: At least they don't appear to know that you are in William's company – and anyone local is going to assume that you and William always travel together now – so they won't link William with the story that way."

Franklin hadn't considered that and the, by now, normal feeling of being impressed with Maisie's quick, logical mind overcame him. "In that case," he said, "I'd better make sure I'm not in London for too long."

"Absolutely," Maisie agreed. "And now, I'll cook you some breakfast," she paused and looked at the clock, "Well, some lunch, anyway."

"So, how does it feel to be a wanted man?" Franklin asked when Maisie had left.

"To be honest, my lad, it doesn't seem to have had any effect on me. I suppose I've always considered myself that way since we left," Bill replied. "Anyway, there's no use fretting over it. We'll just have to hope that you manage to turn something up in town."

"That," Franklin promised solemnly, "I will try my hardest to do."

"And, in the meantime, we shall eat," Bill continued, "Let us away to the kitchen and assist the dear lady." He led Franklin through to where Maisie was preparing lunch, and, despite her protestations, they eventually convinced her to let them help. There was a forced jollity in their preparations as they considered the days ahead, but this gradually gave way to a more relaxed atmosphere as a series of mishaps, all perpetrated by a suddenly clumsy Maisie, dogged their efforts.

While he was clearing up the shattered remnants of a mixing bowl, Franklin slipped and ended up wedged between the refrigerator and the cooker. Maisie couldn't help him up for giggling and when Bill attempted, and slipped on the same mess, ending up on his own bottom, she ended up in hysterics and with a highly amusing case of hiccups which lasted a further ten minutes.

By the time the meal was served (or, as Bill put it, spread around the plates) their collective mood had become one of optimism and good humour. It was matched by a marked increase in their appetites, and they sat back afterwards with bellies bloated and contented sighs, Bill nursing a large tumbler of whisky. The afternoon passed in a collective doze until it was time to walk with Franklin to the door where a taxi arrived to take him directly into Norwich and the train that would carry him to each of their destinies.

Maisie pecked him on the cheek, wishing him the very best of luck, and quickly ran through a checklist to ensure that he had all of the money, addresses, telephone numbers and so forth that he needed. The only missing item was the sports bag containing all of his clothes, and Maisie ran back into the house to fetch it for him.

While she was retrieving it, Bill took Franklin's hand. "I wish you the very best of luck, my dear friend," he said, "And not just for my own sake. Hurry back, Franklin, for, surprising as it seems, even to my poor self, I shall miss your company."

Franklin nodded, signalling clearly that he understood. His vocabulary wasn't nearly good enough to voice his own thoughts and emotions in a single sentence, so he simply replied, "Me too, man," and surprised himself by awkwardly hugging his friend.

Maisie returned with the bag and the contact between Bill and Franklin was broken. With a final reminder to him to telephone as soon as he was settled that evening, Maisie handed him the holdall and he climbed into the cab. Shutting the door behind him he waved once as the taxi sped away and then breathed deeply and a little shakily. "Oh, well," he muttered to no-one in particular, "Here goes."

* * * * *

Jenny Thomsett woke slowly, for the second day running her head and stomach indicated that, just maybe, the previous night's drinking had got a little out of hand. She realised quickly that Susan was missing from the small bed and peered blearily around the room in search of her friend. It was a moment or two before she recognised the fact that they weren't in their own flat and the disorientation made her close her eyes once more.

Water was running in the en suite bathroom, and the door stood slightly ajar. Susan appeared naked and with a towel wrapped around her head. She picked up another towel from the chair by the bed and made to return to the steaming room. Jenny sat up awkwardly. "Morning, Suze."

"Hiya, sleepy head," the bright and cheerful reply came, making the heavy-headed Jenny wince. She watched Susan return to the bathroom and reached for the tumbler of water on the bedside table. Susan had obviously refreshed it recently and the cool liquid tasted like nectar to her. She lay back and waited for Susan to complete her ablutions.

She dozed and was wakened by a gentle shake. She came awake quickly and was surprised to find that her head had cleared in the few minutes she had slept. Susan was standing over her, still naked, but now a shade pinker. She felt dirty, sweaty and somehow unclean, but when Susan pulled back the sheet and climbed into the bed beside her, those perceptions vanished, and she surrendered herself to the wordless, gentle, sensual, erotic caresses of her girlfriend.

Half an hour later she sat up, sated, and smiled at Susan. "What would I do without you?" she asked.

Susan laughed. "I don't know what's come over you," she said, "except possibly me, but this sea air is really showing me a new side of you. I like it."

Jenny realised that Susan was somehow right. It wasn't just the sea air; the change had been going on for a few days. It had started, perversely, with Franklin's disappearance. She thought back to a number of her colleagues that had finally decided enough was enough and had given up the 'caring' profession. Before they had left, they had suddenly gone through a mental metamorphosis – their character had changed perceptibly. She realised now, the realisation deep and strong, that she had made an awful mistake with a young life. She could easily blame the pressure of her work, the myriad responsibilities that distracted her – even Franklin himself, for his continuous brushes with disaster. But that wasn't quite right.

A pressure had been building inside her, unseen. Somehow, some way, a valve had finally opened. She realised, there and then, that she wouldn't – couldn't – go back and be the same person. Her career was over. She laughed aloud, a sudden, choking sound, lacking any depth of humour. *'This is it,'* she thought, *'I've got someone with me that I love. Someone that is strong and good. I know I've had enough of the work. Why couldn't I see that?'* She slumped back against the pillows. The feeling of intense relief was overpowering, and she felt giddy – the cynical part of her mind wondering whether it was merely last night's alcohol, before being overwhelmed by pure reason – and she made herself one last promise. She would find Franklin, whatever it took, and she would apologise. Help him and see him right.

She opened her eyes, tightly shut while the epiphany played itself out, and saw Susan staring down at her, concerned. Tears began to fill her eyes and the view of her dark-haired friend dissipated into a kaleidoscope of images.

"Jen, what's wrong?" she heard Susan say, the voice filled with a deep and genuine concern.

"Nothing," she gasped, "Nothing at all." Her sobs broke over her in a wave and she hugged Susan tightly.

* * * * *

Gerry Cooper awoke slowly and found himself slumped in the armchair in his front room. His mind nagged guiltily at him, but he couldn't begin to wonder why it should. Slowly he began to recall some of the details of the previous day; the arrest, the hours in the police station, returning to the Mucky Duck, drinks.

After that, his powers of recollection failed, and he stared blearily into the murk of his front room, his eyes refusing to focus for a number of minutes. After a while he realised that the television was still on, some inane post-adolescent preaching inanities to the pre-adolescent population. He wondered vaguely whether the average IQ of the audience was really that much higher than the presenter's but decided it didn't matter.

He sat up and cursed as his head throbbed and his cramped back screamed in protest. The nagging guilt feeling persisted and he realised that he might well have made some terrible social gaffe the previous evening. He drank copiously, but seldom to excess, and was only too well aware that when he had downed a few, he was likely to speak too much about too little.

He immediately began to dread the visit to the pub that was his usual Sunday lunchtime habit, but recognised its necessity were he to regain the mental equilibrium that the previous evening's alcohol had so easily disturbed. Besides, if he were lucky, he would learn exactly what he had been up to last night without too much ribbing.

Muscles and joints complaining bitterly, he climbed out of the armchair and made his way gingerly up the stairs and into the bathroom. Twenty minutes later, he stood by the boiling kettle and tried to make a mug of coffee without scalding his fingers and fretted about the guilt cloud that had failed to dissipate in the shower.

It was nearly one o'clock when he left the house and, grateful for the overcast as being easier on his eyes, made his way gingerly along to the pub. He did not notice the furtive man with the newspaper who followed him discreetly along the tree-lined street.

When he entered the pub, he expected a few raucous calls and some general ribbing about his behaviour the previous evening. What he didn't expect was being grabbed firmly by the arm and led into the furthest corner of the pub by none other than Richie Bates.

"What?" he asked numbly, his head pounding all the louder.

"If just *half* of what you said last night is true, I hope for your sake that no-one let's on!" Richie uncharacteristically stormed at him.

Gerry desperately tried to process the information being yelled at him by Richie and failed miserably. "What?" he asked again.

"Don't you remember anything, moron?" Richie enquired.

Gerry shook his head and immediately regretted the action. However, the motion and subsequent flare of pain seemed to shift aside a large mental block. He dimly recalled mentioning something about Bill. He was immediately panicked. "Oh, God!" he exclaimed.

"Quite," Richie replied dryly, "I hope for your sake someone up there is listening, because it would take a miracle if this information isn't going to spread."

Although he knew he had said something, Gerry couldn't for the life of him remember just how much he had let on. "What on earth did I tell everyone?" he asked, plaintively.

"Oh, not a great deal," Richie replied sarcastically, "Just that you ensured that Bill made a clean getaway, that you helped Bill get cash, that he was in the company of a young man who was also in trouble. Jesus fucking wept, Gerry..." Richie trailed off, lost for words.

Gerry closed his eyes and cursed himself and his own stupidity. "It was all an exaggeration," he began, desperately trying to undo some of the damage. The look on Richie's face stopped him in his tracks.

"Gerald, I'm well aware of what happened that Saturday afternoon a week ago. You were absent all afternoon – the afternoon that Bill left for Brighton. You really did help him, didn't you?'"

Gerry nodded miserably.

"Ok," Richie went on, calming himself, "We'd better consider what our next actions are. There's no way we should leave it all to you with your track record."

Gerry was suddenly relieved to be sharing his burden. He nodded, the pounding in his head subsiding a little. "Over a drink?" he suggested.

Richie looked at him. "Don't be so stupid, Gerald. *Of course* over a drink. And before you're re-arrested!"

They walked over to the bar leaving a delighted detective constable fumbling surreptitiously for his phone.

* * * * *

Dave Phillips awoke to the sound of running water when he sneezed violently enough to launch himself off the side of the bed. He had slept fitfully, a grand total of about an hour in the past eight, he imagined. Scrambling himself into a sitting position he peered at his wristwatch. At first, he thought it must have stopped. The digital display read 10:18. Peering at the dust-encrusted glass of the window, he paused for thought. It was certainly very bright outside, but he doubted very much that it was that late. Looking down at his watch once more, he was surprised to see the display now reading 10:19. He had evidently slept a great deal longer than he had thought.

He was still fully dressed, if somewhat rumpled, and his stomach decided that he needed to eat. He struggled to his feet and elected to risk whatever breakfast the establishment might offer. Without even realising it, he had chosen to abandon the sleuthing. Grabbing his coat from the bed where it had served as a blanket during the night, he left the room and made his way downstairs. Ten minutes later he was sharing a slice of buttered toast with two flies.

*****

Susan had ordered breakfast to be served in their room and she and Jenny had slowly eaten their way through a massive fried breakfast, drunk a reservoir of coffee and pored through the Sunday newspapers that had appeared, unbidden, with the meal. When they had finished, they had showered, Susan for the second time, and planned the rest of their day.

Jenny's mood had lightened immeasurably, and she seemed, to Susan, almost preternaturally happy. For her own part, Jenny felt a hundred pounds lighter, as if an unseen burden had been suddenly removed from her shoulders. As they chatted about what they would do for the rest of the day, her mind kept drifting to Franklin, and she wondered what he was doing at that very minute. However, it didn't bother her because she made her mind up to enjoy the rest of their short break – Monday afternoon would do to start fretting over her wayward ward.

They opted for a visit to one of the local cinemas, a treat they hadn't seemed to have had time for in the past few weeks, and the landlady let them use her computer which was set up to loop through local entertainment websites which included details of the films on offer, together with the times they would be shown. They agreed that the vast breakfast would suffice them until the evening and opted for a couple of drinks before a matinee showing of the latest Mars-based blockbuster.

They left the New Rotterdam cheerfully and contentedly, wandering into the town centre in glorious June sunshine, unaware of the overcast that had dampened the spirits of early risers elsewhere in the country. En route, Jenny chatted and capered, Susan amazed at the change in her friend and eventually caught up in her buoyant mood. They arrived at the Lord Wellington pub near the station, giggling, and entered the bar where they had enjoyed sampling the cocktails the previous evening.

The barman, Paul, who had maintained a remarkable level of cheerfulness in the face of their drunken behaviour the previous evening, greeted them

198

with a smile and asked them what they required 'this time'. Jenny asked for a bottle of Budweiser and Susan opted for a Holsten.

"Did you see that story about your home town in the news this morning?" Paul asked them when he returned with the bottles.

Jenny, insisting on paying, handed him a twenty-pound note. "As in London?" she asked.

"No," Paul replied, from the till, "As in Walthamstow. That is where you come from, isn't it?"

"I haven't been checking my phone today, so no I haven't seen anything," Jenny said, when he returned with her change, "What's it about?"

"A murder, no less," the barman explained, "Apparently some bloke topped his sister. The police are looking for him along the south coast somewhere."

"Good God!" Susan exclaimed, "I bet that must have been about old Bill Taylor. What site was it on?"

Paul handed them his tablet from beneath the bar counter, still open at the page. Susan took it from him and Jenny peered over her shoulder as they read the brief article. "Good God!" Susan exclaimed again when they had finished, "I can't believe he really did it."

"Well," Jenny replied doubtfully, "There's no smoke and all that, but I must agree – he just isn't the type."

"Know him, do you?" Paul asked.

Jenny nodded emphatically, "Lovely bloke, really intelligent. Bit of a piss-head, mind you, and a memory like a sieve, but he just isn't the type."

Susan agreed with her, "He'd probably double the take in this place single-handedly," she told the barman, "But he's a real pussy cat. A real gentleman too, one of the old school."

Paul and Susan chatted on, Susan relating stories about Bill Taylor and his drunken friends, the Losers' Club, and Paul responding with roars of laughter. Jenny sat silently, scanning the story once again. Something about it bothered her deeply, in a way that she couldn't define. She wasn't prone to deep belief in anything or anyone (with the possible exception of Susan) but she couldn't accept that Bill Taylor would ever harm anyone – let alone 'brutally' murder them. Despite the unease she felt, the story on the site didn't deflate her optimistic, buoyant mood. If anything, it brought her new-found recognition of herself and her circumstances into clearer focus. She wondered if there was anything that she could do to help the unfortunate Bill and eventually determined that she would put herself forward as a character witness should that be required. Satisfied with the decision, she returned to the conversation and helped provide a little colour to Susan's narrative.

The pub quickly filled up with the Sunday lunchtime trade and Paul was called away ever more frequently to cater to the demands, leaving Susan and Jenny alone at the counter.

"He definitely fancies you," Susan told her.

"That, my angel, is all very nice. But I really don't want anyone – let alone a man – except you," Jenny replied. She smiled at Susan and then leaned forward and kissed her lightly, quickly on the mouth.

Susan stared in surprise for a moment and then laughed. "When I said I could quite get used to the new you," she said when her laughter had subsided, "I was wrong. The new you is just *full* of surprises – but don't you dare change back."

They finished their drinks and ordered more, Jenny flirting outrageously with Paul, and left the pub an hour later in search of the cinema.

Chapter 11

Sunday 15th June 2014

Franklin arrived in Liverpool Street Station just one week and one day after his first ever visit there and found himself outside the glass concourse and back on the streets of London. His first stop was the Macdonald's restaurant where, despite the massive lunch he had eaten earlier, he gorged himself on burgers and fries, unaware until then of how much he had missed them. His belly once more bloated, he waddled uncomfortably outside and looked around for a taxi.

The temporary rank was little more than twenty metres distant and he was relieved to see a number of the distinctive black cars parked there. As he crossed the street, he suddenly noticed the numbers of people drifting around. Even though it was Sunday evening and he was more-or-less in the City's business district, there were more people on the streets than he had seen in all the time since he had left the previous week. He was surprised to find himself missing the peace and relative solitude of the countryside already.

He approached the driver of the cab at the front of the rank who viewed him with immediate suspicion. It was another thing that he had already forgotten about, and one that he missed as much as a broken leg. After he had waved a bundle of twenty-pound notes in front of the driver's face, and presumably changed from thug to pimp in the man's mind, the driver gracelessly told him to 'park his arse' in the back and then took him on an impromptu tour of the environs before arriving at the hotel which Franklin and Maisie had selected.

The hotel was like nothing he had ever seen or experienced. Glass and chrome glittered everywhere he looked and the carpets under his feet were lush. He felt like he was wading through a sunlit meadow as he made his way to the fifteen-metre long desk marked 'reception'. A number of people were being dealt with at the desk as he approached, but by the time he had crossed the hotel foyer, yet another member of staff had appeared and was waiting for him, smiling in, what Franklin thought, was a rather false manner.

"Good evening, sir," the young woman greeted him.

Franklin had to struggle hard to suppress the notion that she was talking to someone behind him – he couldn't remember the last time someone had addressed him as 'sir' and wondered briefly if it was the first time ever. "Good evening," he replied, striving hard to recall the procedure that followed as advised by Maisie and Bill, "I'm looking for a single room."

"Certainly, sir," the young lady, Anthea, her name badge read, replied. "How long will you be staying?"

"At least one night," Franklin replied promptly, remembering his lines, "but possibly two or three if that's alright."

"Very well, sir. Could you please fill in this registration form," she handed him a tablet and an ornate stylus, emblazoned with the hotel's name and crest.

Franklin accepted both, setting his bag on the floor, and began filling in the requested details. The first box requested his surname and forenames and he smiled to himself as he entered the details as 'Taylor' and 'Frank'. Five minutes later his entirely fabricated personal information was complete and he returned the equipment to Anthea.

"How would sir like to pay?" she continued when she had finished rattling her own keyboard with a less than delicate touch.

Franklin fished the roll of bank notes out of his pocket and the receptionist referred to her computer monitor before requesting one hundred pounds 'for the first night, and please pay before two p.m. tomorrow if you are going to be staying on'.

Franklin counted out five twenty-pound notes and finally received a piece of plastic that very closely resembled a credit card. This, he was informed, was the key to room two hundred and eleven.

"We have a cocktail bar on the first floor, a saloon bar just beyond the reception on your right, the Peacock Restaurant, also on the first floor, and the Palm Grill on the fourth floor, please enjoy your stay with Gate House Hotels," Anthea intoned without pausing for breath.

Franklin judged that the process was over when her eyes glazed over and, thanking her briefly, he picked up his bag and made his way towards the palatial lifts.

He let himself into the room after wandering aimlessly along plush-carpeted corridors for a few minutes and was amazed to find himself in a room no bigger than the one he had left at Maisie's guest house just a few hours earlier. He peered into every corner and finally located the en suite bathroom in what he had assumed to be a second wardrobe. Fluffy towels hung from a heated rack next to the shower and a complimentary wash kit was arranged on a broad shelf behind the wash basin. The bathroom was almost as large as the bedroom.

He returned to the bedroom and read the card placed next to the television screen. Apparently, for a small charge, he could watch 'tasteful adult' movies all night. Next to the dressing table there was a small refrigerator and he opened it to find small bottles of spirits, wines and beers. He wondered briefly how much each would cost but decided that he'd earned at least one beer for putting up with the electronic grilling at the reception desk. He opened the bottle with an opener chained unobtrusively to the side of the minibar.

He moved to the bed with the drink in his hand and unpacked his clothes slowly, flicking the television on as he passed. It was the normal Sunday evening fare on the first fifteen channels he flicked through and he decided there and then that he would spend the evening in the bar before retiring, ready for his detective work due to start early the next morning. He hung his last sweatshirt in the capacious wardrobe and stowed the sports bag underneath the dressing table.

He looked around him at the relative luxury of the small room and it suddenly struck him that just a week before he had been just another teenager en route to nowhere. Somehow, in a way and by means he couldn't place let alone understand, he now had a real chance of making something of himself. It wasn't really thanks to Bill, more a response to the circumstances – but either way, his life would only stand that chance, somehow, if he could help prove Bill's innocence – and, of course, stay out of trouble himself. If he couldn't achieve both of those ends, the multifarious opportunities that now represented his future would be lost – probably irrevocably.

He smiled a little, a curiously adult, knowing smile and drained the dregs of his now warm lager. He lobbed the bottle gently into the room's bin and picked up a thick notepad bound in faux leather from the dressing table. The temptation to stow it away in the empty sports bag was initially strong but something else had changed within him. He replaced it gently on the polished surface and smiled again.

A sense of soft loneliness overcame him, and he quickly crossed to the television screen and switched it off. Grabbing the plastic key from the bedside table, he stuffed it into the back pocket of his chinos and, checking that he still had the money on him, he left the room in search of some human company.

* * * * *

"William, you're fretting again," Maisie chided him softly. She crossed the sitting room to where Bill was slumped in an armchair, turning an empty whisky tumbler around and around in his hands.

He looked up at her as she approached and smiled ruefully. "Strangely enough," he said, "It's not just worry about what happens next, it has more than a little something to do with our Franklin."

"Oh, I'm sure he can take care of himself," Maisie told him reassuringly.

"Of that, I have not the slightest iota of doubt," Bill explained, "It's just that I seem to be missing him a little. I didn't realise until he departed just how much I like the lad."

"I know what you mean," Maisie sighed.

"I really couldn't bear to think that I might not see him again – or, God in heaven and all other deities please note, that his association with me might lead him into any trouble." Bill trailed off into contemplative silence once more.

Maisie perched herself lightly on the arm of the chair and laid a hand on his shoulder, offering whatever comfort she could. When Bill's own hand left the glass and covered hers, she shivered slightly, delightedly. '*Whatever else happens,*' she thought, '*I'll do my damnedest to make sure they don't lock you away from me. If only things were different for me...*' Instead of voicing her thoughts, which she hadn't the courage to do, she simply squeezed his shoulder. "Would you like another drink, William?"

He broke his silence with a lively, "What a splendid idea. And in a short while we should take a stroll. Get some air in our lungs and all that."

"Marvellous," Maisie agreed, happy to see his normal buoyancy returning after the dolorous mood of the afternoon. She took his glass and refilled it. Returning it to him she announced that she would 'just pop upstairs and make myself pretty'.

"See you in just one second, then," Bill replied, making the lady blush and giggle in the way that so delighted him. When she left, he sipped his whisky, relishing the taste and a little easier in his mind. 'Que sera, sera,' he mentally shrugged as another thought – an alien but somehow very appealing one – came to him. 'Oh yes, William old thing,' he mused, 'What a wonderful idea...' Suddenly the planned stroll took on new meaning – as, indeed, did his wasteful life.

* * * * *

Jenny and Susan left the cinema shortly before dusk, still giggling at the antics of the digitally wonderful but artistically hilariously camp Martians.

"That was great," Jenny commented, her mood even lighter than lunchtime, "And it's definitely given me an appetite. How about a burger?"

Susan stopped in her tracks, "You? Junk food?"

"Well, why not?" Jenny shrugged, "Truth be told, I used to quite enjoy a burger now and again."

Susan laughed delightedly, "This is truly amazing," she chuckled, "What other little secrets will the new Jenny reveal?"

Jenny smiled knowingly at her, "More revelations later. Now let's go buy some cholesterol." She peered along the High Street and spotted the familiar crown of the Burger King, "Over there," she pointed.

Ten minutes later they were tucking in to a mound of fries and burgers, unwittingly mimicking Franklin, their supposed quarry, eighty miles north.

* * * * *

Gerry Cooper was far less happy, and the prospect of any food, let alone a Whopper or two, had receded into the far distance.

"Mr Cooper," DS Craig asked him for what seemed like the hundredth time, "Will you please cut all the bullshit and just tell me where the *flying fuck* Bill Taylor has holed up?"

The detective's voice grated on the re-arrested Gerry's still sensitive nerves and he winced visibly. Rather than reply verbally, he just shook his head.

Craig stared at him with open contempt ingrained in every feature. "You realise that he really did kill her?" he asked, darkly. In actual fact, the forensic team had yet to ascertain that fact and one of the squad had even gone so far as to say he was beginning to doubt it. Craig had studiously ignored this information. If he could get hold of Taylor, regardless of his guilt or innocence, it would look very good on his record when the next round of promotions came up.

Gerry sighed and looked evenly back at the sergeant, "And you say I'm full of bullshit?"

Craig gave up. He had been pounding question after question at the witness for over four hours and his throat was beginning to get very sore. In other interview rooms along the corridor a number of the people present in the Mucky Duck the previous evening had also been questioned. To a man, and in the case of the barmaid, to a woman, they had denied any knowledge. One, Richard Bates, had even gone so far as to say the only unusual thing that he had heard the previous evening was one of the police officers singing drunkenly in the corner of the pub.

He sighed and left the room, not even bothering to slam the door behind him. Dave Blake was waiting in the corridor and stood up when Craig emerged. "What has he said?"

Craig snorted. "Other than nothing at all, he just says Taylor didn't do it. How stupid can you get?"

The question was voiced in a rhetorical tone which Blake was happy about – he didn't really want to voice his own opinion which tied in very closely with Gerry Cooper's.

"What next then, sarge?"

"I suppose we might as well try letting him go again. But this time, I want him followed every second of the day and night. I want to know everything he says, everything he does, everything he even thinks!"

"Am I going to be on the team?" Blake asked hopefully.

"No point," Craig replied, "They all know you, anyway. They're hardly likely to say anything while you're hanging around." Craig stopped suddenly and looked thoughtfully at the junior officer. After a moment he asked him, "You still go along to that amateur drama nonsense with that girlfriend of yours?"

Blake shrugged, not seeing what the question had to do with the ongoing investigation into Bill Taylor's departure, "Well, after the last few days I might well be going alone, but I suppose the answer is yes."

Craig smiled, an evil smile that any self-respecting devil or demon would have been proud of. "Let's have a cup of coffee and a brief chat, shall we?"

* * * * *

Half an hour later Gerry Cooper was woken from a light sleep by the interview room door opening noisily. His headache had cleared somewhat but the return of DS Craig brought him no further comfort. The detective wandered into the room and sat himself in the chair opposite the yawning Gerry.

"Well then, Gerry," he began, "Have you anything to tell me yet?"

"I'm thirsty and I could kill for a cigarette," he replied and yawned loudly again.

"Very well,' Craig replied slowly. He rose to his feet and went to the door which he opened quickly. "Constable! Some coffee in interview room three!" he yelled.

Gerry was a little surprised in this shift in the detective's mood but held his silence.

Craig returned to the chair and produced a packet of Camel which he opened and offered to his witness, "Sorry, no Marlboro left in the machine," he commented.

Gerry accepted the proffered cigarette and held it to his lips while Craig lit it with a match. "Thanks," he muttered after taking a long satisfying drag.

Craig waved the gratitude away and began wearily going through the same old questions until a knock sounded on the door. He broke off from the latest rendition of the 'Where the hell is he?' question and yelled "Come!" with a ferocity that nearly sent Gerry slithering from his chair and Blake, outside the door struggling to maintain his grip on the tea tray.

With a silent curse Blake opened the door and entered the room precariously balancing the tray on one hand.

"Ah, refreshments!" Craig exclaimed as if he had forgotten that he had requested them earlier, "On the table, constable."

Blake crossed the room and set the tray on the small, cigarette scarred table. "Will that be all, sir?" he asked.

Craig paused a minute as if he were about to dismiss the officer and then changed his mind. "Here's a thought," he began slowly, "PC Blake. You know the suspect here, don't you?"

"Yes, sir," Blake replied, following the hastily prepared script that Craig had devised.

"You also know Bill Taylor?"

Blake nodded.

"Listen to this for a minute," Craig instructed. "Gerry, before our coffee break, let us just run through the questions once more for the benefit of PC Blake, here." With that he began to go through the monotonous routine once again.

Gerry guessed that he would at least save Dave Blake some time if he deigned to answer the questions this time round, even if they were all in the negative. He responded, often mono-syllabically, to the questions which he now knew by heart.

When Craig had run through the list he sat back and turned slightly to look at Blake, "Well, firstly, do you think Cooper is telling the truth, and secondly, do you think Taylor is guilty?"

Blake took a deep breath. Even though the next few words he was about to say were rehearsed, he still felt uncomfortable with them. "It's obvious even to me," he began and flinched as Craig spun around completely in the seat to face him directly, "Gerry here is no bullshitter, anyone can tell that just by listening." He paused as Craig rose to his feet, "And also, anyone with half a brain knows that Taylor wouldn't have topped his sister–"

Craig interrupted him savagely, "Are you standing there telling me I don't know my job?" he said threateningly.

Blake shrugged, sweat breaking out on his forehead, "I suppose if you put it like that..." he trailed off.

"Well?"

"Well, yes, I suppose so. I mean you don't really believe Gerry's lying, do you?"

"Outside!" Craig roared at him. As Blake scuttled out the detective turned back and looked at Gerry, "And don't think that just because some wet-behind-the-ears plod believes you, I should as well. I'll be back to you in a minute." He stormed out of the office and slammed the door behind him.

Gerry blinked in surprise. '*Wouldn't want to be in his shoes,*' he thought as the sound of raised voices in the corridor came to his ears. He could make out a few words and none of those exactly complimentary. He was also surprised by the contribution from the mouth of Dave Blake who sounded as if he were giving as good as he got. If anything, his voice was more powerful and more insistent than that of his superior officer.

The din continued for another minute until, finally, Dave Blake fell silent. With one final roar which announced that Blake was 'suspended until the end of the investigation' and that he should go get his clothes and 'piss off home', Craig slammed the door open and stalked into the room. His face was red, and Gerry could see incipient cardiac problems in the officer's near future.

"Right!" Craig exclaimed sitting down, panting. "Anything to add to the garbage you've already slung at me?" he demanded of Gerry.

Gerry, his headache returning, simply shook his head, unwilling to give the sergeant cause for a further outburst but powerless to stop himself. To his surprise, Craig simply shrugged.

"Well," the detective said quietly, his face a complete emotionless blank, "You might as well piss off as well. I've had quite enough of you wasting my time." Craig stood up. "As I said before, don't go anywhere without letting me know. And as I also said, don't think for a minute that I won't have Taylor, because I promise you I will."

Gerry, his head reeling from the conflicting emotions generated by the past few minutes, simply stared up at the detective.

"Well? What are you waiting for?" Craig asked him.

Dumbly, Gerry stood and, without a word, made for the door. As he departed along the corridor, Craig alone now in the interview room, smiled to himself. "Good luck, Blakey," he muttered to himself.

* * * * *

As he had done just twenty-four hours previously, when Gerry reached the relatively fresh air outside the station he paused and breathed deeply. As he was about to make his way through the gates and towards the somewhat dubious haven of the Mucky Duck, the station's door slammed open. He turned back to view the cause of the commotion. PC Dave Blake stormed through the doors.

"What's up?" Gerry asked him.

The constable looked up, seemingly surprised to see Gerry standing there. "Oh!" he exclaimed, he paused a moment before explaining, "I've just been suspended after that little outburst."

"I heard something similar," Gerry replied.

"Bloody typical," Blake moaned, "That Craig is useless."

Gerry laughed, "Now there you're not wrong," he agreed, "What are you going to do now?"

Blake shrugged, "Nothing much I can do until they catch up with Bill. Although, with a bit of luck it'll all be sorted out before they do get hold of him."

Gerry eyed the constable carefully, wondering whether he had found an ally. "Fancy a pint?" he asked him casually.

Blake looked up at him in surprise, "Well, yes. Why not? Off to the Mucky Duck?"

"Eventually," Gerry replied, "But first, I want to pop into the Green Man. There might be some work on offer."

Blake shrugged, "Ok, the Green Man it is."

The two men made their way towards the glowing sign, visible from the station, and towards a pub that both of them knew was never frequented by the police. Both were more than delighted to be on their way to such neutral territory.

When they were seated at the tiny bar, Gerry began his own interrogation, "You really don't think Bill did it, do you?"

Blake smiled, at ease for the first time in a couple of days. He shook his head, "No. No way," he replied honestly. He looked closely at his companion before continuing, "You can keep a secret, can't you?" he asked, unnecessarily. Gerry nodded. "Well," the officer continued, "I've heard word that forensic can't quite link it all together. I really am beginning to believe that Bill is somehow innocent – at least as far as the act goes."

Gerry stared back in surprise. he hadn't expected any such revelations, he was merely looking for information that might help him avoid any further silly mistakes. Somehow, some way, he had to warn Bill of what was going on. "That," he replied, "Is very interesting. But why are they still going after him?"

"That's fairly obvious," Blake explained, "Whether he committed the crime or not, Bill is a vital witness. Even if he's innocent, he must have some information which can be of help."

"So why the press release?" Gerry pressed him.

Blake laughed. "Politics. Pig-headedness. Craig's superior is not exactly flavour of the month at the minute. He has to be seen to be on top of everything or he's likely to find himself squeezed out. The release is his way of saying that everything's under control. If nothing else, it gives him some breathing space, and an operation like this, a manhunt, will also give him the budget to put a few more men on the case."

Gerry snorted in disgust, "That stinks."

"True," Blake agreed, "But these days, virtually all operations are carried on like that. I sometimes wonder while I bother."

Gerry, impressed by his candour and apparent honesty decided to risk asking Blake the question which had been uppermost in his mind since he offered the man a drink, "What do you think I should do now?"

Blake paused a moment, staring down into the dregs of his pint glass. He was torn between duty and a genuine desire to help in a case that was rapidly

211

becoming an injustice. Eventually his innate sense of justice prevailed. "Before I can risk my entire career suggesting anything that might help you to help Bill, I'll need to know just what you do know of what has happened. If you can't trust me with that, then I really can't help, and we'd better go our separate ways." It was all he could do to try to maintain the balance between his duty to the force and his duty to people.

Gerry's mind raced. If he really could trust Blake, then he could get the help he needed. If he, in turn, could then help Bill, he would be able to atone for his mistakes and also assist him in ways that Bill could not have imagined. Finally, his desire to help won through. "Fancy another?" he asked, gesturing at Blake's now empty pint glass, "This could take some time."

Three quarters of an hour later Gerry had finished telling Blake everything he knew about the previous weekend's activities, and his own part in the intervening period. He offered up a prayer to whatever deities that might be listening, that he hadn't made the most awful mistake – and waited for Blake's reactions. Throughout the narrative Blake had remained silent, although he had begun smiling and shaking his head when Gerry explained how he and Bill had discovered their stowaway.

Now, Blake laughed. "Good God!" he exclaimed, "That's quite some tale."

"All true, I assure you," Gerry told him.

Blake nodded, "Of that I'm in no doubt. But there's quite an amazing coincidence going on here."

Gerry looked at him quizzically, "Such as?"

"This morning," Blake explained, "I had a telephone call from my aunt down in Southampton. Seems she was visited yesterday afternoon by Jenny Thomsett and her girlfriend. They were looking for a young tearaway."

"Your aunt?" Gerry exclaimed in surprise.

"That's right. Kathleen Blake. She used to work for the social services around this way. She retired to the coast a few years ago. Quite a tartar, but a lovely old girl."

"And it was me that sent them off after Franklin in the first place," Gerry said slowly. "You're right, that is some coincidence."

"Something else springs to mind," Blake mused, "If Bill is still with this Franklin lad, and by the sound of it I hope he is for his sake, then they'd be quite an easy couple to spot. That sort of information should definitely not become public knowledge."

Gerry nodded eagerly, "But what else can we do to help?"

Blake sighed. He was fairly sure that he, himself, would be under surveillance of some sort, and any overt actions by either him or Gerry would soon be recognised for what they were. An idea began to form in his mind. "What do you know of this Jenny Thomsett and her mate?" he asked Gerry.

Gerry shrugged, unsure where the question would lead. "Nice enough couple I suppose," he replied, "Jenny sounds as if she'll be like your aunt in a few years, but Susan's really nice."

"Are they really committed to their work, do you think?" Blake persisted.

Gerry shrugged again, "They're always going on about it and I suppose you could say that if they took the trouble of going all the way to Southampton to look for a runaway on the most dubious of leads, they must be pretty much committed."

"That's what I was thinking," Blake agreed. "If we can't do anything too obvious to help Bill and Franklin, then how about them? After all, no-one seems to know that Bill and Franklin are together, the girls know both of them, no-one will suspect if Jenny or her friend go off to Norfolk for a day or two. If anyone does notice, they'll simply think that they've gone off in search of the runaway." He stopped triumphantly.

Gerry stared back at him impressed. "You just might have something there," he mused, "But how do we get in touch with them? I don't remember where they live, and it might be a bit awkward going in to their office – we'll be seen. Besides, can we wait 'til tomorrow?"

Blake laughed. "No need. Aunt Kathleen said they were staying on for the rest of the weekend in some hotel and that she was to call them if Franklin showed up." He reached into his pocket for his mobile. "I'll call my aunt, get her to call them, and she can ask them to call here. Simple – and no-one is going to be any the wiser."

"That's it!" Gerry exclaimed, his optimism rising for the first time since his arrest at the cash point the previous morning. "Get to it."

Blake clapped him on the shoulder and quickly scrolled through the contacts on his phone. Five minutes later he rang off happily. "Settled," he said, "Aunt Kathleen was her usual self, wanting to know all the ins and outs of what was going on, but I just said that we'd had some news about Franklin back here and needed to speak to the girls to confirm a few details. When I mentioned Franklin, she got all professional and said she'd do it straight away. Now all we have to do is wait. Another pint?"

Gerry shook his head in admiration. "That's great. And yes please."

The mobile rang less than five minutes later, and Blake snatched it up. Gerry watched on and tried to work out how the discussion was going. Occasionally Blake rolled his eyes, once he laughed, but generally he simply talked rapidly. When he nodded once, vigorously, and then pressed the 'end call' button, Gerry realised that he'd been holding his breath, "Well?"

"Seems we have doubled the number of people willing to help. They're coming back tonight," Blake replied happily.

"That's great!" Gerry exclaimed, "But how are we going to work this? I mean, how are we going to meet up with them, or whatever? If we're being followed..."

Blake held up his hand to interrupt him, "Simple. You and I are going to take a short taxi ride. That should shake off anyone following us. After that, we'll travel to Victoria and meet them at the station. We should be there by nine-thirty," he continued glancing at his watch, "And we'll sort out the rest from there."

Gerry sighed contentedly and leant back on his stool. "That's marvellous. One for the road?" he asked, before downing the remains of his pint.

"We've earned it," Blake agreed.

* * * * *

Dave Phillips stood snuffling on the platform at Southampton's railway station and sipped at the weak mug of coffee he had purchased in the Traveller's Fare. He glanced up at the station's digital clock and groaned aloud when he realised that the train was now twenty minutes late. He sneezed violently and slopped scalding coffee over his hand. Cursing he cast the polystyrene beaker into a nearby litter bin and begun pacing the platform once more.

214

A couple of minutes later a nearly unintelligible public address system informed him – probably – that the train would be arriving in two minutes. He stared up at a loudspeaker above his head and laughed mirthlessly – it was the fourth time he had been told that in the past twenty minutes. He was still staring at the infernal object when the thrumming of the tracks beside him alerted him to the approach of the promised train. He turned and watched it pull smoothly into the station. As the doors opened, he sighed in contentment and bustled aboard in search of a nice quiet corner where he could doze his way back to London. At least in this direction he didn't have to worry about missing his stop – the train terminated at Victoria and he was moderately sure that a passing guard would wake him if he was still aboard ten minutes after it arrived.

The alarm buzzer sounded shortly afterwards, indicating that the train was ready to leave, and the doors were about to close, when he was disturbed by a commotion behind him. A loud thud as a heavy bag was thrown into the carriage made him sit up and look round. Two women, gasping for breath, followed the bag into the train and collapsed against the back of his seat. He stared dumbly at them for a few seconds before hurriedly turning around so that they couldn't see his face. '*Good God*,' he thought, almost in despair, '*It's that bloody pair again!*'

* * * * *

"Thank God we made it," Jenny gasped when she had got her breath back.

"Yes," Susan agreed without enthusiasm. They had argued a little about cutting short their weekend away after Miss Blake's telephone call about Franklin, the subsequent call to her nephew, the policeman, and Jenny's assurances that they would have a whole week away when she had finally sorted out the runaway weren't as believable as they might have been. It wasn't that Susan doubted the change in Jenny – it was just too much to hope for.

Jenny picked up the heavy bag and, still panting, made her way along the near empty carriage until she found a seat to her liking. Susan followed her and announced that she would go in search of the buffet car for some drinks.

"Good idea," Jenny said, "I've got a feeling that this could be a long night."

"Me too," Susan grumbled, leaving Jenny to recover her breath.

Jenny didn't mind Susan's somewhat negative response. It wasn't her fault that she didn't realise just how much this meant to her, and besides, the quicker she could get this sorted out, the sooner they would be able to concentrate on the important things in life. She settled back in her seat and replayed the conversation with Dave Blake. That Franklin had fallen in with a possible murderer somehow didn't surprise her. But, there again, she didn't believe for a minute that Bill Taylor was guilty. Taylor might even be a good influence on the lad, she mused, and smiled to herself. She had been a little concerned at first by the idea of potentially helping a wanted man, but, as Susan had so sensibly pointed out, she wasn't really going to be helping Bill as such – simply going to the aid of one of her wards. If Bill Taylor happened to be there... Well, how was she to know?

She was still grinning happily to herself, satisfied that things were working themselves out so quickly, when Susan returned bearing a large brown paper bag bulging with liquid goodies. "Thought you'd got lost," she teased.

Susan grinned despite herself, "This new you is definitely going to take a lot of getting used to."

* * * * *

Bill and Maisie stepped from the front door of her guesthouse and paused a moment, watching the last of the day seep gently out of the sky.

"Do you realise, my dear Maisie," Bill commented, "that this is the first time we have been outside the house together?"

Maisie laughed gently, "I'm very aware of that, William. It feels nice."

Bill turned and looked at her earnest features. "An understatement, I am sure. To me it feels as if we're taking a far larger step than the few inches to your driveway. A veritable leap for Bill-kind."

Maisie looked back at him and grinned shyly, "You're making a mature lady very happy, William."

"Not so old, at that. But I'm really very pleased. The feeling, as they so rightly say, is mutual – even if the gender is wrong."

216

She laughed again, "Shall we promenade?"

"If you can bear to be seen in the company of such a one as myself, I would be delighted to take your arm." Bill replied, offering her his crooked limb.

Maisie ignored it and groped for his hand, taking Bill a little by surprise, "Let's walk," she suggested, quietly.

Bill smiled at her and they began strolling gently into the twilight. As they walked, they said little, a comment here about the bird calls, a remark there as Maisie spotted a neighbour. They paused for a while at the very stile that Franklin had climbed on their first evening in Wroxham and stared across the fields beyond.

"I wonder where I shall be a week from now," Bill mused, "Of course, I am unable to answer that question but all I do know is that if I'm not to have you by my side, then I shall be all the poorer for it."

"That's lovely," Maisie sighed happily, "And if I have anything to do with it, I'll definitely be here for you."

Bill stopped walking and stood quietly for a moment, apparently admiring the view. Maisie halted her own progress and stilled herself, a slightly puzzled frown appearing above the top of her spectacles.

"William, is anything wr– "

"Maisie, my wonderful lady, let me think for a moment." His interruption was gentle but firm enough to quieten the curious woman by his side.

He stood in silence for a full minute before he said, "I'm about to say some things that may sound strange and even alien to my own ears but please – a very serious request – hear me out before you say a word in response."

Maisie shrugged before nodding firmly.

"It's been just a week, I am well aware," Bill continued, "and to say the circumstances are far from, shall we say *normal*, is litotes of the highest order. When, though, you say that if you have anything to do with things then you shall be here for me, well that really does make this ageing heart soar." He paused and took a deep breath, "Everything about you seems to have said organ soaring, in truth, and that is why – regardless of the brevity of our knowledge of each other, contrary to these dire circumstances... in fact, in the face of all of these adversities, true or merely feared – I want to declare to you right at this very instant... that... I can only see a future featuring you at my side."

He turned to face her, "Maisie Baxter, would you do me the greatest honour by pledging yourself to me, as I would delight in pledging myself to you. In more common parlance, would you marry me, Maisie Baxter?"

Maisie had turned to face Bill and now her jaw dropped. The affirmative word almost tumbled from her lips before tears welled in her eyes and she swivelled away taking a single step before stopping, her shoulders now shuddering.

"Maisie?" His voice full of concern, Bill stood behind her, unsure of what to do, uncertain of what to say, "I had no desire to upset you in any way," he tried, "Could you, might you, explain what I have said to so cause you grief? My words were true and honest, but I never intended hurt in any form..."

She span back to face him then, the misery replaced by anger, "Well they do hurt, William! And you don't and never will understand why!"

His unflappable calm washed through him, "Maisie, my angel, elucidate. I may be a whisky-sodden fool in the eyes of many, but I assure you my levels of understanding have remarkable bounds."

"Do they really?" her uncharacteristic demeanour persisted, "Then see if you can 'understand' just how much it hurts me to be forced to say no to you!"

"Forced?" he remained the epitome of calm.

"Precisely that, yes. I can't marry you no matter if I want to!"

His expression deliberately blank, he said, "And what stops you?"

She stared into his eyes for fully ten seconds before her shoulders slumped and the quiet, reserved Maisie took back her place, "William, you don't want to burden yourself with me no matter what you might believe. I have a medical condition, one that will worsen over time, one that will prevent me from being the partner you deserve, one that–"

Her jaw almost hit the ground at her feet when he shrugged and said, "The MS?"

"What... how did you... who told...?"

Bill let out a soft laugh, "I may not be neurosurgeon, Maisie, but I'm learned in many ways, and I watch people. You have spells when you... drop things that seem to be firmly in your grasp. There are times when you tire so easily and others when you are so full of life. Whether you know it or not, you massage a constant pressure around your diaphragm. And yes, I couldn't be sure of such a condition in so short a space of time, but it seemed to fit best with your symptoms, and it one that is not unknown to me." He reached for one of her hands as she remained open-mouthed before him, "I knew there was something awry, dear Maisie, but my request was made with that uncertain knowledge in mind. Now that your condition is fully known to me, I will ask you again. Maisie Baxter, will you – you with your multiple sclerosis – marry me?"

It was almost too much for Maisie to take in, and something deep inside her was trying to lay every obstacle it could find in her path, "You live in London, though..."

"When this whole horrid business is done and dusted, my dear, I intend to move to somewhere quieter – such as Wroxham. Undoubtedly there will be times when I find need of the Capital in one form or another, and perchance I have an inkling of a plan involving your Franklin one day – but that is for then and not now." He turned and stared across the dim landscape, "I crave all of this more and I crave your company yet further."

"But the MS..."

"A horrible beast, I'm aware, but it will never change the essential you, Maisie, my dear lady. This proposal, I assure you with every fibre of my mortal being, is not in any way born of sympathy and I am aware of what the future may bring – and will hang true to the matrimonial vows. I have not considered this lightly or without reality of thought. Now, please say yes, will you do that for me?"

Still staring at the fields, Maisie's mind raced – but in one direction only now. "Yes, William. Oh my goodness, yes!"

They turned and embraced for a moment, clumsy at first, and then more certainly. A car passed them by, headlights piercing the growing dark, and they parted slowly staring intently into each other's eyes.

"A truly remarkable lady," Bill whispered softly, "To melt a man's heart such as this."

Maisie's pulse raced, and she shivered involuntarily, "And a quite remarkable man," she whispered in reply.

Bill mistook the shiver for a temperature-induced reaction and quickly took off his jacket and wrapped it around Maisie's shoulders. "Make that, a quite remarkable *gentleman*," Maisie laughed, unwilling to tell him that she was quite warm enough.

"Let us wander into the village," Bill suggested, "I suddenly have an unshakeable desire to be seen with you on my arm."

"Not to mention," Maisie teased him, "An unshakeable thirst, no doubt?"

Bill laughed loudly, "My little angel," he said, "There's a phrase I have used to describe the young Franklin which seems just as fitting when used to describe yourself. You are very perspicacious."

Maisie laughed too, "Thank you, kind sir," she replied, imitating his cultured accent, "Now let's go before you freeze."

They strolled briskly into the village, Bill trying not to shiver too noticeably, and arrived at the pub where he had spent the previous evening with Franklin. "Shall we?" he suggested, pointing to the still-boarded doorway.

"Why not?" she replied, "It must be more than a year since I've seen old George at work."

Bill led her to the door and made a great show of opening it for her. He followed her in to the noticeably warm and friendly interior to find the rotund landlord bearing down on Maisie at a remarkable and somewhat alarming speed.

"Maisie!" the large man boomed, "So nice to see you. Come in, come in! And Tom! What a sight to please the eye."

Maisie laughed, "Enough, George, you'll frighten us away."

"Good evening to you, George," Bill greeted him, "My usual, please, whatever my dear Maisie would like and, of course, a drink for your good self."

George hugged Maisie briefly, Bill surprised that he didn't hear the sound of bones cracking, and then hurried back to the bar to dispense Bill's order. "'My dear Maisie', is it?" George grinned at them.

Maisie blushed deeply, and Bill laughed. He glanced quickly at Maisie and she nodded almost imperceptibly. "Most certainly," he said, interpreting the gesture, "I appear to have been bewitched by her magic charms. A most unusual thing but not so unusual that I cannot announce here and now our betrothal."

George looked on delightedly, "Now that," he said in his broad accent, "Is the best news I've had all this cursed weekend. Have these on me," he added, passing Bill a large whisky and Maisie a sherry which he evidently knew to be her preferred tipple.

Bill tried to protest but surrendered in the face of George's joy. "Many, many thanks, George," He sipped at the warming liquid, grateful for the gentle burn that radiated from his mouth to his stomach.

"Wonderful news, indeed," a voice behind them added.

Maisie and Bill looked around, surprised that they hadn't noticed anyone else during their entrance, "Oh, it's you George!" Maisie exclaimed.

Sitting behind them in the furthest corner, Maisie's brother, out of uniform, was grinning at the scene, "Evenin', sis, evenin' Tom," he greeted them.

"Good evening, Sergeant," Bill replied, trying hard to suppress a sudden feeling of unease in the policeman's presence.

"Call me George," he replied, standing and joining them. "since it seems I am to be your in-law! Nice to see you out and about, sis."

"You can thank B... Tom for that," Maisie replied, a little flustered.

"And thank him I most certainly do," her brother laughed, "Let me buy you both a drink before I get on home."

Bill tried in vain to protest once more, but eventually relented. "Thank you most kindly, George. And I promise I'll not keep your delightful sister out too long – or lead her into bad habits."

George Baxter laughed long and loud. "Bad habits? After all those tales she told you about me yesterday, I still haven't had a chance to tell you a few things that my little sis, here, used to get up to. Real wild child, this one," he began.

"George!" Maisie protested, blushing once more.

"I'd better let her tell you herself," George teased, "My dinner's about ready and it'd take hours to tell you all about her wild ways."

"Are you sure you can't stay?" Bill enquired, joining in the teasing, "I'm fascinated to learn all I can about Maisie's chequered past."

Maisie batted him playfully around the ear, "Enough! Both of you. And you've no right to go misleading him about my past," this latter to George who was laughing at the by-play.

"Sorry, sis," he replied with as much sincerity as he could manage, "Anyway, that's cheered me up no end. It's a shame, but I really 'ad better be going." He picked up a dark green jacket from the back of a chair and bade everyone 'goodnight' before disappearing into the darkness.

"You realise that this will be all around the village by noon tomorrow, don't you?" she asked Bill with a half-smile.

"Undoubtedly," Bill replied, "Does it concern you?"

She looked long and hard at him before smiling broadly. "Not at all," she answered softly, "Not at all."

They stayed in the pub for another hour, chatting happily and getting used to being the centre of attention as the landlord informed every new customer of their burgeoning relationship and forthcoming nuptials. When George finally called time, they left and strolled back to the guest house chatting animatedly about cooking techniques.

Maisie let them in and then hurried to stoke the embers of the fire which still glowed in the sitting room's massive fireplace. Bill fetched the whisky bottle for himself and the sherry bottle for Maisie and they settled down together on the sofa, taking pleasure from each other and the flames dancing merrily before them. At one o'clock Maisie fidgeted against Bill and he looked down at her upturned face. It appeared red, but he couldn't decide whether that was just a reflection of the fire or something else.

She yawned gently and was about to speak but closed her mouth quickly.

"What?" Bill asked softly.

Maisie looked away from him and spoke rapidly, one hand tugging at her blonde tresses, "It's just that I'm tired and want to go up now," she paused and then plunged on, "And I feel so happy and I don't really want to be alone tonight, and I don't want to make you think bad of me and..."

Bill reached down and gently turned her face towards him, quietening her flow. He leant forward slightly and gently kissed her. "I've been sitting here for half an hour wondering whether I could ask you and if so, *how* I could ask you. More than anything else in the world, I'd love to share a night with you. In fact, many nights as you well know. You are the most remarkably wonderful women I can ever recall meeting, my dear Maisie," he paused and gently kissed her upturned nose before continuing, "I can tell you right now something I thought I'd never want to say to anyone. Maisie, I have, without a shadow of doubt, fallen helplessly for you. I love you, my sweet angel. It's the kernel of my proposal, the seed of my need, shall we say? I simply love you."

Maisie smiled, shivering. "Oh, William," she sighed, "And I you." She gestured towards the stairs. "Shall we?" she asked.

Bill nodded, and they set their glasses down and went upstairs together hand-in-hand.

Chapter 12

Monday 16th June 2014

Franklin awoke to the warbling of the telephone on his bedside table. Yawning hugely, he fumbled for the handset and dragged it underneath the bedclothes where his head still lay submerged on his pillow. "Yes?" he mumbled.

"Good morning, sir," an unnaturally cheerful voice said, "It's half past five and this is your early morning alarm call. Will you require a further call, sir?"

"Thanks, and, er, no thanks," Franklin replied, his sleep-befuddled mind working the question out slowly. He heard the click as the caller replaced the receiver without a further word and fumbled around until he managed to replace his own.

Still yawning, he pulled back the bedclothes and flicked on the bedside lamp, flinching and closing his eyes again as the light penetrated his brain. He sat up and slowly opened his eyes. He glanced at the clock, it's digital display confirming that it really was some godforsaken pre-dawn (ish) hour and yawned yet again. Despite turning in early the previous evening, he felt as if he could sleep for another week at least and swung his legs out of the bed before his head decided to replace itself on the soft, warm and highly inviting pillows.

He showered slowly and dressed in dirty jeans and a clean sweatshirt in preparation for the disguise he might need later in the day, and then wandered down to the breakfast room. In spite of the vast volumes of food he had consumed the previous day, he was surprised to find himself ravenous and ordered a full English breakfast after first pleading for the waitress to bring him some coffee – 'strong enough so the spoon stands up in it'.

He had collected two newspapers on his way to his table and pored through them while waiting for the breakfast to materialise. The Telegraph didn't appear to have followed up the article from the previous day, but the Daily Mirror, in its normal sensationalistic style, carried four column inches under the headline 'The Sibling Murder – Massive Manhunt Under Way in Brighton'. The rest of the article carried more information about 'South Coast

Murderers' than it did about the case in question and Franklin was pleased to see that they, too, had used the blurred print that had appeared the previous day.

Franklin guessed that the pattern would be repeated in the other tabloids and prayed that he would be able to get somewhere before a particularly diligent reporter dug up any more information. All in all, he felt that a reporter was far more likely to locate Bill than any policeman.

His breakfast arrived, and he demolished the somewhat meagre fare in a few short minutes. '*They*,' he thought, '*could take a good few lessons from our Maisie.*'

When he had finished the last dregs of his coffee he returned to his room and gathered together the various pieces of paper bearing the addresses that he would be visiting. He left his key-card at the reception desk and wandered out into the chill morning air, pulling his jacket closer around him.

A taxi rank stood before him, most of the drivers sipping coffee from polystyrene beakers, newspapers spread across their steering wheels. He approached the foremost vehicle and tapped gently on the window. The driver stared around at him and gave him a weary wave, indicating that he should climb aboard. Once inside he told the driver the road he wanted him to take him to and settled back trying to ignore the grumbling emanating from the front of the cab.

The journey, along relatively empty London streets, still took a good fifteen minutes and he was deposited on the corner of Courteney Road in a light drizzle and with the comment 'Thanks a bunch' after he had given the driver a fifty-pence tip.

He looked down for the fourth time at the address on the sheet of paper. According to it, Jarvis lived at number eleven, and he peered across at the nearest house. '*Typical*,' he thought when he saw that it was number two hundred and forty-eight. He was even on the wrong side of the road. He *could* have given the taxi driver the exact postcode but of course hadn't wanted to be too obvious. Surely, he was taking 'being careful' too far now?

He crossed quickly and walked along, head down, occasionally glancing to his right to determine how far he still had to go before he reached the correct property. He glanced at his watch and was surprised to find that it was nearly eight o'clock – he had intended to be in place at least half an hour earlier. He increased his pace and quickly checked the number of the house he was passing – fifteen. As he looked forward to the property that he was his destination, the front door opened. He stopped in his tracks, unsure what to do, and waited.

A figure emerged, hunched in a large raincoat, and fumbled the door closed before double locking it. The man glanced quickly around him but seemed not to notice the young black man standing in the middle of the pavement no more than ten metres away. He put the keys into his jacket pocket and buttoned the overcoat before making his way quickly down the front path to his gate.

"Oh, well. Here goes," Franklin muttered aloud and walked towards his quarry.

The man was fumbling with the latch on the gate when Franklin tapped him on the shoulder, "Excuse me," Franklin said, making him jump.

The man spun round and stared wildly at Franklin, "Y... yes?" he stammered.

"Jarvis?" Franklin asked, "'Mr Paul Jarvis?"

"Er, yes," Jarvis replied, "I mean, that depends."

Franklin snorted a laugh.

"What do you want?" Jarvis asked him nervously, "Are you a policeman?"

The question intrigued Franklin. Why was this man expecting a policeman to call? He decided that the question might well prove to be very important but decided to ignore it for now. At least he must look old enough... "I'm not a policeman," Franklin assured him, "But I would like to ask you a few questions."

"Who sent you?" the frightened Jarvis demanded querulously.

"No," Franklin intoned slowly, "*I* want to ask *you* some questions." The man looked blankly at him as if Franklin were speaking in Swahili. "About the church?"

Recognition dawned on Jarvis's face before he quickly drew a veil over his features. "What church?" he asked Franklin in mock innocence.

Franklin sighed as if disappointed by a recalcitrant child. He could see that Jarvis was scared and decided to play things a little heavily. "Mr Jarvis," he began darkly, "I'm not here to play games. Let's go and talk somewhere quietly."

Jarvis flinched from the tone and then his shoulders slumped. He had spent the weekend expecting a call from the police or from Brother Jacob and had hardly slept a wink. During the darkest hours of the previous morning he had almost decided to admit everything if the police did call on him – but the thought of Brother Jacob and his strange ways of finding things out had pushed the idea from his mind. This young man, a hulking black youth who reminded him of every young heavy portrayed on the silver screen, was obviously from neither camp. He didn't appear to have much of a choice and a little flicker of hope began to glow inside him. Perhaps there was some protection to be had from him at the very least – perhaps even a little help.

"Very well then," he replied in resignation. "Where do you suggest?"

Franklin was a little surprised to find that his hard man act had apparently produced the desired result, and quickly replayed the loosely planned response before replying, "I'm staying in a hotel in the City. We can talk safely there."

Jarvis shrugged. What did he have to lose? When Franklin asked him where the best place to hail a cab would be around here, he pointed to the main road at the end of the street.

"Come on then, Jarvis. We've got a lot of things to discuss," Franklin told him and pushed him into motion.

They reached the end of the street and spent five minutes trying to stop the passing cabs, most full of businessmen on their way into town. Just as Franklin was beginning to despair, a familiar black shape pulled up to the curb.

"Where to gents?" the driver called cheerfully.

Franklin gave him the name of the hotel and tried to ignore the knowing smile the cabby gave him. They climbed into the taxi unaware of the Peugeot 308 that followed them into the rush hour traffic.

* * * * *

Jenny awoke to unfamiliar surroundings and took a full minute to recognise the interior of yet another hotel room. Beside her, Susan lay on her back snoring gently, a pillow covering the top half of her face.

After they had arrived at Victoria Station the previous night they had met up with Gerry Cooper and the policeman, David Blake, and had retreated to a nearby public house to discuss matters. They were gently but firmly thrown out a few minutes later, Gerry cursing the 'ludicrous' interpretations of the licensing laws that some pubs followed, and had decided, for safety reasons to book into one of the many hotels in the area. Here, they had met up again in the room Blake and Cooper were to share and the two men related the events of the previous week.

When they had finished, Blake, who had essentially chaired the discussion, asked Jenny and Susan what they thought. Susan, characteristically, remained silent while Jenny asked a few more questions. When they had been answered to her satisfaction, she reached her decision.

"We've got to help them," she said simply and looked at Susan to see her reaction.

"Most unlike you it may be," Susan had replied, "But it's the only choice. Especially if you really are just going to help sort out Franklin and then quit."

The comment brought a barrage of questions from Gerry and Dave, and Jenny was forced to explain her decision.

"Hope you didn't tell my aunt that," Dave remarked.

Jenny laughed, "No," she replied, "I'm not sure she would have approved."

"But I'm sure she would have approved of our helping out this way," Susan added.

Between them, the four decided that it would be best to try to contact Bill and Franklin by telephone, and Blake said he was sure that he could find out what the number was using his contacts, given that Gerry knew the address. It was generally agreed that Gerry should make the first call, since he was likely to get a far better reception from Bill than Jenny would from Franklin.

By the time their initial plans were laid it was nearly two-thirty in the morning and they decided to postpone any activity until they had all had a few hours' sleep. Dave was worried, privately, that Craig would be missing him, and suspected that his superior was already striving to locate himself and Gerry. He shelved his concerns – if this turned out as he suspected, he could always cobble together some story to cover his back.

They arranged to meet up at breakfast by about half past seven, and Jenny and Susan had returned to their room, Jenny feeling suddenly exhausted. They had undressed quickly and set their mobile phone alarms for six-thirty.

Jenny rolled over and looked at the bedside table. The clock there read seven fifteen. Groaning she rolled back and shook Susan gently awake. "We're late," she explained when Susan registered a few signs of awareness.

"Oh goody," Susan moaned, struggling to get back to sleep.

Jenny slid a cool hand down Susan's belly and between her thighs. Susan squirmed. "No fair," she complained, but struggled awake once again.

Jenny, tired herself, sympathised, "I know, I know. But we really must get going. If we're going to be any help, I get the impression we should start soon. It can't be long before we'll be too late."

Susan yawned and stretched, "Since when were you the practical one?" she asked, smiling up at Jenny.

"Since you got to be the lazy one," Jenny grinned back. She slapped Susan's bared thigh lightly and swung herself out of the bed. She went quickly to the bathroom and appeared less than five minutes later fully dressed, if a little damp around the edges.

"I saved the biggest towel for you," she explained as she dripped her way around the room.

"You're *so* kind," Susan replied shuffling into the tiny bathroom.

When Susan re-appeared, Jenny hustled her down to the breakfast lounge-cum-bar and joined the two men at a large table where they were poring through the day's news sites on their phones.

"Morning, guys. Any news?" Jenny greeted them.

"Hi girls," Gerry replied, "Nothing much. What will you have, we've already ordered?"

Jenny opted for the full breakfast and Susan, her eyebrows still raised at this sudden increase in Jenny's appetite, ordered toast and 'several gallons of caffeine'.

All four of them seemed pre-occupied throughout the meal and spent their time smearing their fingerprints over their mobile screens. When Susan had drained the last of the coffee from the third pot, she pronounced herself ready for action.

"Ok then, Dave," Gerry remarked, "It's over to you. Let's have that number."

Blake nodded and left the table in search of the receptionist with his warrant card in his hand. The remaining three chatted easily while he was gone, mainly about the coincidences that had brought them together in a fairly tatty West End hotel. When Dave returned a few minutes later, they were laughing happily and each of them felt ready for the coming day.

The policeman handed Gerry a piece of paper. "That," he explained, "is the number. Let's get to it."

The four of them rose and went upstairs together to the men's room where Gerry was to make the call.

*****

Bill awoke to the most unfamiliar of sensations. He was curled on his side facing the window and in his arms Maisie was stirring as the sound of the milkman who had woken Bill retreated along the drive below the window.

"Good morning, dear lady," Bill whispered into her ear.

Maisie woke with a little start, "Oh, William, it's you," she mumbled sleepily.

"Whoever did you think?" he teased her.

Maisie came fully awake and rolled over to face him. She smiled happily. "Only you," she replied, and kissed him lightly.

Bill chuckled, as content as he could ever remember being. "I hate to break this cosy moment," he said, "But it is nearly six-thirty and we really should be up and ready for Franklin's telephone call."

Maisie sighed at him, contentment radiating from every pore, "Very true," she replied, "But a shame."

Bill chuckled again and, with a final kiss, disentangled himself from both Maisie and the bedclothes. He swung himself out of bed feeling younger than he had for many a year and donned his dressing gown before virtually skipping along to the bathroom.

When he reappeared a few minutes later, Maisie was dressed and was drying her hair with a hand towel, her glasses perched precariously on the very tip of her nose. "Ah lovely lady," he beamed, "A sight I wish to see many more times whilst I shuffle along this mortal coil. May I prepare you some breakfast?"

Maisie giggled, "Why, thank you, William. And yes, you may. I'll be down to help you in a moment or two. Must make myself pretty for you, mustn't I?"

"You, my dear," Bill replied courteously, "Could never look prettier." With the delicate sound of Maisie's laughter ringing in his ears, he descended to the kitchen and began the preparations by brewing coffee.

Maisie joined him a few minutes later and they dined at leisure, both of them poring through the daily newspapers and finding the same story that Franklin had found a little earlier and a lot further south.

It was eight o'clock before they rose and washed up the breakfast things and then retreated to the sitting room once more to await news from the lad. Bill was a little restless, but passed the time filling in crosswords and scanning the previous day's Sunday Supplements. Maisie read the Times from cover to cover and occasionally glanced at the clock.

At around nine o'clock Maisie suggested that they have a coffee and Bill agreed, happy to have something mundane to concentrate his mind on even if only for a few seconds. It was while Maisie was in the kitchen preparing their drinks that the telephone rang.

* * * * *

Jenny, Susan and Dave crowded around Gerry as he dialled the number and waited for the reply. He misdialled for a second time and held the mobile away from his ear as an irate voice explained that not everyone worked day shifts.

On the third attempt the telephone at the other end rang at least eight times before a quiet, feminine voice said, "Hello, Rose Arbour guest house."

Gerry smiled and gave the thumbs up to the spectators, then switching on the speakerphone. 'Hi,' he began in a friendly voice, "May I speak to Tom?" He felt relieved that he had remembered to use the alias Bill had decided on.

He paused, listening with growing alarm to the voice at the other end, "But I'm sure he's there," he said, "Tell him that this is Gerry. Gerry Cooper. It's really very important that I speak to him." He glanced round at the others and shrugged as they once more listened to the woman's voice.

"Look," he said eventually, exasperation creeping into his tone, "I know he's there. He's with – or at least was with – a young black lad by the name of..." he paused for a second trying to remember if Bill had told him the alias that Franklin was using, and then in desperation said "Franklin." He held his breath and listened to the woman for a few seconds.

Suddenly he spun round and faced the others. Quickly covering the mouthpiece, he said, somewhat unnecessarily, "He's there. She's just going to get him for me. And," he said meaningfully, "She just called out 'William', I heard her in the background – didn't you all hear that too?' he broke off his narrative as a familiar voice spoke into his ear.

"Gerald, dear boy! What's afoot?"

"Bill! How are you? What's going on?"

Gerry listened in silence for a while as Bill told him of the events of the previous few days as succinctly as he could. "Good God!" Gerry exclaimed when Bill had finished, "And you trust her?"

He nodded and half-shrugged at the affirmative reply before Jenny interrupted, asking about Franklin. Gerry asked if Bill had heard the social worker.

"He's fine," Gerry translated Bill's long response, then began to explain their own situation to Bill. He told him what he knew of the police involvement and that Dave Blake was currently helping them in any way he could, he related the involvement of Jenny and Susan, and finally he explained what they were going to try to do to help – which in truth amounted to very little other than offering support and information.

He fell silent as Bill explained how the investigations were going from their end and whistled in admiration when he heard how the three of them had made contact with the mysterious church. After a few minutes he nodded at

232

the phone and said, "Ok then, Bill. Call me or Dave or Jenny when you hear from him, and in the meantime, take care." He gave Bill both Dave Blake's and Jenny Thomsett's numbers before finally ending the call.

"Well, I think we can certainly help the lad out for starters," he said letting out a long breath, "Do you need me to find out where the hotel is that Franklin's staying–"

"Yes," Jenny interrupted. "I've got a map here on my phone. Let's go."

Gerry shook his head, "No, not yet. You heard them – they're waiting for Franklin to call them with any news. For all any of us know he could still be sat outside the guy's house or his office or whatever. Bill will call us when he hears from him, tell him that we're available and all that, and we'll work out the next move from there."

Blake nodded in agreement, "Seems sensible."

Jenny was less sure, "What if the boy's out of his depth? Surely one or two of us can at least go over there and see if he is about and if he needs any help know?"

Gerry thought for a moment and then shook his head again, "According to their plan he won't be there anyway. He's going to call Bill as soon as he gets back. As soon as Bill knows, we'll know."

When they had eventually reached a unanimous decision to stay where they were Gerry suggested coffees all round and Susan was dispatched to the reception to order them – they didn't want to even tie up the hotel phone for a second.

* * * * *

By the time Franklin had regained the sanctuary of his room, he had become quite used to the knowing – but wrong, so wrong – stares of other members of the public. He opened the door with the plastic key and let Jarvis into the room, wondering if the taciturn guy would ever say another word. On the cab ride back to the hotel the man had said nothing and at times had even appeared ready to throw himself out of the vehicle and into the path of any passing double-decker bus. Franklin had begun to think that the man really must have something very dark and secret locked away within his mind and was torn between optimism and despair. It seemed as if it was going to be a question of whether the guy would reveal all first or top himself.

With the door shut and locked behind him, Franklin faced the dissolute character standing miserably by the bed. "Sit down," he suggested.

Jarvis responded by slumping onto the bed covers and staring back at him with a look more closely associated with rabbits and headlights. Franklin felt completely out of his depth but decided that he was probably still in far more control than the hapless individual currently awaiting his forthcoming interrogation. "Coffee?" he asked, his own mouth dry with anxiety and tension.

Jarvis nodded, seemingly a little surprised at the civilised hospitality on offer. "Er, black, please, no sugar. And, er, no offense!"

Franklin crossed to the kettle on the dressing table, switched it on after checking the water level and set up the cups. He also switched on the recording function of a small burner phone in his jeans' pocket that Maisie had somehow found and made him carry to this meet – although he seriously doubted that it would pick up the voices clearly enough. *Where was he to start*? He watched the man out of the corner of his eye as he prepared the drinks and decided that he really had nothing to lose. Jarvis had retreated into a docile state and seemed determined to stay there. Franklin wondered whether he should call Maisie and ask her to conduct the interrogation, but a spark of personal pride prevented him. In a way that he couldn't quite comprehend, he felt that he owed Bill Taylor something, and here, on the bed, was an opportunity to pay back that elusive something.

The kettle boiled and Franklin, with deliberate slowness, poured the steaming water into the cups and stirred them thoughtfully. His stomach appeared full of butterflies and he tried to ignore the feeling of nervousness that seemed so out of place in the circumstances. "Here you go, man," he said, offering Jarvis one of the cups.

Jarvis took it without meeting Franklin's eyes and mumbled a quiet 'thank you'.

Franklin drew up the room's only chair and set it beside the dressing table, facing the bed and his 'captive'. He stared at the man and frantically racked his brain for a good starting point.

Jarvis stirred and looked up at him. "Are you sure you want to do this?" he asked Franklin, a tone of pleading in his quiet voice.

Franklin nodded, confused and disoriented by the man's attitude.

"Ok, then," Jarvis said, a deep sigh escaping him, "I suppose this is all to do with the Taylors?" He looked hard at Franklin for a moment before dropping his eyes. "Yes, I see it is."

Franklin decided to remain silent. Jarvis evidently wanted to talk, and he didn't want to disturb him. After all, if Jarvis was about to tell him what he needed to know, who was to guess that it wasn't Franklin's own interrogation techniques that had wheedled the information out of the man?

Jarvis began talking slowly, his eyes fixed on either the carpet in front of the bed or on the coffee cup in his hands. After a few faltering words, he began to speak more rapidly, seemingly desperate to tell the entire story before he lost his nerve.

"The church, it's... it's not really a church as such. We call each other 'brother' – even Jacob, and he's the, sort of... no, not *sort of*, he *is* the leader – and we're basically just a bunch of people who have fallen on hard times." Jarvis paused and sought for the right words. "Jacob helps us. He seems to know what we've done and how to put it right." He glanced at the ceiling and all around the room as if he expected to see some evidence of Jacob's presence and then closed his eyes firmly before he went on. "Take me for example. I've got – or rather, had – a bad habit or two which got out of hand. I gambled. Lost everything – and not just my own money. Borrowed from the company I work for, had to keep covering up. It all got too much, and I was desperate. Suddenly, there it was. A note. Dropped on my desk for me to find one morning when I came in. It was simply a message for me to attend a church meeting where I was sure to find my 'salvation'. There were other things in it, I don't recall them all, but I was sure from what was written that someone, somewhere knew what I was up to."

He paused and sighed deeply at some long distant memory before he went on, ever more rapidly. "I didn't think for a minute that there was any salvation to be had in any *church*," he almost spat the word as if it offended his very tongue, "But the threat was there, and I had to go along and find out who it was that knew what I was doing. Well, I won't bore you with too many details, but needless to say, I turned up at this address – an old warehouse in the East End – and everything was weird. I mean *really* weird. When I entered the room, everyone seemed to know my name and without asking, I was sure right from the start that they all knew what I'd done – what I'd been doing.

"I don't mind telling you that I was scared. I just couldn't accept the whole thing – anything. Now, I don't even remember too much about that first evening; I'd probably even swear that they did something to me, gave me a drugged drink or something, that ensured that I wouldn't remember too much. Perhaps it was the whole situation, perhaps it was the drink, I really can't say."

Jarvis paused again, evidently looking for a way to continue. Franklin realised that he was holding his breath – this was obviously going to be everything that he could hope for and he consciously and unconsciously didn't want to break the flow. Questions – and he already had a dozen or more – could wait.

"Well," Jarvis sighed deeply, "the long and the short of it was – and, I suppose, is – that all of the members of the church were in the same boat one way and another. Or *had* been," he corrected himself, "The message that was given to me that night was pure and simple. Jacob and the church could and would help me if I promised to help them in the future. There were no details, nothing definite, no *specifics* – but afterwards I was left with the impression that there was a direct threat involved. As simply as I can put it, I felt that I had sold my soul, somehow – and probably to the devil.

"The devil is Jacob," he continued, shaking his head as if in awareness that what he was saying would not be believed, "Even now, I can't conceive of how he seems to know so much. It's nonsense, of course, but there really does seem to be something... unnatural, other-worldly, about how he carries on.

"Of course, what I have learned about the methods the church employ is that they are all too 'worldly'. They're nothing but a bunch of crooks, shysters." Jarvis imbued the word 'They' with as much meaning as he could in an effort to ensure that Franklin realised that he didn't mean 'us'. "Their scam is really quite simple. They sucker people into believing that they are some sort of charitable organisation – old biddies that want to do good before they pop their clogs, retired businessmen that had spent a lifetime stepping on the toes of others and wanted to atone for their sins, that sort of person."

Jarvis paused again and shook his head, trembling a little at the magnitude of the sins he had been a part of. "Basically, I suppose," he went on reluctantly, "They are nothing more than murderers."

Franklin, unable to contain himself any longer, sat bolt upright. "What do you mean?"

Jarvis glanced up at him for the first time and for a second Franklin thought that the man was going to clam up on him. But Jarvis sighed again and resumed the hang-dog, droop-shouldered, thoroughly defeated posture. "What do I mean?", he echoed. "Simply that. They are murderers. They prey on these would-be do-gooders. Spin them tales of how the 'church' help out unfortunate souls who have fallen on hard times; how the 'church' helps these unfortunates to rehabilitate themselves." Jarvis stopped in mid flow and sighed deeply, capping the well of anger that had begun to stir within him and make its presence felt. "And in a way, I suppose they do."

Franklin, for the first time in his life, suddenly knew what the word 'speechless' really meant. He was close to it, but forced himself to ask, "But how do they do it? *Why* do they do it?"

Jarvis snorted as if at some private joke. "The 'how' is easy to answer, the 'why' I'm not so sure about." He seemed glad to have some direction in which to take his confession, "Take my case, for example. I first went along to the church nearly eighteen months ago. Since then, all of my debts have been paid off – and that's how they catch you. By the time the debts have been cleared, you find out how the church has obtained the money to do it. Then you're in their control. Or rather, his control, Jacob's." Jarvis shuddered deeply and then continued, grimacing as each word left his mouth, "The do-gooders become part of the church, they give money, help organise fund raising events and all of that bullshit. But, somehow, that's not enough for Jacob.

"He gains their confidence – the 'feelgood' syndrome, he calls it – and then makes them believe that they can still be of help when they die. That's the token nod towards faith and belief and that religious shit. In practical terms what they are told to do – what they end up *wanting* to do – is make sure that when they die, all of their worldly worth is given to the church.

"But even *that* is not good enough for Jacob. He's... impatient. Why wait ten, twenty years for someone to die if there's an alternative. Not that he arranges '*accidents*' – oh no. Once someone changes their will in favour of the church they are usually murdered."

Jarvis said it simply and seemed on the verge of hysterical laughter. Franklin didn't for a minute doubt what the man had said, as far-fetched as it seemed, but he was worried that Jarvis was on the point of cracking up altogether. He was relieved when the man continued.

"Normally, they set up someone in the family. They kill the person and the blame is laid firmly at the doorstep of one of the person's relatives. That way there's a motive. After all, the deceased has just changed their will to the benefit of a third party and to the detriment of the family member – that's as good a motive as the police seem to need these days. And, before you say it, the church has apparently got many guises – there's no direct link between all of these will changes. Sometimes the church is a cat's home, sometimes it's an orphanage. They're just all controlled by Jacob, and god knows how many identities that man has got.

"As to why he does it, who knows? I don't even know the half of it – how the church operates, who else is involved. We're all kept in virtual ignorance – we only know enough to know that if we ever go against them, it's prison at best." Jarvis shuddered uncontrollably, "At worst..." he whispered and trailed off into silence.

Franklin was having serious difficulties in coming to terms with what he was hearing although he believed every word. A creeping sense of dread was shrouding him – as if every word he heard was a threat in itself, and they were all now multiplying. Still, he needed to know more. "How many people...?"

Jarvis snorted. "I've no idea," he replied, "I don't even know how far Jacob's net spreads – or even if he's the top man. To my knowledge, he's had at least eight people killed in the last eighteen months."

"What about Bill Taylor?" Franklin asked, finally summoning up the courage, afraid of breaking the spell that had been cast.

Jarvis snorted, "More to the point, it's Mary Taylor. Not for the first time, something went wrong. In fact, recently, there seem to have been a number of 'errors of judgement'. I wasn't there when it actually happened," Jarvis looked up at Franklin, desperate for the youth to believe him, as if he believed that Franklin would act as judge and executioner, "but I do know some of it." He continued when Franklin, silent and stony-faced, but breathing heavily, motioned for him to do so, "Apparently, Jacob and another brother, Mark, were supposed to meet her at her brother's house in an effort to convert him. That was the cover. Somehow, Mary Taylor had gotten suspicious, checked up on the church, and found out something that very evening which made her scared for her life. God knows what it was, but by the time Jacob arrived, she was ready for him.

"She made him wait inside and kept watch for her brother. When he turned up, he was drunk and whatever message she tried to get to him, he couldn't understand – it was some sort of sign language, something to do with when they were kids. She was livid, raged at him, or something, but he didn't understand the warning. Instead of calling for help or whatever he was supposed to do, he tried to get indoors. Mark arrived about the same time, and alerted by whatever Mary was doing, he knocked the old boy around and forced them both inside.

"Jacob took a chance on Taylor being too drunk to recall what went on and carried out the murder as planned. Even if the old boy did remember, who was going to believe him? They drugged him to ensure that he stayed out of things for the night and arranged for someone to call in the morning and 'discover' the crime.

"Apparently, Taylor came round before he was supposed to, and the guy that was supposed to call at the house was arrested for some petty crime – something to do with his foster children. There was nothing much Jacob could do without arousing suspicion. He waited a week and then he got Mark and me around to the house and," Jarvis paused and swallowed hard, "I had to help him dispose of her body."

Jarvis trailed into silence and awaited the young man's reaction. He was truly shocked when Franklin yelled, "Yes! I knew it!"

Jarvis eyed the lad nervously as Franklin got up and began to pace the room.

"It all makes sense now!" Franklin made for the bedside table, his progress taking him close enough to Jarvis so that the man flinched in fear. "You," Jarvis was told, "Are going to sit tight. I'm going to phone someone, and we'll sort this out from there."

Jarvis was suddenly alarmed. It was only now that he realised just what danger he had put himself into. "But what about Jacob?" he pleaded.

"What about him?" Franklin replied, the telephone receiver in his hand.

"I tell you, he knows everything that's going on. If you tell anyone else what I've said, your life won't be worth living, let alone mine."

Jarvis' pleading fell on deaf ears. "Don't be stupid. No-one knows we're here – no-one will know until everything's been sorted, my man. All we've got to do now is let Bill Taylor know – he and Maisie will sort it all out."

"But... didn't you hear what I said? You can't be the first to hear someone say what was going on, someone's confession. And no one else has managed to stop things!"

"You don't know how smart Bill and Maisie are, man."

Jarvis stared incomprehensively at Franklin. *Didn't he realise just what Jacob was capable of after all I've told him!* He couldn't put any more thoughts into words. His mind, relieved of its terrible burden refused to co-operate. Numbly he sat and stared at the young man as he dialled the number and waited for the reply.

* * * * *

By the time the telephone rang for the second time that morning, Bill's nerves had stretched as taut as they possibly could. Despite the early hour, he had liberated a bottle of whisky from Maisie's depleted stock and had been pacing the sitting room sipping rapidly from a never-empty tumbler. Maisie had sat and fretted silently, offering words of solace at frequent intervals, but feeling generally helpless.

Bill dropped the tumbler when the strident bell rang and leapt for the telephone, beating Maisie by a stride.

"Hello!" he almost yelled, and then to Maisie, "It's the boy!"

She reached around him and flipped the speakerphone switch, then watched in helpless silence as Bill's face told the tale of what they were hearing. After nearly two minutes in which Bill had said nothing, she saw his face crumple and a tear leak from under his tightly shut left eye. "Thank God!" he whispered. He nodded at the receiver, oblivious to the futility of such an action and then began to talk.

"And Jarvis is still with you? Good.'"

Maisie breathed a sigh of relief that she would hardly have credited anyone was capable of. They now clearly had the witness who could help to prove William's innocence.

"Perfect," Bill continued after a pause to listen to Franklin's explanation, "Ok, now my news. Gerald has telephoned me not an hour ago. What I suggest is that he and PC Blake come over to you and..." Suddenly Bill paused.

"Franklin!" he turned wild eyes at Maisie. "Something's wrong. Franklin!" he called again, desperately, into the receiver.

Quickly he pressed the cradle down and began dialling Franklin's mobile number.

"William! What's wrong? What was that noise?" Maisie asked suddenly, coldly, very alarmed.

"I don't know," Bill replied, pressing the cradle once more, and dialling again, "But I don't like the sound of it. You heard Franklin was only telling me about this Jarvis fellow when I heard that sudden crash in the background. The lad called out in alarm and then we both heard that most terrible bang. I fear it might have been a gun. The lad's phone just went dead..." He broke off and listened to the handset as a telephone began to ring at the other end of the line.

Panic broke over Maisie in waves, pounding her already raw nerves, "Who are you calling now? That wasn't Franklin's number as ir?" she asked querulously.

"Gerald!" Bill said, both in answer to her and in answer to a voice that had answered the telephone. Without waiting for any pleasantries and without pause, he spoke rapidly to his friend.

"Gerald. No questions. Get yourself and Blake over to Franklin's hotel. Something terrible has happened, I fear. Please, go now. Just one other thing – I know for sure that I'm innocent, and Franklin was there with the person that could prove it; someone has burst in on them. Please, Gerald, hurry."

Bill nodded once as Gerry replied and muttered a quick 'Good Luck' before replacing the handset. He sighed, a deep shuddering breath, and turned to face Maisie. "We heard him cry out," he moaned plaintively, "I think... I think someone shot him!" Tears streamed, then, from his eyes and Maisie hugged him, her own tears mingling on their faces.

*****

Gerry threw the handset back into its cradle. Ignoring the wide eyed, inquisitive stares he snapped commands. "Get your jackets. Susan, go and hail a cab. We'll be down in two seconds."

Jenny looked at him frantically as Susan, sensing the urgency, hurried from the small room. "What...?" she began.

Dave Blake silenced her. "Should I call my lot?" he asked Gerry.

Gerry shrugged in desperation. He shook his head but replied, "Yes," then grabbed his coat and shrugged it on to his shoulders. "Bill thinks there's been some trouble – bad trouble – at Franklin's hotel; guns, maybe."

"Oh dear God!" Jenny moaned.

Blake grabbed the telephone and dialled quickly, "Get your jackets and I'll meet you outside," he told them while he waited for a reply.

Gerry and Jenny shot from the room and hustled down the stairs, too urgent to wait for the ancient lift. Outside, Susan was standing on the curb waving frantically at every passing cab. Unfortunately, the volume of cars parked along the road made her difficult to spot.

Blake shot from the front door of the hotel and, quickly sizing up the situation, he strode into the middle of the rode, his warrant card in his hand. Vehicles screeched to a standstill and he spotted the familiar black cab a few cars further back in the line facing East. Signalling to the others to follow him he strode between the stationary vehicles and, ignoring the imprecations of the drivers, reached the taxi.

By the time the others had caught up with him, he had ejected a complaining American tourist from the back of the cab and was giving the driver instructions. They piled into the taxi, Gerry thoughtfully hurling the American's luggage into the road as they pulled away.

The journey, a shade under two miles, took twenty minutes and the four of them, cursing the traffic and constantly glancing at their watches, fumed and fidgeted. Susan held tightly on to Jenny's hand throughout and worried about both her friend and the poor unfortunate Franklin. The taxi driver, once clear of the most congested roads, revelled in the instructions of the police officer and drove like a maniac. For him, at least, the journey was fun.

He screeched to a halt outside the hotel immediately behind a police Range Rover, its blue lights flashing in the morning sun. A second police car drew up alongside them and an ambulance, its sirens still wailing mournfully, lurched into view as they disembarked.

Gerry and Dave raced into the hotel foyer and were tackled by two burly City of London policemen.

"We know all about it," Blake yelled at them, struggling loose. He flashed his warrant card at them, "It's part of an ongoing enquiry. Which room?"

The officers, noting the card and Blake's plain clothes decided that discretion was the better part of duty and let both men loose. "Room 211," one of them yelled after the men's retreating figures.

Jenny and Susan dashed after them, the officers ignored, and the four of them raced up the ornate central stairwell. Blake reached the second-floor landing well ahead of the other three, his more physical lifestyle lending him speed which the other's lacked. The hotel's discreet signs were initially confusing, and the rest had caught up with him before he realised that signs were unnecessary. To his right, through a fire door, he could now see two figures, one prone, the other standing over the first.

He pushed his way through the door and the man standing there looked up briefly. "About time!" he drawled, a Bronx accent unmistakable.

"Who's that?" Blake snapped pointing at the figure on the floor

"Dunno," the American replied, "but he burst into the room next door to me and started blasting. Luckily for me, I always carry this."

The man gestured with the handgun that he had trained on the prone figure and Blake wondered how the man had smuggled it through customs. he glanced behind him and saw uniformed officers appearing at the top of the staircase. "Ok," he said, "Let them handle him. Where's 211?"

The American glanced up at the policeman briefly before shaking his head in disgust. "Try that one," he suggested indicating the room behind him, its door hanging off the hinges.

Blake and Gerry skirted round him and entered the room. The smell of cordite was strong in the air and feathers still fluttered in the breeze caused by the shattered window. Blake was the first to spot the two figures lying on the bed and quickly turned to block Jenny and Susan who were trying to push past. "Get the paramedics up here," he told them.

Susan, wordlessly, backed away and dragged Jenny, nearly hysterical, with her.

Blake turned back to see Gerry bending over the bed. "Don't touch anything," he told him.

Gerry turned back to him, his eyes burning, "He shot him!"

On the bed, Franklin lay still.

Chapter 13

Monday 16th June 2014

The ambulance crew arrived within seconds and Blake guessed that the police officers must have called them up. He stood back and dragged Gerry to the side of the room to let them work, his heart racing.

"This one's gone," one of the men announced and Gerry thought for one horrible moment that he was referring to Franklin until the other pointed at a dark-skinned arm and said, "This one's alive – but only just."

One of the crew began to snap orders into a radio and Blake immediately understood that another vehicle had arrived on the scene. "How bad?" he called to the other paramedic who was bending over Franklin's prone body and working to free his clothing.

"He's losing blood fast," the woman replied, not looking up, "He's been winged, but I can't see how bad it is. What is it, another drug hit?"

Blake snorted. "Anything but. Let me know how he is as soon as you can, ok?"

The paramedic grunted and continued to work away while her colleague began to assemble a drip at the bedside. Blake pulled Gerry from the room aware that there was nothing more they could do. He ignored Jenny and Susan's questioning eyes and made for the captive man, now handcuffed and upright.

They were about to lead him away when Blake caught hold of them. "Just a sec," he said, "I need a quiet word with this guy."

The officers looked at each other and one shrugged. Who were they to interfere? "We'll be right outside," the taller of the two said and gestured to the fire door.

Blake nodded and waited for them to leave. The American was already at the top of the staircase and being interviewed by another officer. He turned to the prisoner.

"Name?" he snapped.

The man grinned at him, a smile of pure loathing. "Mark," he replied lightly, "And before you even bother. I'm a nutter. Just passing through. Whatever you think you know about me and why I'm here is pointless. Nothing will be proved. Taylor will still go down."

Gerry stared dumbfounded at this blatant statement and Blake sensed the closing of a door. This had been a highly professional hit and the man before him would obviously rather die than admit anything at all. He stared hard into the man's eyes and saw only his own reflection.

"I don't know what hold they've got over you," he said quietly, "But I do hope, most sincerely, you rot in hell."

The man laughed, dark humour resonant in every sound. "You know," he said, conversationally, when the laughter had subsided, "I just might do that."

Blake punched him once, hard, in the stomach and was not unduly surprised when the man merely flinched and then straightened up. He glanced up to see if the other officers had noticed his actions and was relieved to see one of them glancing hurriedly away. "I could beat it out of you," he suggested to this Mark.

The man laughed again. "You don't honestly believe it, do you? A little beating from you is nothing compared to what would happen if I said anything wrong. And, before you say it, 'policeman', I don't doubt for a single minute that my boss would find out. I told you already - Taylor's going down. This will never even be linked. You might be able to talk to your God on a Sunday. Me, I've got friends in really high places - and they talk back."

Blake understood that his investigation had come to an end and when he looked at the despair on Gerry's face he realised that Cooper knew it too. Whatever Franklin had been able to achieve was to no avail. This was the end of the road and Franklin had paid a price far greater than it was all worth. He shook his head in admiration at the friendship and self-sacrifice that Bill Taylor had earned and then realised that, for Bill Taylor, despite his innocence, this really *was* the end of the road. There was no longer any way of protecting the man - that had ended here in this hotel. He resigned himself to the interview that he would be undergoing in just a few short hours and wondered what he might be able to do in the meantime - was there any way he could save himself and Taylor?

Gerry leant against the wall and alternately cursed and prayed. His eyes kept travelling back to the shattered doorway and he could just make out one foot, shoeless, hanging from the end of the bed. The foot of a dead man. He prayed fervently that Franklin wouldn't be the same in a few minutes.

The five people in the corridor looked up as one when the female paramedic emerged. She was shaking her head and Gerry cried out involuntarily. Dear God! How was he going to tell Bill?

Jenny rushed forward and grabbed the woman by the collar. "He's not...?" she asked, plaintively.

The woman looked up, seemingly in surprise, and laughed. "Not in the least. He's a very lucky young man – if you can call being shot through the shoulder lucky. He's lost some blood, but he'll be alright in no time. The stretcher is on its way up."

The collective sigh of relief made the paramedic start. "Friend of yours is he?"

"I never thought I'd ever say it," Jenny replied, sobbing and laughing in relief, "But yes. A very good little friend." Without another word she pushed past the woman and entered the room.

From the hallway Gerry and Susan could clearly hear her first words. "Where the hell have you been you stupid little..."

Susan hugged Gerry and Dave briefly and then, ignoring the protests of the paramedic, joined Jenny in the room.

The next hour was chaotic for everyone concerned. Gerry, on Blake's advice, tried to slip away from the crowded hotel to telephone Bill but his way was blocked at every turn by the presence of police officers who had seemed to crawl out of the woodwork. Franklin was left in the room, the scene of crime team wanting to interview him immediately, and Jenny and Susan defended him the best they could, constantly interrupting until they were forcibly removed.

DS Craig appeared towards midday and immediately whisked Blake away for a de-briefing that could be heard throughout most of the hotel. When he re-appeared, forty minutes later, rubbing his ears gingerly, Gerry stopped him and pulled him aside.

"What now?" he demanded.

Blake shrugged. "I've not let on about Bill's whereabouts, but it's not going to take long. Craig wants to charge Franklin with aiding and abetting and I can't see the lad being able to hold out for too long."

At that point Susan and Jenny, still fuming, joined them. "What's going to happen to Franklin now then?"

"As far as I know, he'll be taken along to Barts, given a check-up and then released into police custody. I suppose he'll then be taken in and questioned until he coughs up what they want to know. And, incidentally, all four of us are likely to be in the same boat."

Jenny sighed deeply. "There must be something we can do."

Gerry reached down and picked up a yellow jacket, dropped carelessly in the corridor by one of the paramedics. "You know," he mused, "I think there is."

*****

The ambulance sped along the crowded streets, it's siren wailing and lights of various hues splashing intermittently across the surrounding buildings.

"Weirdest ambulance crew I ever saw," Franklin commented.

"Shut up and recover," Jenny scolded him, "You're ill."

"Where are we going?" Franklin asked, the painkillers that he had been administered clouding his thought processes.

"Not far," Blake replied, "These buggers are easy to spot," he explained meaning the ambulance.

Gerry pulled in to the side of a road and switched off the systems. He hurried round to the back of the vehicle and threw open the doors. "Last stop!" he called, "That radio telephone is really rather good."

A car drew up behind the ambulance and a familiar figure climbed out of the driver's side.

"Folks," Gerry intoned, formally, "I'd like you to meet Richard Bates. For once in his life he's sober, but don't let that put you off him."

Richie bowed and gestured to the battered Mini. "Your carriage awaits, young sir. And so do your friends."

Franklin was helped into the passenger seat and the seatbelt placed over his shoulder as delicately as possible. Richie climbed in and the others gathered by Franklin's open window.

"Thanks guys," he said simply, not able to articulate the feelings that, albeit clouded by drugs, were roiling around inside him. "But aren't you all in deep shit?"

Blake laughed. "Me more than most I suppose, but, without any real evidence, it'll all blow over in time. Don't worry, we'll be ok."

"Definitely," Gerry concurred.

Jenny leaned in the window and pecked Franklin lightly on the cheek. "Think of it as my way of saying sorry," she told him.

"And don't forget," Susan added, "You won't have long."

Franklin nodded. "Thanks is just about all I can say. But I mean a hell of a lot more than that. Wish Bill was here now, he'd know what to say."

"I don't really think you've got that long," Gerry said, and immediately regretted it as Franklin laughed and then winced in pain. "Go on, Richie," he urged the driver, "Get him out of here."

Richie nodded and started the engine, "I'll make sure he's there on time," he promised.

The four looked on as the battered little car sped away into the lunchtime traffic. "Hope it all works out," Blake commented.

"If nothing else," Susan said, "We've done our best. Let's just hope that Bill and Maisie manage to get everything sorted.

*****

"Have they pulled out yet?" Dave Blake asked Gerry, re-joining him outside Euston Station.

Gerry nodded. "God knows how, but they're away. How are the girls? Did you manage to get through to them?'"

Dave nodded, "Despite the vagaries of the phone network I finally got through. I spoke to Susan and she said that Jenny has already re-opened the guest house and that Maisie's brother has agreed to stay quiet. Apparently he even helped them with the bank details and that sort of thing."

Gerry nodded in satisfaction. "Have you phoned your station yet?"

Blake laughed and nodded, "Apparently everyone is blaming everyone else and it looks as if we're off Scot free. They bought my story about us two pursuing the 'other man', and no-one even noticed Jenny and Susan at the scene. As long as no-one grasses me up about how I helped you out, we've got nothing else to worry about."

"Well, that's that then"' Gerry said, smiling and relieved. "I get the distinct impression we've earned a pint or two. What do you say?"

Blake laughed, "Lead me to the beer."

The two men sauntered through the milling crowds towards one of the station's bars and Dave Phillips watched them go in a speechless frustrated rage. It had taken him four days to finally get back on their trail – four days during which he had sneezed better than eight hundred times and had only achieved about six hours sleep. If only he'd managed to get a glimpse of the people Blake and Cooper had driven to the station! He spun on his heel, his only thought being to get home and get into bed with a cup of something hot and lemon flavoured, and clattered into the armed security guard, his arm knocking the man's automatic rifle flying across the concourse. His last thought as he fell under the weight of several more armed guards was a simple plea: '*Please don't let me wake up for at least a week...*'

* * * * *

The stewardess laughed as the gentleman in seat D12 waved a crumpled twenty-pound note at her. "Excuse me kind lady, I have a picture of the Queen who looks most displeased to be in the company of such a miserable reprobate. Perhaps you could separate us in return for a large measure of something warming?"

"Certainly, sir," she replied, reaching for the rapidly depleting stock of miniatures that she maintained on her trolley.

"And of course," the man continued, "Please provide whatever my protege and his nurse here require," he gestured to his left where the other two passengers in his party were sitting quietly.

Once the stewardess had moved on with her trolley Maisie nudged Bill's arm. She whispered, "Are you sure we should be running off like this for a few days, William?"

Bill laughed, "Of course, Maisie my dear. We've left Franklin's burner phone thingy with Dave Blake and knowing our wonderful constabulary it will take them a few days at least to get everything sorted out. In fact," he added, "knowing them it will probably take a few weeks. Once it's all settled though we can get our happy future all planned and progressed."

Maisie nodded, "I do believe you're right, my lovely man."

"As ever, my lovely lady," Bill laughed, his voice louder now, "As ever and hopefully a day or a two at the very, very least!"

A teenage girl in the set directly in front of Bill raised her improbably green-haired head and turned to face Bill, "'Ere! Do you mind givin' the bleedin' posh git yammerin' a rest for five minutes?"

He laughed again, "Oh I do so apologise, young lady! I fear I am suffering from an exuberant mood brought about by multifarious joys that have swung my way these past four-and-twenty hours. Rest assured I shall endeavour to restrain my enthusiasms for the remainder of our little Odyssey."

The girl, somewhere around fifteen, stared at him with a look in her eyes that was much closer to fifty, "You're one weird git, ain't you?"

"Says the young lady with bright green hair," Bill teased, smiling broadly.

Whatever protest or insult the girl has been about to add was cut short by her sudden need to smother a smile.

"And never cage the beast of an expression of your happiness," he added, "I'm sure a smile becomes you well. Where, though, are my manners? I'm... Tom, Thomas Williams, travelling with my dearly beloved companion and betrothed Maisie, and my quite well-liked dusky friend Frederick."

The girl shrugged, giving in to the strange guy, "I'm Dot Kom."

Bill raised an eyebrow, "A pseudonym for the digital, ethereal age, perchance?"

"A pseud... oh, I get it. No," finally she smiled, "It's just my real names cut kinda short, you know? Dot for, well, Dorothy and Kom for Kominski."

"How marvellously modern," Bill said, "And are you an expert in the interweb thingy?"

"The... oh, I get that too. And yeah I can 'andle a keyboard."

Bill nodded, "And, it would appear, handle your thought processing at high speed." He turned for a moment to Maisie, "Do you recall the idea I mentioned to you in the early house of this very morning, my dear?"

Maisie giggled, "Surely that's not a subject... oh, sorry, you mean the one about the agency don't you?"

"I do, indeed," he smiled, "But I thank you for the order in which you recalled the ideas! But in all seriousness, I do believe this young lady is precisely the sort of wildcard we would need, do you not agree?"

Maisie looked up at the now-inquisitive stare that she and Bill were being scrutinised with, "I dare say you are, as ever, correct – but surely this is not the correct circumstance, and Dorothy here–"

"Dot not Dorothy!"

"My apologies, dear. And surely *Dot* here–"

"Thanks!"

"You're most welcome. Surely Dot here is both a tad young and also headed in the wrong direction?"

Bill laughed, "Most perspicacious, Maisie my dear, but my life has suddenly become somewhat full of marvellous fortune." He pulled a small notebook out of his pocket and hurriedly wrote his phone number on a blank page. "Maisie, I will say nothing more now, but will leave things entirely in the hands of providence."

He turned back to Dot Kom and handed her the page he had now torn out of the notebook, "This, young lady, is my telephone number. Should you happen to be in the southern part of this sceptred isle and are seeking an opportunity to follow your skills with an electronic keyboard then perchance contact me. I make no promises whatsoever at this juncture, but there is a slender possibility that I may be able to furnish you with said opportunity."

"You what? You're not some kinda weirdo into teens are you?"

Bill raised an eyebrow, "Save for young Frederick here, I find teenagers to be a somewhat alien species, believe me."

"Gee, thanks, man!" Franklin tried to suppress a smile.

Maisie sat forward a little, "I assure you Doro... *Dot*, my beloved here is merely pursuing one of his many strange business ideas and he's a most honourable man." She pushed her glasses back up her nose.

Franklin winced more upright, "What business idea?"

"Later, dear boy," Bill said, "Dot, please assure yourself that this is merely a very aimless shot into the darkness, but it's nevertheless genuine. I have a very strange sensation about this now, so simply take the number and keep it safe. One day it may become a true opportunity for all of us. We shall, as they say, see."

Dot was about to say something else, but the situation had become rather odd, although not uncomfortably so. She shook the green hair instead and slid back down into her seat.

Bill turned to look into Maisie's amused eyes, "Well," he said, "As I said to the young lady, there have been two major fortunate events in the last day – and the cosmic system suggests that three is the number that befall us in such circumstances. Perhaps her appearance – here rather than her hair – is the missing link, as it were."

Maisie patted his hand, ignoring the 'Oi, I 'eard that' emanating from row 11, and said, "I no longer have the capacity to think you might not be correct, my love."

"What business idea?" Franklin asked again.

Bill laughed, "We'll have a proper discourse once we're settled in the shadow of Ben Nevis, but for now, dear boy, rest that shoulder and the few brain cells that you seem to be developing."

Shrugging, and then in too much discomfort to argue the point, Franklin settled back in his seat.

* * * * *

At the front of the carriage the stewardess who had served Bill re-joined her colleagues as the train prepared to pass close by Loch Lomond. "It's a real pleasure when you get someone like that on the Fort William run," she commented.

"He's some sort of rock star manager, isn't he?" one of the others asked.

The stewardess nodded. "Yes, Tom something or other. The young black lad, Freddie, had an accident on tour and they're taking a break in Scotland with a private nurse. Personally," she confided, "I think Maisie the nurse is soft on the guy. Can't stop smiling at each other, they can't."

* * * * *

In row 12, Bill and Maisie held each other's hand. "I think the boy's a little jealous," Bill commented.

Franklin stared balefully at him, and then laughed easily.

"Why do you think that might be?" Maisie asked, smiling.

"I'm not sure," Bill replied, "But he's definitely giving us black looks."

The End

Epilogue

Spoiler Alert!   1

If you don't want to know what happens next and haven't already read The Dark Side where all is revealed (why not!?), then you'd better skip to the last page!

Bill and Franklin went on to form all sorts of liaisons:

Together in the form of a fledgling detective agency where they find themselves deep under the streets of London seeking out the mystery of two old tribes and a pseudo Guy Fawkes, and together as well in the employment of a certain spiky green-haired teenager by the name of Dot (never, ever Dorothy) Kom.

And *separately* where we find out that Bill does indeed marry his new love, the fine Maisie, although he spends a lot of his time still in London giving the new agency the benefit of his wide knowledge, and giving his new wife's ears a well-deserved rest. And Franklin... well, let's just say he's a very friendly young man – and a *very* popular one...

For those who haven't read it yet, here's an excerpt from the start of The Dark Side:

Chapter 1

Monday 12th November 2018

As he hurried along Cheapside, Franklin Richardson was beginning to think that the old saw about bad things coming in threes was absolutely accurate. He was cold and getting colder, wet and getting wetter, late and, as is the natural order, getting later. November had never been his favourite month and this year was no exception. He hated the dark evenings, the seemingly incessant rain and sleet, the plunging temperatures, and, in particular, taxi drivers who managed to spray pedestrians with filthy water as they passed. His right shoe squelched with every stride he took.

Franklin glanced up at the clock on the tower of St. Mary-le-Bow and cursed under his breath. It was five-forty and he should have picked up the files and computer discs almost an hour earlier. If the office was closed by the time he got there, Dot would not be a happy bunny.

Not that she ever was these days, or so it seemed.

A loud rumble from his mid-section reminded him that he'd had to skip lunch and since he was late already, he decided to make a quick stop at the nearest burger bar for some much-needed sustenance. As far as he could recall, the closest place was a Burger King at the end of Bow Lane and he ducked into the narrow passage. It was, he reasoned, pretty much on his route anyway.

The streets were filling up with office workers heading for their trains or, more likely, the nearest bars and restaurants and as he squeezed past them Franklin felt a pang of envy. Okay, so he had his own office these days, but sometimes the prospect of a steady nine-to-fiver appealed. It appealed even more as someone's umbrella deposited what felt like a pint of cold water down the back of his neck as he ducked past them. Life as a private investigator was not nearly as glamorous as it sounded.

Near the end of the tiny street a crowd of people were standing shoulder-to-shoulder by the entrance to Mansion House tube station, their forms outlined by flashing blue lights and it quickly become clear to Franklin that further progress would either prove painful or impossible. Muttering another mild curse, he turned and was about to make his empty-bellied way back to the main thoroughfare, when a voice from waist level stopped him in his tracks.

"Spare a smidgen of your fortune for an unfortunate like myself?"

Franklin was used to the beggars that over-populated the streets of London these days and would normally have turned a blind eye, continuing on his way. This voice, though, was cultured and sober. It took him a moment before he could make out the figure in the gloom.

The man was sitting on the doorstep of an empty shop, long legs crossed underneath him. As Franklin paused, the man rose to his feet, the movement fluid, almost graceful.

"Actually, it's a little of my fortune that I wish to share with your good self."

Franklin was at a loss, "Sorry?"

"It is the famous Franklin Richardson, is it not?"

Now that the man was upright, Franklin could make out his features. A long mane of dark hair framed a face almost entirely covered with a luxuriant dark beard. Only the eyes, a piercing blue, and a rudder-like nose, gave any indication that the man was white.

"You know me, man?" Franklin asked, puzzled, "I mean I'm not the "famous' anything."

"Yet it would seem I do know you, would it not?" White teeth glittered in the gloom.

Franklin had been used to the occasional stranger recognising him since the Courtney case the previous year with all its attendant publicity, but since he was black, and Bow Lane was dark even in daylight, he couldn't imagine how the man could have identified him so easily.

"Well, yeah," he shrugged, "I'm Franklin Richardson. But how the–"

"Let's just put it down to a fortunate coincidence, shall we?" the man said.

"Just who are you?"

"How terribly remiss of me. Peter Charno." The man held out his hand.

Franklin shook it involuntarily, "I still don't get how you recognised me, man."

"As I said, serendipity."

Making a mental note to ask his partner, Bill, exactly what *that* was supposed to mean, Franklin shrugged, "Well, it's me, but I'm in a bit of a rush Mr. Charno. I suggest you call my office if it's business you're interested in."

Charno smiled once more, "Just give me one minute of your time, Mr. Richardson. I'm sure you will find it beneficial. Perhaps this will convince you." He handed Franklin a large brown envelope.

It was unsealed, and Franklin peered warily inside. Then he *reached* inside to confirm by touch what his eyes had told him. They hadn't lied – the envelope was crammed full of banknotes. Large denomination banknotes, at that. "Okay," he said, "Let's say that you've got my interest. What's this all about?"

"An intriguing and... complex problem," Charno said, "It will take me a good deal more than a few minutes to fully describe the situation, but broadly speaking I want you to undertake an investigation on my behalf."

"What sort of investigation? Missing persons? Suspected infidelity?"

Charno paused before answering, a smile playing around his mouth under the thick beard, "I suppose 'missing persons' is the most fitting term, but as I say, the issue is a great deal more complex than it might at first appear."

Everything was conspiring to pique Franklin's curiosity, "Okay, Mr. Charno. I hear where you're coming from and missing persons are my speciality, but I really am in a hurry right now. Why don't we arrange to meet up somewhere tomorrow?" He offered the stranger the envelope.

"Keep it, Mr. Richardson," Charno said, "Call it an advance. A show of faith, if you prefer. I'm positive that you *will* accept this case once you have heard a little more detail, and I'm equally certain that you're the ideal man for the job. However, I'm afraid that I won't be able to meet up with you after tonight. If you really must continue with your errand right now, may I suggest we meet later this evening?"

"No can do,' Franklin said, "I gotta get some stuff back to my office or one of my assistants will fry my sorry ass."

"Ah!" Charno nodded, "And how is the delectable Miss Kominski?"

"You know–"

"As I said, Mr. Richardson, I'm certain you're the man for the job. To be that certain, I've had to make a few enquiries of my own."

Franklin shook his head in disbelief, "You're freakin' me out, man."

"That was never my intention, I assure you," Charno went on, "And I apologise if this all seems a little... *strange* at the moment. However, I'm sure things will become clear when you've more information at your disposal."

"I sure as shit hope so," Franklin muttered under his breath.

Charno appeared not to hear, "If you are really positive that you cannot spare me a couple of hours this evening, then I will have to leave you in the capable hands of my own assistant. I will arrange for her to contact you at your office sometime tomorrow if that is suitable?'"

Franklin shrugged, "Fine by me, I guess."

"Splendid! As I say, I'll be... *away* for a while. But I look forward to seeing you on my return Mr. Richardson."

Without waiting for a reply, Charno turned and strode away towards the crowd outside the tube station. Franklin, his jaw hanging open, stared after him.

"Just what the *fuck* was all that about?" he muttered aloud.

Charno was quickly lost from sight and Franklin turned his attention back to the envelope. Another cursory examination of its contents assured him that whatever it was all about, it was looking pretty certain that he'd earn well from it. With another shrug, he thrust the cash into the inside pocket of his drenched overcoat...

And Black Looks 3...

The third instalment, **Summer Cottage**, is well under way now, and it sees Bill and Franklin – with Dot Kom in tow – heading off for a quiet break with Maisie up in Norfolk. What they don't know is that Summer Cottage, a run-down old property close by Bill and Maisie's guest house, has new occupants – and that doesn't just refer to the young couple who have moved in.

In their quirkiest story yet, the two wannabe detectives and their personal partners find themselves pitched into a very, very strange meeting of past and present...

Summer Cottage, the third Black Looks mystery, will appear in early 2020

More Information

As I mentioned in the preface, this book would never have made it to the shelves were it not for the help and encouragement of a number of people – and the publication of The Dark Side in January 2019.

Specialist publishers (and lovely people) **Regency Rainbow** can be found at:

https://www.regencyrainbow.com/

Cover designer *par excellence* **Maria Spada** can be found at:

https://www.mariaspada.com/

And then there's **me**, I guess. News, book links and my blog can be found at:

http://www.johnmoneywrites.com/home.html

The second book in the Black Looks Series, The Dark Side, can be found at:

https://www.amazon.co.uk/Dark-Side-Black-Looks-Book-ebook/dp/B07MZ8B2Z7/ref=asap_bc?ie=UTF8

My final words though, must be:

Thank you for reading **Black Looks**, and I truly hope you enjoyed it!